I0761676

MOB QUEEN

Books by Erin Bledsoe

NOVELS

Mob Queen

The Forty Elephants

MOB QUEEN

ERIN BLEDSOE

Published in 2025 by Blackstone Publishing
Cover and book design by Alenka Vdovič Linaschke

Printed in the United States of America

First edition: 2025
ISBN 979-8-8746-9548-4
Fiction / Historical / General

Version 1

Blackstone Publishing
31 Mistletoe Rd.
Ashland, OR 97520

www.BlackstonePublishing.com

For all the women who have survived men like Ben,
and Justin, who taught me to write darkness without shame.

On March 24, 1966, passersby walking on a footpath beside a picturesque brook near Salzburg, Austria, found the body of a woman in the snow beside a tree. Her coat was neatly folded on the ground. A possible suicide note indicated the person was simply "tired of life." The woman was Virginia Hill, the onetime so-called "Queen of the Mob," a courtesan and entrusted cash courier for household-name American gangsters from the mid-1930s through the 1940s.

—Excerpt from the biography for
Virginia Hill at TheMobMuseum.org

Part 1

Chapter One

CHICAGO WORLD'S FAIR, 1933

"He's here again," said Rosa, barreling into the kitchen with two plates stained red from our meatball special. "Third time this week, Virginia. Have you told him you divorced him?"

"Not today." I let out a hard breath to blow some hair out of my face, a messy red curl that not even my favorite ribbon-trimmed bandeau could save from the Avenue of Flags. I was long gone from the bannered entrance at the north end of the Chicago World's Fair, but I could still feel the wind beating off Lake Michigan, threatening to knock me over.

I leaned down to rinse my hands under a nearby faucet in the small but homey restaurant kitchen, where you couldn't take a step without bumping into jars of oils and dried pasta. Cooks shuffled plates of ravioli genovese and mustaccioli into the window, giving each dish a final sniff of approval before the waitresses trayed them for serving. It was barely noon, and my stomach growled with hunger.

"He better not cause another scene today. Ma won't have it."

I pulled off my hat and combed my fingers through my hair to tame the mess. Georgie was the least of my worries. I was far more concerned with the woman I'd seen on my way in, standing by the gladiolas near the terrace. My missing friend, with rapeseed-yellow hair framing her slender face and long neck, sporting a lilac day dress with a bell-shaped skirt and puffed sleeves. She waited in a sea of customers in line at the front of the restaurant. A man chatted with her, holding her hand in a delicate way, looking deep into her unremarkable brown eyes she hated so much.

"Madeline," I called for her, loud enough to catch the attention of others in the line. They cast me questioning looks while I used both arms to shove past them like I was running from something. I reached out for her shoulder, but like all the times before, when she turned to face me, I saw only a stranger.

Just another tourist with good fashion sense, observing the Italian Pavilion with wonder. It was shaped like a giant airplane, the entrance resembling the tail fin, adorned with "Italia" in large red letters, and left most visitors in awe.

I quickly withdrew my hand, tucking it behind my back while giving them both a smile. "Excuse me."

I turned back to the restaurant and overheard her asking the man where to find the Sears and Roebuck building, gushing about how she longed to do some shopping. My friend knew the fair like the back of her hand.

She wasn't Madeline—no matter how much I'd wanted her to be.

That feeling of suspended hope resided in my stomach even now. And you'd think after making this mistake at least a dozen times, I'd stop assuming every fair-haired girl was Madeline, but I couldn't help it. Between the two of us, all we had were a couple of lowlife ex-husbands and each other. If I didn't keep looking for her, who else would?

Rosa snapped her fingers, pulling me back to the noisy kitchen.

"Let me get dressed, Rosa, then I'll take care of Georgie."

She tossed the red-stained plates into the sink of soapy water, then searched the kitchen for a dry towel. "You better hurry. You've got a regular out front asking for you. Big tipper."

I took the towel and dabbed my hands dry. "Which one?"

"Joey Ep."

"Same time every day."

"Same soup every day," she groaned in response.

I pulled my apron over my cranberry-red dress and lazily tied the knot around my waist. Rosa stepped in to help me adjust and flatten my peaked cuffs and sleeves. Her dress mirrored mine, a spun rayon, firmly tailored with stitched pleats; only she fit it better with her dainty frame and small bust. I was envious, frankly. Momma always said I had more curves than an old dirt road.

She moved behind me, pulling any loose hair from my dress collar. "Why didn't you come in through the front?"

"Your ma doesn't like it when I come in the front without my uniform on," I answered with a huff, searching my purse for a tube of matching cranberry lipstick to give my lips a dab of color. "I don't have a life outside this joint, but I'll be damned if I'm walking through the fair in my apron."

"She likes you," she insisted with a comforting smile. "Might not always seem like it, but she does. You work well. Don't date any of the customers. More than she can say for the rest of the girls that work here. They'd do anything to be a filly to one of these joes."

"Can you blame them? Gangsters are about the only folks in this town with any money," I reasoned. I didn't like the truth, but I knew it.

She leaned in a little, eyebrows narrowing suggestively. "Why don't you go on any dates?"

"Four years of trying to keep a man happy was plenty enough for me."

"Better looking men in here than your ex-husband. More dough too."

Sweet Rosa. She yearned for a date, but her ma ran this place, and her with it. Nobody touched her, and that wasn't going to change anytime soon. The best kind of fun she could have was living vicariously through the other girls. And they had plenty of stories to tell.

The San Carlo, Al Capone's favorite place to eat and talk business before his lockup, was still buzzing with the city's most dangerous criminals. And for the girls that worked here, the most eligible bachelors.

"Money isn't everything," I countered, though admittedly, I didn't believe my own words. I'd never had real money, despite Georgie's promises of getting us better lives. I had grown up in a withered old farmhouse on a small plot of land, with cows, chickens, and shit-stained feet. But money through men always came with a price. Maybe I'd work the rest of my life to have something decent, but at least it would be mine. "What about love, Rosa?"

She let out a boisterous laugh, then leaned against the nearest wall, too close to the oven. A wave of heat hit us both, leaving a black tendril of hair stuck to her forehead. "I don't care what they say, money *can* buy happiness . . . I'm sure it can buy love too. It worked for Madeline. She wasn't here two weeks before she had herself a man and a ticket outta this joint." She looked up, placed a hand on her chest, and let out a long, dramatic sigh. "There's not a girl here who isn't trying to walk in her shadow."

My gaze fell as my stomach twisted into a familiar knot. The truth was, I had no evidence anything bad had happened to her. Nobody did, really. Rosa believed Madeline had gotten herself a man to take care of her, then kissed Chicago goodbye—and in all fairness, that's precisely what happened. Only Rosa didn't know her like I did; she was my best friend, and she wouldn't not write me. Two months since her last postcard was all the warning bell I needed.

"Not everyone can be Madeline," I said before drawing a breath.

I reached into my apron, checking that the two items that kept me grounded in my search were still there—a photo of her and her fair souvenir booklet. I lightly ran my fingers along the brochure's spine, its pages littered with notes about all the men who dined at the San Carlo. Madeline was a hunter, so most nights she didn't know the special, but there wasn't a detail she didn't know about every man in this joint. What they ate, who they fancied or married, and who was free for the taking.

She would talk the same way about this place and all the promises it held. That all she needed to do was catch her a big fish, and she'd be set for life.

"But she must have taught you some things," Rosa pried, as if she wanted to pull out a notepad and jot down some pointers. "You two were so close when she worked here."

I felt my throat grow dry and dismissed her assumption with a wave.

"These mooks tip me good. Why would I want to mess that up with a date gone wrong? Madeline could make anyone fall in love with her . . . but me, well, my mouth is always getting me in trouble."

Rosa frowned in response.

"But if I ever get naked with one of them, you'll be the first to know."

A blush soaked her cheeks, and she looked around timidly, as if the word *naked* might trigger her ma to spontaneously appear to pop her on the hand.

I took a deep breath and quickly changed the subject, forcing myself to wear the same mask I had worn for months. Just another girl, another waitress. "Get Joey some creamy tomato for me? I'll get the rest of his order after I run Georgie off."

"You want me to run him off?" My favorite cook, Robbie, peeked over a pot of boiling noodles, the steam rising and filling the kitchen.

I held my smile and gave him a peck on the cheek. "You know I like to do the running off myself, Robbie."

His skin was oily, and he smelled like an onion, but he was the best cook here. If you kept the cooks happy, they fed you on the house, and there was nothing better than sneaking home with boxes of leftovers to hold me over for a few days. Before I started working here, I waited in soup lines or got up early to see which churches were handing out bread to the unemployed. If all I needed to do was kiss a man on the cheek to eat, it was a small price to pay.

He pulled open the oven and tossed me a piece of fresh bread. I caught it with my apron to cool it off while exiting the kitchen through the back door. Outside, the clatter of silverware and feverish staff were replaced with a dull alley where yesterday's trash waited for pickup.

I placed my hands on my hips. "You're going to get me tossed, Georgie!"

He lingered by the trash in a clean, pressed, button-down shirt and seersucker slacks. He was mostly legs, with a short torso and broad shoulders. I hadn't liked how lanky he was when we first met, how hard it was to stretch up and kiss him, but I'd ignored the things I didn't like for the things I did. I was fifteen years old and would have done anything to get out of the Southern hell that was Marietta. Georgie had said all the right things: *"Marry me, and I'll take you away."*

A good head of hair on top of it all? Momma said I wasn't going to do any better.

"I ain't giving up on you, Virginia." He rushed up to me and reached for my face to give me a kiss. I shuddered away and lifted my hands to push him off. Tragic was the only way I could possibly describe going from thinking the world of someone to being repulsed at the thought of touching them again.

I hadn't known the first thing about being a wife when we got married, but I'd played the part the best I could, taken the beatings he dished out when the money troubles and drinking started weighing him down. All of Chicago was fighting to eat, to breathe. I thought I was lucky to have a room and food in my belly. But when I cried myself to sleep at night with his arms wrapped around me, I knew I'd become my mother. And once you start hitting back, there's no getting back to the way things used to be.

The divorce was messy, and the judge wanted proof beyond the flesh. A witness to fight back against Georgie's Southern charm. If not for Madeline's gripping testimony in a four-page letter, I'd still be under his thumb.

"You've got to stop doing this," I said with a sigh, thinking about Joey Ep finishing his soup and impatiently waiting for me to scribble down his lunch order. I couldn't afford to piss off one of my best tippers. "I need to get—"

"I'm going back home," he told me urgently. "Come with me! Chicago ain't done nothing for us. We can go back and start over. I'll get a good job, and we can make some babies. A fresh start."

I picked at the warm piece of bread, my lips flattening into a line. Just a request like that proved how little he knew me. "You know why I left Marietta."

"We'll live far away from your pa."

"There's nothing farther away from my pa than here."

"I love you, Virginia."

"I don't love you, Georgie. How many times do you want me to say it? I have friends here."

"One more chance."

Despite my new independence and desire to see how far I could take it, the sound of his voice pulled at my resilience. He'd gotten me to cave before, to try again. It was difficult surviving without him, I couldn't deny it. Living was just easier with a man, maybe because life came easier for them.

"I'm staying here," I said firmly.

"And slinging meatballs for tips? You can't make it this way." He looked at the restaurant, and a muscle ticked in his jaw. The old Italian atmosphere, a favorite with tourists visiting the World's Fair, wasn't fooling any Chicago natives. "You know the crowd here. You could get hurt if you say the wrong thing. They might have Al Capone behind bars, but Chicago still belongs to the Mob. Everyone knows it. This place is nothing but trouble."

I shrugged and tossed him the bread with a fearless smirk. "I'm not afraid of a little trouble."

And I wasn't going anywhere without Madeline.

He caught the bread and threw it at the door behind me, too close to my head for comfort. "I'm not clowning around, Virginia!"

"Does it look like I'm joking?"

"Your place is with me. You're my wife."

I rolled my eyes, sucking in some air to calm myself. "I'm your ex-wife. Are you honestly scared for me, Georgie? Or scared of what I might do without you?"

He growled at my tone and took a step forward, puffing out his chest like a child. "Don't mock me, Virginia."

I involuntarily flinched and briefly wondered if I'd be able to cover up a black eye to finish my shift before snapping out of it. I had done this before . . . stood up to men that hurt me.

I picked up the bread and threw it at him. It bounced off his forehead, absurdly slow, and his face heated into a rage that brought out his freckles.

"I'm not afraid of you anymore. I almost killed my pa with a frying pan full of grease before I left because he thought he needed to remind me of my place in this world. It ain't with him, and it ain't with you."

I reached for the door and opened it swiftly, maneuvering one foot inside. Predicting my movement, Georgie lunged, snatching me by the upper arm to pull me away. Just as the pressure of his fingers began to burn my flesh, someone on the other side of the door jerked it open with a fierce swing. Robbie stood tall, sauce stained along his white shirt, bushy brows steady. The only thing moving was the toothpick in his mouth, twisting with his grinding teeth. He had a single oven mitt in his hand, certainly not anyone's weapon of choice, but something about his foreboding presence compelled Georgie to retreat. Perhaps it was the unknown? Robbie might be nothing more than a cook, but he still worked at the Mob's favorite spot. He was too close to men that could snap their fingers and make people disappear.

People like Madeline.

"You got customers," he told me, then pulled the toothpick out and pointed it at Georgie. "You best be going."

Before I made it inside, I overheard Georgie mutter, "God be with the next man you marry, Virginia. Have the decency to warn him that you're just a devil with nice hips."

Chapter Two

Robbie slammed the door, and his flat smile curved up. I knew the look too well. It was the same look Georgie gave me on our wedding night. Having played the hero and saved me from my abusive father and dull, small-town fate, he longed for a reward, praise, something to satisfy his ego. Men could be so drearily predictable.

"You know how to pick them, don't you?"

I ran my hands along my apron and dress, adjusting any piece of fabric that got ruffled in the struggle. "I'd say that's my business, not yours." I paused for a moment before adding, "Thank you."

I moved through the crowded tables of chattering guests, placing my hand on my chest to soothe my racing heart. *Breathe, Virginia. Breathe.* Georgie always left me a nervous wreck.

I continued walking, finding that the deeper I ventured into the restaurant, the easier it was to forget there was even a world outside the place.

The San Carlo looked as if it had been plucked from old Italy, with arched windows, string lights, and terra-cotta flooring that appeared more worn down daily. Ma believed the shoe scuffs tarnishing the flooring were the mark of a flourishing business. Each imperfection was a new or returning customer, sinking money into her place when nearly half of Chicago's workforce was unemployed. She was right. I was lucky to have the job.

Sometimes, while closing up, I'd drift through this place, gliding my fingers along the fresco paintings and dancing under the lights to an Italian opera. I'd imagine I was somewhere far away, a little Italian village in the countryside. I'd never be happy there, of course, just like I was never happy on the farm. But the thrill of being someone else always left me dizzy with excitement.

Months before Madeline left for New York, we thought about packing our bags and moving to California. She claimed we could be the next Loretta Young and Katharine Hepburn, and I played along with her dreamy words for a few weeks. I'd fallen in love with Hepburn after seeing *A Bill of Divorcement* but had no illusions I'd ever make it to the screen. I had one dream: a life of my own that didn't depend on a husband. Madeline didn't mind a husband if he was able to give her what she wanted—everything.

I sighed deeply at the thought.

How far did you go for everything, Madeline?

"Where have you been?" Ma's round face burned red at the sight of me. She heaved a tray of empty plates to a nearby busboy, and he nearly toppled over trying to balance them. "Joey Ep has been waiting—"

"I've got him," I assured her, though that didn't seem to bring her any sense of relief.

I passed men in fitted, stylish suits with two-button notch-lapel coats. They sat at tables draped in crisp white cloths, their drinks half full, with only the buzz of a whisper between them. I could never make out the conversations. It was as if they'd been trained to speak a language all their own.

I swallowed down a cough while walking through a plume of cigar smoke.

Joey Ep was at his usual table on the veranda that overlooked the bustling World's Fair. He was a cool drink of water if I ever saw one, plenty rugged, with a warm smile. His suit was action black, a signature diamond weave pattern with a black felt fedora to match. As usual, he had a paper in his hand, reading it slowly while adjusting his thick black glasses. Glasses I'd usually want to take off to get a better look at a man's peepers, but not his. His eyes were large and blue and always ever clear.

As I predicted, he was all done with his soup. He had the empty bowl strategically placed at the edge of the table for pickup.

I pulled out a pad, tucked under Madeline's booklet, from my apron and hurried over. "The usual?"

He folded down the paper and observed me leisurely, from shoes to hair. But he didn't undress me with his eyes like the other joes here. He looked at me the same way he looked at the books scattered across his table every Friday. Numbers in need of crunching. Money in need of moving.

"I do like that color on you, Virginia."

It was the cranberry color I wore every day, the standard uniform, but he always paid me the same compliment. Joey Ep thrived on routine. He was never late, ordered the soup and the special, had a suit for every day of the week, and loathed change. A few weeks ago, I caught a bug and needed to rest in bed for the day. When Rosa told him I wouldn't be in, he folded up his paper and left.

I shrugged a bit, giving him my usual response: "Too bad I'm not on the menu, Joey."

There were so many secrets passing in and out of this place every day, but it was a well-known fact that Joey Ep was in charge of every nickel and dime for the Chicago Outfit. If he wanted something, he got it.

Too bad that rule didn't apply to me.

He half grinned, the endearment leaving his eyes bright. "How many times do I need to ask you to dinner before you say yes?"

My conversation with Rosa crossed my mind, and I paused a moment. When I didn't deliver my usual quip fast enough, his eyes narrowed.

I flashed him a charming smile, one I reserved for a few select men—one I should have given Robbie but didn't want him getting the wrong idea. I wasn't really interested in Joey Ep, but I wanted to keep playing the game of *will they, won't they* with him because of all the men listed in Madeline's notes, his name was the only one circled.

And that made him my only lead.

I'd worked plenty of shifts with Madeline before she started traveling with her mystery man, one she'd always promised to tell me more about, but she never got around to doing it. I knew it was one of these goons, knew she kept him a secret because secrecy kept the Mob thriving.

I would never have guessed Joey Ep; he just wasn't her brutish type.

"We have dinner together all the time," I teased, gesturing to the restaurant.

He chuckled a little and pressed his lips together. A tic of his—a sign he didn't particularly like my response but didn't want to show it. "I'll have the special."

Shocking, Joey.

I scribbled it down and turned on my heel but spotted Georgie at the front, shouting demands to a very uncomfortable Rosa, who stood rigidly at the host stand. She stepped around the podium and lifted her hands up to block him from busting inside, where all the customers turned their heads to the commotion.

I left Joey Ep without a word and rushed to the scene. Ma bolted from the kitchen to save Rosa with a firm grip of her shoulders and a shove back. Then she stepped between her daughter and Georgie. "You need to leave," she growled, her voice as robust as her six-foot-tall stature. "You leave, or I make you leave."

And she wasn't lying either. I'd seen her do it.

I reached for Georgie's arm and pulled him back. "Georgie, let's go."

"I told you to take care of this, Virginia," yelled Ma, throwing her anger between us. Her chin trembled, and she called for Robbie. He stormed out of the kitchen with a baseball bat, eyes holding Georgie in a deathly stare.

I knew what happened next—I'd seen him knock a man down with a quick swing to the head, then drag him to the alley to get him out of view. Nobody knew what happened after that, and I had no interest in taking any guesses.

I pulled at Georgie until he gave in, letting me drag him a good distance away.

"Are you out of your fucking mind? I just served Charles Fischetti and Jake Guzik ravioli last night. I am begging you to leave, right now."

"I'm not leaving without you." He took my arm and yanked me forward so hard that I tripped over my shoes and stumbled. It was a mess of a scene, one that caught the eyes of several fairgoers. I flushed with shame, and before I could even find my balance, he pulled me like a child, and for one tragic moment, I let him.

I'd just settle him down and then escape in the night. Anything to get him away from my job, my only chance at finding Madeline.

But then I thought about her and how much we both fought to see the divorce through. I stopped moving, planting my feet firmly. "No."

"I can change, Gin. You just have to give me a chance. I know I hurt you. I got this anger inside me . . . I don't want it. I'd do anything to get rid of it. You make me better. I know that's hard to believe, but it's the truth."

My bottom lip began to quiver. "You can't change, Georgie. We both got anger." Sometimes it felt like a sickness, festering inside me, turning everything black. "You're going to hit me again."

"No, I won't," he rushed out.

"And when you do, I'm going to kill you." I could hardly believe I'd said it, but the words tasted sweet on my tongue. I had never been more certain of anything in my life. I was going to kill him, and then both our lives would be over.

He stood there a moment, picking at the lining of his pants; then his face turned ravaged, and I waited for him to spit his venom—the harsh insults he often handed out when he felt cornered. He couldn't use his fists here, so only his mouth would do.

"The truth is, you're a whore. Your pa paid me money to marry you, said you ruined yourself with some farm boy. That's why you live at that massage parlor, isn't it? That's all you're good for, Virginia. All you'll ever be good for. I'm glad I'm rid of you."

I tried to concentrate on the fairgrounds, the noise of the children skipping by with balloons, pointing up at the Sky Ride towers. I wanted to control it, that sense of deaf rage my pa handed down to me. It was like another person inside me, a woman I didn't want to know—a woman I'd do anything to silence.

Georgie talked a lot of silver-tongued nonsense, but *"I got this anger inside me . . . I don't want it, I'd do anything to get rid of it"* felt like the most honest thing he'd ever said to me.

We fought the same battle, and if I didn't keep fighting it, I'd be just like him and my pa, and I'd have no room to talk of change.

When I said nothing, Georgie continued viciously, "You sleeping with that cook, now? When I get back to Marietta, I'll make sure the entire town knows the kind of woman you turned into. That your pa was right."

My breathing hitched.

"You'll never be worth a damn thing."

"Go home, Georgie." My words came out slow, breathless.

"We would have been a family if you had just been a wife and done what I told you to do," he uttered, the anger and sadness clashing to create a strangled sound. "If you didn't make me hurt you, we'd have that baby right now."

"We'd have that baby right now." The words burned me like he knew they would, branding along my stomach as a reminder of what I lost, and what I never had.

Then there were no sounds, just the beat of my own heart, hammering like a drum in my chest. I stood, curled my fingers into a fist, pulled my arm back, and swung it into his face. The noise came back to me just as the pain made my entire arm tremor. I cursed and cradled my hand. Georgie stumbled back, clutching his bleeding nose. "I'm fucking bleeding, Virginia!"

Suddenly I was a child again, staring at the bruise on my mother's cheek, demanding she stand up to my pa. *"Women like us must take what we can get,"* she'd tell me. *"I'll do better, listen more, obey him. Be a better wife."*

Ten years later, I was staring at the same bruise on my face, compliments of my pa for pulling him off my mother. She held a cold cloth to my swelling jawbone, muttering another lesson into my ear: *"Don't hit back, you'll just make it worse."*

Why did hitting him back feel so good, then? Why did I always find peace in my pa's rage? The very rage that had stolen my childhood.

Robbie positioned himself between us with two giant steps, holding the bat so tightly his knuckles looked white and knotted. Georgie lifted his hands in surrender. "I'll go! I'll go."

My fingers felt crushed inside my hand, and try as I might to stretch them, they throbbed from the pain.

With Georgie off into the crowd, Robbie rushed me inside by the waist, past an awestruck Ma and an applauding Rosa, nestling me into a corner table near the kitchen.

"Give me your hand," he insisted, pulling it toward him to observe my swollen knuckles. He stretched out each finger, and I ground my teeth through the pain. "Not broken. I'll get some ice."

Ma was in front of me in a split second, hands on her hips with distaste. I closed my eyes and waited for it. I was losing this damn job over my ex-husband, likely without a reference for another position. No job, no money, and no Madeline.

Her eyebrows knitted together. "What a greaseball."

"I sent him off earlier," I told her. "I thought he took the hint."

She gave me a dubious look. "I think he got the hint now."

Robbie returned with the ice and reached for my hand, but Ma snapped her fingers. "Back to work, Robbie. We got orders waiting."

He cleared his throat and handed her the ice, wrapped in a napkin. She took my hand in her own and placed the ice on my knuckles with little delicacy. I tried not to wince.

"The only reason I'm not tossing you is that was a damn beautiful sight, Virginia." She leaned in, not allowing me a moment to accept the compliment before squeezing my sore hand until my elbow jerked from the pain. "But you bring that kind of nonsense in here again and mess with my business, you're done. You are not the only one around here that can throw a good punch. Do we understand each other?"

I smiled through the pain. "Yes, ma'am."

"Good girl." She looked back outside to the veranda. "Now, shake a leg. Clean up your hand and go check on your tables."

I jumped from my seat and headed to the bathroom to wash up, only momentarily glancing in the mirror to smooth my frazzled mess of hair. I wanted to splash some water on my face to calm myself down, but I didn't want to chance ruining my makeup too.

I breathed in, then out, until the buzzing in my head stopped. I lost myself again, but it was over now. I rinsed my hand off and wrapped it with the napkin before leaving the bathroom. Rosa stopped me on the way out with a tender grip on my shoulders. "That was something else! A great kiss-off to a lousy marriage, if you ask me!" She bounced on the balls of her feet. "I wish I could throw a punch like that. Can you teach me?"

I shook my head, resisting the urge to snap at her. "The best thing you can learn from that is don't go marrying a man you need to punch, Rosa." I maneuvered around her, her ma's words fresh in my head. "I need to get back out there before your ma kills me."

"Joey Ep paid out," she said, handing me his ticket—a hundred-dollar tip on a less than five-dollar tab. I stared at the money for a few long seconds, shaking my head in disbelief. He always tipped well, but never this good. Why today when I didn't even get him the rest of his order?

Rosa rolled her eyes. "Ma really needs to let me start waitressing."

Tangled up in the money, a note read, "Party tonight. I'll pick you up at eight."

Chapter Three

I spent the fifteen-minute bus ride from the fair to my little place in Cicero considering Joey Ep, his very generous tip, and, most importantly: Was he bluffing? Or did Al Capone's money man have my address and every intention of taking me on a date tonight?

The other waitresses claimed he was a gentleman—a good one. Whatever the hell that meant. Gentle men only existed for gentle women, and I was far from soft. All rough and unkempt, my mother liked to say. And what if I was wrong? Maybe Joey Ep's name was circled for an entirely different reason. Maybe he wasn't her mysterious benefactor. My nerves cried with warning. What had I gotten myself into and how was I going to get out of it?

I knew the only way to find out was to get closer to him, but the idea made my stomach flip. All that talk with Rosa about staying away, and here I was about to dine with the devil.

I hopped from the bus with sore feet and peeled off my black kids at the entrance to one of Cicero's finest massage parlors, Lady Luck—where fifty cents could get you a classic rubdown and five dollars could get you a lot more. Not that I was one to judge. I could hear Madeline's voice in my head, clear as the rumble of the streets below the bus wheels. *"From her luscious head of hair to her tiny, delicate toes, a woman's body is pure magic. Why shouldn't a man pay for the pleasure?"*

And these girls working down in Cicero were worth every penny. Miss Suzannah, the madam, ruled with an iron fist. She'd hired Georgie as security when the factory laid him off, and let us rent a room on the bottom floor. When we split, she favored me but gave me no sympathy when it came to rent. If I wanted a place to stay, I had to work, so I agreed to do the laundry.

I cleaned every scrap that passed through this place, from lacy undergarments to damp hand towels, and still paid a little cash to keep Miss Suzannah from insisting I earn my keep with skin. Wash day was tomorrow, when I'd wake up around six in the morning to get started wringing and mangling clothes into the copper for boiling, then hang them in Miss Suzannah's very particular order along a clothesline.

To get a jump, I entered Lady Luck and strolled past the front parlor. Miss Suzannah was at her post near the door, smoking a cigarette and leisurely sprawled out on a small chaise—covered in a resourceful washable leather—next to a deep-blue wall. Beside her, in red lacquered chairs, men waited to be called back to rooms.

Her eyes glanced my way but didn't linger, while the men looked me over with a hunger that was easy to recognize.

I kept my head low and headed to the laundry room. It was a small space and the only modest-looking room in this joint, with nothing but tubs, rollers, and several baskets. I sorted the woolens, cotton, colors, and whites to soak them in the tubs overnight with soap flakes.

I kept Joey Ep on my mind the entire time, only occasionally glancing at the clock, waiting for eight to come and pass. The tip he left me was still in my apron, burning a hole there. Should I have given it back to him?

My fingers began to prune, and when I looked down at them, wrinkled and mushy, my mind did something funny, clawing at a memory and pulling at it until I was in it. The silky nightgown in my hand was coated in something dark, alcohol by the smell of it. I had six of them beside me, all with parallel stains. The girls had often done this to me—stained their items on purpose and forced me to blot them out for hours into the night.

"Don't forget mine," said Madeline from the doorway, and when I looked up, there she was. Her condescending smile spread while she tossed her nightdress on top of all the others. I felt the venom on my tongue, the need to scream at her. The girls were cruel in their antics to give me more work. I just kept telling myself it was better than being on the streets.

"Now, now, Virginia," she teased while placing a hand on her hip. "You know the rules. If you can't get the stain out, Miss Suzannah makes you pay for it. We wouldn't want that, would we? If you can't make your rent, well . . ."

"I'll get it out," I said firmly, feeling my bottom lip twitch.

"You could always start the real work, like the rest of us." Her tone was sharp. "If you did that, maybe the girls wouldn't treat you like this."

"I don't need your advice, Madeline," I said her name just as sharp.

"You think you're special because she doesn't make you open your legs?"

I kept working on the stain, forcing my eyes down so I didn't have to look at her. I didn't even hear her step toward me, slow and determined. She leaned down behind me, voice right in my ear, smelling of flowers and sweat. "You're just Southern trash she picked up, and when she tires of you, she'll throw you out."

My instincts took over, and the heat inside me burned. I jerked my head back into her forehead, and she shrieked in response. I turned around and she was on me like a cat, claws out, pulling at my hair and arms. Everything around me faded; all I could see was a lump of color—soft pink skin I wanted to hurt. I grabbed her by the chin and forced her back into the window, and she just kept clawing at my skin. We were both bleeding, panting, until Miss Suzannah rushed in and shoved us apart like children.

"Enough," she ground out. She looked at the nightgowns, then at both of us, and drew her own conclusions in a split second. "Your last client just left?" Her eyes veered to Madeline.

"Yes," she said, but it came out as more of a growl in my direction.

"Good." Miss Suzannah reached for one of the nightgowns and

shoved at Madeline. "You'll help her get the stains out tonight. Both of you will work until it's done, or both of you will pay for the fabric."

Madeline parted her mouth to say something, to protest, but Miss Suzannah glared to silence her before leaving the room. I didn't like the idea of needing to stare at her face for hours into the night, but getting some help brought me some relief. Two of us would get through the stains faster.

I taught her how to get them out—blot the stain, rinse in cold water, then use soap. Repeat until the stain was gone. A few hours later, when her hands were raw like mine, she finally broke the silence.

"Who taught you to fight?"

"My brothers," I said quietly. "My dad was rough with my mom, and they thought if I knew a few things, I'd be able to fight him off if he ever came for me."

"Did he come for you?"

I didn't answer her, just kept working through the fabric.

"Is that why Miss Suzannah kicked Georgie out of your room? Because he was hitting you? The girls said they heard crying in your room sometimes."

Again, I didn't answer. I didn't want to.

"Are you going to divorce him?"

I finally gave her my eyes. "Are you and the girls going to keep tormenting me?"

She smirked in response. "It's just a little fun. Can you blame us? Miss Suzannah wouldn't hesitate to kick us out of the house if we stopped taking clients. Here you come along, getting hired by her to do laundry."

I took a deep, shaky breath, feeling my arms burn from nails sinking into my skin. "I tried taking clients," I told her honestly. "I tried being like you, but my husband did a number on me, I guess, and when men touch me now, I—"

"Don't," she said quickly, hushing me with a shake of her head. "You don't have to say anything else." She finished one nightdress, took it over to the hanging wire, and lapped it over. Then, a soft chuckle escaped her lips, and I looked up, waiting for her to explain what on earth was humorous about anything I'd just said.

With her hand lifted to her mouth, she tried to suppress the smile. "Sorry, it's just that I whispered into your ear, and you threw me into a window. I can't imagine what you did to that poor man Miss Suzannah sent your way."

A smile began to tug at my mouth when I thought about it. "I didn't hurt him, I just screamed, and he stumbled a bit out of the room . . . without his trousers on."

She roared with laughter then, and the fight was long behind us.

The laundry room door creaked open, bringing me back to the present. I cleared my throat and blinked. One of the girls dropped off a basket of linens, and I checked the time again—nearly seven. I ran my fingers through my hair and quickly finished up, then exited the laundry room.

I drifted through the halls, up the stairs, past room after room, where muted sounds of pleasure escaped from cracks in the doors. I picked up my pace until I spotted Madeline's door ajar. It had been closed since she left for New York, so for a short moment, I thought my mind was playing tricks on me until I heard the faint shuffle of someone inside.

I opened the door and threw a frantic look around. Helen, one of Miss Suzannah's favorites, was cleaning the place up. I watched her delicately pack Madeline's dresses and shoes into a traveling case. I stood motionless until she dared to reach for the Persian lamb coat at the edge of the bed, one I knew Madeline would return for, come hell or high water. It was the only thing she had left of her mother.

I snapped out of my haze. "What are you doing in here?"

Helen jerked around with a gasp. "Scared the right shit out of me, Virginia." With a hand on her chest, she used the other to wave at the clothing on the neatly made bed. "Miss Suzannah said I needed to get this room cleaned out. We've got more girls moving in, and we need the space."

A lump rose in my throat. "You can't," I started to say before Miss Suzannah joined us in the room, positioning herself between me and

Helen. She lifted one hand, as if to silence any rebuttal that might escape my lips. "I need the room. I gave you two months when we agreed to one. I've gotten no rent from her in sixty days."

"And that doesn't strike you as strange? She was paying on time every month, a little bit more, if I recall."

She nodded grimly. "I am aware that when she had money, she was generous with it."

"Then why can't we return the favor? I'm working on finding her," I insisted, and I was. I couldn't storm the San Carlo and demand answers, even though I wanted to. It wouldn't get me anywhere, except likely dead. "I just need more time."

Her expression didn't soften, but she released a sigh in response. "Madeline was one of my best girls."

And she hated every day of it, I wanted to say back, but held my tongue.

"That's why I gave you time to find her . . . but I have girls that need the room. Real earners. I'll keep her things tucked away, so when she comes back, we'll find her a new room."

Nothing about what she said was at all reassuring, but I stood silently and tried to reason with myself. It was only a room, it didn't mean anything, but I couldn't convince the pain in my chest. The dreadful thought that once someone else moved into her room, she was never coming back.

I fished Joey's tip from my apron. "How long will this buy me?"

Her eyes narrowed at the money. "What are you doing down at the San Carlo to bring in that kind of cash?"

I jutted out my chin. "Not what you think."

"Two more weeks."

She reached for the money, long fingers stretching out in a spider-like fashion, but I pulled it back. "I pay eighteen a month for my room."

"It's not personal, Virginia, it's just business. Every day that we waste this space, girls are looking for food on the streets with nowhere warm to sleep. You let that sink in while you're waiting for Madeline to come back through that door with another failed story of trapping some man . . . how her ticket out was just a tragic mistake." Another sigh escaped her lips, and though she seemed fond of Madeline, her words were harsh. "It's always the same with that girl. She'll be back."

I wanted to believe her. It would be a whole hell of a lot easier to just take her word for it. But my mouth kept opening, spewing out protests. "Every few weeks, a new postcard from her. Every month, rent paid to you at the same time. Now nothing? How can you just brush this off?"

"She got distracted, she's off having fun." Miss Suzannah waved her hand in the air at a list of invisible reasons.

"Fine, but her mother's coat? Just left behind? Has she ever done that before?"

The defense in her eyes seemed to lessen at the comment, and she observed the coat on the bed. Because her stone face was impossible to read, I could only imagine what she was thinking. She muttered something, a string of curse words, I thought, before walking to the bed. She reached down to touch the fur sleeve of the coat.

Had I finally gotten through to her?

Without looking at me, she muttered, "One month."

I felt the muscles in my shoulders ease into their natural state. One month wasn't much, but I'd take it. I handed her the bill, and she tucked it into the strap of her dress, then gave Helen a nod. I waited for her to stop packing Madeline's things before leaving for my own room.

Contrary to the lush interior of the floors below with checkerboard flooring and plaster moldings, my place consisted of nothing but a love seat in my living room, a kitchen nook separated by a sheer curtain, and a small twin bed. The walls were yellow, the paint chipped, and there wasn't a lacquer chair in sight.

It wasn't the large ground-floor apartment I'd shared with Georgie, but I wouldn't dare complain. The Depression had nearly killed this city. A man was searching for work or begging for some food on every corner. I had a place to lay my head, to call my own, and a job that paid me decent.

I had more than most. More than Georgie thought I'd have when I left him.

I pulled off my apron, and Madeline's book fumbled onto the bed. Miss Suzannah's speech plagued my thoughts. Maybe she was right, and Madeline's disappearing act was nothing to worry about, but I just couldn't shake the feeling something had happened to her.

I reached for my dress buttons, but a cough startled me into jumping around, hurling myself back onto the bed. Behind the curtain hiding the kitchen nook, I could see the shadow of a figure looming over my small two-chair table. I searched my room for a weapon, anything to hurt the intruder with, and settled for a metal flower stand near the bed with dead lilies in it.

I lurched forward like a cat in a dark alley, unhurriedly getting closer, but something about the outline of the intruder soothed my concern. One leg crossed over the other, with square shoulders back in a somber yet relaxed manner.

I set the flower stand down and rushed over to pull back the curtain to find Joey Ep, sitting in my kitchen as casually as he would in the San Carlo. Tonight, he was wearing a summer suit with a gray windowpane pattern and a matching hat.

"What are you doing here?" I asked with little delicacy. "Who let you in?" I shuddered, considering I'd somehow walked right past him. Was it possible for someone to be so deadly quiet?

He chuckled a little, too cocky for my tastes. "I have a hand in every massage parlor in Chicago. Sex is just like all the other businesses I count the cash for, only more honest." He checked the gold watch on his wrist, then looked me up and down the same inspecting way he always did. "It's about eight. You should change." He motioned to a box on the table—a large white one with a red bow. "I bought you a dress. Had to guess your size."

I placed my hands on my hips. "Your ears thick or something? I said no. I meant it. I don't date my customers." Maybe he was my only lead in Madeline's disappearance, and I needed to play nice, but a man who entered a home without asking wasn't one I planned on spending any time alone with.

The girls at the San Carlo were wrong. Joey Ep was far from a gentleman.

He adjusted his glasses and looked down at the box, a small hint of disappointment in his eyes as if he had expected me to jump up at the gift.

He motioned at the seat across the table. "Let's talk."

I pointed to the door. "We can talk at the San Carlo."

"I don't like when things are hard to get, Virginia. Get dressed, I'm hungry."

His audacity tugged at my patience. "If I wanted a man to tell me what to do, I'd still be married. I don't care who you are, you don't get to make decisions for me, and you sure as hell don't get to decide what I wear." I reached over and tore at the ribbon, then flipped the box open with a dramatic heave.

A gasp escaped my lips at the contents of the box, and my jaw nearly hit the floor. A metallic-gold lamé evening gown with ruffled sleeves spilled out. I placed my hand over my chest at the sight of it. It was something you'd see on Carole Lombard, not a divorced waitress from Georgia.

"I have good taste," he reasoned with a broad grin.

I momentarily lost my ground and reached down to touch it, but he cleared his throat, and I shook myself out of the trance with a step back.

It was a dress, a drop-dead gorgeous dress, but I couldn't be distracted by the finer things like Madeline. I had to stay focused. I relented. "I don't want your money or this dress." Only, I'd already spent the tip and couldn't return it. Why had I been so quick to give Miss Suzannah that money? "You want to take me out, we do it the proper way."

"And what is the proper way?" He quirked a brow.

"You ask me out."

"I did that."

"I didn't say yes, and even if I had, you can't show up in my home like this."

He fixed his gaze on me. "Will you let me take you to dinner, wearing this dress?"

I swallowed—he'd done what I asked, but even if I needed him, I couldn't find it in me to say yes. "Not tonight."

His fingers shuffled into his suit pocket, searching for something, then pulled out a polished gold cigarette case. He placed it onto the table in front of him, popped it open, and retrieved a single cigarette irritatingly slow, as if my words meant nothing to him. He pulled out a match from the same tin and flicked it against my table, lighting the cigarette.

Several puffs later, he motioned at the seat in front of him once more. "What do you want, Virginia? You see, it's my job to solve problems. I'm a solutions man. There's nothing I can't fix. No mystery I can't solve. Except you. You're a first for me."

"I'd hardly constitute a woman refusing you a mystery you can't solve."

"What would you call it, then?"

"It's called rejection, Joey Ep."

"Call me Joe," he said warmly. Another drag, and he pointed his finger at me, firmly shaking it for a few seconds. "The girls working at the San Carlo know what they can achieve if they catch the right fish. They're creatures of survival. They're easy to understand. You don't operate like them. Maybe you haven't found the right fish?"

Catch the right fish. The words rang in my head like an alarm bell, a phrase Madeline had said time and time again.

I remained still, frozen in place, with my eyes locked on him. He considered his own question, internally debating in front of me while scratching his chin. His entire forehead wrinkled up in thought, then smoothed out a moment later as something dawned on him. "Or maybe you're after something else?"

Everything became real so violently that the sense of panic sweeping over me kept me from being able to speak. I'd longed to find out what happened to her and why Joey Ep's name was circled in her book, but now it was too frightening. Too close.

His eyes squinted, and he used his foot to shove out the chair from underneath the table far more aggressively than he had before. The scraping of the chair's legs on the floor sent a chill down my spine.

My inner voice of reason screamed at me to run, but how could I? How could I abandon her? I'd finally found a real lead, and he was sitting across from me. I pulled myself together after a quiet sigh, but when I opened my mouth, no words came out.

With his empty hand, he tapped the box with the dress. I avoided looking directly at it, afraid it would call my name again, and I'd melt into it. "I saw your eyes when you opened it. I can give you more dresses like this, Virginia. What keeps you saying no? Your husband?"

"Ex-husband," I corrected grimly.

"Did he ruin you? Are you afraid every man will treat you the same?"

I choked out a laugh. "Every man has treated me the same."

"I'm not every—"

I lifted a hand to stop him. "I don't want the 'I'm the exception' speech because I've seen the way the men at the San Carlo treat the dames they dine with."

"Then it is about money. You're after money." He made the conclusion with a look of relief, as if he'd finally solved the mystery.

I took pleasure in my next words: "I'm not after money."

He blinked with surprise, then let out a sigh of impatience. "Everyone is after money."

"Not the way you get it," I snapped, and felt a tinge of regret. I was getting too lippy with a powerful man, even if I didn't want to admit he had it.

His upper lip twitched. "You women and your games."

"Men play games too."

He rolled his eyes. "I don't. I deal in numbers. I hate theatrics."

"You want to talk about theatrics?" I eased into the seat in front of him, carefully pulling my hands up to the table to fold them. "When you come to eat with your friends, you joke around with them about wanting to look up my skirt or take me out for a nice dinner and have me for dessert. You look when they look, laugh when they laugh. But when you're alone, Joey Ep, you look me in the eyes. You never look at my breasts or legs or make any lewd remark about what I taste like."

He didn't even hold my gaze when he said, "What's your point?"

"I catch you staring . . . but not at me. At the busboy, Giovanni." I sighed deeply to myself, knowing I was taking a risk at the assumption but wanting to find some power in the situation. He believed I had none, and I needed to change that. "And I don't blame you . . . he's beautiful. As beautiful as this dress in front of me . . . So if you're going to ask me what I want, I think you should answer the same question. What do you want with me?"

What did you want with Madeline?

Without missing a beat or showing any sign of discomfort from my words, he retrieved a black gun—a Colt—from the lining of his suit and placed it on the whitewashed table between us. A pinch of fear broke my confidence, and I pulled back my shoulders firmly. Would he kill me for saying it aloud? Am I the only one that noticed? I swallowed down a lump building in my throat.

Stay calm. Don't break in front of him. Don't cry.

"Last chance," he said, not a hint of anger in his butter-smooth tone. "You've already proven what I suspected—you're not after a man. If you're not after a man, why are you working at the San Carlo?"

"Is it so hard to believe I like the job?"

"You think I didn't notice you watching me? Studying me?"

Panic lodged in my throat.

"You're going to tell me what you want right now, or we're going to have a problem." He reached out for the gun between us, and for a fleeting, terrifying moment, my entire world halted. Every ounce of pride and self-respect hurled out the window, and I imagined all the things I'd say to him while begging for my life until finally I shouted, "I want to know what you did to Madeline!"

Her name was enough, and the second it hit his ears, he released the gun. He left it at the center of the table, and with the gift box between me and the weapon, there was no chance for me to make a grab at it.

He fidgeted with his hands, searching the details of my place. "Madeline was a waitress, and we had some fun together. That's the beginning and end of my involvement with her."

"That's a damn lie."

"Is it? Did Madeline tell you about me?"

"No," I said quickly.

"Madeline had fun with plenty of men at the San Carlo."

I thought about it a moment. Madeline helped me get hired at the San Carlo just a few weeks before she started traveling, and she was the same way with all the men—contagiously flirtatious. I didn't have solid evidence Joey Ep was her mystery man aside from his circled name. "I trust my gut, and she's missing."

He cleared his throat, and any unease building behind his eyes shed. He was back to blank, staring at me firmly. "A shame, but that has nothing to do with me."

"Catching a big fish," I mocked his words. "She used to say that same thing . . . In fact, she said she caught one. Suddenly, she's wearing nice dresses and jewelry, and traveling." I rushed to the armoire beside my bed to retrieve the postcards. I scattered them across the table, pointing to the very last one she sent. "Last stop, New York. Two months since her last postcard, when I was getting these weekly."

"Ah," he said, eyeing the postcards with callous indifference. He reached out to touch the last postcard, scribbled brightly with Madeline's messy penmanship, but I stopped him with a shoo of my hand.

"You're right, I don't have evidence you were her man, but I do know that she was hunting for one, and your name was circled in her notes."

"She kept notes?" His eyes narrowed.

"On men, yes," I said simply. "What she liked about them, what she didn't."

"And what did she say about me?"

"That you were a gentleman."

He placed a hand on his chin, and his bottom lip turned in. "You're the friend, the reason she insisted on keeping her god-awful room here instead of moving into a new place with me. I'd see her writing those silly postcards and ask her about you. She kept you a secret."

I understood the words separately, but trying to put them together left me puzzled. "So, you are the man she was traveling with?"

"Yes, I was her companion."

Heat rose inside me at his words—he was confirming the truth. Madeline's mystery man was sitting right in front of me. If anyone knew how to find her, it was him.

He sighed, then cleaned the palms of his hands on his pants. "You're going to forget this conversation happened . . . and move on. You're also going to find another job, Virginia. No more spying on me."

He gathered himself to leave, straightening the fold in his suit. But I couldn't let him go, not when he'd told me so much and yet nothing at all. The adrenaline that hit me felt impulsive and unpredictable, like my pa's rage. I tried to control it, overcome it, but I couldn't talk sense into my body. Maybe I was still riding the punch I gave Georgie, or maybe I was tired of men telling me what to do. Whatever the reason, I shoved the dress box out of the way and snatched up the gun off the table.

The box hit the floor, and the fabric spilled out in a tragic fashion. I gripped the handle and fingered the trigger. The only gun I'd ever fired was a shotgun to scare off birds in the fields on the farm. I'd liked the weight of it in my eight-year-old hands. How, just for a moment, while my pa recovered from a drunken stupor, he'd given me some sense of power. This gun was different, and tiny. I had to aim carefully and watch the position of my fingers.

But the power was the same.

Joey Ep's face sported a hint of surprise, but he never showed it in his body language. He reached out, palm flat, and said, "Give me my gun."

"Tell me where my friend is," I said, trying not to let the nerves get the better of me.

"What's your plan here?" He looked around briefly with a smug expression. "Kill me? What then? How are you going to get rid of my body?"

"Plenty of men come in here getting too rough. You think you're the first man to die in one of these rooms? That Miss Suzannah doesn't have people she calls to get rid of bodies?" The lie came out so well rehearsed that I amazed myself.

A moment of silence lingered between us, and he just stared at me. He studied my body, my eyes, and then the way I held the gun. His gaze was trained on it for so long that the silence grew thick enough to make the air in the room unpleasant. What was he thinking?

"I'm the people she calls," he finally answered.

I opened my mouth to come up with another lie, but only air came out. My throat felt dry, parched. I could hardly swallow, I was so nervous. But I had nothing but this gun as leverage, and even if I didn't intend on firing it, I wasn't giving it up.

"But you did well," he complimented. "If I didn't already know, you might have convinced me."

He was praising me?

"Did you want to be an actress, like her?"

A pain filled my chest at the mention of Madeline, and I briefly relived the hours we spent dreaming of Hollywood. "I'm going to shoot you," I said instead, finding my strength and forcing my voice to remain steady.

"Have you ever even fired a gun before?"

I aimed at the floor-length mirror and pulled the trigger. The bullet punctured the glass, then shattered it. I jerked at the sound, and while the broken pieces littered the floor, my door opened with a bang. Miss Suzannah exchanged a glance between Joey Ep and me before a fire lit behind her eyes. I waited for the lecture, prepared myself for the consequences of such a brash action. Would she send me packing?

"What is going on in here? What did you do to her?"

His mouth dropped open at the comment. "She's the one holding my gun."

"I know my girls and Virginia wouldn't be firing a gun unless you did something to provoke her." Then, it dawned on her, and her expression twisted. "How did you get into this room? Who let you in?"

Calmly, he sighed. "Do I need to remind you who owns this place?"

She shrugged out of her coat, revealing her thick shoulders and meaty arms, prowling closer until she was eye to eye with him. I'd seen her body plenty of times, but the way it transformed in the face of an adversary made me all the more grateful I lived under her roof. "You have my replacement in mind? Is there a long list of women waiting to run one of your brothels you've got tucked away in your books?"

Joey Ep cleared his throat, and though he still seemed awfully composed, his eyes held no sense of defiance. "We wouldn't dream of replacing you, Miss Suzannah. I know what these girls mean to you. Forgive me."

"It's not me you need forgiveness from."

He turned to me and cleared his throat. "Forgive me, Virginia. Now, if you'll kindly return my gun?"

I could have said everything in front of Miss Suzannah. Maybe that would put pressure on him to tell me something—anything. Despite her dismissal earlier, I knew she cared for Madeline. But I didn't want to involve her too deeply or put her in danger.

I placed the gun back on the table with a thud.

"Who let you in?" she asked again, refusing to let it go.

"One of your boys, and I paid him handsomely," he said. "I'm not going to give you his name . . . because this is a onetime occurrence."

Without acknowledging his statement, she waved him to the door. "Time to leave, Joey Ep. You want to visit again, you do it right and ask me." Her lips thinned while she looked my way. "And pick one of the working girls, yeah? Virginia does the laundry."

"We're just talking," I said. "It'll only be a few more minutes. I'll clean up the glass."

She didn't buy it but agreed to leave if the door stayed cracked open, and Joey Ep paid her for the mirror. When she was gone, I felt a sudden urge to break down, and it took everything inside me to keep tears from escaping my eyes. My next words came out in a shaky whisper. "Is she dead?"

"I don't know," he admitted, his eyes solemn.

"How can you not know? You were her man, weren't you?"

He laughed a little at the idea, then sank back into the chair. "We were friends." For the first time since I'd known him, his shoulders dipped, and his tight posture eased into a slump. His very emphasis on the word *friends* made me question everything I'd assumed about him. "She wanted a job, Virginia. All I did was show her how to get it."

"A job with you?" I questioned. "Madeline worked for the Mob?"

His eyebrows perked up, and a sense of longing washed over his features. "She was damn good at it too. One of the best I've worked with."

"*Was?*"

I didn't know if I even wanted him to answer me, but before I could recant, he said, "If I tell you, you'll leave this alone? You'll keep your mouth shut? The consequences if you don't will be dire."

I said it though I had no intention of following through: "I'll keep my mouth shut."

Chapter Four

He spent the next half hour telling me all about Madeline's involvement with the Outfit. She started laundering money for them, then had some fun at the racecourses, but she wanted to travel, so Joey Ep arranged for her to transport stolen goods across state lines. At first, his stories felt comforting to me. I had fought her when she quit the San Carlo, claiming she had a new job, but wouldn't tell me anything about it. I could recall every instance she'd come home with a new coat, a fresh cut, or a costly dress, and though I'd question how she got it, grow upset that each visit stretched longer, she beamed with newfound life. Her world was finally materializing into something out of a dream, and watching as she flourished, I both adored and envied her. I had never seen her so happy, and I wanted to feel the same way.

But as he continued detailing more dangerous ventures, my heart sank. He gazed down at the New York postcard with a sense of unease. He'd finally made it to the most important story of all: What had happened in New York? What had happened to my friend? I waited for him to carry on, but he held the pause a moment too long.

"Go on," I insisted. "Tell me."

"Before I explain what happened, you need to understand what she walked into," he finally said. "There was a war with Masseria and Maranzano, two rival Italian bosses, each seeking control of the other. It was a bloody mess." His voice wavered from its calculated flow. "When the war ended, a truce was proposed. We stop fighting each other and start making decisions together."

"You call it the Commission." I cut him off with a wave of my hand. His eyes went wide, wider than I'd ever seen them. "It's intended to keep the peace between the major crime heads. Chicago would have stakes in New York, and New York would have stakes here. Shared interest, no cheating each other."

He just kept staring at me, perplexed. "How did you know that?"

"Men talk at the San Carlo. I listen. What does any of that have to do with her?"

"She was to meet with Joe Adonis, one of the prominent figureheads in New York. I'd sent her with a case of stolen diamonds and jewels. Adonis agreed to help her find a buyer for them. It was supposed to be a onetime transaction."

"But?" I pressed him on.

"But Adonis liked her, as most men do. He wanted to see her more. I played along and kept sending her back because it was beneficial to me." He hesitated, and an emotion I couldn't place crossed his features. "I've long suspected Adonis of cheating us out of our stakes, or not giving us the proper amounts owed. This peace between the organizations is all very new, and while there's an adjustment period, I'm a numbers man, and the numbers weren't adding up."

I shook my head, pondering his words. "You wanted her there to spy on New York?"

"I wanted her there to spy on New York," he repeated with a nod.

"Doesn't that defeat the purpose of a truce? One spying on the other?" I didn't understand the dynamic between crime families, or what it took to maintain peace, but it felt more like children trying to share than grown men.

"You don't know how many died to get here, the bodies we walked on to achieve the alliance. I didn't want him to threaten it. Adonis worked for Masseria during the war with Maranzano."

"But he betrayed Masseria . . . switched sides when it looked like the tide was turning?"

A breath escaped his mouth, and he leaned in, less surprised now and more on edge. His shoulders tensed. "Stop doing that."

"Interrupting you?"

"Showing off knowledge that could get you killed. Knowledge is only power when you're in a position of power."

I swallowed—I'd overplayed, run my mouth.

He cleared his throat. "As I was saying, Adonis knows no loyalty. But worse, he's violent, impulsive. I didn't think Madeline was ready for him and I was right."

A sense of dread washed through me, and I stood up, pulling a glass from the cabinet beside my sink. I turned on the faucet, let the water fill the cup, and then took a long drink. When I came up, gasping for air, I faced the sink and asked, "Did they find out she was spying?"

"Adonis says she never arrived with her last shipment of jewels," he answered. "They claim she ran off with them. With Madeline's habit of disappearing, it didn't seem wild to think she might have."

"She wouldn't do that," I snapped back, twisting around, feeling my stomach starting to roll and knot. "Stealing from the Chicago Mob? She doesn't have a death wish."

"I'm inclined to agree." He stood up and lightly placed his hat atop his head. "But I can't storm New York and demand answers. She might have been important to you and me, but she's just a body to the organization. Replaceable." He straightened his suit and reached down for his gun, preparing to leave me with a story that would forever haunt my days and nights.

"That's it?" I knew tears had collected in my eyes, but I couldn't feel them running down my face yet. "No answers, no justice?"

He glanced down at the dress on the floor. "Keep it, Virginia. It will look lovely on you." Tucking his gun away, he took steady, determined steps to the door. He'd told me what I needed to know, but it wasn't enough. What if she was still in New York, hiding away? What if they'd done something to her, and they'd never have to answer for it? She'd stood by me through the divorce, even testified against Georgie. She'd been a friend when I had none, a companion in a city full of strangers.

How could I leave her behind like this?

I stared down at the postcard, and a wild idea crossed my mind, one I barely had time to consider before my mouth opened, spilling out the words: "You can't storm New York demanding answers, but maybe I can?"

He halted at the door, hand gripping the side, then looked over his shoulder. "What are you asking me?"

Heat ran up my body, settling in my cheeks. "You'll need a replacement, won't you?" What was I thinking? I couldn't join the Mob. Not on some wild pursuit for a missing friend, and yet, the words kept falling from my mouth with the same ease as Georgie's venom. "A woman to do all the things Madeline did. I'll do it."

"I can't let you."

"Why?"

He peered out the door before shutting it quietly. "Because Madeline was a mistake, one I have no intention of making again."

"You already know I have good ears," I protested. "That I am determined, that I will see this through. You want proof New York is cheating Chicago, I want to find out what happened to my friend. Let's help each other."

I thought he might leave, certain I didn't have it in me to pull it off. I wasn't even convinced myself. I was often in awe of Madeline's fearlessness. The leaps and risks she took to feel something new, experience something better. I was only just getting on my feet and learning to be alone. At night, I still felt a pull to run back to Georgie, just so I'd have arms around me, keeping me warm.

I wasn't her.

I wasn't fearless.

I waited and waited, but he never opened the door. It occurred to me then, perhaps Joey Ep needed me more than he cared to admit. He shifted around to face me, hands in his pockets.

"Make no mistake, this isn't the kind of thing you can just walk away from when you please and take a bus back to Georgia. When you're in, you're in, meaning we will expect you to continue your work even after we find out what happened."

"There's no way out?" I asked with disbelief. "What if I do find the proof you need on Adonis? Could we use that?"

He looked down, then back up with curious, narrowed eyes, as if the very idea was a darker thought than he'd imagined I was capable of voicing. "You get the evidence, I can agree not to turn it over until they let you go. It's not foolproof. There's room for error, but it's worth a shot." He took long strides forward with a finger pointed at me. "You'll have to earn your way to New York, just like Madeline did. It won't happen overnight."

I buried any sense of fear lingering in my stomach and said, "What do I have to do?"

"It's not up to me," he said with a sigh. "I have a say in the kind of men we bring into this organization, but the women are a different story." He reached down for the dress on the floor, inspecting it for damage, then collected it and gently placed it on the bed. "Get dressed. We'll go to a party. If you can impress her, you're in."

I arched both my brows slowly. "Her?"

I squeezed into the dress and dolled myself up while Joey Ep anxiously checked his watch but didn't say a word to rush me off, even as I struggled to pick the right shoes to wear. I numbed myself to thinking about the consequences and all the ways this could go wrong. I'd never make it out of this building if I let the voice inside my head, begging me to reconsider, win.

We walked through the massage parlor together, my hand hooked in his arm, and unlike earlier—when men had shamelessly gawked my way to envision me naked—they glanced up at Joey Ep and then back down in a rush.

I anticipated Miss Suzannah to appear in her ghostly fashion to stop me. Maybe a small part of me hoped she would, but the hustle and shuffle of the parlor continued, and with nothing to keep me inside, we left without a word.

"If a girl wants to change her life, all she needs to do is take a big, fat risk." Madeline drifted into my head, her usual wispy voice sounding clearer than ever before. *"Nothing changes without risk."*

I let out a harsh sigh. If only this risk couldn't get me killed.

Outside, he opened the passenger door to his parked Cadillac V-16, and I sunk into the seat with a weightless feeling. Like the dress, it was classy . . . beautiful. I didn't belong inside it.

He told me we were going to his Madison Street suite but gave me no information on the mysterious woman I needed to impress. The drive was quiet, and though Chicago's nightlife was on display, the city felt lonely. Dark. At night, I craved the fairgrounds, with the colorful exhibits and busy fairgoers. The rest of the drive was a blur. I blinked, and we were at the suite door.

I pinched at the fabric of my dress until my fingers ached. He took my hand with little delicacy. "The woman who grabbed the gun off the table, where is she?"

I blinked.

"Find her. She's the only way you're going to survive this."

I forced myself to smile, and we stepped inside. My ears were greeted by blues music playing from a gramophone near the door and a sea of chattering men and women clanking glasses and shouting Italian at one another.

"*Cazzo!*" (fuck)

"*Figlio di puttana!*" (son of a bitch)

I grinned a little. Not quite a sophisticated party where politicians talked strategy or socialites gossiped over dinner, but I felt comforted at the reminder of the San Carlo. I took another step forward, leaving his arm in a trancelike state. "This is where you live?" I asked aloud, decidedly far more fascinated with the interior of his suite than the guests I should be conversing with.

"One of my homes," he answered.

I sucked in a big breath. A long, mirrored wall led like a catwalk to the suite's crowded living room with etched opal glass lights hanging above me to light the way. Maple furnishings with vermilion trim surrounded me—a handsome look, but there were hints of his unique style in the orange upholstered sofa, leather chairs, and grand piano.

Joey Ep had class.

The men and women greeted him with a head tilt or casual wave but then resumed socializing. Instead of gesturing me to a group of women huddled in a corner near the bar, he snapped his fingers to the left, where men sat together in a parallel alcove.

"You said I was meeting a woman?" I asked, desperately trying to keep any nerves from shaking my voice and betraying me.

"Velma," said Joey Ep to a man in a swanky gray silk suit with stripes. He spun around and startled me with his, no, *her*, face—buttermilk skin, sharp eyes like a dragon, and a mess of blonde waves pinned beneath a fashionable matching hat. Her cheekbones could cut glass, and there was this raw, animalistic beauty about her. I'd never seen a woman in a suit before, and I imagined I'd never see another pull it off like she did.

"Vel, I want you to meet someone," said Joey Ep, then turned to me with a comforting smile. "Virginia, this is Velma Capone, wife to Bottles."

"Bottles?" I asked. "As in, Ralph Capone? Al's brother?"

"How about you ask me the questions?" Velma reached up for my face, fingers holding my chin as if she was sizing me up. And for the moment, I let her. "What a pretty dame she is. What's your plan for her, Joey?"

"How about you ask me the questions?" I repeated her words and lifted my hand to move her fingers away from my chin. "I got a name. Use it."

"I like her," she declared robustly, with a haughty laugh to follow. "But that's not enough. Everyone has to be tested. The men have their tests . . . battles over who has the bigger cock through gunplay or bets." She strolled past me, heels clicking on the black linoleum floor to a credenza where, with just one touch of a hidden button, a bar emerged. "But we don't have cocks, so we'll do this the old-fashioned way. Two glasses, one bottle of Cutty." She retrieved the glasses and Scotch, then placed them atop the oak bar top. "We drink together, one shot each until the bottle is empty."

"A drinking game?" I glanced at Joey Ep and folded my arms. "This is the test?"

The men around us huddled in to get a better look.

"You make it through the bottle without passing out or chucking up, and you're in."

"Is this necessary, Vel?" asked Joey Ep, pursing his lips with distaste. This wasn't what he had in mind either. "I need her to have a level head tomorrow for our trip to the track."

"The track?" I cut in.

Velma poured us two shot glasses, filling them to the brim with careful precision, not letting a drop of the amber liquid fall to waste on the polished bar. I reached out for my glass, getting close enough to Velma to smell her Chanel No. 5 perfume. This was all it took? A drinking game with Al Capone's sister-in-law? Had Madeline done the same thing?

I grinned a little to myself. My entire family had a complicated, deeply rooted relationship with alcohol. Though I tried to stay away from it—sometimes just the smell brought memories I longed to forget—I knew how to hold my liquor. I'd been drinking away my anger since the ripe age of nine.

She lifted one eyebrow, and I took it as a green flag. I reached for my glass and downed it quickly, desperately trying to keep my lipstick from smudging all over my mouth. The whiskey burned my tongue and throat, a sensation that used to make me shudder as a child.

Another round, and another, and another.

Velma's careful, steady hands were long gone by round five. The shot glasses overflowed onto Joey Ep's bar, and he hurried between us to clean it off.

I smoothed a hand across my forehead, and the men around us cheered and laughed while the wives in the corner rolled their eyes in repulsion.

We kept it up until there was one round left for both of us. I was sweating off my makeup, and the armless love seats, where the wives sat and lounged by the fireplace, all started to blur into nothing but a mess of colors. Cigar smoke billowed around me, the smell distressing my head into a dull pound, and the spaghetti I had for lunch threatened to betray me. Just the thought of the vomit burning my already whiskey-sore throat made me grimace.

Velma didn't look much better, blinking quickly to steady the likely swiveling world around her. One more glass. Just one more drink.

I could do this.

I took it quickly alongside Velma, and with significant effort, kept the bile from rising in my throat. I was done for; I could feel it. My knees grew weak, and my arms felt heavy. If I took a step in any direction, I'd fall to the floor like honey on my momma's charred biscuits.

Joey Ep circled behind me, two hands taking hold of my shoulders with a firm but comforting squeeze. Velma poured us both a tall glass of water, and a few men brought us each a plate loaded with hors d'oeuvres. I crammed a cheese soufflé and anchovy croûtes into my mouth until I couldn't breathe, then downed the entire glass of water.

I'd regret this in the morning, but right now? I felt more alive than ever. The alcohol did what it always did—made me forget. All the worry and fears I'd collected since Madeline's disappearance vanished, and despite the very dangerous situation I was willingly stepping into, I felt good.

Joey Ep led me to one of the love seats, shooing off a head-shaking wife to plop me down. He carefully pulled my hair from my face and tucked it behind my ears, wearing a look of what I could only assume was pride. "That was impressive. Who taught you to drink like that?"

"The same person who taught me how to shoot a gun," I said.

He grinned.

My pa was good for nothing, scum of the earth, but I couldn't say he didn't leave me without the anger and drive to survive the world.

Velma shoved him off with a push and plopped down into my lap as if we were two schoolgirls greeting one another after a long, fun-filled summer.

"Welcome to the family, Virginia Hill. Now let's get out of here and have some real fun."

"I told you, Vel, we have plans in the morning," cut in Joey Ep, sounding more paternal than ever.

Velma stood and pulled me off the chair with a playful grin, waving his words away. "Don't worry, Joe, I'll have her home before breakfast."

On the way out, Joey Ep took hold of my arm and leaned down to whisper, "Try to keep up, but don't let your guard down."

Velma and I spent the night bouncing from club to club until finally settling in at Villa Venice, where she was welcomed like an old friend. A big band played jazz for hours with guest star Eddie South, followed by a nude chorus line Velma joined. Madeline had been wild enough for me, the first person I'd met in Chicago who didn't seem to care about the proper womanhood rules we'd been taught as girls. I thought I'd never meet another like her, but here was Velma, unhinged and out of control.

We drank cocktails, danced, and talked men and sex until around three in the morning. I couldn't keep up with her, so I didn't try. She'd order me a drink, and I'd pretend to finish it or quietly signal the bartender to water mine down.

I knew I had already passed her test, but that didn't mean I'd earned her respect. *She'll know if you're soft.*

When she finally slumped over into the small booth beside me, I prayed this was it. The end of her exploits. A moment to rest my aching feet and burning throat. "You know the only way out is death or divorce, right?"

"What?" I asked, spitting out the olive in my mouth with a light cough.

Her eyes widened, and she shook her head, as if she'd been in a trance. "I'm drunk," she said in response. "I talk when I'm drunk."

Only she made sense to me, and her words would resonate in my mind, burned there for good. The only way out is *death.*

"Are you going to be his woman?" She quickly changed the subject. "Can't say I've ever seen a woman stick around Joe too long. He's a particular son of a bitch, but with great taste."

"If I can help it, I won't be anyone's woman again."

"You been married before?"

"Recently divorced."

"Don't fall in love, Virginia," she warned, taking my hand and squeezing it tightly. "Not with these men, not with any of them, you hear me? They don't know love outside of power, and the second you give up yours, you're done for."

Men were the very least of my concerns. I was here to find my friend, not love, but I couldn't tell her that. "I won't," I assured her. "I'd never get involved with a Mob man."

She shot me a look. "You think you're better than me or something?"

I straightened my shoulders, swallowing over a lump in my throat. *Don't stumble and don't apologize.* I mocked her words. "I talk when I'm drunk."

She opened her mouth again, and I waited at the edge of the booth, ready to soak up some more of her drunken wisdom. Maybe I could ask her questions about Madeline? But instead of words, she swiveled around and threw up into a wine bucket. The smell almost caused me to do the same, a reaction I avoided by glancing back to the nude chorus line.

I didn't know much about Vel, but I did know that she was tragically unhappy and drank to fix something inside her. I knew because my pa did the same.

I shook off the judgment, the cruel thoughts, and reminded myself that not so long ago, I was tragically unhappy too. Regardless, it was in my best interest to use this moment to my advantage. "What happens after this? They send me to the track to clean some money, then maybe I start traveling?"

"If everything goes well," she said simply. "It doesn't always go well. Not every girl makes it that far."

Only I knew Madeline did.

"What about the girls that do?"

"It doesn't matter," she said angrily. "Aren't you listening? You're just a body to them. Keep your mouth shut, do what you're told, and you'll make so much money." She smiled dreamily, but something cut it short, some thought that consumed her and twisted her expression. "Your soul, though, you won't be getting that back."

I tamped down the nauseous feeling and shifted in the booth, reaching for her hair, gently trying to clean her up. Waitstaff loomed closer, attempting to scrub down the floor and collect the mess before other patrons noticed. I pulled one of her arms around the back of my neck and heaved her out of the booth. On wobbly legs, she leaned against me, flushed with embarrassment.

"I don't need your help," she muttered in my ear.

"It sure as hell seems like you do," I said back, gripping her arm and waist tightly to keep her from toppling over.

"I saw you drink as much as I did, what's your stomach made of?"

"I pretended to drink to impress you," I admitted, wondering if she'd even be able to remember tonight when she woke up in the morning.

Her brows pinched together, and she stopped moving her feet, forcing us both to halt in the busy club. "Why would you do that?"

"Joey Ep said you're my ticket in, that I need your approval."

"They don't really care what I think. Besides, why would you want this? This life?"

"Money," I muttered. "I don't want to ask a man for a damn thing again."

She was wobbly, leaning against me. "Good answer, but you'll need to work on your lying."

I played the fool. "I have no idea what you're talking about."

"You're not like the other one."

I stopped, felt my chest heave in response. "The other one?"

"The one before you . . . she couldn't hold her liquor, but she was a better liar."

Velma started moving again, and we made it outside, where the cool Chicago air greeted me with a refreshing gust, taking some of the cigar smoke caked to my hair and skin with it. A bellhop jumped into action, dashing off to retrieve Vel's shiny black coupe.

She pulled herself together, straightening her posture and cleaning the drool from the edge of her lips. "Maybe you've passed my silly little drinking test, but if it were up to me, I'd say no."

I eyed her seriously. "I just held your hair while you vomited in front of a crowd of people, and you're going to say no?"

"I want to say no," she reasoned. "You're too nice, you're not going to survive this." She made a motion with her arm, as if her drunken state should be enough to ward me off. "But they don't really care what I think. They just wanted to find me a place, something to do."

"Did you give the one before me this same lecture?" I inquired, knowing I needed to be careful with what I asked. But in her drunken state, how much could she possibly remember?

Her eyes closed and she pulled her plush fur coat tightly around her shoulders. "I didn't," she said. "That one would have done anything we told her to do, but you . . ." Her voice trailed, and she turned to face me. As if she were a creature and not a woman, she transformed before me. Her weakened expression and woozy disposition snapped together. Her eyes were focused, narrowed, and watching me. Had this all been some kind of act?

"I can follow orders," I said, rather hesitant.

"Can you?"

Her car arrived, and the bellhop handed her the keys. I thought about intervening, unsure she could even drive after so much to drink, but I was beginning to suspect that some of this, if not all, was an act. "Get inside, I'm going to take you somewhere."

I watched Chicago blend into a flash of colors and darkened streets until she pulled into a quiet neighborhood on the outskirts of the city. She pointed to a spot, a building, nestled between two others. "That's the morgue," she said.

I leaned in heavily to the idea she was still drunk because I knew morgues tended to be closer to the police stations and hospitals. Why would one be operating out here?

"That's where they take the bodies . . . if they're not throwing them into Lake Michigan."

I shuddered at the words but didn't let it show. The thought of Madeline being carried into the building in a bag left me on edge. Nothing about the building would lead me to believe it held the bodies of murdered men and women, families that had wronged the Mob. Red brick, clean windows with simple white trim, and well-tended flower beds. It looked comfortable, inviting.

"Why are you showing me this?"

"I think you got a right to know where you'll end up if you don't follow orders," she said. Her voice was hard now, cold like ice. "It should scare you, Virginia. I know it scared me when they first drove me here. You choose to go to that racetrack tomorrow, and after that, they do the deciding."

I sucked in a breath and tried to come up with my next question, something about Madeline, maybe? I could ask about the girls before me. But just like earlier while waiting for her car, she shook off her stony expression and arched her brows playfully. "Let's hit another club? Joey Ep would think something was wrong if I didn't bring you back sloshed."

My stomach groaned in response. "He wants me in good shape tomorrow, doesn't he?"

"I make the rules tonight, and I say we hit another club. You want my approval, don't you?"

I managed a smile in return, but I knew it had to be hardly convincing. What had I gotten myself into? What had Madeline gotten herself into?

I drank with her until every thought I had was a mushy collection of images and words, but that didn't stop the nightmares of the morgue. Madeline's body, still and cold, her lips stained cranberry red in the brick house with nice windows.

Chapter Five

I awoke to Joey Ep's voice, carrying through the door into the room with a quiet but demanding tenor. He gave the door a few gentle taps. "Time to wake up, Virginia. Join me for breakfast when you're ready."

In a rush, I lifted and grabbed at the sheets to cover my usually half-naked, slumbering body. But when I reached to cover myself, my fingers brushed against a silk nightgown, so light and airy that I hadn't even realized I was wearing it.

The pounding in my head began without mercy, a relentless, mounting ache, and my mouth was dry, reminding me of the mistakes I'd made the night before.

I glanced around the room and realized I was not at my little home above the parlor. White walls surrounded me, matching lacquer drawers with silver moldings and black accents along the walls. The sofa next to the bed had a splash of coral in the upholstery, and as if the room were made for a woman, there was a mirrored dressing table. Did Madeline ever sleep here?

"There's a selection of dresses in the closet," continued Joey Ep from behind the door, tossing me back to reality.

Who changed me last night? How did I even get back to Joey Ep's place?

I got up and took a long bath in the polished marble tub, soaking longer than I should to soothe my head, then bounced out in a robe to investigate the two dresses hanging in the closet—both summer cotton crepe frocks, one yellow and one navy, with embroidery along the bust. I pulled out the navy one and slipped into it. Right at the door, he'd left me a pair of brand-new ghillie tie heels. I slipped them on slowly.

Just my size.

I studied the room, surveyed the photos littered about the room. A different woman in each, and in some of them, he was kissing them. I continued on, spotting a framed photo on the dresser, hopeful it was Madeline. When I got closer, disappointment shook me. It wasn't her.

Was I wrong in assuming Joey Ep preferred men? Or were all these women just a collection to him? Girls he'd recruited? Friends?

I walked through the foyer to the dining room, where he sat at the glass table, eating his breakfast of fresh eggs and sausage. He had the morning paper in front of him and several notebooks set beside his coffee. They were scribbled with numbers and dates, page by page, in neat rows. He smiled rather triumphantly while looking me over. "I'm glad you chose the navy one."

He stood up to retrieve something from another room. I sat and picked at the bacon on my plate, then took a long swallow of my orange juice. He returned with a French beret, just like ones I'd seen in shop windows at the World's Fair, and a silk chiffon scarf. He handed them both to me, and I took them tentatively, noticing that upon closer inspection, the scarf was hand-painted.

"What is going on?" I asked bluntly, placing the scarf and hat down. "What is all this?"

"All what?"

"The dressing me, the feeding me. I'm not a child."

"I don't think you're a child."

"Did you undress me last night?" I knew the answer, but a part of me hoped he'd tell me Vel had done it.

"You didn't expect me to let you sleep in my guest bed after God knows what you and Vel were up to all night. And the clothes are a gift, a necessary gift for the racetrack today. I told you last night, we have plans. You asked for a place in all this, I'm finding it for you. Most would just say thank you."

"In my experience, men don't give gifts like this without getting something in return."

"And I must want to fuck you because all men want the same thing? You women are terribly predictable sometimes." He neatly cut a piece of sausage, plucked it with his fork, then chewed it leisurely. "You're not my type."

"What is your type, then?" I poured some milk and a few spoons of sugar into my coffee, then took a slow sip. "Chiseled and bronze?" He hadn't confirmed it yet, and I felt gross not knowing. Not knowing if, when he undressed me last night, he'd stared at parts of me that he had no right to see.

I thought I saw a grin pull at his mouth. "In my line of business, in our grand Chicago, if the world knew my type, I'd be gutted from head to toe by my own friends and family. I've worked hard for what I have. I have no intention of letting anything take it from me, even my own preferences."

"Strictly business then?" I asked.

"So that's settled," he said mildly.

I exhaled sharply, deciding to draw the line, damned be the consequences. "Moving forward, I can dress myself."

He crossed his legs, eyes on his food. "I enjoy taking care of things . . . my home, my books, my clothes, my—"

"People?"

"Madeline didn't mind it. In fact, she rather enjoyed being catered to."

"I'm not Madeline," I retorted.

"I see that."

"It's been four long years since my body has belonged to me. I want to have a say in the men that see it."

Though his eyes were void of any readable emotion, his voice lowered a bit. "It will not happen again." His eyebrows lifted, and he used his fork to point at the scarf and hat. "Finish eating, then dress. We're off to the races in twenty minutes."

My heart began to thump wildly in my chest, but then I remembered my shift at the San Carlo today. "I can't," I said quickly, startling him. "I work today."

It looked like he might laugh, but his lips fell into a straight line before he said, "You can't work at the San Carlo anymore. You won't need to."

"I don't want to quit my job. I like working there, and I make good tips." And it was the first place I'd felt an ounce of independence since leaving Georgie. "I can do both."

He sucked in a fast breath, as if he were growing impatient with the conversation. "You're going to be working at the track, convincing the rich that you are one of them. We can't risk them wandering into the San Carlo and seeing you with your apron on. Do you understand?"

He held my gaze as if I were a child, the same one he'd dressed and fed this morning. It was patronizing and got under my skin. Maybe there was logic in his words, but that didn't mean I had to like them.

"Can I say goodbye?" I asked after a prolonged moment of silence.

"Certainly." He paused. "Through letter only."

A warm July breeze hit us as we exited his car at the Washington Park Race Track. The sun was high in the cornflower-blue sky, and despite the beautiful sway of the trees, I could smell the horse manure with every updraft, carrying from the grassy infield. I should have been slinging meatballs and cleaning sauce off my apron at the World's Fair, but through the most unforeseen events, I was here.

Joey Ep held out his arm, and I wrapped my hand in for the long walk. We passed through the tiered grandstand seating, where spectators chatted, shouting bets at nearby booths and tables. He leaned in. "After what happened with Capone and the IRS, every penny coming into our organization has to be accounted for and cleaned. Every penny."

His voice deepened a bit. "Every week, I find a new way to launder money, but this is by far the most lucrative. I bet on a horse with dirty money, it cycles through the ticket window and comes back to us clean, and if the IRS ever wanted to take a look at the books, I can record it as track winnings."

I looked around briefly and lowered my voice when I asked, "But how do you know which horse will win?"

He smiled sheepishly.

I stopped dead in my tracks and gave him a look.

"I have my connections, so rest assured, when I send you in to place a bet, you're going to win."

He was sending *me* in to make a bet? "You want me to launder money here?"

"That's the idea."

"So you'll tell me who will win and I bet everything on that horse?" I was confused, trying to piece together how this worked.

"We never make straight bets to win. We never put everything on one horse. Too risky," he said simply. "I don't care if God himself came down and told me which horse was going to win. Anything can happen, anything can change out there. And it would draw too much attention. We play it safe. We bet on horses to show or place, meaning they might win, or they might finish second or third."

I peered past him at the oval-shaped track, flags flapping in the wind as men and women chatted over the next race. A man passed us with a crumpled-up ticket, swearing at the sky and tossing it to the ground with a spiteful hiss. How much money had he lost betting on a horse that hadn't won? A small pinch of guilt struck me. Men like Joey Ep came here and won every time, while others wholeheartedly believed that the odds were out of their hands.

"You're going with me, aren't you?" I asked, mid-thought.

His cheeks reddened considerably, face tightening with irritation. "If I could do that, we wouldn't need you. My associates and I draw too much attention. But a sweet-looking dame like you can get as lucky as she wants at the tracks without the IRS catching on." He adjusted his fedora and cleared his throat.

"What's my take?" I asked, a question I only now considered. I was determined to find out what had happened to Madeline, but I wasn't going to break the law for nothing. Maybe I was in over my head, too soft for this kind of work. Maybe my mother was right, that we women should take what we can get.

Maybe, maybe, maybe.

On the other hand, if I ignored the doubt brewing inside me and decided to take this seriously—be the girl unafraid to sock Georgie in the mouth and pick up a mobster's gun—maybe I'd surprise myself.

What if I could be good at this? What if this could help me create a life of my own?

His eyes widened. "You pass this test, then we'll talk about a take."

I breathed in a newfound confidence. "I think I'd like to talk about percentages now. You're a numbers man, aren't you?"

"Three percent of the winnings."

I pretended to think about it. "Ten."

"Five."

"Five, then."

I smiled rather triumphantly, and he handed me an envelope so loaded with cash that it didn't quite close. I peeked into it, and my jaw dropped. "How much is this?"

He snapped his fingers to grab my attention, then pulled out a small piece of paper and handed it to me. "Four thousand on this horse to place, two thousand on this horse to show. I'll have a car wait for you outside the track, and we'll meet later at your place." Again, I opened my mouth, unsure what I wanted to ask next, but he cleared his throat and disappeared before I could get another word in.

Now that I was alone, a mild panic hit me. I was at the track, with an envelope of money from the Mob. I let out a breath of apprehension, and once it left my body, drifting into the summer air, I pulled in another. Again, my mother's voice plagued my thoughts. *"Where's your gumption, Virginia? Find it."*

I did what he said and placed my bets, then awaited the start of the race in the grandstand with all the other gamblers on rows of benches above and below me. I looked around slowly, taking in the crowd, and then glanced up at the top of the grandstand, where there were shaded boxes for the wealthier gamblers—the big spenders.

A bell signaled the call to the post. Jockeys in beautiful silks mounted their horses and rode into the starting gate, and then it clanged open. The thrill of it all had me jumping up from the benches to get a closer look as if I couldn't possibly trust Joey Ep's sources. A cold sweat trickled down the nape of my neck, worsened by the summer heat. Thank God I chose to wear the navy. Once the sweat started coming, it usually didn't stop.

What if Joey Ep was wrong? What if I lost all that money? Would I be the next body they dragged through the morgue doors? I closed my eyes to drown out the voice over the loudspeaker and focused on the hooves pounding against the dirt, just barely breathing while clutching my chest.

I glanced at the man beside me, shouting at the horses and jockeys. I snatched the beer out of his hand for a long sip. He gave me a quizzical look as I handed it back to him.

He chuckled and shouted, "First time at the tracks?"

I nodded tersely.

He handed me back the drink. "You're going to need this."

I took another drink. "Thanks, stranger." He was a tall, gaunt man, wearing cassimere slacks and a striped summer vest. Unlike Joey Ep, groomed and clean, he had a week's stubble along his chin, and despite his dreamy blue eyes, there was something dark about them. Two exhausted, lifeless voids staring back at me. I couldn't place if I felt sympathy toward him or unease.

I stared a long moment before I was startled by a bell that signaled the end of the race. I missed the horses crossing the finish line, but when the crowd shouted the winners, and the announcer followed, I screamed like a little girl on Christmas morning.

"I won! Can you believe it, I won!"

I had never won anything in my life, and though this hardly qualified as good luck, I couldn't help my racing heart, fueled by a delight I'd never felt before.

The stranger lit up with me, chuckling with praise, and reached out to embrace me. The action threw me out of my blissful shock, and I shuddered away from his hands.

"Pardon me," he said, and despite his haunted look, a brimming confidence emerged before me. He wasn't shaken by my rejection, as most men would be. Instead, his lips pulled into a wolfish grin, and his face flushed. "Wish I'd won myself. It would have been a nice send-off for my last night in Chicago."

"Last night?" I inquired.

"Headed to Hollywood for bigger things."

"The movies?"

"Something like that."

I moved my fingers up, shaping them into a rectangle, closed one eye, and pretended to take a picture of him. "I'll have to remember your face."

"I don't think I'll forget yours."

I felt a knot form in my throat, and he grinned. His smile was wide and engaging, his teeth sparkling white. He was attractive in a brooding kind of way but didn't look like he had money. I guess I had a type. I groaned at my own ridiculousness.

"Say, how about celebrating? We can go have some drinks . . . but you're buying."

"I'm married," I said, a lie that just slipped out far too easily—my mouth's only defense against myself. A man was the very last thing I needed, another problem I'd have to solve.

"No ring, and at the track alone? What kind of husband do you have?" He cocked his head to the side. "He's either dead or a figment of your imagination, or . . ." He paused, eyes narrowing, leaning in a little too close. "You're a liar."

He was taunting me and enjoying it. I struggled to repress my own smile. "Apparently not a very good liar." I'd have to get better at it.

I handed him back his beer and ran my hands down my dress to straighten any wrinkles, then turned to collect my winnings. He reached out for my arm but retreated quickly, as if the memory of how I'd reacted earlier suddenly dawned on him. I appreciated him for it. "Wait. At least give me your name?"

I grinned over my shoulder at him. "If I see you again, I'll tell you."

Back at my place, Joey Ep counted the money carefully and logged it into a giant black book. I couldn't see specifics of what was in it, but there were at least a hundred numbers and dates.

"I'm going to need a bigger purse next time," I said, motioning at my poor, overstuffed handbag.

"You're going to need more than just a purse," he said without looking up at me or taking a break from his notes. "You still look like a working girl. If we want to get away with higher bets without catching unwanted attention, you need to look like you have money. Dress like it, sound like it."

I pulled my shoulders back. "I just brought you twenty thousand dollars. Save the insults, will you?"

"A fact is not an insult, Virginia. You want to move through the ranks like Madeline did and get to New York?"

"Yes. You think I can't do that?"

"It's not a matter of can't . . . it's a matter of want and will. Do you want to find Madeline? Do you want nicer things?" He combined the two with ease, gazing around my little space with a look of critical indifference. It wasn't like his home, new and clean. A work of art. But I worked hard for this place, and even though I had very little in comparison to him, I was proud of it.

And yet, his words rang inside my head, rooting there. This dangerous venture came with an advantage—money. Money I could spend freely.

I fiddled with my fingers and looked around my place. No more working for tips or ringing sauce out of my apron. No more doing laundry for Miss Suzannah until my hands were weak and pruned. Was I willing, he asked. Maybe. Did I want it like he wanted me to want it? I wasn't sure.

He broke from his notes and gazed at me through his wide glasses with a grin. He used the pen to point to a tinier stack of money. "Your cut."

I reached out to touch it, then counted it slowly, just like Joey Ep. One thousand dollars, and I had no idea what to do with it.

"I'm looking into getting you a new place. Let's see how you do a few more weeks at the tracks. If everything is still going smoothly, we'll tour some apartments."

"There are nice places up the road." The words slipped out, mostly because I'd grown to love my home. It was where I'd met Madeline, where I'd gotten a taste of independence, and I could already predict the foreseeable lecture from Miss Suzannah.

"No." He cut me off with a wave of his hand, as if the idea of continuing to live here was preposterous. "Think bigger, Virginia. Think bigger."

"You didn't make Madeline move," I protested. "She still has her room here."

"She lived with me and insisted on paying her rent here. Now I know that was because of you." He didn't seem pleased with the revelation. "Letting her come and go here was a mistake, and I won't make the same mistake with you. I need you to commit to this new life, and in order to do that, I think it's best that we leave your old one behind entirely."

"But I . . ."

He raised his hand to stop me. "This decision is not up for debate. I didn't offer to fund Madeline her own apartment, Virginia. You're going to have your own place, buy nice things with your own money."

"But it's bad money. How can I feel good about buying things with bad money?"

"There's no such thing as bad money. It's all the same. You're taking a risk trying to find Madeline, but that doesn't mean you can't enjoy the fruits of your labor. You are done with the massage parlor. Have I made myself clear?"

He left me no room to argue, but I didn't hide the sadness in my tone when I said, "Yes."

When he left, I drifted to my bed, staring at the money on the table from across the room. I couldn't possibly sleep, so I pulled on my robe and left my room, trailing down the stairs to the bottom floor to exit into the laundry room. Along the windowsill, Madeline and I had stashed half-smoked cigarettes. I reached for one, and the door opened swiftly behind me.

I jerked around.

"I just passed Joey Ep on his way out." Miss Suzannah's deep voice joined me in the quiet room. I braced myself for what was coming, the words of reason she'd force me to hear, filling me with unshakable doubt.

"I know what you're going to say," I said. "Why don't we skip to the end of it?"

She lit a match, lighting the cigarette for me, eyes sharp. "Very well."

I cracked the laundry room window, took a long puff, then blew the smoke out into the night air.

"They steal women, you know. The Mob men will pillage the countryside, looking for stray young girls to snatch from their homes. Little, sweet girls, with good families, that can be broken easily. They ship them here, to Chicago, where women like me are forced to mold them. Teach them how to please a man, how to make money with their bodies, how to take away everything that makes them unique. They make me turn them into objects." Her words haunted me, but even more so, her eyes. They were nothing like I had seen before. They were tired and distant, with a layer of water that glistened in the moonlight streaming through the window. It was a tragic sight. I had never seen her cry. Not this woman, who had the men of this joint cowering in her presence.

"That's who you're working for," she finished, inhaling sharply. She took the cigarette from my hand for a smoke. "I didn't want to believe it, not my Virginia. Not my headstrong laundry girl who wants to work honest, clean, so that she can make something of herself."

Before I broke down myself, I swallowed over the lump in my throat and said, "He's going to help me find Madeline. She was working for him; she was working for the Mob."

"Fuck, Virginia," she snapped before I could tell her the rest. Her bottom lip curled in. "You're going to get yourself killed for that girl?"

That girl?

"You know how many times Georgie almost killed me?"

She said nothing.

"Just once." I placed my hand over the skin of my neck instinctively. "He followed me here one night, attacked me before I could get inside. He was drunk, out of his mind. He's always been quick to slap me around . . . but he was different that night. He was angry that I'd thrown him out, that I was staying here. He was squeezing my neck so tight. I'd seen my pa do it to my mother a dozen times, but he always stopped before she started turning blue. Georgie wasn't going to stop. He was going to kill me. Madeline was outside for a smoke and found us. She didn't like me much. You'd made an exception for me, and like all the girls here, she was wondering what the hell was so special about me. And the answer is nothing. There is nothing special about me. You just felt sorry for me."

Miss Suzannah's eyes lowered.

"She pulled him off me . . . saved my life that night. Maybe all the things you say about her are true, but to me, she's important. I need to find her, or at least, find out what happened to her. I owe her that much."

"What about what you owe me?" Her tone matched her eyes, sharp, unrelenting. There was no sense of compassion anymore—it had vanished so quickly that I wondered if I'd imagined it. "What about what I've given you?"

"What do you want from me?" I asked, shattered by the notion that even Miss Suzannah wanted something in return for her charity.

"I want you to live." The words were weighted, raw, and delivered with expert precision. “You have two roads. One, you do some illegal things for the Mob . . . and maybe find out what happened to your friend. Two, you let all this go, stay here, work hard, and eventually have what you need to start a new life. One that belongs to you.”

But if I took road two, I’d never find out what happened to her. I’d also never see one thousand dollars sitting on my kitchen table again. If I’d never seen the money, never been given a look at what it gave people like Joey Ep, maybe the choice would have seemed simple.

“The money I make can set me up with a new life, a good one, and when I find Madeline—”

“If,” she countered.

“*When* I find her, I’ll have the money to get us far away from these people.”

“You think it’s going to be that simple? This fairy-tale ending where you two run off and live somewhere and leave this dark mark on your history behind? You don’t think it will follow you forever?”

I opened my mouth to reply, but her words choked me.

“I want you out, Virginia. I will not watch you disappear like her.”

I sucked in a fast breath and decided to leave out the fact that Joey Ep already wanted me gone. Somehow being kicked out hurt less than walking out voluntarily. I held back the tears and uttered, “I’ll leave.”

Chapter Six

"Honestly, you're an idiot," said Madeline, soaked from the pouring rain. It dripped down her frock while she examined the skin of my neck, bruised and purple. I couldn't talk back, not yet—I still felt as if my voice had been stolen from me, squeezed so tightly that my final squeal for help was all that was left of it.

She handed me a glass of water, then paced my room, hands on her hips, staring at the barren walls. I had nothing but a bed and a few articles of clothing. Georgie had taken everything that was his, leaving me with the suitcase I'd left Marietta with.

She found a long mirror leaning against the wall and grimaced. There was a bruise near her left eye from Georgie trying to shove her back. It was big and seemed to have grown over the past few minutes. It wouldn't go unnoticed when the men entered the parlor, looking for the prettiest girl to spend time with.

"I'm sorry," I muttered.

"Why do women like you . . ." She stopped, as if she couldn't form the words. "You've lived here four years. What took you so long?"

The truth? I was scared to be alone, scared to death, but I wasn't going to tell her that. "Divorce is a sin," I managed with a raspy voice, not bothering to hide my wry tone.

She rolled her eyes. "I'm not in the mood for your daft sense of humor."

I nodded. "I know. Miss Suzannah kicked him out when I asked her to."

"Not nearly soon enough. Don't think the girls and I didn't hear you two arguing all the time. It's no wonder Miss Suzannah favors you . . . you're a mess. She's always had a soft spot for tragedy."

She wasn't telling me anything I didn't already know, but the words stung. I didn't need a reminder, not when I was working hard to find my place in this city with nothing but the clothing on my back. Every day I woke up and feared I'd drown, but I kept trying, pushing, and wanting.

"Thank you for your help, but could you just fuck off, please? I want to be alone."

"Virginia!" Her voice almost squeaked. "Did you just tell me to fuck off after I saved your damn life?"

"I don't need this," I exclaimed. "What opportunities do I have? No education, no money, no family to lean on. I just had Georgie when I got to Chicago. I stayed to eat, to be warm in a city where thousands are out of work. All I have is a pretty face, and the only job for a pretty face is—"

I stopped before I went too far, but her brows were already coming together. A heat filled her cheeks. "The only job for a pretty face is being on her back?"

"I didn't say that."

"You didn't have to." Her hands found her hips again. "I'll have you know that my favorite position is on top, slapping a man around while he screams my name."

Her brash words left my mouth agape.

"That's right," she said confidently. "I don't know who taught you that sex is the loss of power. When I'm with a man in the bedroom, I run the show. I make the rules. What other job can you say allows a woman to do that?" She scoffed. "And you wonder why the other girls here don't like you. Take your judgment and shove it."

I was speechless, sitting there like a child being lectured, until finally I uttered, "If only I didn't hate men."

"I hate men," she countered strongly, then lifted her shoulders into a casual shrug. "And I love them. Not all men are the same. You decide you're going to go to war with men and love, you'll end up alone. Or worse, running a place like this."

Her dig at Miss Suzannah didn't go unnoted, but I decided not to address it.

She gathered her wet gloves and coat, then shuffled to the door. Before she left, I stood up quickly. "I shouldn't have told you to fuck off. Nobody was coming for me, nobody but you. I won't forget it."

"Well, that makes one of us." She breathed heavily at the door, using her fingers to touch the bruise on her face. "Not that my face will let me. When are you going to divorce him? He's going to keep coming back. He still thinks he's got some ownership of you. You need to do things right and give him back his last name."

"It's not easy."

"I divorced mine. You just need a witness."

The revelation filled me with relief. If she could do it, why couldn't I? Except . . . "Not a line of people waiting to testify against a violent man, and I don't have friends here."

Her mouth dropped. "I'm offended. I scrubbed those nightgowns with you until nearly morning."

"You stained one of them," I reminded her. "And Miss Suzannah made you help me."

"I didn't complain, did I? If that doesn't make us friends, I don't know what does."

I gave her a weak smile. "I need a serious witness, Madeline. I just want to get to sleep. I have to get up early and start looking for a second job. Otherwise, four years from now, I'll still be renting a room here."

She pursed her lips, and her shoulders dropped. Instead of walking out, she returned to the bed and reached out, her palm up. "Let's get a drink."

"I don't want your sympathy," I countered, and I didn't, but I couldn't deny the urge to take her hand.

"Well, you have it." She didn't move her hand, just waited patiently for me to take it.

I eyed the bruise on her face more carefully, a reminder that anyone who decided to get too close to me would eventually get his fist. Without meeting her gaze, I said, "I just want to be alone."

The lie came out strong, as if I'd spent years rehearsing it. And though it was awfully cynical, I considered how long it would be like this. Would I be alone in this city for the rest of my life? What choice did I have aside from catching a bus back to Georgia to a family that wouldn't embrace me? I could already see my father shaking his head from the porch while I lugged my traveling case down the dirt road.

I couldn't go back.

"That's a damn lie." She called me on it. "You owe me, Virginia. Let's be alone together, and drink until we feel nothing. It's my favorite medicine, and it works every time."

Nothing . . . Why did the absence of feeling sound so inviting? Without letting my mind talk me out of it, I placed my hand in hers.

I awoke in a cold sweat to the faint sound of someone at my door—a tapper I couldn't ignore. I jumped up, feet on the cold floor, but my eyes were still heavy. I pried my lids open by using the pressure from the palm of my hand. I was in my room, alone, no Madeline in sight.

The thump at the door continued.

"Virginia." Miss Suzannah's voice was but a whisper.

I searched for my robe, pulled it from the small wardrobe near my bed, and shuffled to the door. When I opened it, the beam of sunlight flooding in from my dainty curtains gave me a clear view. Miss Suzannah was standing next to an elderly woman with smooth, aging skin and yellow hair. She wore a black satin afternoon dress, with a checked coat and sizable cravat tie-fastening. It looked costly, and certainly too warm for a Chicago summer. She clutched a handbag in front of her, her gloves pulled tautly, eyes weary but steady.

I blinked twice because, for a moment, I thought I might still be in the dream. She looked like Madeline, only older. I stared at the freckles along her nose until she cleared her throat, and I shook myself from the daze.

"This is Madeline's mother, Doris," said Miss Suzannah, confirming what I already suspected. "She'd like to speak with you."

I opened my door to allow her inside, expecting Miss Suzannah to slip away into the dark hallway. She didn't, and instead stalked behind Doris until the two sat at my table. Somehow in the past week, I'd had more company than in my last four years in Chicago. "I can make you some tea," I offered, though I suspected it wouldn't compare to what she drank at home.

"No need, dear," she said with a lift of her hand. "Please, sit. Miss Suzannah tells me you and Madeline were close . . . ?"

"Friends," I confirmed.

The word seemed to bring her a sense of comfort. Her lips turned up in a weak smile.

I sank down onto the bed. "I thought you might be dead," I blurted out. "She spoke about you—about all her family—in a way that made me think . . ."

"Not dead, but dead to her." Doris held her smile, but it didn't reach her eyes. "My husband didn't approve of her divorce; he didn't approve much of anything she did. Madeline wasn't conventional . . . or proper."

A deep sigh escaped her mouth, one I could only associate with disappointment. "She kept threatening to leave one day, but I never believed her." She placed her handbag on the table tentatively. "Her father had set her up with an inheritance on the condition she stay married. When she went through with the divorce, he disowned her . . . and forbade her from ever coming home."

Madeline came from money?

"Is there anything you can tell me? Anywhere I should start looking? Miss Suzannah says she left months ago . . . Did she tell you where she was going?"

For a moment, my mind drifted to the very same conversation I'd had with Joey Ep at this same table when he told me everything. All the frightening details of how deep Madeline had gotten into the Chicago Mob. I couldn't tell Doris the truth. What would happen to her if she went sniffing around the San Carlo?

I decided I needed to lie but couldn't possibly come up with something convincing in the short, demanding moment. I sucked in a breath.

"Why now, Doris?" Miss Suzannah asked with little delicacy, her sharp tone piercing the night air. "I watched that girl, taught that girl, for years. She lived under my roof, ate my food . . . We shared laughs and love and moments you decided weren't important enough to have with her. Why now?"

I watched Miss Suzannah's fists curl into her palms. If she cared this much, why was she dismissing all my attempts at finding her?

Doris held her composure well, shoulders straight, eyes even, but her voice shook when she said, "I was forbidden by her father. He didn't want her to be found. I know it's hard to imagine, but she was a stain on our name, and to my husband, our name was everything."

Not hard to imagine, no, but the bitter taste in my mouth thickened.

"Now that he's dead, I make my own decisions." The way she uttered the word *dead* told me everything I needed to know about their marriage. "I need to find my daughter."

I knew what it felt like to have no control over my choices, bound to my husband's guidance and rules. I understood, maybe even sympathized, but I also felt a rage. Madeline's father didn't beat her, but he abandoned her. And like my mother, Doris did nothing to stop it.

"Have you heard from her?" Doris leaned in, her voice shifting into a plea.

"California," I said. "She's always wanted to be in the movies."

Miss Suzannah cast me a look but stayed quiet.

"Her dream as a girl," she agreed with a nod, but then, tears streamed down her face, as if she'd been holding them in since the moment she walked through my door. "You see, she rang the house a few months ago. She sounded like she was in trouble, and not the kind of trouble I'm used to with her . . . This time she sounded"—a pause lingered while she struggled to find the right word—"scared."

I pulled myself to the edge of my seat. I'd gotten postcards, plenty of them, but never a call.

"She asked to come home, she said she just needed a few days and then she'd be on her way." Another soft sob escaped her lips. "I begged him to let her come home, but he wouldn't budge. I told her no."

I glanced up at Miss Suzannah, but she was far away, eyes fixed on the wall next to the door. The fire in her was gone, and I wasn't sure why.

"I just have this awful feeling," she blubbered on. "If there's something I should know, anything, please tell me. I can't possibly get her out of trouble if I don't understand the trouble."

The pain in my chest urged me to voice the truth, to give her some relief, but the sense of loathing grew like a mold inside me, poisoning the softness. Maybe I'd still have my friend if her mother and father had allowed her to come home. For that, it didn't matter how deep Doris's sorrow was; I saw her as less of a mother with each passing second.

My lips dipped into a frown, and I reached for her hands. "I wish I had more to tell you, but I don't."

We sat a little while longer as she recalled her favorite memories of Madeline. In them, she was proper and well behaved. She lived on an estate in Virginia that had been in her family for generations. She played the piano beautifully, spoke fluent French, and wore the latest fashions. She'd met her husband at a country club, and the wedding was well attended. This woman didn't take risks, didn't live in a rundown massage parlor, and wouldn't dare be seen in ripped stockings.

She didn't bed men for money or befriend women like me.

It pained me to do it, but I retrieved Madeline's coat and gave it back to Doris. She sobbed into it for a few long minutes before leaving me with all the information I'd need to find her again.

She embraced me warmly, but I stiffened in her arms, still lost in my own thoughts. Madeline had had everything, and it hadn't been enough. All this time I'd thought she was chasing wealth, that her "ticket out" was some dream to have beautiful things, when really, we'd always wanted the same thing.

A life that belonged to us.

Miss Suzannah walked her out, and I sat back down, feeling the need to fall apart. I hadn't once cried since Madeline disappeared, clinging to the hope that she'd return with a story of her latest adventure and all would be well. But now, with the call in my mind, I couldn't stop the plaguing thought that my friend might be dead.

I cried fast and hard, my chest heaving up and down rhythmically until I felt some sense of release. I heard footsteps down the hallway and cleaned my face off before the door opened.

"I've changed my mind," Miss Suzannah announced firmly. "Go get our girl."

I blinked, trying to make sure I understood her. As I opened my mouth to respond, she retrieved something from her coat. A black revolver. She swung the gun toward me, and I stood up urgently. "Put that thing back in your coat!"

"You're taking this with you," she ordered.

"I don't need a gun."

"I already know you can shoot," she said, pointing at the shattered mirror. "But can you aim? Do you need me to teach you?"

"I can aim," I told her, surveying her features. They were twisted and wild, eyes bulged and watery. "What changed your mind? Doris?"

The unease in her expression made me tighten up. What wasn't she telling me?

"Doris wasn't the only call Madeline made."

My heart dropped into my stomach. "You heard from her? You heard from her and you didn't tell me?"

"I couldn't let her bring her trouble back here. I have other girls to worry about and what kind of protection can I offer her when the Mob owns this place?"

Maybe all her words made sense, but none of them soothed the anger inside me. She'd watched me sit nightly, worried for my friend. She had me pay rent for her room and then dismissed my fears with some excuse.

"'Oh, Madeline will be Madeline, she always comes home,'" I mocked her dismissive comments with a sneer. "Only, she tried to come home, and you wouldn't let her."

She placed the revolver on the table with a thud. "I'm not going to talk you out of this, so take this gun to protect yourself."

"I don't want your help." The words came out in a spiteful hiss.

"Well, you have it." Her hand pulled up to run through her curly brown mane tensely. "I can't promise much, but I can promise that when you need me—" Her voice broke, but she cleared her throat to pull herself together. "I won't leave you behind like I did her."

The silence between us grew dark and unsettling. She craned her neck until it cracked, then heaved in a deep breath. The emotion on her face, the pain, was gone. How had she learned to turn it off so easily?

With nothing left between us but my rage, she walked out the door without a word.

I didn't sleep at all that night, just lay restless, tossing until my legs couldn't take it. I sprang from my sheets and moved to the gun on the table. I snatched it up and stared at the broken fragments of my mirror, where my reflection was a messy patch of images.

All the doubt inside me, the fear of the unknown, dissipated.

Dead or not, I was going to find out what had happened to Madeline. When I did, come hell or high water, I'd make them pay.

Chapter Seven

I spent the next month following Joey Ep's orders—making bets at the races according to his mysterious sources. He dressed me from head to toe in wealth—fine mulberry silk and slimming floral frocks. He even let me borrow one of his cars, a gorgeous green Buick roadster. Despite my desire to remain impartial, disconnected from the entire ordeal, I couldn't deny how much I'd grown attached to the vehicle.

There was something about the purr of the engine, the way it vibrated against my seat, that left me in a state of bliss.

Today, I arrived at the track with the same little piece of paper—my orders from Joey Ep. A crowd awaited me, a select bunch of rich and poor, eager to see if I'd continue my lucky streak. My story was easy enough to believe. After all, I'd stolen it from Madeline. Rich heiress from Virginia, spending Daddy's money before he tracked me down. I played the part well, often letting myself fall into the ditzy state a girl with too much in her pockets might.

It was all a big show, and the onlookers loved it—particularly the other high rollers. One man, Wayne Fitzgerald, an oil tycoon from Texas, loomed closer today. He'd made a habit of stalking me after my third or fourth big win. I loved the spotlight feeling more than I'd ever admit. It wasn't the dirty attention I got in the parlors or at the San Carlo. It was intimidating and powerful.

After I made my bets, I took a seat and tried to ignore his piercing gaze. Thankfully, any pretty dame was able to catch his attention long enough to give me a break. I grew comfortable, holding a drink in my hand, glancing down the stands from my box—one reserved for a chosen few—wondering if I might see my stranger again.

The repetition over the last thirty days had me eager for something new. Something different. Even if it was just a man with an unkempt beard and a dark smile.

I pulled out the latest issue of *Vogue*. In my head, Joey Ep was scolding me for doing it. *Rich women don't read in public, it's unbecoming.* But the excitement of the races had faded over the weeks, and I longed for an escape. I wasn't well read, though I'd never admit it aloud. My ma pulled me from school to help on the farm, leaving the learning up to me. After all, burying my head in a book wasn't going to find me a husband.

I struggled with words at times but pushed through, dragging my way from page to page until the sentences grew smoother. I picked out words from "Summer Synopsis" by Marya Mannes, mouthing them to myself. "Hello, darling, what a scorcher. Why yes, yes, I'm swell."

"*Vogue*?" a woman's voice asked from beside me. "I've read that one. Did you see the page on Mrs. Marshall Field? The Chanel suit she's wearing is just divine." She sunk down close, her voice dropping to a whisper, before handing me a tiny piece of paper that said, *Trigger*.

I was so startled by the intrusion that I looked around her, thinking I might see someone chasing down a lost, mad woman. But I knew the face well, just not the voice—Wayne's wife, who hadn't spoken a word to me over the last month.

With a deep sigh I didn't bother to hide, I tucked the magazine down beside me. "What can I do for you? More mocking from your husband about how I don't belong at the track without a man or a keeper?" I thought more about it, all the little phrases he'd used over the last few weeks that had trickled their way back to me through the gossip and mumblings of all the other big bettors. "That eventually I'm going to lose all Daddy's money and come crawling back to a man just like him?"

"Nobody hates my husband more than I do," she said, too proudly. "Maybe we can help each other . . . This is the horse that's supposed to win today." She pointed to the name on the piece of paper.

Trigger was an awkward little chestnut-colored thing with misshapen hooves and an unpredictable gallop. One moment he was in the lead, the next he was stalled. I couldn't fathom how he'd come to win. Was she trying to get me to make a mistake to appease Wayne's ego? I groaned at the thought.

"No, thank you." I motioned her up and down. "I don't want any part in what you and your husband are cooking up. There's no way Trigger is going to win today."

I studied her flushed cheeks and mossy eyes, which stared at me earnestly. She was not a young beauty anymore but had a sense of class that couldn't be found in Georgia. A grace and sophistication I often tried to mimic. Even her tight posture made me straighten my own shoulders.

"His sources have never been wrong before. Well, until now," she pointed out.

I knew that to be true because, over the last month, Wayne had won every race. But how could it be true if the races were fixed? I had thought he knew the winners because he just knew the horses, but now it seemed that, like me, he was getting names to bet on. Who was his inside source?

I blinked, lowering my voice. "Who is giving him the names?"

"I don't know, and I don't ask. What does it matter? You have the name of the winner, and he's got a different name. I made the switch this morning. Today, he's making all the wrong moves."

I still didn't understand. "You're making him lose?"

Her lips were pursed. "I told the bastard if he had another affair, I'd be volatile. I want him to hurt, and this is the best way to do it. We don't have to be friends, Virginia, we can just make this a simple transaction. I give you the name of the winner, you make the bet. He has a different name, he loses big."

"He's going to lose regardless today if you gave him the wrong name. Why involve me?"

I watched her eyes steal a glance behind us, where all the high bettors conversed in a private section, each tailored and neat, with wives sitting quietly in corners with hand fans. "You're his enemy here. He spends countless hours talking about ways to get rid of you. He doesn't like the competition. Worse, he doesn't like that you're a woman. He can handle losing, but he cannot handle losing to you. I want to teach him a lesson, a real one."

I couldn't get over the gall of her, and though admirable, how could I trust it?

Joey Ep had different names listed for today, bets he wanted me to make on horses to show and place. If Trigger was going to win, why not bet everything on him? Why wouldn't Joey Ep want a bigger cash flow? A massive win? I thought about his words, his fear of betting on a winner—the uncertainty behind it.

Maybe a big win would get me out of the races and off to more important things. New York. Madeline. The mystery I needed to solve instead of sitting here, basking in the sun.

"I can't," I finally told her, because though the idea was tempting, I couldn't trust she wasn't secretly plotting with Wayne. Not just that, but betting on a different horse would be going against Joey Ep's orders.

I'd done well the last few months; I couldn't get greedy or stupid.

"Listen—" Before she could continue, Wayne emerged, casting a shadow over us both. He reached for her and scooped her along, his hand so tight around her pale arm that it looked painful. "Go sit down," he gave the order, and with a snarl, she did.

"What are you and my wife gossiping about?"

I shrugged lightly, leaning on how I had dampened Georgie's temper with playful stupidity. "Men, of course, and fashion."

He then took her place, and I grabbed my magazine and bag, fully intent on finding a new spot for myself. He reached up for my wrist and circled the bone, giving me a pull back down.

I gasped at the audacity but had an unpleasant memory of Georgie yanking me along outside the San Carlo and sank down like the woman I used to be, surviving on compliance. I couldn't hit him, couldn't lose my temper. I couldn't make a scene.

"I don't know what part of Virginia you came from, but I've got friends there that never heard of you. Not your father, not his money." He twisted my wrist harder, and I eyed my bag, where the gun rested snuggly inside.

I snapped out of it. "Get your hand off me."

"Sir, you're in my seat," called a man behind us. I looked up to find my stranger, neatly dressed, but still bearded and unkempt. His eyes held the same darkness as they had that first day, only now they narrowed fiercely, staring at Wayne with unmatched aggression. I had never seen someone smile in such a frightening way.

Wayne didn't move. "The lady and I are having a discussion."

"The discussion is over," he said simply.

The two men stared a moment longer, to the point of discomfort. I shifted in my seat, noting that the scene was drawing attention.

Wayne stood briskly, running his hand along his vest pocket before tipping his hat to me. "I should be joining my wife. Best of luck today."

Wayne shoved past him, a shoulder brush that didn't make my stranger stumble. He gave Wayne a grin as he walked away. When he took his place, I thought about what I could have possibly done differently today to have three separate people sitting next to me in a matter of minutes. One with a desperate plan, the other a threat . . . Now what did my stranger want?

"If you're going to bet with the big boys and not be . . . well"—he paused and motioned at my figure—"a boy, you should hire some protection. It all seems very civilized, but men with big money can be animals."

"Are you one of them?" I dared to ask, unable to ignore his threatening stare at Wayne.

He barked a laugh. "We're all animals."

I eyed him curiously, trying to figure him out. I could easily blame one chance meetup on coincidence, but a second was edging on suspicious. "I thought you were going to California a month ago?"

"I'm a traveling salesman with a gambling addiction." He placed a hand on his chest. "I always find my way back to the racetrack."

"What do you sell?" I asked without looking him directly in the eyes.

"Shoes."

I stole a glance at his polished oxfords and nodded. It all seemed believable enough, but I didn't buy it. Not with his grim expression and two haunted voids.

"Thank you for your help with Wayne, but I can handle myself." I tried to shoo him off with my words, my demeanor, but he was unshaken.

"I don't doubt that."

His response surprised me.

"But since I'm here in town for a little longer, I'll sit with you? Keep you company to keep the wolves from your door?"

"What's in it for you?" I arched both my brows and turned to face him. "I won't be sleeping with you." The words slipped out before I had time to catch them. I knew not every man wanted to take me to bed, and yet, my defensive nature kicked in any time a man offered to do me a favor.

The amusement made his dark eyes sparkle for the first time. He flashed me his hand, where a gold band rested on his ring finger. "I'm married, doll, to a good woman. Honestly, nothing in it for me, except maybe learning a thing or two from you."

I sighed. I wasn't disappointed, I'd only just met the man, but there was something thrilling about the idea of him. My stranger at the track, stealing longing glances at me from his seat, desperate to know my name. We'd never speak again, but always wonder. I liked the fantasy of it.

I looked down at my wrist, where Wayne's fingers had left a small imprint. If it was only sitting, company during the long morning races, what harm could it do?

"Fine," I relented. "I'll take your company."

He loosened up his shoulders, threw one leg over the other, then sank into a relaxed state. With a hand on his knee, he began to tap with one finger. "You promised me your name."

I pressed my lips to keep myself from grinning.

"Virginia."

He offered me his hand for a shake. I accepted it, but he quickly tightened his fingers around mine, flipped my hand, then lifted it to his mouth for a kiss. The scruff of his facial hair tickled my fingers. I blushed in response, to my own disappointment.

He then turned my hand back over and trailed a few light kisses from my palm to my inner wrist, where I felt like my heartbeat might betray me through the spiderweb of veins.

I gave him an eye roll. The mysterious air he had before seemed to be vanishing before my eyes, as if the world had decided to tell me—once again—that men are not imaginary or made-up. I couldn't conjure what I wanted and expect it to materialize. My stranger did not disclose his motives freely, but now, I knew what they were.

I pulled my hand away, waiting for him to tell me his name. A long silence followed, and he returned to watching the races as if he had no intention of telling me at all.

"Are you going to tell me your name?" I pressed rather forwardly.

He took note of my aggression and leaned over, face still lit with amusement. "You didn't like me kissing your hand, did you?"

His bluntness left me rigid.

"You make a habit of kissing women's hands? How would your wife feel about it?"

"Does it bother you that I have a wife, Virginia?"

I swallowed, feeling the beads of sweat on my forehead. I liked the way he said my name, like it was slowly melting on his tongue, and he needed to draw it out longer before he lost the taste of it.

"No. It bothers me when men kiss me without asking."

"It was innocent, truly. A good show for the watchers. We don't want them thinking we're not familiar."

I exhaled slowly, looking over my shoulder to find Wayne staring the same way he always did—closely, and with intent.

Maybe I was too quick to judge, but my history was working against me.

"My name is Ben," he finally offered.

It wasn't grand or mysterious, but instead, rather simple. Easy to remember.

"Nice to meet you, Ben."

That day, the race ended with a winner—Trigger. I couldn't believe it, not even after the crowd began to chant the horse's name. I hadn't made the bet out of caution, and the regret made me see red. But I soaked in the pleasure of watching Wayne rage and his wife grin beside him. I waited for it to happen again the next week. Only, it didn't. He continued his unnatural pattern of winning while his wife sat behind him, glowering at him while he followed attractive women to the concessions.

I felt a pang of guilt but reminded myself that I couldn't help every lost woman. Madeline needed to stay my focus, and every week spent at the tracks left me on edge. Often, I'd completely forget my role and just chew at my nails in the most unladylike fashion, imagining how much harder and longer I'd need to work to finally get to New York.

"I lost every race today," I told Joe one night over drinks. The empty feeling, the sinking conclusion of loss, sat with me—left me uneasy. I wasn't supposed to lose, and it didn't make much sense to me. His organization thrived on winning, beating the odds, or rather, creating them. I watched Wayne win again and then leave the tracks with his mocking expression. How did he do it? And if I had all the connections to win every time, why wouldn't they let me?

"You've lost before," he reasoned. Joe took a slow sip of his coffee. "We've been over this. Sometimes you need to lose."

I looked down at my own coffee and tapped on the porcelain cup. "How do you imagine it looks to the spectators? I'm supposed to be good at this, making connections, creating a name for myself there. That's what you told me you wanted."

"You're laundering money, Virginia, and if you win all the time, you're going to draw the wrong kind of attention. We need this to look real, and real gambling requires loss."

I needed him to make it all make sense to me. "I can accept losing, but why can't I bet everything on one horse? Just once? I know you said it's a risk, but the payoff—"

"Nothing is exact about this. God himself could tell me the winner tomorrow and I still wouldn't send you in to put everything on the name. We fix the races to the best of our abilities, but nothing is certain." He flashed me his little ledger, crowded with numbers in fine, pristine handwriting. "We pay off the jockeys, but all it takes is one moment, in that split second before those horses cross the finish line, for him to decide he's done taking orders from us."

I opened my mouth to reply, but he wasn't done.

"Or the animal gets hurt, or there's a collision of sorts. It's all unpredictable."

"The same thing could happen with the horses that place second or third," I said quickly.

"True," he agreed. "But we can take a hundred small hits, Virginia. When losses get too big, they want someone to blame. I will protect you." His voice cracked, and though I couldn't determine why, it felt as if I'd just cut him, and he was bleeding in front of me, giving me the much-needed assurance that he was human. "I will do better by you."

He returned to his books with a sigh, and though his words should have been enough, they weren't. I couldn't shake the feeling that I was still in the dark.

For the most part, Ben sat quietly beside me, like any other spectator. He didn't barrage me when I read my magazine, nor did he press me to tell him more about myself. It had been weeks and we hadn't discussed anything outside the race and the heat. In his silence, I found an unusual sense of peace. When I was with him, there was no pressure to perform, no judgment when I didn't, and though he did act curious when I placed my bets, he didn't ask for advice.

"Virginia, did you hear me? Do you want to get out of here?" He reached over, his hand delicately pulling my fingernails from my mouth. Sometimes, I had no idea I was even doing it. I made the choice not to look down at my nails to see the damage.

I blinked determinedly, shaking my head. "Of course not. Has the race started?" I peered out to check. I expected to see the horses thundering down the track, riders bucking them on with spurs, only to find it was long over. I sighed at the realization that I was quickly blowing my act. "I'm tired," I lied, then leaned back in my chair. "Maybe the next race will wake me up."

"What's going on inside that head of yours?" He folded his newspaper and placed it neatly in his lap. "Sometimes you do this thing where you just disappear."

"I don't know what you mean."

"You're here, but you're not," he continued to try to explain. "Your eyes get far off, like you're thinking about something very seriously. It can't possibly be the horses."

I pulled my shoulders back at the notion that he was studying me, or worse, seeing through me. Perhaps our moments of quiet reflection weren't so quiet after all. I wondered how I could possibly explain myself without giving too much away. "I've been thinking about something," I began, not entirely sure if I planned to reveal what yet.

"I'm all ears."

"Do you think the races can be fixed?"

"No," he said quickly, and it caught me off guard. It felt like he was trying to shut down the thought. "Too many factors. Two boxers, sure, easy enough. But even if you could bribe every jockey, animals are unpredictable."

"Then how do you imagine Wayne wins so often?"

"Dumb luck." He shrugged. "Men like Wayne come from a long line of men just like him, rich and bored and with plenty of time to learn the ins and outs of the race. Not just that, but how to gamble smart. He's got a keen eye, analyzes the past races, the form of the horses and the jockeys, then makes calculated bets."

I grimaced at all the compliments he paid him. I fanned myself a moment, feeling like I couldn't distinguish what was making me sweat: the Chicago sun or my racing thoughts. "But humor me . . . if the races were fixed—"

"But they aren't," he cut me off.

If only you knew, Ben. "If they were," I repeated, "and you had the winner's name in the palm of your hand, would you make the bet?"

"No," he said again, staring gravely at me, as if he could read my mind. "I don't know how Wayne keeps winning, but it's not because the race is fixed." His fingers moved to my wrist, giving it a firm squeeze, and it dawned on me that he'd been holding my hand since he pulled it from my mouth. "What you're doing now works, why change it?"

I studied the way his fingers pressed into my skin, and my memory flooded with thoughts of Georgie. The way he dragged me outside the San Carlo before I socked him. The tendencies of a violent man I ignored, too distracted by a smug grin or a pretty face. There was one right here, sitting next to me, and I'd invited him in. But it wasn't just that . . . The way he'd lectured me, so similar to Joey Ep, made a tension fill my chest.

I jerked my hand away, placing it back into my lap. Who was he, *really*?

A part of me didn't want to push it. What we had worked here. He sat with me and kept Wayne at bay and didn't ask me for anything in return. I didn't need to know everything, did I?

I tried to put my thoughts into words without sounding accusing. "You haven't told me anything about you."

"You know I sell shoes, and I'm not a very good gambler," he reasoned. "What else do you want to know?"

"Why are you here every day? Don't you work? What about your wife? I'm certain she gives you hell when you come home smelling of horse manure and cigarettes."

A muscle in his jaw ticked, but his engaged smile didn't falter. "Why don't you ask me what you really want to ask me, Virginia? Why have I been here, sitting with you, the last two weeks?"

His honesty felt crude, and sharp. I didn't like it.

"You're a smart woman, keen. Why do you think I'm here?"

I sucked in a breath but tried to keep my mouth flat. This wasn't fun to me. Every question he asked was shattering the sense of peace he'd given me. "You want something from me."

"We already established we're not sleeping together," he noted.

"Doesn't mean you're not thinking about it."

"If I wanted to sleep with you, I'd have you already." He said it too matter-of-fact, like bedding women outside of his marriage was a sport. One he excelled at. "I'd take you to the clubhouse, buy you some oysters, tell you everything you want to hear. Don't think I haven't imagined what that red hair would look like sticking to your forehead while you sweat beneath me."

Warning bells rang inside my head, and my instincts tugged at my composure. His face lit with amusement, pure joy—this was just good fun to him.

"Who said I'd be beneath you?" I shot back.

His dark eyes found mine, and surprise replaced the amusement. I thought of Madeline, her words. "My favorite position is on top, slapping a man around while he screams my name."

He shifted uncomfortably in his seat.

"Am I being too loud for you?" I questioned. "You can spit filth but can't take it?"

He ran his hands down his trousers, adjusting them, desperately attempting to regain his composure. I covered my mouth to keep myself from laughing.

"You've got a cruel sense of humor," he said, cheeks flushed, nearly laughing himself. "But that was fair. Let's start over? Honest to God, I'm just here to watch you. You're good at this, and I'd like to not lose so much."

I wanted to believe him and let it go, but it just didn't add up. "You've been at this two weeks with me, and I haven't seen you cash in a single ticket, which means you aren't betting on any horses."

"I'm being careful," he countered. "I'm a shoe salesman from the New York slums. Not all of us have money to throw around. If I don't get better about where I put it, I'll be right back where I started. Now, the race is about to go off. Can we get to know each other better later?"

"I don't believe you," I told him.

"You don't need to believe me. I'm useful to you, let's just leave it at that."

He wasn't wrong. I glanced back at Wayne, far off in his private box, unsurprisingly preoccupied with another woman while his wife stared at the cloudless sky. I wanted to talk to her, find out more information about Wayne and his sources. If I didn't get the full story, I'd never stop thinking about what would have happened if I'd bet on Trigger.

I took a deep breath and stood up. "I'll be back."

"Should I go with you?"

"Just need to visit the ladies'. Finish reading your paper."

He didn't argue with me and flipped it back open. "Shake a leg, will you? Wayne strikes me as the type of fella that might follow you."

I gave him a nod and dashed up the stairs, cautiously avoiding Wayne's foreboding gaze but giving his wife wide, beckoning eyes. I tilted my head, a sign to follow, and she slithered away from the group of wives. Together, without getting too close to one another, we made it through the crowds to the ladies'. The adrenaline left my heart racing. I stopped before getting too close to the bathroom.

"Was making him lose once always the plan?" I asked, wondering why nothing had happened since Trigger.

"He's gotten clever," she admitted with a snarl. "Usually, the name of the horse is delivered in an envelope and placed at his desk. Since the Trigger loss, he's been meeting the courier to be handed the name directly."

I gave it some thought. "Find a way to get the name tomorrow," I insisted.

"How?"

"Meet the courier before he does? You know your husband. If you find a way, I'm in."

She straightened, and though she didn't look entirely convinced, she gave me a firm nod in agreement. "Meet me here in the morning before the race?"

I left her in a rush, feeling weightless, brimming with the hope that maybe this was it. If I could supply Joey Ep with a win, a fat amount of cash, it could prove to them that I was ready for New York.

"What are you doing with Wayne's wife?" The voice was right behind me, and it was so low and deep that I felt it radiate inside my skull. I shivered and jerked around to find Ben, hands in his pockets, eyes staring me down in a primal way that left me with the urge to flee.

"Are you following me?"

"How else do you expect me to keep you safe?"

"Keep me company," I corrected him. "I don't need—"

"Virginia," he cut me off. "Let's sit down."

I opened my mouth to fight him, lecture him, and ultimately push him away entirely. I didn't need a keeper. But something about his expression, those dark eyes, made my mind reel with memories of our first meeting and every moment that followed. How the timing seemed so bizarre and perfect that maybe like the racing odds—it was all fixed. My earlier instincts were right; he was confirming them.

We returned to our seats, and I reached for my bag, letting it rest in my lap. I clutched it tightly, feeling the outline of the gun inside.

"I'm not going to hurt you," he said.

I snorted. "What are you going to do with me, then? No more lies."

"Keep you company, like we agreed."

"I don't want your company any longer."

"You don't have much of a choice."

He took a deep breath and positioned himself more comfortably in an unhurried manner that made me fume.

"You're not a shoe salesman, are you?"

"No more than you're a rich socialite."

I felt queasy thinking about my first race, him standing next to me, the innocence of the memory burning away in my mind. "Did you even go to California?"

He sighed deeply. "I travel all over the place. I recently got into a little bit of trouble in Miami, need to lie low, so I took this job. That's all."

Job? I was a job to him?

"You were hired to watch me?"

"We both do what we're told, and we both get to move on." He reached for my bag and shoved it back to the ground.

"You didn't answer the question."

"I've answered enough of your questions today."

I couldn't fathom how the man who'd charmed his way into sitting next to me could now speak with such cold indifference. We were laughing moments ago, and though I suspected he wasn't telling me everything, I hadn't expected this. I hadn't expected another Mob man.

"The first time we met, was that . . ."

"Romantic, wasn't it?"

My bottom lip quivered, and I wanted to scream. He'd made a fool of me.

"Now be a good girl and watch the race with some semblance of interest? You're not going to be to using that gun on me anytime soon."

My mouth went agape. Good girl? Did he just call me a good girl? "Fuck you, Ben," I spat, and his grim expression shifted into a look of surprise. "You made me think that you were—"

"What?" He leaned in eagerly, waiting for my next words.

"Different," I said, but it pained me to do it.

"You were starting to like me, weren't you?"

"No," I hissed.

"There's still time," he reasoned. "I've rather enjoyed our days together."

We both turned our attention to the next race, but all I could do was imagine all the ways I wanted to slip away. Joey Ep didn't trust me to do the job; he couldn't if he'd sent someone to watch me. "Do all new recruits require a keeper or only the women?"

He gave me a bored look but didn't answer.

"Virginia!" A woman's voice squealed from the staircase. Her arm was looped with another woman, both fashionably dressed, fanning away the heat. "Tell me you're coming to the brunch at my estate. The other girls are dying to meet you."

"Ada," I said with a forced smile, remembering my role, despite the tension between my seat and Ben's. I stood up and walked to greet her on the stairs. "Yes, I've marked my calendar."

She fished the invitation out of her clutch and handed it to me. "It's a charity event, but we'll be drinking, and there's a pool to keep cool." Ada's eyes surveyed Ben briefly. "Will your friend be joining you? My brother will be so disappointed. He was hoping to whisk you away for the afternoon to tour the gardens."

"No, tell your brother I'll be coming alone," I said without a thought, smiling.

Ada smiled and, after a few minutes of gushing over fashion, left. I moved back to my seat and eased down. Ben's face was still unmoved, expressionless.

"Is anything you told me true?"

"I have sold shoes before," he said. "I am married. I do travel. I have thought about you sweaty and naked. What else do you want to know?"

"How do I know you won't lie or make something up?"

"I don't lie to women if I don't have to," he said simply. "Not my wife, not the women I sleep with, not even my own mother."

His voice wasn't smooth or convincing, just forward and sharp. "What you said about the New York slums?"

He huffed in response. "I'm a Jewish immigrant. What do you think?"

"I don't know what to think."

"I had a choice . . . be poor or start climbing."

All the allure was gone, and I wondered if it had all been an act—the same one Joey Ep expected me to play. I quickly decided to test it by asking a question I wasn't entirely sure I wanted the answer to.

"Have you ever killed someone?" I whispered.

"Told you I got into trouble in Miami, didn't I?"

I winced.

I couldn't say I hadn't asked for it, but was the truth really something I wanted? Would I feel better if he'd never revealed his identity and just continued being my mysterious stranger? I looked down at his smooth hands, wondering how many times those fingers, which had so delicately reached for mine earlier, had been soaked in blood.

"You're not scared of me, though." He tilted his head, eyes hard. "Why aren't you scared?"

I wanted to say I'd already seen every kind of monster between the men who raised and married me, but I resisted giving him anything personal. "I don't think you want me to be scared of you," I countered, hardening my eyes in return. If I played his game, maybe he'd tell me more.

He grinned in response.

The day continued on, and we returned to our quiet contemplation throughout the next race until I finally decided on another question, one that had been plaguing my thoughts since this morning. "Honestly," I said, breaking the silence. "How long is it going to take me to move on from this? The races?"

"A couple more months, maybe."

"That's too long."

"For what?" He leaned over. "What's the rush?"

"I want to travel," I lied. "Just like you."

He laughed, a sound that I found entirely too pleasant. "You joined the Mob so you could travel?"

I felt my face drop. "Well . . . yes."

"I don't believe you," he said, voice leveled. "But it doesn't matter. Stay away from Wayne's wife, follow the rules, or we're going to have a problem."

My father's rage began to simmer in my belly. Until Madeline, I had always followed the rules—obedient daughter, submissive wife. I played the part given to me and became who I needed to be to survive. It was always the same dreadful pattern. This was no different. Ben's words echoed inside my head: *"Follow the rules."*

But what if this time, I made my own rules?

"You could have told me someone was going to be watching me," I said to Joey Ep later that night while he meticulously counted the winnings on the table in my room.

"What was that?" he said, still not giving me eyes while he reached for his coffee cup, nearly empty, and took a final sip.

"Someone is watching me," I told him again, louder this time.

He finally gave me his eyes. "How do you know?"

I opened my mouth to tell him everything, but something stopped me. I didn't want him to think I'd been too trusting—that I'd invited the enemy in. "He made it very clear to me." I decided to leave out how careless I'd been by allowing him to get so close.

"You don't think you're just paranoid?"

"I know when someone is watching me, Joe."

He leaned back in his chair and neatly folded one hand over the other, looking out my narrow window, where the Chicago sky was cloaked in shadows. His face was still smooth and thoughtful, and there was no hint of surprise in it.

"Joe?" I pressed.

"It's fine," he reasoned. "It's unnerving that one mistake has them watching my new recruits, but it's to be expected after Madeline."

"What are you saying?" I shook my head.

"Madeline was a disaster in the eyes of the organization. I trained her, sent her off to New York where she"—he paused, as if he were deciding with great effort which word to say next—"supposedly ran off with some money. They want to make sure you're a good investment."

"I don't like it," I said simply. "Even if it's a smart business decision."

"If you're doing everything you're supposed to do, there shouldn't be any issues."

I had told him nothing about Ben, or Wayne's wife and her tempting proposition, but his words made me feel as if he knew everything.

"How long do I need to work the racetrack?"

He leaned back in to continue counting. "Until you impress them."

"What did Madeline do to impress them? I know her, and there's no way in hell she sat and watched races for months. The girl could barely sit still for a single bus ride."

He cleared his throat and hesitated in his response. "She did something unorthodox . . . She recruited someone."

I blinked, wondering if I'd heard him right.

"What?"

"She recruited someone, someone important to us."

"That's all you're going to tell me?"

"That's all you need to know. Keep doing what you're doing, and you'll move up."

"Every day I waste at the tracks is another day she's lost somewhere in New York, or on the run, or dead."

It was the first time I'd ever said it out loud, and when I did, my throat felt like it might close up.

His eyes met mine, and though there wasn't anything soft about them, he uncharacteristically reached out and patted my fingers before pulling his hand back to the safety of his lap. "We don't know anything yet about what really happened in New York, but I do know Madeline. She's a survivor. Be patient and get through this. If they're watching, put on a brilliant show . . . prove to them you're ready."

Or maybe, do something unorthodox like Madeline? Bet on a winning horse and supply them with a load of cash they couldn't possibly ignore?

I closed my eyes and breathed out slowly. Ben's gaze was there, in my mind, foreboding . . . haunting. I'd need to sneak around to meet Wayne's wife, show up to the tracks off schedule to place the bet, and somehow avoid him on the way out. He could still catch me and stop everything, but I had to try.

In the morning, I'd bet on the winner, not the horses on Joe's list. If they wanted a brilliant show, they'd get one.

Chapter Eight

"What have you done?" Ben shouted after me while I shoved through the crowded lot, spotting the Buick and dashing for it. The bright sun bounced off the hood, creating a sparkling green hue that made it stand out among a sea of dimly tinted Fords. My heart was hammering in my chest, beating so profoundly that my breathing grew staggered. I'd made the bet, won the money, but had no intention of explaining myself to Ben. If everything went right, this would be my very last time at the tracks.

The bag of cash hung from my arm, somehow both heavy and light. I needed to get back to my place, somewhere safe, until I met up with Joey Ep later tonight.

As I reached for the door, two hands took me by the shoulders and jerked me around. I felt a sense of panic, but my survival instincts kicked in. "Fuck off, Ben!" I shouted the words and pushed at him, only to find Wayne in his place.

"Get in the car," he ground out.

He opened the passenger door with one hand while the other was wound tightly in my hair and shoved me inside. I bounced along the leather seat, and he pushed me to the driver's seat, then shut the door. With both of us snug in such a small area, I felt my stomach start to roll.

My mind reeled, my memories getting the better of me. He had the same look Georgie had—he wanted to kill me. But this wasn't an isolated alleyway in the middle of the night next to a massage parlor. This was a very busy place; surely someone would notice.

He pulled out a gun, a small one like mine. "Drive."

"Where?" I cried out.

"Anywhere, just drive!"

I started the engine and left the safety of the track, where, despite Ben's rage, at the very least, I could depend on him not to let someone else kill me. I followed my routine from the track to Lady Luck, where I knew I was safe the second I entered the establishment. I just had to make it there.

As we drew closer and Wayne registered the lower-end neighborhood in Cicero, he cast me a glare and tapped the gun on the steering wheel. "Where are we? Pull over."

I wasn't close enough. A few blocks down near a tavern on Forty-Eighth. I could run inside, leap from the car, and beg for help from the patrons. I let out a shaky exhale and pulled over. I reached for my door, not needing a moment to decide on the gamble. Get shot in the car or get shot on the run. I'd run away from Georgie plenty of times and often surprised myself with how far my bare feet could take me.

Just as I maneuvered to get out, discreetly slipping out of my heels, he said something I never saw coming: "What do they have on you? You're working for Chicago, aren't you?"

I turned to him, my mouth agape. How could I have been so naive? When his wife told me someone gave him the winners before every race, how could I not have put it together? But if Wayne was just another cash cleaner, why hadn't Joey Ep told me? Why hadn't Ben told me?

"Nothing," I finally admitted, settling back into my seat. "I'm not working for Chicago."

"Then who are you working for?"

I wasn't about to tell anyone I worked for the Mob. This could all be some terrible setup I'd walked right into. I shook off the idea and played defense, recalling Ben's words and repeating them with breathless confidence. "Honestly, I don't know what you're talking about. I analyze the races, study the forms of the horses and jockeys, and make calculated bets."

He looked down, trying to figure out how any of this made sense. "Then why were you talking to my wife?"

Again, I fumbled out a lie. "We chatted about fashion; she's got fine tastes."

He reached for my hair, gathering red locks, and yanked my head back. I moved to fight and claw at him, but then he slammed my face into the wheel. I yelped, and the pressure in my nose had blood running down my face.

"Why were you talking to my wife!" Any sense of coolness or Southern charm in his voice left the air between us.

I grabbed at my nose and decided, despite the pain and swelling, I wasn't going to sob. My father's rage tickled at me, taunting me. The revolver was still in my bag, but what would I do with Wayne's body? How would I make him disappear?

I turned to him with a bitter expression. The lies were gone, and all that remained was a wild woman with blood on her face and a newly bald patch on her scalp. My thoughts turned violent, and then, my words did too. "She gave me the name because you're a cheating fucking bastard."

The revelation had his mouth twitching. "She gave you the name of the winner?"

"And gave you the wrong name," I said, hoping to twist the knife. "She wanted you to lose everything."

"She wanted attention," he shouted, then balled his hands into tight fists, and slammed them into the car window. I was certain he'd break the glass, but it stood firm under the pressure. "She's going to get us both killed."

"Get out of my car," I finally said, reaching into the bag between us slowly. Cautiously.

He let out a burst of laughter tinged with hysteria, a sound that hovered on the edge of a sob. "They've blackmailed me, you know. The one before you, a pretty girl . . . she tricked me into it."

His words made everything around me stop. "Madeline?"

"You knew her?"

"No," I lied, nearly stuttering. "Just heard of her."

"She found something on me and gave it to them, and they blackmailed me into laundering money for them." I couldn't be sure, but it looked as if his eyes were starting to glisten. "She ruined my entire life."

I couldn't make sense of it—Madeline, my Madeline?

"Is that why you've had it out for me since day one?" I dared to ask.

He shook his head. "I thought maybe they'd sent you to spy on me, but the more I watched you, the more I noticed you were just like me." He turned to me, eyes pleading. "Why did you make the bet? You get a list of names too, but you didn't bet on the right horse today. Why did you do it? Don't you know that they'll kill you for not following orders?"

I didn't know what came over me, but when I opened my mouth, the truth came flooding out, and with it, tears. "I thought if I bet on the winner and won a bunch of money, I could impress them. I wanted to move on from the tracks, do something bigger."

"You stupid girl."

I didn't fight him on it because the truth was right in front of me. I had bet on the winner and won the money, money that already belonged to the Mob through Wayne's bet. I hadn't done anything but prove to them I couldn't follow the rules or be trusted.

Silence lingered between us until he finally said, "They believe they control me, but they don't." He nodded, as if affirming his own resolve, and his gaze shifted toward the street, where the sun began its descent, casting a gentle amber glow upon the buildings. I stopped my pursuit of the gun.

"What do they have on you?"

"What don't they have on me?" he questioned, his gaze growing cold as he suppressed any trace of the earlier vulnerability. His mouth turned up into a half grin. "But I've got connections, and I'm working with law enforcement. I'm going to bring them down . . . all of them.

I just have to keep playing this role a little longer." He pointed the gun at me firmly. "Which means, I cannot lose money. You need to give me your winnings, winnings that belonged to me before you schemed with my wife, and I'll leave you alone."

I shook my head in protest. "I can't do that."

"I was supposed to win today," he reminded me. "You weren't."

"That doesn't mean I can return with nothing. I put everything on the winning horse, and even if we make this right and you get your winnings, I still lost their money. I can't come back to them with nothing."

"You're not my problem. My wife might detest me, but if I don't get them the money they're owed, I lose everything and so does she."

Admittedly, I felt a pang of sympathy for him, but if the Mob was going to decide which one of us was the more valuable asset, they'd undoubtedly pick him. He was rich, had power, and was easily manipulated.

I was still training, learning. Even if I managed to escape without giving him the winnings, he could tell the Mob, and my fate would be all the same.

My heart began to pound. I'd thought, for just a moment, that I'd made a big move with an advantageous reward. That I was one step closer to Madeline. But I'd read the situation entirely wrong, meaning Ben was right.

I wasn't going to get anywhere if I didn't play by the rules.

I blinked slowly, feeling the world start to spin around me. My instincts kicked in, and a single terrifying thought entered my head: Was I going to be killed over this?

The passenger door opened with a violent swing, and I watched Wayne's body get dragged out, saw his head hit the ground with an awful thud. In the amber light, Ben's fists pounded into his face, knocking the gun from his hand. I didn't dare scream, just watched the moment with a frozen horror I couldn't begin to fight.

Ben's entire face was red and wet with sweat. He looked more animal than human. Every time his fist hit Wayne's flesh, a growl escaped his mouth. I frantically looked around for any help, expecting someone to notice. A single man or woman to eye the grotesque scene and shout for help. But in the hours before sunset, there was only a desolate Cicero in front of me, waiting for nightlife to invade the streets.

Ben kept going until Wayne was motionless on the ground, and when his face turned, chest heaving with staggered breaths, I felt a sense that I was next.

I snatched the bag of money, leaped from the car barefoot, and ran to the parlor. I'd spent months carrying around a sense of shame that I lived there, and told no one at the San Carlo. Now, I was eager to reach those doors, rip them open, and find solace in my tiny undecorated room. The ground below my feet grew rigid, my toes cutting along the jagged, unpaved surfaces of broken brick and pavement. In the city, the roads were well maintained, but the Depression had left the slum areas like Cicero forgotten.

I wouldn't forget it, though.

No matter how far away I ended up, I'd never forget the place that saved me.

I threw open the doors, and Miss Suzannah shoved away a gentleman speaking with her to take me by the shoulders.

"Is Joey Ep here? He's supposed to be here," I blubbered on. He always came at night to collect the money.

"Caught up in business. He left word he'd come in the morning," she said in a panic.

Her questions filtered into my head, demanding to know what had happened, but I sank into the warmth of her arms and sobbed.

I didn't have a clue what was going to happen in the morning or what kind of repercussions I'd face from Joey Ep, and at that moment, I didn't care. My mind was busy with images of Wayne's battered face, and the animal that took his life. A man I'd sat so comfortably with for weeks.

My stranger was a monster, and I never saw it coming.

During the night, I drifted and awakened, always on the edge of dreaming but never leaping in. I'd made a mistake, and I knew it. Not just at the tracks, but going after Madeline. If Ben was just a glimpse into what the men of the Mob could do, had she ever stood a chance? Was I chasing a ghost? I'd considered it before, that she was dead and buried and the only sense of justice I could give her was finding out who did it. But until I knew the truth, I kept clinging to the idea that she was on the run. How very like Madeline to stash away in a little motel somewhere or run off and start a new life with a new name.

I drifted too long and jerked awake, the thick fog of panic lingering. Sweat beaded down my forehead, and I searched my dim surroundings, reminding myself I wasn't in that car anymore.

Just as a wave of relief filled me, I noticed a shadow in the corner of the room, an outline in the chair near the window. The very one Madeline had sat in when she lectured me on divorce. I couldn't make out any features, not even with the light filtering in from the streetlights outside. But I knew who it was; I just knew.

The dark silhouette was my monster, and he'd come to kill me.

How did he get in? Was I still dreaming?

I masked the panic and thought about my options. My revolver was in my bag under the bed, stuffed between the stacks of cash. I reached over to flick on the lamp, still not convinced I wasn't dreaming. When the lamp invaded the room with a soft light, Ben was a mess of blood and sweat.

"Don't scream," he warned, but I had no intention of listening.

I opened my mouth to yell out, but he pulled *my revolver* from his lap and pointed it in my direction. "I don't know what happened at the tracks, so I need you to explain it to me."

I flinched and spotted the bag of money next to him. He'd searched my room while I slept, watched me in the dark. "Are you going to kill me?"

"I don't want to, but you need to tell me the truth."

I let out a frightened laugh. "You could have told me the truth when

I was asking about Wayne. You knew he was cleaner, didn't you? You said you weren't a liar."

"I said I don't lie if I don't have to. I was trying to protect you from yourself . . . and what you were cooking up with Wayne's wife. What happened, Virginia?"

My feet were sore, and the escape to the door wasn't going to be easy. I had to navigate the room and run around furniture, but I decided to chance it. I sprang from the bed and made it inches from the door before his hand was around my mouth. He pulled my back into his chest and nuzzled his face into my hair. I didn't feel the gun, but I knew he still had it.

Lips on my ear, he ground out, "Tell me what happened so I can help you."

Help me?

My heart was pounding in my chest, and I could hardly breathe. He turned me around, shoving me down into the chair. My slip pulled up my waist with the throw, and I felt so awfully exposed. I caught his eyes staring at my bare legs and nudged the slip back down my thighs. Without meeting his gaze, I looked at the gun, still firm in his hand. He loomed over me, then took three polite steps back. He glanced around the room, in search of something. When he finally found it, he pulled my robe from the hanger on the door of my wardrobe, then tossed it at me softly.

"No more running. What happened?"

I slipped my arms in, too stubborn to say thank you. After another moment of tense silence, I told him everything. The deal I'd made with Wayne's wife, then Wayne's revelation in the Buick. Ben took a seat on the edge of the bed and, for what seemed like the first time since he appeared in my room, breathed. He used one hand to pinch the bridge of his nose, then wiped that same hand down his face.

The gun in his hand lowered.

"I was just trying to impress them . . . do something big to get their attention," I said.

"You should have bet on the horses you were told to bet on. If this was a test, you would have failed."

I stiffened. "Why was the winner reserved for Wayne? I was told that making a bet like that was risky and would draw too much attention . . . Why was he allowed to make it then?"

Again, he ran his hand down his face. "The rich get richer, and nobody blinks. The poor get rich? Something must be wrong. Wayne can keep winning, you needed to be careful."

I considered his words. "If I'd been told the truth, I would have—"

"You would have what?" His eyebrows raised a bit. "Followed orders? I highly doubt that."

"You don't know me," I said, finding my boldness mixed in with the lingering fear.

He sighed, as if exasperated with the conversation. "I know enough. You got some vendetta against men . . . something to prove, right? That explains the conspiring with a woman you barely know to take down her husband."

I lowered my eyes—I didn't have a retort. His words felt awfully similar to Madeline's lecture on how hating men wasn't going to get me anywhere. And now, it might get me killed.

"Too trusting, too naive . . ." He counted off with his empty hand. "Too fucking proud."

"I made a mistake," I said, just barely above a whisper. "What happens now? You'll tell them everything?"

A moment of silence fell between us, and I couldn't read his expression. It was far off.

"I wasn't hired to watch you, Virginia," he revealed slowly. "I was told there might be a new cleaner at the tracks, but to avoid you. I was hired to watch Wayne. There's a rumor he's talking with the feds. Chicago typically takes care of their own problems, but I have a very unique skill set, and I owed them a favor."

"You mean beating a man to death?" I uttered.

"Yes," he said with no sense of shame.

All I could do to keep myself from running was pretend the single word *yes* didn't terrify me. That it was just another word with nothing haunting behind it. I focused instead on the other words: *hired to watch Wayne, but to avoid you.*

It made little sense to me.

"You weren't hired to watch me?" I needed him to say it again.

"No, you weren't my job, until you became my job."

"I don't understand," I admitted, because I didn't.

He gazed blindly at the window, and in that moment, I knew I could make another run for it but decided not to test him again.

"I wanted to be near you," he finally said after some pause. His voice changed, his shoulders lurched, and the menacing demeanor I'd felt earlier seemed to be lifting. Only, I knew the feeling well. Georgie would snap, then pepper me with love and compliments after to show me that his rage was just a moment. A memory. That I'd never see that side of him again.

I knew better.

Georgie had hit me; Ben had murdered a man in front of me.

"So I pushed off Wayne. I told them I'd run into some delays, that I needed more time to get proof. I just wanted to sit with you for a few more days."

"You're married," I reminded him.

"Something tells me you understand that marriage doesn't mean happiness."

I pulled my robe tightly around my slip, looking down. His dark eyes found mine, locking in my gaze with an intensity I still found jarring, but the fear of him began to dissipate. "Couldn't you get in trouble if they found out?"

"I do what I want," he reasoned. "As long as, in the end, I give them the body they ask for."

A chill ran through me.

"At first, I just wanted to fuck you," he said simply, and my stomach pulled into a knot. Nobody had ever spoken to me so brashly. "It would have been easier if that's all this was."

I swallowed.

"But I liked to watch you read and study the crowds, and smile at my awful jokes. You saw through me so quickly, maybe because we both got a chip on our shoulder." A smile edged at the corner of his mouth. "You did a fine job convincing the elite you were one of them, but with me . . ." He paused and considered his next words. "You were someone else with me . . . a mystery I wanted to solve, and I knew after I found proof on Wayne, it would be over."

"I gave you the wrong impression," I told him meekly. "There's nothing between us, Ben."

"Then why did you let me sit next to you?"

The truth was that he made me feel safe and that he was the first person since Madeline to do that. But I had no idea what he'd do with the truth, so I lied. "You kept Wayne out of my hair."

"You like me too, I know you do."

I shook my head in response, but no words escaped my mouth.

His expression softened to the point of reminding me of the bearded stranger I'd met my first day at the tracks. He was right. I did like him, though I hated myself for it. He was married, and that should have been enough.

But even if he weren't married, he was prone to the same violence as Georgie and my pa. Why did men like him find me, and why did I let them? I belonged in a room somewhere, with doctors studying me, making articulate notes about the mental case in front of them. The tragedy of a broken woman seeking broken men.

"I don't."

He stood then, straightened his wrinkled summer suit, and cleared his throat. "You're going to have to own up to the mistake of betting on the winner."

I didn't want to because that would mean I couldn't be trusted. If they couldn't trust me to do what I was told, what use was I to them?

"Will they kill me for it?"

"If they got the money, they didn't lose anything . . . except any faith they had in you. It will come down to whether they believe you can keep your mouth shut. Either way, you're done with us." He glanced at the bag next to the chair.

"That's the only option?"

His brows perked. "You want another one?"

I calmed myself down in a snap, feeling like if I didn't, I'd never get answers out of him. "I want another one."

He laughed richly. "You want to stay? After what you just saw?"

I held his gaze coolly. "That was nothing I haven't seen before." A lie, of course. I'd seen my pa beat my mother plenty of times, but never until her face was a mess of blood and flesh. I was all lies tonight, but for once I was convincing. The truth was just too terrifying. Too wrong.

"You're not cut out for this," he said with absolute certainty. "You're just too soft, Virginia . . . and too angry. You're going to make more mistakes when it comes to men, and I got news for you, this organization is run by men. Men that will kill you if you don't do what they say. I'm doing you a favor, doll. Own the mistake, tell them you're not cut out for this, beg them to let you go."

He took a step toward the window, leaving his words hanging in the air behind him. *"Too soft, too angry, own the mistake. Do what they say."*

I leaped up. "You don't get to decide I'm soft. Give me the other option."

He didn't listen: He was on his way through the cracked window, reaching for the bottom to pry it open further. I rushed at him and grabbed his forearm, my fingers digging into his suit, pulling at him with every bit of strength I had. "Give me the other option!"

I could have sworn I heard him growl when he faced me head-on, but the hint of aggression quickly faded, and his endearing smile returned. I spotted a glint of challenge in his eyes. "You clean up this mess tonight, you'll prove to them you're bought in."

"What do you mean, clean it up?" I didn't know the details yet, but I imagined it had something to do with Wayne's dead body. I drifted back to the chair to put distance between us.

"I think you understand what I mean. But first, you need to prove to me I can trust you." He folded his arms across his chest.

I scoffed. "You expect me to do that in one night?"

"I want you to admit it."

"Admit what?"

"That you like me."

"Are you that vain?"

"Yes. Say it, Virginia."

"No." I was being stubborn and too proud, like he'd just said. If I said yes, maybe this would end, and he'd trust me enough to help me. I'd lied plenty of times tonight, why couldn't I lie now? Perhaps, I thought, because it wasn't a lie. Those three words, *I like you*, would mean I was no different from my mother, drawn to men like him. That I couldn't change, that I'd never deserve better than Georgie.

He stalked closer, getting down on his knees in front of me and jerking the chair forward. I whimpered in response, frozen in panic, knowing my breathing was staggered and loud. My chest heaved up and down to a rhythm I had no control over. The bravado I'd had moments before was long gone. He had me caged.

"How many other things do you deny yourself because you're scared?"

"I gave you the wrong impression. I'm sorry, Ben. I'm sorry." I just kept repeating it, thinking he'd politely understand, even though my mind warned me otherwise.

"Every time I touched you, you'd cross your legs and turn away from me, but I could see your skin." His eyes wandered back down to my legs, but he caught himself and looked back into my eyes. "The little bumps on your arm, the way your face turned cherry."

His hand moved between my legs, grazing my thighs, fingers pulling at the fabric of my slip. I shoved at his shoulders, the only protest I offered him.

"You still want another chance?"

Was he saying I had to do this? The lack of choice left me in a rage. I was just like the girls here, exchanging sex for survival. For Madeline.

Nostrils flared, I tried to get up, but he shoved me back down, eyes never leaving mine. I needed to say no, but *no* meant it was over. Everything I'd done so far to find her would be useless. But how far could I go for her? For the truth?

"Answer me."

"You don't make the rules."

"I do right now. You were reckless at the racetrack. I need to know you can follow orders. I need to know I can trust you to help me clean this up . . . even if it makes you uncomfortable, or makes you feel dirty, or challenges all those little things that you were taught make you a proper woman." He reached up to tap the side of my head with his finger, and I wanted to bite it off. "I don't need proper, Virginia. Proper isn't going to survive in this organization. They're having you launder money now, but make no mistake, they're going to want your body next."

"You keep trying to put your hands between my legs, and I'll break your fingers," I said, the words like venom. "How's that for proper?"

"There's that anger, that pride." He tsked, then grew frustrated with the tension of my hand pushing his shoulders and yanked me off the chair, maneuvering his body to sit down instead. "Stand by the bed and take off your clothes."

"N-no." I stuttered the word out, standing in front of him awkwardly.

"Do you still want this?"

"Yes, but that doesn't mean I want you."

He huffed out a mock laugh. "I'm not going to fuck you, not until you're begging for it." His voice was grave, eyes leveled and serious. "And you will eventually beg me, Virginia. That's not what's happening here. Now be a good girl and take off your clothes."

"Or?" I pressed, the word lingering on my tongue.

"Or it's over."

"You want to humiliate me then? Is that the lesson?" My voice shook, betraying me all at once. "My punishment?"

He gave me a soft laugh in return. "It's just skin, Virginia."

"But it's my skin to show."

A determined glint shone in his eyes, and I knew there was no talking him out of it.

My throat dried up, and I took deliberate steps away from him, closer to the bed. With a quiet huff, I listened, drifted into the woman I used to be to keep a man tame, and obeyed. I shuddered out of the robe and slip in a hurried motion, feeling my face heat. I just wanted to be done—another memory I could bury and pray it wouldn't haunt my dreams. My breasts were exposed and cold, and the humiliation made my cheeks heat.

He leaned back in the chair, placing a hand on his chin, staring at me, memorizing every inch of my body. The slip hung stubbornly on my hips, and he made a sound in response, but I couldn't figure out if it was pleasure or frustration.

I reached for the soft fabric, starting to push it down my hips, feeling my eyes water.

"Stop," he said, then drew a ragged breath.

He stood and I jerked back, the heel of my foot hitting the bed frame. He stalked closer and reached out for me. I closed my eyes while his fingers toiled with the slip, pulling it back up my arms. His thumb purposely grazed my hardened nipple, and my stomach buckled, my body wanting to sink into itself. "Too soft," he whispered, using the same thumb to brush away a tear that had escaped my eye.

I turned my head away at his touch.

"Now imagine I didn't tell you to stop," he said, eyeing the skin of my neck. "Imagine I took you on this bed, and I expected you to enjoy it. Imagine then, days later, I came back again . . . and again. Then, maybe I share you with a friend."

I swallowed and willed myself not to cry anymore. He leaned in, lips grazing my neck. Every nerve in my body was on fire—rage, heat, and bitter shame. "But I buy you things, beautiful things. I give you every luxury you could ever want or need. You can own anything but your body. That's mine, and you'll never get it back."

His breathing was still heavy against my skin, and I waited for him to go further. His mouth ventured up, lips on my ear. "Do you still want this, Virginia?"

"I know what you're trying to do. You're trying to scare me away." I gave his shoulder a violent shrug, reaching down for my robe. On my way back up, he captured my face with his hands. His grip was firm, but not painful, with just the right amount of pressure needed to keep my face still and staring up. The robe fell from my hands as I reached up for his wrists, digging my nails into his flesh, wanting to draw blood.

"Are you scared now?" He searched my face, looking for something. His eyes suddenly appeared sunken and far off.

I was scared; I felt it down to my core, but I was quickly beginning to understand Ben. This was a lesson, a sick test. I needed to match his challenge, even if I wasn't certain I could trust the outcome. Through gritted teeth, I said, "You want to hurt me? Do it. Get it over with. But when I come to, I'm going to hurt you back."

He retreated as if he'd been spooked, and something dawned on him—something he didn't like. "You've been hit before."

"Like you said, marriage doesn't mean happiness."

For a moment, we just stared at each other and breathed. I had a hundred things I wanted to say, to wound him with words, but I needed to stop my heart first. Calm myself. He looked primal again, like he had with Wayne. I didn't move, didn't blink, just waited for him to find himself again.

When he did, he adjusted his clothing. "Get dressed and meet me downstairs. I brought your car back for you. Don't tell anyone where you're going."

The moment he slipped out the window, tears sprang from my eyes. I still felt naked, exposed, and though he was long gone, his words rang in my ears—the dreadful thought that maybe there was truth to them. That this awful, worthless feeling in the pit of my stomach was just the beginning? I could hear him down on the streets below, the thud of him slamming my car door. I didn't have time to cry or think.

I got dressed and followed him.

We said nothing on the drive, the air tense and strange. I kept my eyes low, not even bothering to look out the window to determine where we were going. I let the anger build until I knew I'd explode if I didn't say something to him. "Do you feel proud of what you did to me back there?"

"You think I'm the only man you're going to have to listen to? You think that's the only time you're going to have to do something that makes you hate yourself? You made this choice, and you said you wanted it. Here it is, Virginia."

My breath caught in my throat because I knew he wasn't lying. In his own, awful way, he was trying to warn me. Help me.

"Your ex? What's his name? Is he still in Chicago?"

I stared him down, trying to read the motive in his question. "I'm not telling you that."

"I'd like to pay him a visit on my way out of town."

My mouth went agape. "You're not killing my ex-husband."

"I'll make it clean." His lips turned up. "Bring you a souvenir, if you want."

"You're sick."

His fingers tightened along the steering wheel. "I shouldn't have asked you to undress," he reasoned. "I just needed you to break, to give up that pride. That's not how I want to see your body." He breathed deeply, as if he were reliving it.

"Is that your way of apologizing?"

"Take it or leave it."

"You're never seeing my body again," I told him, then looked down at my hands and toyed with the fabric of my dress. Just as he stopped the car, I breathed out my next words. "You got what you wanted. You scared me."

He turned to face me. I didn't look up, but I could feel him. "Were you scared of me, or scared of what would have happened if I didn't ask you to stop? If I had fucked you on that bed?"

I twisted around and threw my hand across his face, then I curled my fingers into a fist and pulled my arm to my chest, holding it there so I didn't do it again.

His face stayed cold, detached, but then, the grin returned. "Not to worry, Virginia. I'll never judge you for being just as fucked up as I am. Get out of the car."

I reached for the door and swung it open, stepping out to finally take in my surroundings. My heart sank. We were in the small Chicago suburb Vel had driven me to, right outside the perfectly normal-looking house that served as a morgue. "What are we doing here?"

"Don't scream," he warned me. "You want to cry, do it quietly."

Before I could question the demand, he opened the trunk of the car to reveal two mangled bodies, squished together. I recognized Wayne's brown boots, but the second body had the acid in my stomach rising, scratching my throat. Wayne's wife, in her beautiful dress and fine features, purple and dead.

I doubled over, throwing up beside the car, gasping for breath.

He pulled me up, made me face him, then cleaned the vomit with the sleeve of his suit.

A man jogged up, the undertaker, and helped him retrieve the bodies from the trunk discreetly. We moved into the funeral home together, but each step left me feeling like I might faint. I couldn't faint. Not here, where it was so easy to get rid of someone.

Inside the basement, Ben gave the undertaker clear instructions to prepare the bodies but paused and looked back at me. "Who recruited you? We need to call them, give them the story. They'll need to explain to the higher-ups what happened."

I hesitated, already seeing Joe's look of disappointment in my mind. "Joey Ep."

"Fuck," he spat, casting the undertaker a look of pure discomfort. One I'd never seen on his face before. "Call Joey Ep, tell him his girl is here."

There was history there, I could see it in his tense expression, but I didn't care to pry. I watched the undertaker place the bodies on white sheets, where they were laid close together. I imagined what they wore on their wedding day, how they loved one another, and what crossed their minds in those final moments. And then, I wondered how long it took for all the beauty and life in their skin to fade into the ghastly shells before me.

I had never seen a dead body, and I knew I'd never be able to forget it.

We waited for a short twenty minutes, during which the undertaker brought in various items and placed them beside the bodies. When Joe arrived, his gun was drawn. He thundered past me and shoved it in Ben's face. Ben didn't react, just lifted his hands in surrender, matching Joe's cold indifference. Joe looked to me. "Did he hurt you?"

"I didn't hurt her," he said in response. "You want to take that gun out of my face so I can explain what happened?"

"What the fuck are you doing in Chicago, Siegel?"

"Business. We're all friends now, remember?"

Joe spit at his feet, and the fire in his expression burned. He loathed Ben, it was so easy to see, but why? What had he done?

Ben sighed. "We both know we're too valuable to kill, so let's clean this mess up together and maybe we never have to see each other again."

"He didn't do anything to me," I finally spoke up. Another lie.

Joe lowered the gun but took several steps back to pace the room. When nothing was said, he waved at Ben. "Get on with it, what happened?"

Ben gave him the details, and each new revelation left Joey in a trancelike state of stress. He'd look my way and then back to Ben, close his eyes, and breathe. It was the first time I'd ever seen him have a reaction that wasn't passive or calm. I was convinced, until now, that nothing could shake him.

"What were you thinking?" he asked, finally addressing me, lip twitching.

"You said you never put everything on a win," I reasoned, pleading with him to understand my motive. "But I knew I had a sure win, and you also told me to do something to impress them."

He itched the back of his head.

"You should have told her about Wayne," Ben advised.

Joe snapped his fingers in his direction. "Don't say another fucking word about my business, Siegel." He brought his eyes back to me. "What did I tell you? Even if we fix the races, something can go wrong . . . For instance, a jealous wife can plot with another woman to mix up names on a piece of paper. What do we have then?"

"A loss," I uttered.

"A major loss."

Ben said nothing in response.

Joe began to undress, removing his suit and meticulously folding each garment to fit in a single pile. Ben began to do the same, and I looked to the ground, forcing my eyes to hold the dark flooring. I didn't know what they were doing, but my mouth had gotten me in enough trouble already.

The undertaker brought in two meat cleavers and handed one to each man. They all quietly spoke to one another, and I dreaded what was going to happen next. Was Joe going to make me watch?

"Step into that room, Virginia," said Joe, pointing to a small storage closet.

My mind couldn't possibly accept their plan, or the sense in it. "Joe . . . you're going to bury them, aren't you?"

"We're going to cut them up," said Ben forwardly. "Bodies burn quicker that way."

My stomach rolled again, but I had nothing left in it, so I just felt the muscles tighten with pain. "What if they have children, family—they'll have no one visit."

I remember how angry I'd been that my pa didn't tell me where he'd buried the family dog, so I spent a year visiting a tree near our house where we'd hid in the shade together. "You have to bury them."

"It would be different if the feds weren't involved," explained Ben, a look of compassion twisting his hardened features. "We can't leave bodies behind. No trace of them. Do you understand?"

I hoped I never would.

I stared at the ground, frozen in place. Joe turned to put some sort of sheet over his shoes, and Ben hovered in front of me. He placed a hand on my shoulder and gave the muscle a light squeeze. "They're not your ghosts to carry. Look at me, Virginia."

I resisted.

"Look," he whispered into my ear.

I gave him my eyes.

"They're not your ghosts, they're mine. Now go to the closet."

I nodded, and to keep myself from sobbing in front of them, I opened the door in a rush and sat quietly inside. I was surrounded by closed boxes and the faint smell of alcohol. The sounds grew louder with each passing minute, flesh and bone breaking, far worse than the sounds Ben's fists had made slamming into Wayne's cheekbone.

I covered my ears, and for the first time since I was a child, dragged to church by my pa for simply looking at a boy who worked at our local grocery, I prayed.

Let this be a nightmare. Let me wake up at the parlor. Let me wake up.

Chapter Nine

I peeled off my shoes, caked in dried blood from the walk out, and stared at them. Joe sat quietly by the window, glowing in the moonlight with a waft of cigarette smoke clinging to his suit. His shoulders were slumped, not at all tense, and when he finally made conversation with me, his voice was flat. "We're going to tell them that Wayne was mad for you, in love, and told you about the winning horse to impress you."

I said nothing in response and didn't avert my eyes from the shoes.

"During your time spent with him, you found out he was talking to the feds and told Siegel. They will be angry with you for reaching too high, but impressed with the information you found, and further impressed that you helped get rid of them. You'll get your wish and be done with the tracks."

"I didn't help," I finally said, needing to hear it myself. "I sat in a closet."

"Ben and I are in agreement on the story. They'll believe what we tell them." He stubbed the cigarette out and drifted to the bed to sit next to me. "Did Ben do anything to you?"

I shook my head.

"Virginia?"

I closed my eyes, willing myself to be just like him. Detached, strong. "He helped me."

Joe's upper lip twitched. "Did he touch you?"

"Are you hearing me, Joe? He helped me, what does the rest matter?" I paused, thinking back to the exchange they had. "What has gone on between you two?"

He tensed up. "Too much history. As I've said before, this alliance, this friendship, is far more complicated than I can even begin to explain." He took a deep, steadying breath. "You'll never have to see him again."

Maybe he was right. I'd never have to see Ben Siegel again, but that wouldn't stop him from haunting my dreams. With tears streaming down my face, I said quietly, "I really liked those shoes."

Joe reached around for my shoulder and, in a tender moment I didn't fight, pulled me into the crook of his arm. We stayed like that for so long that I wanted to drift to sleep but kept heaving myself awake with sobs. Finally, Joe stood and made a drink, stirring something into it before handing it to me. I hesitated, wary. "What's in it?"

"You'll sleep. You need it. It's a new day tomorrow."

I took the glass and gulped it down, decidedly thrilled to quiet my mind long enough to feel nothing.

Joe was right, they weren't angry with me—quite the opposite. They'd lost no money, just a cleaner who was in league with the feds, and I'd earned their trust with a clear warning never to gamble with their money again. Joey Ep was given the go for me to move on to bigger scams, and within the week, I'd be crossing state lines with stolen goods.

I spent the next week shopping Chicago's Michigan Avenue with Joey Ep, setting up my wardrobe, and discussing future, bigger racing scams. He showed me off at fancy Loop and North Side restaurants to get the buzz going—the rich heiress from Virginia with money to blow—and by the end of every day, the Buick was loaded to the brim with shopping bags. Chic Schiaparelli and Chanel dresses, stylish hats, and a luxurious mink coat, but regrettably, not even the pearls around my neck could keep my thoughts from drifting.

At the strangest of times, in a sea of people in bustling department stores or while strolling sidewalks, I'd see two bodies on the floor below me and imagine them burning.

"How long are you going to be angry with me?" I asked Joe on the drive back to his place. "You're playing along at the lunch dates and the shops, but you've barely spoken a word since . . ." I couldn't even say it.

His mouth tensed at the corners, but he said nothing.

"I'm sorry," I said.

"The word *sorry* is for children," he snapped back. "You're lucky, Virginia. Lucky they didn't ask more questions, pry into why Wayne bet on the wrong horse that day. After what happened with Madeline, we have to be careful. We cannot afford any mistakes."

I nodded in response because he wasn't telling me anything I didn't know.

"Don't go behind my back again." His voice dropped, and I knew there was a threat behind the words. A warning that he wouldn't be so forgiving next time.

He pulled the Buick to a stop, and I glanced at the window to find we'd driven to the Edgewater Beach Hotel, a grand lakefront property I saw in a magazine once. I couldn't believe I'd missed the sweeping views of Lake Michigan from the car window.

The beach that stretched alongside the water glowed in the ocher sunset, and it seemed to go on forever. The waves broke and thrashed at the shore, and I closed my eyes for a moment, struck by a memory I thought I'd buried.

Georgie took me to the ocean on our honeymoon. We took a detour to Tybee Island, where we could only afford a one-night stay at a bed-and-breakfast. Georgie kept me naked most of the time, but in the early morning, I drifted off to the beach to watch the seagulls have breakfast.

I could still feel the warm gold sand between my toes and taste the salty waves in my mouth. And then my mind wandered—the sound of bones breaking, warm pink skin turning purple and blue. My belly ached with dread, and my palms sweated.

I thought of Ben again, the words he left me with. *"They're not your ghosts to carry."* Then my mind did something even more horrifying—I imagined Ben stalking toward me, his haunting eyes, the way he looked at me in the dim light of my room.

I leaned down to bury my head into my hands, but Joe got out and walked around to open the passenger door.

"Why are we here?" I asked.

"Come on, now," he said, taking me by the arm to lead me away from the pink hotel to a set of apartments to the north. They stood as tall as the hotel; only instead of the flamingo pink, they were the color of butter. He stopped at the entrance to the apartments, where a doorman gave Joe a curt nod and welcomed us inside the lobby.

My feet tapped against the terra-cotta flooring, and I looked up at ornate walls and high dramatic ceilings that gleamed and soared. My gaze moved from the elaborate chandelier above me to where men and women sporting swanky suits and lamé gowns strolled along an open second-story lookout. They gave Joe and me pleasant smiles. He was one of them, and they thought I was too.

He pulled my hand up and placed a set of keys in it. "I've had your things brought to your new apartment. Let's put this behind us. All of it. A new start?"

A thrill consumed me as I glanced down at the keys. I had never had a place of my own. For the moment, the buzz of excitement swallowed up the pang of guilt. "My apartment? I'm staying here?"

He leaned in to kiss me on the cheek but stopped himself and drew back. He lifted his hand up to shake mine. "A new partnership? No more secrets?"

It was all so dazzling, and yet, I felt only a sense of dread wash over me. Was this what he'd done with Madeline? I could imagine her now, melting into his arms. She would have done anything he asked to keep this life, even if that meant running off to New York, far away from his protection.

Now he wanted me to do the same, and all I felt was pressure and a heavy warning inside me. I didn't want to be so far from Miss Suzannah. I wouldn't call her the mother I never had to her face, but I felt it in my heart. And though she treated every girl at the parlor like a daughter, a small extension of herself, I liked to believe our connection was special.

Joe had mentioned getting me away from Cicero before, and now, he was disguising this grand gesture as a way to do just that. He wanted me isolated, alone, and all to himself. Otherwise, how could he possibly control me?

A new apartment was no different from the flowers my father presented to my mother after a beating, or the gifts Georgie left for me on the kitchen table after one of his "rough" nights.

With them, I thought I'd never get out, but I'd proven myself wrong.

I intended to do the same with Joe and the Mob. But not yet. For now, I focused on Ben's advice. I needed to play the game, and that meant convincing Joe I wasn't going to let him down. I reached out to shake his hand while letting my fingers toy with the keys. "A partnership."

"Can I walk you up? I'd like to show you the place. Designed it myself."

"Now you're a designer?"

He threw me a playful wink. "I've been quite obsessed with Jean-Michel Frank as of late. He's a pure genius. Our little secret, of course."

"One of many," I said aloud. How many more secrets would we acquire together over the next few years?

He stopped at the elevator, but I motioned to the stairs, preferring them to the lift.

"Stairs?" he inquired curiously, opening the stairwell door, one flight for each floor.

"Something about being caged in four walls, hanging in the air, doesn't sound so appealing to me."

He huffed under his breath before agreeing to the stairs.

When we stopped at the door to my new apartment, he gestured to the lock. I sank the key inside and turned it open. For a moment, I was at a loss for words, far too breathless to speak. The walls were covered in gray lacquered wood, the ceiling white, and there was ebony flooring beneath my feet that gave everything a warm touch. The living room was lush, with white leather furniture, satin draperies, and an S-shaped settee in black velvet. I sank down in awe, trying to remember to breathe. This couldn't all be mine? I continued to look around, where from beyond the settee, I could see my dining room—similar to his—and my kitchen.

"This is a white bearskin rug," he said, pointing below my feet. "Take off your shoes," he insisted. "Let your feet sink into it."

I did as he said, and my toes felt like they were being caressed by the fur.

He continued to point around, mentioning both the chromium lamps and marble mantelpiece. "I added some floral wallpaper in your bathroom for a feminine touch. Come, let's see your room."

I got up to follow him to the bedroom. A delicate, soft interior welcomed me, a distinctive contrast to my sharply modern living room. Chartreuse furniture, a satiny chaise, and a closet filled with new things. Shiny, expensive new things. Gowns, coats, and bags I'd never seen before, not even in dress shop windows. "You've outdone yourself," I uttered, forcing my voice to sound blissfully unaware that all of this came with a price.

Joe pulled out a smoke, then strolled back into the living room to have a seat. I followed him, continuing to note all the little details that he had worked so tirelessly on. I played with a switch near the fireplace, and the light fixtures along the mantelpiece flicked on. "It's the most beautiful thing I've ever seen."

And that was the truth, at least.

"You have other talents, Joe. Did you always want to be a Mob accountant?"

He gave it some thought, his cigarette smoke filling the air, then shook his head unhurriedly. "Numbers are easy, they don't lie, they're not complicated. I was at this job before I turned twenty and it's all I've known since."

I tried to pry deeper. "You don't ever feel wrong?"

"Wrong?"

"Wayne and his wife are dead, and you can carry on like it means nothing, like it's just another day." I waited for his face to change, the emotion to strike him, but it never did. He just continued to observe the apartment like a work of art. "Don't you feel something? Anything?"

His eyes fixed on me. "Feelings aren't going to get you anywhere, Virginia. They're just going to make every man in this business think you're just *another* woman. That you have a weakness, like all the others. They'll use it, abuse it, manipulate it. You can't feel anything if you want to rise in the ranks. You can't succumb to your emotions. Power is not given, it's taken."

I eyed him more seriously. "I don't want power, I just want my friend back."

"Sadly, the two are connected." His voice dipped, and I sensed dismay. "We're one step closer. You got out of working the racecourse circuit. Now, we doll you up and get your story straight, and we can have you start transporting goods. Stolen cash, diamonds, and furs across state lines. Given you breeze through inspection, as I imagine you will, you'll catch the right attention from the right people."

My palms sweat at the thought—what if I didn't "breeze through"? He handed me his lit cigarette, and I accepted it. "Fooling men and women at the racetrack is one thing, but deceiving the state border inspections is entirely different. You have too much faith in me."

"You don't have enough in yourself," he countered, leaning over to snatch the cigarette from me and stub it out in a sharply cut ashtray next to the sofa. "I'll supply this place, set you up with a bank account that will replenish weekly. You can have your own life, buy what you want, and do what you want, but never forget who is supplying you with it. You have an obligation to us before anything else."

I already knew I'd made a deal with the devil, but hearing him set out the terms sent shivers down my spine. He was all but confirming that if I didn't do what I was told, I'd end up just like Wayne's wife.

Joe got up to leave.

"Where are you going?"

He straightened his suit at the door, brushing his hand down the lapels. "This is your home now. Not just this apartment, but Chicago. Make friends, have lavish parties, call Vel and set up some nightclub exploits. Start your new life. Nobody should suspect you are a poor girl from the country. Nobody should even know but me. Do you understand what I'm saying to you?"

I took a deep breath and straightened my shoulders. "Become someone else?"

"Someone better," he corrected me, and didn't blink.

I thought about Joe's words for the next few hours, walking through my new place with a strange sense of loneliness I hadn't expected, then took myself to dinner at a small private café for residents. I ordered an old-fashioned, but before I could order dinner, Vel interrupted with a wave from across the café.

She swaggered over in a sage-green evening gown, a striking contrast to her flamboyant suit the last time we met. "Virginia!"

"Vel?"

"Joe called me and said you might want some company, help getting adjusted."

I swallowed, startled by the idea. I could hardly keep up that single night we'd spent together. How long did she expect to stay?

"A week?" I asked.

She waved her small clutch around carelessly. "A month, Virginia. We need to have you rise in popularity and reputation. That takes time, too much time." She got a little closer, leaning against the table, voice dropping to a whisper. "So, Joe says we create our own narrative. Tell the story we want! It sounds like tremendous fun, doesn't it?"

I gathered she'd done this before, and was tempted to ask about

Madeline but didn't want to give anything away. I knew so very little about Velma Capone and had no idea if she could be trusted based on the sole fact that she was a woman.

I fought the urge to down my drink. "Tremendous fun."

Over the next few weeks, we did just that—created our own narrative. Inheriting a substantial fortune from my late father, whose tragic passing left me as his sole heir, I opted to venture beyond the confines of the South and explore the world. Chicago became my temporary home, and the city's high society eagerly embraced my presence. After all, why would a Southern belle like myself fabricate a story when I possessed the wealth and means to back it?

I graced elegant parties, indulged in extravagant dinners, all-night treasure hunts, and dined at the most notorious restaurants in town. I even hosted my own soirees, using them as opportunities to rally influential men and women to contribute to my carefully selected causes and charities—causes that were, unbeknownst to them, backed by the Mob.

My story and reputation ended up working fabulously for Joe's new plan to make me a carrier.

"You can't be serious," said Vel, staring at the boxes of jewelry littering the apartment in odd places, spilling glittering diamonds from their casings. My heart thudded at the sight, but more important were the words Joe repeated next.

"We need to get them to New York. You two will be responsible for doing that."

"New York?" I tore my eyes from the jewelry at the words that had been tied to Madeline since I agreed to this.

"Just a drop-off," he said, with some dismay. "But if it goes well . . ." He didn't finish the thought, just allowed me to make my own conclusion. I needed to pull this off, regardless of the threat that came with it, one Vel had no issue voicing.

"This is the jewelry from that robbery," she reminded Joe like he didn't know. "It's all over the papers." She searched my apartment to find a paper, then noticed one rolled tightly, tucked into Joe's armpit. She thundered over and snatched it up, flashing me the first page. The robbery was all anyone could talk about, and Joe had smuggled the evidence into my apartment.

"We get caught with this jewelry and we're dead," she said. "There's no way in hell I'm smuggling this to New York. There's too much heat."

"Security is lax at the train station . . . It's not like we're asking you to fly."

"Why don't we just drive ourselves?" I asked.

"Too risky," he said. "They've got officers stationed at every state border. They're checking every car."

"What's going to stop them from checking our things at the station?" Vel snapped.

Joe threw his arms up in frustration. "You've played the part well enough to fool much of Chicago's elite, what's stopping you now? You're not who they're looking for. All you have to do is convince them of that."

Vel, mouth agape, was still clearly unconvinced. "Virginia, aren't you going to say something? Fancy dinner parties and charity events are entirely different than illegally transporting stolen jewels."

"Vel . . ." Joe cleared his throat after saying her name. "Given your behavior lately—"

"Don't you dare, Joe," she spat, lifting her hand to silence him. Her behavior had been frantic, to say the least. When she wasn't sloshed or tripping into my apartment at night, she was doing every drug offered to her. And when she was hazy, her mouth would run. There had been too many close calls, and too many nights I looped my finger into her throat to make her throw up.

I shuddered at the reminder.

"It might be smart to do what you're told, just this once," he resumed cautiously, as if he were trying to avoid stepping on broken glass. I'd noticed a change in his usual straight-faced manner since he'd begun managing two women. He handled conversations differently, listened to our concerns, fought for us at every turn when higher-ups made suggestions. At times, I sensed he loathed his situation, wishing he could retreat to his numbers and books. Other times, I got the feeling he enjoyed it, taking care of something. Someone.

Vel looked down in consideration, placing her hands on her hips. It was a warm fall morning, the sun beaming through my curtained windows, the light reflecting off the jewelry and dancing along the ceiling. I knew the risks, but I buried the anxiety, too tempted by the reward. If everything went according to plan, New York was finally in my sights.

"We'll do it," I said, making the decision for us.

Six bags between us, jewelry stuffed into different parts of our coats, stockings, and shoes—I had never been more frightened, and I couldn't dare show it. I tried to find comfort in the facts: Vel and I had perfected the con. Maybe she was brash, and often drunk, but even I couldn't deny that we played elite well—too well. If we treated this like another charity event, where we convinced the rich to donate to a false cause, we could fool the train inspectors.

The second our feet stepped onto the platform, we left ourselves behind in the Windy City. With shoulders back, lips pursed, a walk that could kill, we moved in unison. Neither the clatter of luggage carts nor the hiss of steam distracted us from the role, and when we passed travelers less fortunate, we cast them judgmental looks.

We didn't need to be discreet, we needed to make a scene. The rich loved to flaunt, and the more we did, the more convincing we were.

The uniformed officers, usually thin at the station, crowded the area, checking passengers, tickets, and suspicious luggage. We joined the line, and I glanced up at the sign overhead that listed prohibited items—no mention of stolen jewelry, but they'd be looking for it.

Vel looked my way, and I wished she could hear my inner voice, urging her to relax, saying that we could do this. I took her hand instead, letting our fingers graze, and the tension in her face eased. When we reached the front of the line, the officers split us into two directions, and finally, I felt panic set in. If we weren't together, we couldn't use each other to compensate for our weaknesses. I tended to be awful in conversations, but Vel could make conversation with a horse. However, she faltered under pressure, but when the adrenaline hit me, I rose to the occasion.

I gave her a pleading look, willing her to manage. We just had to fool two men, and we would be free.

My officer, stern faced but youthful looking, took one look at me and smiled. Warm, eager, so inviting. I flashed him a smile back, and he checked my ticket, then eyed my three bags. I controlled the panic, shrugging off some of my coat to reveal my bare collarbone, fanning myself with my ticket. "It's warm in here," I said lightly.

His eyes found my skin, and he cleared his throat. "Yes, it is, miss. The crowds can do that. I hope it's more pleasant for you on the train. Please, take your seat." He nodded at a train attendant, who quickly moved over to scoop up the bags and load them in. *Too easy.*

I looked over to Vel, and her security officer, silver haired and brooding, offered her no such pleasantries. He reached down to inspect her bags, and Vel's face dropped.

I rushed over. "Why are you touching my sister's bags?"

Another thing I'd come to learn over the last few months: The rich loved theatrics.

The officer straightened up, pulling his shoulders back. "It's standard, miss. We're checking everyone's bags."

"You're not touching her bags," I spat out, prissy and loud. I was going to make a scene, I had to. "This is ridiculous. Do you have any idea who our father is?"

"Are you traveling with him?" He looked around the train station at the bustling crowds. "Perhaps I can discuss this with him."

"We are meeting him in New York," I said sternly. "What's your name? I'll certainly be telling him about the officer who touched and searched our things simply because we are two women traveling alone."

"That is not—"

"Then what is it?"

My heart raced—this was fun.

"Perhaps you've heard about the recent jewelry theft, one of the biggest our city has seen," he revealed quietly. "We are just trying to find—"

"Now we're thieves?" Vel finally chimed in with a gasp, placing a hand over her heart. It was a nice touch.

"Certainly not, miss, it's just procedure," he insisted.

The younger officer who had handled my ticket and bags hurried over. "We're holding up the line, here, Jack. Take the woman's ticket and let her through."

Another uniformed attendant joined the mess with a quick, affirming nod. "We need to get this train going."

Jack took a moment to gather his thoughts before handing Vel back her ticket. "Have a safe trip, ladies."

Again, we waited for the bags to get loaded before stepping onto the train. Minutes later, the station chaos was gone, and we settled into our private cabin with nothing but the rhythmic clacking of the wheels on the tracks between us.

I breathed a sigh, leaning my head back and closing my eyes.

"You were incredible back there," Vel said, but there was nothing warm about the compliment. "You're good at this, Virginia."

I opened my eyes and looked out the train window, watching Chicago disappear. "You've been looking out for me since the night you met me. I owed you." I took a moment, thinking back on her expression at the station. "I didn't think you were scared of anything, Vel."

Her shoulders moved up, then down. "I can play the part for society, that's fun, but this . . . this isn't fun. This isn't having drinks and making deals, this is too real. Our entire lives could have ended there. Why didn't it scare you?"

I wanted to tell her that something inside me was wrong now, that

I had changed. That nothing could scare me more than the two bodies I'd seen and what I'd heard from that small storage closet, but then I'd relive it again, and I'd only just stopped having nightmares.

I opened my mouth to say something, but when I did, she reached for my hands and squeezed them tightly. "You know they're just going to want you to do more now? Take bigger risks?" She was looking deeply into my eyes, and I knew she was asking herself all the important questions.

Why was I doing this? What was in it for me? I tried to come up with a lie in my head, but something about her eyes and the way she held my hands made me desperately want to tell her the truth. The truth that I was tired of living alone. "There's something I want to tell you, but I need to know I can trust you."

She leaned back, releasing my hands, eyes studying me. "After what you just did for me, doll, there's not a damn thing in this world I wouldn't do for you."

When I started talking about Madeline, I didn't stop, not until deep into the train ride when an attendant began walking through first class, asking if he could be of any assistance. I lowered my voice quickly. "I need to find her, that's why I'm here."

"I took her drinking," she said, with a sadness to her voice. "It was the only time we spent together, but she was magnificent. A natural. Joe didn't even send me in to help her get adjusted, like he did you."

I looked down, feeling my throat tighten. "She was."

"You think she's still alive?"

I hated the question and tried desperately to avoid it. "I want to believe she is . . . She was resilient, and according to the people who knew her before me, she had a habit of running off and starting over." Miss Suzannah's stories of Madeline's exploits were one of the only things that had left me hopeful when she first disappeared. "But if she is dead, I need to know what happened."

"Joe said she was with Adonis?"

I nodded. "You've heard of him?"

"Reputation only, but I'll see if I can find out more."

"Thank you."

Her eyes started to water, and I couldn't place where the emotion was coming from. "Vel?"

"I must look like a damn fool." She reached up to clean the tears off her face with her hand. "It's just, nobody would come looking for me if I disappeared."

And then, I understood everything about Vel without her telling me anything at all. This time, I switched my seat to move to her side, pulling her into me until her head fell to my shoulder. Somewhere between Chicago and New York, I made my first real friend since Madeline.

After my success with the heist, stolen goods would arrive at my apartment each Monday, delivered by a network of associates. Joe would load me up with an assortment of valuable trinkets, exquisite jewelry, and luxurious furs, transforming me into a walking treasure trove, then send me off to a new destination for delivery.

I thought it might go on forever until Joe suggested traveling to Indiana for a meeting with the bosses. Stunned, I pulled my body up from the tub full of lukewarm water. All the bubbles were gone, but I could still smell the lavender soap.

"We leave in the morning," Joe called from outside the bathroom door, where I could see his shadow pacing underneath.

"What's this about?" I asked, but something inside me already knew the answer.

"Are you ready for your towel?"

"I'm ready." He walked in with his head low, then reached for a towel. He turned politely while handing it to me. I stood and pulled it around my body tightly, stepping out to sit down at the vanity.

"Joe?"

"I'll tell you, but you need to promise before."

I narrowed my eyes.

"You'll play nice with the big boys."

I scoffed. "Why on earth would I do that?"

He strolled into my bedroom and shook his head at the sight of my tousled, unmade bed. He started to make it up while telling me, "The Carnation Club has had plenty of women come in and out over the years, but you're the first to be invited to the back room. Not even Vel has been in the back room."

"The back room?" I repeated, giving him a sideways look. "What's so special about it?"

He didn't blink. "It's where the men talk business . . . where Al Capone talked business. Before you spent so much time with Vel, you knew how to be polite, how to behave. I need the old Virginia."

I wanted to say that he killed the old Virginia the second he made me lie, cheat, and steal for profit, but the "morality" conversation never went well with him. He always brought up Madeline, as if all this was going to be somehow worth it. All I could do was pray that it would be.

I walked out of the bathroom, slipping into the kitchen for a bowl of fruit I hadn't finished at breakfast. "You like to blame Vel for everything."

"Because she's loud and drunk, with no class," he countered.

"Unhappy women tend to be loud."

"I don't want to have this conversation again," he said with a wave of his hand. "Plenty of women get divorced, there's nothing stopping her from doing the same."

I frowned at the thought. "Divorcing Georgie was hard enough. I can't imagine what it would be like trying to leave a Mob man."

He gave me a hard look. "Fair enough."

I chewed a grape as I walked into the living room, and we sat in our normal spots, a strange routine I'd come to enjoy. During the first month, I'd taken the car to Cicero to check in with Miss Suzannah each week. Sometimes, I'd stay the night. I longed for her wisdom and the noisy massage parlor I once called home. When Joe caught me doing it, he made a habit of showing up every few nights to make sure I didn't slip off.

I couldn't say with certainty that we were friends, but we both had a place in each other's lives and understood the importance of it. Typically, we smoked, counted money, and occasionally gossiped, but tonight his mood was grave. This meeting had him on edge. "So, in fewer words, you want me to be like the wives and mistresses?"

"Would that be too terribly difficult?"

"Joe, they didn't invite me into that room to treat them special or gush at how appreciative I am for the honor. I'm not one of their wives or mistresses, and that's why I'm going in there."

He looked at me through narrowed eyes. "These men are hot tempered. They're not the same men you dished out meatballs to at the San Carlo."

"I'm not afraid of them, and I'm not sleeping with them, so I have no reason to play nice," I weighed in. "You know numbers, Joe, and I know men. They don't want another nice girl. Just trust me on this one."

His lips thinned, and for a long moment, he said nothing. He didn't want to trust me. We'd been at this for months, and he still liked to hear my day-to-day in elaborate detail. Any new friends or new conversations. Sometimes he even liked to coach me on what to say and when.

But I was getting the hang of this, and I needed him to see it.

"Well?" I said, the silence beginning to unnerve me.

"I better not come to regret this."

Chapter Ten

The Carnation Club was a remote, out-of-state hideaway secluded behind a long dirt road flanked by rows of thick sugar maple trees that faded from green to crimson. Wildflowers blossomed in thick, open pastures where I spotted horses grazing and livestock baking in the high Indiana sun. Even with our windows up, I could already smell the manure in subtle drafts and began to itch at phantom bug bites along my ankles. I'd long since given up the Southern girl who grew up in a place not so dissimilar to this, and if I'd known coming here would mean facing her again, I'd have stayed in my lavender bathwater.

Joey Ep drove past the carriage house filled with extravagant cars that spilled over onto the graveled driveway. He got out with a breathless kind of moan, inhaling the country air as if these meetings were the most refreshing time of his month. With an eager spring in his step, he ascended the steps of the grand whitewashed mansion, casting an impatient glance back to beckon me to follow.

I didn't move, not yet, because this was far from refreshing for me. I opened the door and leaned out of the car, skin still clinging to my seat, in need of a good rip. My feet hit the ground and the air stuck to my flesh like years of bad memories, and when I shut the car door to glance out at the open pastures, my mouth went dry.

If I were to close my eyes, I'd see my pa, dragging my mother through the field to lock her in the stables as a lesson. I'd sneak out of my room at night in my cotton nightgown to free her, bare feet bolting through the high grass. She'd be sleeping around stacks of hay, trembling from the cold, drafty night air, her lip busted and bleeding. I'd plead with her to come with me, but she'd refuse, afraid of his wrath.

I'd sleep with her on the wet earth and pray that, come morning, he'd be dead.

"Virginia," shouted Joe with a snap of his fingers. "We're late."

I swallowed down the anxiety building in my chest with a sharp breath. I wasn't in Georgia; my pa was nowhere to be found. We'd be back in the city in a few days. I forced my feet forward and pulled my shoulders back to adjust my uneven stride. I wouldn't let the apprehension show.

Joe was greeted by a few stray guards by the door, men in unremarkable suits of dark shades. One of them gave me a look over and pulled the cigarette out of his mouth to say, "This way, doll, I'll show you to the guesthouse. That's where the other women are."

"Other women?" I huffed loudly.

Joe opened his mouth to say something, but I held my hand up to silence him and snatched the cigarette out of the guard's mouth. "I'm right where I need to be, doll, but if you need some help getting to the guesthouse yourself, I'd be happy to escort you."

The other guard snorted out a chuckle.

I took a long drag of the cigarette, coating it with my cranberry lipstick, then tossed it to the ground and stubbed it out with my heel.

"Gentlemen," interrupted Joe, beckoning me forward with a wave. Both guards stepped aside, and we marched in together.

This gathering of men—Charlie Fischetti, Jake Guzik, Paul Ricca, and a dozen others—was only slightly different from their meetings over dinner at the San Carlo, where the world was watching. At least there, the vulgar comments had a sense of humility to them. They wanted me to like them, sleep with them. Now that they knew I wouldn't, there was no such decency.

"Joe won, did he?" Charlie.

"You as good in bed as they say, Virginia?" Jake.

"How about a taste?" Paul.

I placed my hands on my hips and gave Paul a scowl. I thought about what Vel or Madeline would say and surprised myself when I spat out, "How about I head to the guesthouse and fuck your wife for you? God knows she hasn't had any real pleasure since marrying you."

They roared with laughter. Sick, rich laughter.

Joe's eyes widened, and he tipped his hat, the closest thing to him saying, *You were right.* Why did they crave the abuse? If I could make a career out of abusing salt-of-the-earth men like them, I'd do it in a heartbeat. Travel town to town at venues where men filled the audience, and I'd laugh at them. What a career I'd have.

Story after story, there was no sign of business in sight. It was not until they started talking about their kills that all my snide remarks flew out the window. My posture slumped in the chaise, and I averted my eyes to the decor of the home to keep my mind from drifting back to Wayne . . . and Ben. We weren't in the famous "back room," but rather just an informal living room with walnut furniture, chrome wall sconces, and a soft blue shag rug. There was a tasteful nude print above the brick fireplace—a woman spread along a shag rug not so different from the one beneath my feet. High ceilings, crown molding, and a chandelier just as sparkling as the one in the lobby of my apartment building.

"Shot him right between the eyes," said Charlie, his voice like a buzzing bee in my ear, growing more irritating with each passing second.

"Nothing compares to Siegel," said Paul. "Did you hear about what he did to Tony Fabrizzo? Showed up to his home dressed like a detective. He had a real badge and everything."

"Shot him three times in the head," added Jake, then shuddered. "Ben fucking Siegel. He's a madman."

I swallowed over the lump in my throat and looked to Joe, expecting him to say something critical. His eyes met mine with some caution, and then he looked away. Suddenly the room felt warm and small, and their voices collided into a mesh of violent images and strong laughs.

I picked myself up from the chaise and threw open the French doors to leave the room entirely. I strolled past the double staircase to the entry doors and exited with a tightness in my chest that felt as if it might kill me.

The outside air permeated my lungs, and I managed to keep my chin from quivering with one hefty breath at a time. Would I ever be able to sit in a room and talk about murder without feeling something? I hoped never, but the more wrong I did for this organization, the more I wondered if I'd start forgetting good and bad. That they'd somehow blend, and my vision wouldn't allow me to distinguish them.

I took a walk around the estate, past the manicured hedges and scrubs, to a nearby greenhouse, overrun with growing ivy. I saw someone toiling inside, so I tried to sneak past the glass structure quickly, not interested in running into a wife, but stopped when I spotted a bright white bowler hat and broad shoulders.

A man in the greenhouse?

I walked around the entrance and peered inside. He was wearing a brown tweed sport coat with a blue shirt underneath, brown trousers, and a bright red bow tie. He was as tall as Georgie, with thick arms and rough, calloused hands, which I could see even from my distance away. He picked at a basket of strawberries, then moved over to the cherry tomatoes. He popped them into his mouth and pocketed the rest like a thief in a market, passing from stall to stall.

"There's food inside," I said aloud, taking a step into the greenhouse, my heels sinking into the warm soil.

He swirled around to face me and dropped a cherry tomato with a shake. He ran his fingers through his chestnut hair and stuttered out nervously, "Forgive me, ma'am, this just reminds me of home." I took him in from head to toe and noticed a pair of rust-colored leather cowboy boots. He was definitely not from the Chicago Outfit. Was this Wayne's replacement?

"I can never resist a strawberry." He returned to the basket and pulled one out to hand it to me. "Try one, I insist."

He was handsome enough, with a surprisingly youthful face. I took a few steps forward and grabbed the strawberry to try it. It was much fresher than anything I'd had with my breakfast, and even when I was done with it, the juice sat in my mouth and throat, teasing me for more.

"Delicious, isn't it?"

"Very."

He stepped forward, one foot in front and one in back, stuck between each step, as if he were afraid he might spook me into running. "You're Virginia Hill, aren't you?"

"Hardly fair that you know my name and I don't know yours."

He cleared his throat with a cheeky grin, and two dimples emerged. "Major," he answered shyly. "Major Arteburn Riddle."

"Major?" I quirked a brow. "Army?"

He sighed at the question and grumbled out, "Major is my name."

"Your first name?"

He nodded.

"That's an awful first name."

A laugh burst out of him, and some strawberry juice dripped from his mouth. He took a white handkerchief from his suit pocket and cleaned himself up. "They warned me you had a mouth like any man."

"Well, not like any man." I pouted a bit. "I like to think I look better in this lipstick."

"Oh, very much." His cheeks, still caught in a shell-shocked kind of grin, started to blush a warmer shade. "I admit, when they told me a woman would be joining us today, I became rather obsessed with you. I asked them everything I could think of, but you're even more beautiful than they said."

I crossed my arms over my chest with a firm look. "You married, Major?"

"Engaged."

"Your fiancée over there in the guesthouse with all the others?"

"No," he said, quite brusquely. "I'd never bring her here. She's a Georgia peach, and these men . . . they're sharks. You don't bring a peach to the ocean. You leave a peach where she'll grow best, where she's safe."

I looked him over some more and pondered how a man who spoke so fondly of his fiancée could still freely admit his obsession with a perfect stranger. "Do you often refer to women as fruit?"

He parted his lips to speak, but I didn't give him a moment to answer. "What kind of fruit am I, Major Riddle?"

"This is a test, isn't it?" He took a step forward, something about my question giving him the signal he needed, confirmation that I was warming up to him. I wasn't. So far, we were just two strangers on the run from business, seeking solace in nature. That didn't connect us or bond us. Mob men, despite what they said or did, were all the same.

"Well . . ." He cleared his throat. "You looked mighty fine eating that strawberry."

I pinched the bridge of my nose in visible, raw irritation because if this was a test, he had failed miserably. "First mistake, I'm no fruit. I'm a shark, just like every other man in that house. How do you think your fiancée would feel if she were here, watching this exchange of bad lines?"

He visibly swallowed and ran his fingers through his hair again. A nervous habit, I guessed. "She'd feel about the same as I imagine Joe would feel. You're his girl, aren't you?"

I flicked the green nub left of the strawberry at him. "Second mistake, I'm no one's girl."

"I didn't mean to assume."

"And yet you did."

He chuckled and ran a hand down his face. "I really screwed up, didn't I?"

"Virginia," Joe's voice called from the entrance to the greenhouse. He stood rather uncomfortably with an umbrella. He glanced up at the sky and pushed the umbrella open just as the rain started to tap against the roof and walls. He waved at a buzzing bee with a huff as I exited and walked with him back to the main house.

"You know who that is, don't you?"

"I don't want to know," I said with a dismissive wave.

"That's our number one front man. We use him for everything."

"Why would you do that? He doesn't know whether to check his ass or scratch his watch."

"What does that even mean?" His eyes went wide. "You know how I feel about all that Southern talk."

"It means I don't think he's very smart."

"He doesn't need to be smart," he countered. "We learned our lesson with Wayne. Major inherited his father's fortune at a young age and has made a second fortune with his oil and gas drilling company. He's the money. We need him. You were friendly, weren't you? Promise me you were friendly."

I shrugged a bit. "I suppose that depends on how you define *friendly*."

"Virginia!" he scolded, halting mid-path around the house. "You were right. The boys in there love your wit and your mouth. Your brusque charm works wonders on them. But Major? We flatter only."

"Flatter him like all the others . . . How many now, six?" I hated that I'd kept count, wishing I had some ability to wash them all away the second they put their clothes back on and left me alone in the bed to sob. It was a song and dance I knew was coming with every new timely introduction Joe planned.

"We've had this conversation before," he said, rather impatiently. "There are certain things required of your position, especially after you proved yourself so capable with Wayne. Neither of us has to like it, but we don't have to be children about it."

I pushed forward with a roll of my eyes, and he followed without delay. "If Major wants your company, you'll give it to him." He took me by the shoulders and breathed deeply, waiting for me to mimic him. It was rather silly, but when I did it, I always felt a bit calmer. "They're ready for you."

"In this famous back room?" I mocked.

"Yes."

My nerves returned to me suddenly. "What if this isn't it?"

"Then we keep going," he said. "We work harder."

Hardly worth the word *famous.* It was a small room, with a long table set with chairs and a single vase of flowers that looked watered and well tended. Chromium walls with narrow mirrors, and soft, velvet flooring. As each man took his seat, an unusual silence settled upon the room, weighing it down. My confidence faltered, and I found myself clinging to the fabric of my dress, anchored near the door. A dryness crept into my mouth, betraying my nerves.

"Virginia." Joe's voice broke the silence, beckoning me to the chair beside him. "Come, sit."

I forced my feet forward and eased down into the seat. Contrary to the casual banter earlier, there was a heavy, eerie silence among us all, as if entirely different men existed in front of me—men I didn't know. Men I couldn't predict.

"As we've discussed before," began Jake, "our partnership with New York—"

"With the Luciano family," interrupted Paul grimly. "Let's speak plainly about it."

"It's more than just one family," said Charlie, irritated at the introduction. "Regardless, we've been having issues with New York. We need to come up with a better arrangement."

New York? He said New York.

"New York?" I said aloud, and each man averted their eyes to me in terrifying unison. I looked at Joe, who looked right back at me. My heart thudded in my chest again.

Paul lifted his hand. "We'll explain your part in a moment, Virginia."

I laughed aloud, and it echoed in the room. "You invited me into this secret, boring little room to have me sit at this table like a quiet mouse?"

"Of course not," Jake insisted, then pointed a finger at Paul. "Paul, shut the fuck up."

Jake looked at me directly when speaking. "We've already got little agreements here and there with New York, but we need to do something bigger. We allow the Luciano family to buy into our North Shore gambling parlors and brothels, give them a tiny piece of our organization, and in return, we get to expand into the East Coast rackets. But in order to make this happen, we have to work with Joe Adonis."

Paul grimaced, veins pulsing beneath the skin of his neck. "Fuck Adonis."

The name made me shiver, but I only had a single conversation with Joe to reference. The very conversation that had led me to making this decision.

"He's the king of the East Coast gambling rackets," countered Jake.

"He's no king," snapped Paul. "Capone is a king."

Jake lifted his hand. "We can't deny what Adonis has done. He owns more nightclubs, brothels, and gambling joints than any of us. If we want in, in a bigger way, he's how we do it. That's where you come in, Virginia."

Again, all three looked my way. Jake continued steadily, "We send you in there as our liaison to carry profits and launder money. You will play your part but keep your eyes and ears open. Adonis likes to cheat the game, and should he skim or cheat this partnership, we want to know."

In other words, they were sending me to do the very same thing Madeline had done?

"We want to know everything," added Paul gravely. "Everything about that pompous fuck and what he's up to."

"Why a woman?" I finally asked, and though I knew the answer, I hoped they'd surprise me.

"Not just any woman." Jake stroked my ego, while Paul's upper lip twitched, a sign he had more to say.

"Why a woman?" I asked directly of Paul, who I knew wouldn't sugarcoat it.

"Adonis likes women. He's weak around them, stupid." The words came out simple, uncomplicated. They were sending me there to keep him happy, both with laundering and in bed. They'd sent Madeline to do the same. Maybe they hadn't brought her into this famous back room or treated her with any semblance of respect. For that, we were different. But the job they needed done was the same. We weren't special, or important. We just needed to be women.

The conversation grew heated, each man discussing why they didn't like Adonis, and Jake continuing his counterarguments about the advantages of what they were doing. I tuned in and out over the next hour until the meeting was concluded, and they were back to leisure as if nothing had ever happened.

Later that night, I couldn't put myself to sleep, my mind reeling from the conversation we'd had in the private room. On the one hand, I had to find out what had happened to Madeline. Adonis was the last person to see her, know her, and even if it took me a few weeks, I'd find a way to pry it out of him. But on the other hand, what if something terrible had happened to her and that same fate awaited me? As much as I fought with Joe and, at times, hated him, he offered me a sense of protection I would not have in New York.

I sat down on the guest bed in the spacious room, picking out Madeline's postcards from my suitcase. I'd carried them with me through every illegal venture as a much-needed reminder. In each city, she gushed about the weather, the people, the drinking, and the food. She'd write me lists of all the little trinkets she was bringing home, and how her new life was better than she'd ever imagined. Then they changed, the words became fewer, and the emotion in them vanished.

Then that final postcard, and the calls she made to her mother and Miss Suzannah.

I walked out of my room and down the long staircase to the kitchen for some water. As I rounded the corner, I startled to a stop. Alma, Jake's wife, was sipping a cocktail while delicately eating a finger sandwich. After every bite, she cleaned the side of her mouth with an off-white napkin, then took another sip of her cocktail. She was the most intimidating of all the wives, and not because of her brash facial features and short, stylish haircut.

According to Joe, Jake and she had a special kind of marriage. She ran the show when he wasn't around, and if she had something to say, everyone listened. Of all the women Joe told me to stay away from, she was at the top of the list.

I tried to disappear quickly, but she peered my way, and her eyes widened significantly. "Miss Hill? Do come in, I'll make you a drink!"

"I was just coming down for some water," I said, pulling my robe tightly around my body.

"Nonsense!" She grinned and weaved around the island to hand me her cocktail, then started off to make herself another one. I took a small sip, and the alcohol ratio hit my muscles so quickly that my eyes widened.

"You like them strong, Alma?"

She shook and poured hers into another glass, slightly fuller than mine. "Just like my men," she joked, then leaned against the counter to observe me from head to toe. Though, unlike the other wives, I didn't get a sense of harsh judgment in her eyes. "How was your grand meeting? Is the room impressive? I've never seen it."

"It's just a room," I said with a shrug. "I was rather unimpressed."

"Pity." She pouted a bit, then took another sip with a single raised brow. "You hiding from all the wives just gives them more fuel."

"They all think I'm sleeping with their husbands."

"Are you?"

I leveled a serious glare at her. "No."

"Then don't hide. Mistresses hide. When do you head to New York?"

I said nothing for a moment. "You're aware of the business discussed in the room but not allowed inside?"

Her shoulders pulled back. "My husband and I have no secrets."

I placed the cocktail down and folded my hands across my chest. "I haven't decided if I'm even going yet."

She burst into laughter. "It's not like you have a choice, Virginia."

"I'm guessing they wouldn't have brought me into that room if I didn't have a choice." I tried not to let my anger get the best of me. I suspected her to be cross; I knew this was coming. I took a deep, steadying breath.

A look of disappointment crossed her features. "The illusion of choice is hardly a choice."

"What are you getting it? Why don't we skip the small talk, and you get to the point?"

Again, I prepared myself for the worst. I thought about everything my pa had called me, all the terrible things Georgie had said when I asked for a divorce. There was nothing she could say to hurt me that I hadn't heard before.

Stay calm, Virginia.

"You're a very fancy whore, Virginia, with freedoms I do not have, but let's not pretend you have the power to decide anything."

Whore.

It angered me before when Georgie said it because it wasn't true, but now, with everything I'd done under Joe's influence, was she wrong? I'd slept with men for information, money, and position. Just outside, Joe had asked me to sleep with Major if he requested it. How was that any different from the girls at the massage parlor?

I attempted to talk myself out of the haze of fury—I was talented. I'd done things no other woman had. I was a successful carrier, skilled at the con of being who they needed me to be. I'd come so far to get into that room, with men who had never talked business with a woman. I had never felt more powerful than I did today, and yet, the word still haunted me. *Whore.*

"Fuck you, Alma," I spat out, seeing red. My heart began to pound. "I sat at the table . . . How many wives or whores that have come and gone here been able to say that?"

She threw her hand across my face, leaving an awful echo in the large, endless kitchen. I kept my body still, watching her with a sense of unwavering defiance. My cheeks might have been as red as the cherry tomato Major had smuggled earlier in the greenhouse, but the pain was dull. I'd been hit worse. She leveled a strange, terrified gaze at me, then snatched me by the wrist like a child in need of reprimanding. "Come with me, I want to show you something."

"I'm not going with you anywhere!" I pulled against her hold.

"Please," she insisted, her tone changing. "Come with me, and I'll keep my mouth shut about what you said to me tonight."

I didn't think her threat held any merit, but how could I know for certain?

I swallowed down the lump building in my throat and rolled my eyes, following along with clear signs of displeasure in my dragging feet. She exited the kitchen through a servants' entrance and down a tiny corridor to a small door that led to the endless pastures of farmland.

I followed her through the long grass, feeling it along my bare legs as the night breeze tickled my skin. I tried to focus on the smell of woodsmoke in the distance instead of animal flesh as she stopped at a tall, weathered barn, guarded only by a large lock hanging from a chain along the door handles. Alma reached into the folds of her silk night-robe, producing a key that she deftly inserted into the lock. With a satisfying click, the lock surrendered and dropped to the warm earth, startling a small mouse, which darted along the corridor of the barn.

I kept my distance. "What is this, Alma?"

She pushed open the door, and a fleshy, unsettling smell filled my nostrils. With no light, I couldn't see very far into the barn, so she pushed open the door until the moonlight illuminated a group of scarcely dressed women, huddled in different groups, slumbering and shaking in the hay. There was only terror and sadness in their worn features, and in that moment, I thought again about my poor mother. I stepped back and nearly stumbled into the grass.

"What the hell is this?" My voice was breathless, the words choking out of my throat.

"These women are recruited from nearby farms to head back to Chicago with us to join our brothels."

I flicked another gaze at them, bound with rope at the wrists and ankles. "You mean kidnapped? You kidnapped them?"

My mind tugged at the memory. Miss Suzannah telling me that the Mob stole girls from the countryside to ship back to Chicago for her to mold and sell. I had thought she was exaggerating to scare me, that the girls came reluctantly but willingly. But no, they kidnapped and imprisoned them like animals.

"My husband and all those men in that special room you were in today"—she waved down at the litter of girls—"they had no choice, and I have no choice, and you have no choice. We all play a part to survive. We're all in cages. Your body belongs to them. The sooner you understand that, the easier your life is going to be." She took a strong step forward, too close for comfort, voice low and ferocious when she uttered, "And when you feel like you've had enough, just know that it could be worse."

There were a hundred other ways she could have taught me this lesson, but, like Ben, she'd decided on twisted. Cruel, even. I wouldn't forget the two dead bodies I saw on the floor that night in Chicago, and now I wouldn't forget the faces of a dozen innocent girls, waiting for slaughter.

Alma shut the barn doors and locked them securely. "And if you decide New York isn't for you, we'll certainly need someone to keep the girls in line back in Chicago. We're opening another brothel. Did Jake tell you?"

Her casual tone left me rigid.

I watched her disappear through the grass, back to the giant white house, but I stayed behind, staring at the barn until the cold night air got the better of me.

Chapter Eleven

I waited by my window for hours until the early-morning mist covered the vast fields leading out to the barn and two men, the guards from the front of the house, arrived to unlock the barn and feed the women. Joe came for me and called me to breakfast, where he further discussed the New York mission and how all our hope of finding Madeline depended on my success. But all I could think about was Alma. Last night flashed before me in broken scenes until I couldn't decide if she was trying to hurt me or do me a favor. A slash of truth I needed.

I had no control; I belonged to them. Ben had said it, Alma had said it—when was I going to get it through my thick head?

The men drank and played games, only occasionally discussing business, and I played my part. I continued this routine every night; then I woke up and watched, studying the system they had in place to guard the women, feed them, and forcibly bathe them. I knew what Joe would say, that we couldn't afford to be reckless, but I also felt I'd earned a place with them. Even if they found out I'd freed the women, they needed someone to go to New York. How much trouble would I really be in? Would they even know it was me if I didn't get caught? I wasn't supposed to know about the girls.

I thought about it for days until finally, on the fourth night, the last night of our stay, I left my room just after midnight to scour the house in search of proper tools.

I first checked the kitchen, looking for anything I could use to pry off the chain or break it. When nothing of use turned up, I left the house in a rush, eyeing a shed I'd spotted on the drive in, now partly cracked open with a light coming from the inside. I tiptoed around the door, gazing inside cautiously.

Major was smoking a cigarette and reading, using only the light of an old kerosene lamp. He stood in slack navy suit pajamas, a thick robe, and comically fluffy slippers. This boy-man was the money?

I let out a loud huff and pushed open the door. "I'm certain the reading light is better in your room. What are you doing here? Why are you everywhere I'd rather you not be?"

"Virginia!" He dropped his book and cigarette, then fumbled to the ground to find both. "I mean, Miss Hill. Is that what you would prefer?"

"I'll take it over 'strawberry.'"

He chuckled a bit. "Quick wit! I haven't forgotten. What are you doing out here so late?"

"What are *you* doing out here so late?"

His eyes moved from my face to my body, undressing the silk crepe nightgown in a snap. Almost like a switch, he nervously cleared his throat and pressed his lips together firmly. "You must be cold."

He reached for a wool blanket near him and started to walk toward me. I shook my head at the notion. "Save the sweet gestures for your Georgia peach." I rushed around in a hurry, digging through buckets and storage drawers.

"You really don't care for me, do you?"

"Don't think you're special or anything. I treat all men like this until they prove me wrong."

I found a box of tools, but nothing that would be useful against that lock. I thrust it aside and kept hunting.

He shook his head slowly. "How many have proved you wrong?"

I stood up and let out an irritated breath. "Not enough."

"Can I help you look for something?"

I threw my arms up. "Now you want to be useful? I'm looking for something to break a lock with. A pair of bolt cutters, maybe a shovel . . . anything."

"What lock are you trying to break?"

I eyed a small axe hanging from a hook behind him and slipped by to grab it. "The barn has a dozen stolen girls in it, ready to be sent to Chicago brothels. I'm going to free them."

He choked out his next words: "Stolen girls? What are you talking about?"

As I grabbed the axe, I paused to look at him. His body froze mid-movement, his breathing slow and uneven, coming out in short bursts. He looked like a child, devastated at the sudden knowledge that Santa wasn't real. "I was right, then? You haven't got the good sense that God gave a goose. Who do you think you're working for, Major? You're fronting for the Mob. Your money goes to them. Everything they do . . . even the trafficking of innocent girls."

"I don't . . . I didn't . . ." He gripped his throat and rushed to the shed door to gaze out at the barn, fingers trembling. "I'm not on the inside of all this . . . if you hadn't noticed. Otherwise, I'd have been in that room with you. I just do what I'm told."

I gripped the axe and eased forward, narrowing my eyes, thinking about Wayne and the blackmail used to keep him in line. "What do they have on you?"

"Enough," he answered grimly. "But not just me . . . my family . . . my father. Without them, we wouldn't have gotten as far as we have."

Again, Alma's words rang true. I didn't need another woman in my head, whispering wisdom when I hadn't asked for it. Yet there she was.

"You're in a cage too," I muttered to myself.

"A cage?"

I shook my head. "Not enough money and power in the world to get us out of this debt. They own you and they own me."

His gaze moved from the barn to me. "They'll kill you if you do this."

"If this mission to New York is as important as they claim, maybe not." My heartbeat thrummed. "They're not going to have time to train anyone else. This might be the only moment where I have the advantage. Why not use it?"

His expression shifted, somewhere between fear and excitement. "You're going to risk it?"

"I think I am." Any sense of fear swelling inside me was clouded by the ridiculous thought that I needed to help every lost woman. Every hurt little girl. My desperate hunt for Madeline had gotten me into the Mob. I'd nearly got killed in league with Wayne's wife. Now this? What was going to happen to me if I did this? But who would I be if I didn't at least try? The guilt would eat at me, haunt my dreams, just like Wayne and his wife and that dreadful night.

My fingers turned clawlike around the base of the axe, but as I took a step ahead, Major stepped in front of me.

"Allow me?" He reached for the axe.

I pulled it back. "No, you're not getting involved. I can already tell that you're an awful liar."

"I swing this once and break the lock. Your beautiful little arms will make a lot of noise and get us caught before any of the girls are free. Let me help you."

I tilted my head and straightened my shoulders. "You helping me because you want to do the right thing or because you're trying to sleep with me?"

"Yes."

"To what?"

He shrugged. "Both?"

I struggled not to grin, forcibly keeping my mouth clenched shut. He was admittedly growing on me. I opened my mouth to speak but found that no words came out. Instead, I handed him the axe.

We walked together in a rush, and suddenly the spongy ground beneath my feet felt as if it were trying to pull me deep into the earth. Major stopped at the entrance to the barn and studied the chained doors for several seconds, then pulled his shoulders back and gripped the axe tightly with both hands. He drew it down in one swoop, and the axe cut into the chain with astounding ease. It fell to the ground, hushed by the grass, and together, we threw open the doors.

I found myself even more horrified than I'd been that night with Alma, wincing at the sight of all of them shivering in the chilly night air. I imagined them losing hope little by little as the days passed, being treated like cattle, nobody coming to help them. Even now, they all looked at me with weak eyes and little fight.

Major frowned. "This is more than a dozen."

"Then we better get to work."

We managed to get them out of the barn and moving to the road nearby, where even the slightest sounds against the gravel spooked us into nearly crawling. The women, drugged with something to keep them compliant, desperately tried to fight their weakened bodies. Major ushered them into the gravel, where any sense of dizziness plaguing them vanished. Their survival instincts kicked in, and they all started running to the estate entrance, bolting off onto the long road, dashing through trees.

"I'll get my car . . . I'll drive them somewhere," said Major in a breathless plea. "They're not going to stand a chance if we don't help them get into a nearby town."

I opened my mouth to agree, but lights turned on in various rooms of the house, and for a terrible instant, I began to panic. I didn't think through getting caught.

He gripped my shoulders firmly. "Go, now. Get into bed and pretend you know nothing of this."

"I'm not leaving you to take the blame," I snapped.

His gaze dropped to my hand. "What they're going to do to me is going to hurt . . . but they're not going to kill me. They need my face, my company. They need me. It's about time I do something with that fact." He lifted my hand to his mouth for a rushed kiss. "Go now, before it's too late."

I wanted to thank him properly, with a sweet kiss on the mouth and a long, warm embrace, but there was no time. "When will I see you again?"

"I'll find you, Miss Hill."

"Call me Virginia."

He smiled, somehow calm and flushing during the chaotic scene around us. "Virginia."

I ran past the barn to the house, sneaking around the side of it through the same servants' entrance in the kitchen. Inside the house, a commotion was stirring as men and guards awakened to shouts and commands. I slipped back up the stairs and into my room. I stripped my clothes and tossed them into the hamper, then curled into the bed, where I lay awake until my door opened.

"I know you did it!" Alma slammed the door shut behind her and lunged at me with claws out.

I pivoted off the other side with my fists clenched tightly, predicting another slap. "Get out of my room, Alma!"

"Do you have any idea how much money we just lost? I'm telling Jake it was you!"

"Do that, but while you're at it, tell him that you're the one who showed me the girls in the first place."

"Why?" Her eyes nearly watered as the fury spilled out of her quivering lips. "Why would you do that?"

"Because I am not the type of woman that can hold the key to a barn full of stolen girls and not do something about it." But as the words slipped from my mouth, the realization hit me like a punch to the stomach. I gasped for breath. Had I been different, a woman who could just walk away, I'd be far from here. From this. I'd long for Madeline and wonder what had happened to my only friend in Chicago, but I wouldn't be tangled with the Mob. I'd be poor, the same old Virginia without a mink coat to her name, but at least I'd be free.

"They're going to find out . . . When they do, you're dead."

I shook the thought away to keep myself from crying.

"Maybe, maybe not." I walked toward her, and she backed up, inching away from me until her heel hit the bedroom door. "A wife can be replaced with another wife . . . but a really good whore, one that gets results . . ." I pretended to think about it. "They're not so easy to find."

She wanted to hurt me, I could see it in her eyes, but she resisted. Then, her tense shoulders slumped forward, and something inside her broke. I couldn't explain it, or begin to understand it, but Alma—the woman who had threatened me so easily in that kitchen—leaned into me and sobbed. Her forehead pressed to my chest, and I awkwardly pulled a hand around to pat her head, still cautious and unconvinced this wasn't a ploy.

If I were to close my eyes, I could picture a dozen times Vel had done the same thing—sobbed in my arms after a drunken night of foolish fun. I felt a dreadful wave of guilt crash into me. I'd spent so much time avoiding the wives because they detested me, but I should have had more understanding of what they had to endure. After all, I had far more in common with them than the men in the back room.

Quite violently, she shoved away, ending the quiet moment. Before slipping out the door, she uttered, "I hope they throw you into the lake when they're done with you."

In the morning, I slept in and didn't join Joe for breakfast, much to his dismay. He arrived at my room and laid my traveling case on the bed, then began emptying my drawers. He stuffed the case full of my clothing, letting out one impatient sigh after the other. "We need to get going," he insisted. "Last night was a mess, and I'd rather not be associated with it."

"What happened? The noise kept me up," I said, digging a little deeper, stretching my arms wide with a yawn.

Joe sat down on the edge of the bed and pulled a newspaper from the fold of his arm, far more preoccupied with headlines than the business last night. "Some conflict between Riddle and Guzik."

"Conflict?" I sat up slowly, watching him read.

"They were fighting in the yard like pubescent schoolboys."

"Who won?"

"Guzik."

I swallowed. "Is Major Riddle dead?"

He chuckled in response. "Unfortunately, there are some men we can't kill. He left early this morning. Guzik is still in a rage, so I'd like to sneak out quietly and discreetly. Although, I imagine a touch of good news would help. Are you ready to tell them about New York?"

"Yes," I answered quickly. "I'm ready."

My stomach danced with anticipation and fear all the way back to Chicago. Joe insisted on seeing me back to my place, but I pressed for the opposite. I told him I wanted to be alone in Chicago for my last few days, throw a grand party to say goodbye to my following, and only then would we meet back up so he could see me off to New York.

It was a lie, of course. I just wanted to take a few pills, sleep, drink some, and consider how I was going to take on New York.

I opened the door and tossed my bags inside with the plan to phone Major and thank him, but instead, I found him sleeping on my chaise, lounging like a sprawled-out cat and snoring. All sense of admiration I'd felt since leaving vanished in a quick instance. I ran to the kitchen to fetch a glass of water to toss in his face. First Ben watching me sleep in the middle of the night like a proper killer, now Major?

He awakened in a frightful fury, swinging his arms about with a shout.

"Who let you in?" I yelled before he could get out any words.

He stood up and rubbed the water from his eyes, but as soon as he did, I tossed my beret at him. "Tell me, right now! I've come too far for men to think they can come in here without my invitation."

"I bribed the doorman," he insisted with his hands up. "And the front desk . . . I thought I'd take you to dinner, and I just wanted to surprise you. Most women enjoy spontaneity."

All traces of anger sparked into raw annoyance, and I blew some hair out of my face. "You really don't know me at all, do you? Stop comparing me to other women. If I had my gun, I'd have shot you."

He rubbed one temple with his thumb, and the longer I stared, the more I could see all the bruises and cuts along his face and hands. He'd taken a beating, that much was clear, so I swallowed down my temper for the moment.

He handed me back my beret. "I appreciate the dinner invite, but I don't go to dinner with engaged men. Thank you for what you did. Helping me free those women . . . I'm in your debt."

"The thing is," he began with a heavy swallow, "I'm not engaged anymore. You see, I met this woman . . . and I haven't been able to stop thinking about her. Not since the moment I saw her, standing so beautifully in that greenhouse with a hand on her hip. Even as she called me an idiot, and then got me into trouble with my bosses . . . I still can't stop."

A tingle swept down my spine, and suddenly, a butterfly-like feeling filled my stomach. I knew the feeling too well, and it always got me into trouble. "How long did you rehearse that little speech?"

He looked away bashfully, then took a brave step forward, and I allowed it. "Once or twice. I feel like there could be something between us . . . something I can't just let slip away. I'd regret it, and I believe that she would too."

He sounded like Ben to me, urging me that I wanted him, even when I insisted I didn't. Ben was right then, and he was right now. I couldn't just dismiss the attraction for the first man to do something decent, something good.

Another step. I let out a soft breath, desperately trying to keep any kind of blush from changing the hue of my cheeks.

"You're blushing," he said with a grin.

"I'm not."

"You're terribly pink."

Another step, and he was in front of me, breath warm against my face. "Another mistake, Major, leaving your sweet Georgia peach for me. I'm not a good investment. I'm off to New York in a few days."

He reached up for my face, lightly running his hand down my cheek and backward to gather my hair in his hand. I battled for control, the want to resist him. He was the first one Joe had told me to sleep with that I favored, but that didn't make me feel any less dirty for it.

"I supposed I should properly thank you," I whispered, thrusting him down onto the chaise with a shove. Our mouths collided with a similar need, though my aggression seemed to startle him. He removed his hands from my hair, and I guided them down to my dress, where he began pulling at the hem.

I stripped him just enough to mount him, both my legs gripping his waist for dear life until his head thrust back, and he let out a deep moan.

"Virginia, I—"

I placed my hand over his mouth.

"No," I uttered through a moan of my own. "No more talking."

I closed my eyes and rode the wave of pleasure, but like all the men before him, when I opened my eyes to look into his, all I saw was Ben.

We didn't leave bed over the next two days, blissfully unaware if it was day or night. I'd have to drag him from my sheets to eat, but we'd somehow end up tangled back together after only a few short minutes. I forgot about everything—the Mob, the rules, the game . . . and my missing best friend. For just a moment, however fleeting, I was having fun.

"What's going on with you and Riddle?" Joe rang two days later. "He's convinced the boys to give him a few more days with you."

I played the fool, struggling to keep the receiver close to my face while Major trailed kisses down the curve of my back. "I'll call you later, Joe."

As we neared the last day before my trip to New York, we had dinner by the beach and then walked the shores. It grew late, and though I could happily admit the longing for another day was very present, I knew I couldn't put it off any longer. I needed to go to New York. It was my purpose, my only purpose, and when I found out what had happened to Madeline and got Joe the proof he needed on New York, this dark, unsettling moment in my life would be over.

"I have no doubt that you'll return to your Georgia peach after I leave," I said, louder than intended, but wanting to be heard over the crashing waves.

"You think me so bad?" His brows arched. "Perhaps I'll wait for you. Sit around and think about you every day until you get back."

I pouted a bit. "That's too sad. I don't wish it, even for you."

"We could solve all this if you'd just say yes. Marry me and let me take you away."

I cringed at the words, so eerily similar to what Georgie had said to me when he asked me to marry him. But I was young then, desperate.

Now I answered with a roll of my eyes. "We haven't even known each other for a week. You're a madman."

"But we like each other," he countered slyly. "That could turn into love, eventually."

"I don't do marriage." Well, not anymore.

He paused and pulled me into him, where his kiss set me on fire. If not for the hotel guests strolling the beach along the Edgewater, I'd throw him down into the sand right here. He was easy to make love to, and a much-needed distraction, but that was all he could be.

"Let's run away . . ." He leaned down to kiss my mouth, a soft peck, and then he moved to my ear. "We get the hell out of here and leave this behind."

I lifted my chin and exposed my neck. He took the invitation and trailed kisses. "You can't escape . . . Once you're in, you're in." Joe's words, not mine, but the truth. "We can't just do what we want."

"I have money," he whispered. "A couple million in an offshore account. I have been skimming off those bastards for years." He moved back up and tucked some hair behind my ear. "Will you be my escape? There's enough in there to give us a new life if we want it."

My palms sweated, and I pushed him away quickly, letting out a strangled laugh. I hoped he was joking. "What did you say?"

I searched his eyes for playfulness, something to hint this was all a scheme, but I found nothing but a serious gaze. "You're a madman with a death wish, then. If they found out you've been skimming money . . ."

"They can't kill me. They need me." I thought about Wayne's mangled face, Ben's fists, the two bodies on the floor side by side. Riddle had no idea what he was talking about.

"You don't know that."

"You do care for me, then?" The side of his mouth tilted up.

I punched his shoulder. "Care enough to not see you gutted, yes."

He enveloped my hand and held it to his chest warmly. "Run away with me? Don't go to New York."

"I have to go to New York."

"Why?"

Because of Madeline.

"I'm giving you a chance to escape this cage . . . with me."

I started walking, pinching the bridge of my nose, making up any excuse I could think of to avoid accidentally letting the truth slip out. "The money is good."

He reached for my arm to stop me. "Every dollar you make belongs to them in the end. They can take it away as quickly as they give it. I'll give you half of what I have in the account to prove to you I'm serious. That's your money. Not theirs. Yours."

I scoffed lowly. "A million for services rendered. What will you require of me for that money, Major? Marriage?"

His cheeks flushed. "I just want to know you, the real you. And if we grow tired of one another, we move along. You keep your money, I keep my money, and that's it."

It was tempting because even after New York, there was a chance I wouldn't be able to get out of this. That they'd ask more of me, and more, until my name was the only thing left of the woman I used to be. But if I ran now, I'd always be running, and I'd never find Madeline.

"We had fun, that's it," I finally said, shaking off the thought. "Let's not ruin the memory with a bad goodbye."

I began walking back to my apartment, but his next words stopped me dead in the sand. "If you don't agree to come with me, I'll be forced to tell them the truth. That it wasn't me who let those girls out and that I took the fall for you."

My mouth fell open. I couldn't have heard what I thought I'd heard. "What did you just say to me?"

"If the only way to protect you from this organization is to make you leave it, then that's what I'm going to do."

The violent realization that I didn't know him at all hit me with a painful stab in my chest. His silly tendencies to be daft and inept—was it all an act? That boyish charm, playacting? Had I fallen for it?

"You're blackmailing me?" My voice broke, and I couldn't begin to stop it.

"To save you," he insisted.

"Joe will be here to pick me up in the morning. You need to be gone by then."

He retook my hand, but his touch felt cold and strange. Like the touch of a complete stranger, one who harbored a dangerous secret of mine. "I'll be here tomorrow night, on this beach, waiting for you."

Again, I pulled my hand away, this time running through the sand to get as far away from him as I could. Was he bluffing? His words plagued me all night, a nightmare that wouldn't let me sleep, on repeat, until I drowned it out with a sedative and a glass of whiskey.

Chapter Twelve

Joe arrived with gifts. A few new beautiful coats, a dozen dresses and shoes, and a diamond necklace I tried on the moment he flashed it to me. I spritzed myself with Chanel No. 5, then ran my hands along my hips, draped in a sapphire-blue evening gown by Jeanne Lanvin. "Just wait until Adonis sees you in this," he said with a grin, standing behind me, gazing at me through my vanity mirror.

He pulled my hair back to get a better view of how the necklace looked against my skin but grimaced at the marks Major's mouth had left there. "Major finally gone?"

I cringed and pulled my hair around to cover it.

He must have noticed my reaction because his eyes narrowed as he studied my face with a serious glare. "You didn't sleep last night." He ran a thumb along the deep bags under my eyes. "What happened?"

"None of your business, Joe."

"Well, I hope it's out of your system because Adonis doesn't like to share anything, certainly not his women."

"Because I'm going there to sleep with him, right? A Mob whore, like all those women in the barn. I just have fancier clothes when I do it." The words slipped out so fast, and when it dawned on me, I swallowed the air with a gasp.

His eyes hardened, and he raised an eyebrow. "How did you know about the women in the barn? Who's been whispering in your ear?"

"Everyone!" I pushed off the vanity stool and stormed to the kitchen, reaching for a glass to pour something strong.

He followed with a brisk pace, his feet dashing across the floor to snatch the glass away. "You're not going to drink yourself out of this argument. What is going on?"

"Alma."

"Jake's wife?"

"She said I'm being sent there to sleep with Adonis and then proceeded to show me all the girls in the barn being sent to the Chicago brothels. She did it as a reminder of my place in this organization. Just tell me that's what I am, Joe. Was that all Madeline was?"

I desperately tried to keep my voice from breaking with emotion, but I felt the water filling my lids, betraying me.

His eyes softened, and he gathered my hands, pulling them into his chest. The scene was so strangely similar to last night with Major on the beach that I already felt inclined not to believe a word that came out of his mouth. "You know that's not true. You are the first woman to ever be in that room. Maybe you didn't join us with the intention of being good at this, but you are good, Virginia. You are *not* a whore, but the more you allow the word to burn you, the more convinced everyone will be that there's truth to it."

I didn't look at him.

"You can't tell me this big display is because a wife called you a name."

He was right: It was more than that, and I knew I had to tell him. If I didn't, everything we'd both worked for would slip away. Madeline included. After a long pause, while I debated lying, I finally gave up the information. Major had threatened to blackmail me.

Joe tossed my hands away with a grimace. "You helped those girls escape?"

"They were stolen from their families!"

A bitter laugh erupted from his lips, and he rubbed the back of his neck. "We couldn't figure out why Major would decide that day, of all the days, he was going to do something about the girls in the barn."

"He didn't know about them until I told him?" I phrased it like a question because some part of me that always knew the truth decided to resurface in that instance. "He lied to me."

Then came another laugh, louder than the first and far more hysterical. I got a sense he was on the verge of losing control, but I couldn't tell if he was more disappointed in me or enraged at Major. I had never seen Joe lose control, but I always suspected that when he did, I'd wonder how on earth he'd managed to maintain his cool reserve. "Of all the lessons I've taught you, I didn't expect to need to teach you this one."

My bottom lip quivered involuntarily. "What lesson?"

He slammed his hand down on the kitchen counter, and the single ring on his finger made a violent clink. "Trust no man. Major knew about the women in the barn. He's run this scam with Guzik for years! If he told you otherwise, he did it to fool you into his bed."

My entire body stiffened with regret. Why hadn't I questioned Major when he told me he didn't know? I was too quick to believe him, a complete stranger, who'd fooled me into thinking he was dumb as dirt. I recoiled away from Joe, wanting another drink. Something stronger.

He grabbed the bottle of liquor and threw it to the ground. I jumped as the glass bottle broke into large shards, scattering along the kitchen floor. "No drinking. You use it to escape and you're not escaping this."

I shuddered at how well he'd come to understand me, but didn't flee from his towering presence. I didn't know everything about Joe. In many ways, I felt I'd only scratched the surface. But I did know one thing with absolute certainty: He would never hit me.

"The women in the barn, why? I need an answer. I need to know why you'd take a risk like that after what happened with Wayne."

I shuddered at the reminder but didn't answer him, lost in that awful memory.

"Answer me, Virginia."

I glowered at him. "That's easy, because when Miss Suzannah told me that you stole women from their homes to sell them to Chicago brothels, I thought she was being dramatic. I thought she was lying to me to get me to stay away. That maybe you just recruit girls from the country with the promise of a better life, but no, you kidnap them."

He tsked, teeth grinding together. "You, of all people, know the opportunities the city provides. They could have a better life."

"We are not the same," I ground out, and the comparison left me unnerved. How could he find some calculated excuse for this? "I had a choice . . . You're taking their choice away. I have done disgusting things for the sake of finding a friend who is very likely dead." The word *dead* made my stomach roll, my body jerk. The very thought of never seeing her face again made me start to sob.

Joe reached for my shivering body, but I flinched, backing away from him. I wasn't finished. I cleared my throat and swallowed down the breathless spurt of tears. "I will take any opportunity to remind myself of who I am and not who *you* made me."

"We don't know she's dead," he reminded me again, the same words he used every time I began to lose hope. He then retreated to take a seat at the table, burying his face in his hands. "We have to get ahead of this. If he tells them the truth, New York is off the table."

I sank down with him at the opposite end, still wishing I had something strong to burn my throat. "You said he can't be touched, and that must be true—otherwise he'd be dead for the loss of revenue with the girls in the barn."

"Anyone can be touched if they fuck with the right amount of money," he countered.

I lifted my head with newfound rage and determination, a dangerous combination I welcomed more with each passing second. I knew what I needed to do, but I also understood that if I did it, there was a small chance they'd kill him for it. My hesitation must have shown because Joe was quick to tap the table with his knuckle. "What are you thinking?"

"We can get ahead of it. Major did something bad," I revealed.

"Bad?" His brows perked. "How bad?"

"He fucked with the money. Twice, if you include the girls."

"Tell me more?"

I retrieved my gun from my luggage—my handy revolver. I gripped it, held it tightly, considering my inner monologue—what I'd say to him and how I'd say it.

Joe's eyes grew large. "You can't kill him, we need him."

"I don't plan on killing him."

"I know the look in your eyes . . . and I don't trust it. What do you know?"

Major ran late. The moon was high in the sky, and the sounds of the sea and darkness calmed my rage. I peeled off my shoes and let the wet sand stick to my feet. There was a party down the beach, where couples were lying on blankets around a bonfire and dancing to music coming from the nearby pier. I closed my eyes and thought about dancing with Madeline at the parlor, the way her face lit up the moment Billie Holiday graced her ears.

I was so close to New York, and if I kept reminding myself of that, the guilt of what I was about to do wouldn't swallow me whole.

I could hear him jogging through the sand but didn't give him my eyes just yet. A part of me worried that the moment our faces met I'd pull the gun.

"Where are your bags? I've got the car parked."

I took a deep, steadying breath and looked his way. He searched for my bags to see if they were farther up the beach; then a look of disappointment crossed his face. "You came to say goodbye, didn't you? You're going to New York? Don't do this, Virginia. You know what they're going to make you do with Adonis."

"At least Adonis doesn't pretend to be someone he isn't."

"What are you talking about?"

"Aside from the blackmail, you knew about the women in the barn."

I held on to a tiny sense of hope that Joe was wrong. "It's not what you think," he insisted desperately. "I've never felt good about it, and you just gave me the courage to act. I didn't tell you because . . ."

"Because?"

"Because it's shameful. I hardly sleep at night when I'm there, thinking about them in that barn."

I snorted a bit, then shook my head. "I don't believe you."

He drew closer.

"Don't take another step." I folded my arms over my chest. A brisk November wind gust tickled my shoulders beneath my coat, leaving goose bumps as a reminder that winter was here, and the cold would bury this moment of my life with him but never kill it. Come spring, he'd still be another man who had lied to me, fooled me. Another mistake. When would I learn?

"I told Joe about your offshore account, the money you've been skimming."

His upper lip twitched. "You what?"

"Thank you, Major, for proving to me that all men are the same. That they all want something and will do anything to get it."

"That's not who I am," he shouted, his voice booming with the crashing waves.

"You're not the type of man to blackmail a woman into submission?"

His shoulders slumped. "It was an empty threat . . . one I didn't think I'd have to make. I thought we were the same, that we wanted the same thing. Freedom."

I blinked slowly. "We are not the same. I know what it's going to take to get real freedom from this organization. Stealing from men who steal and kill for a living isn't going to do it."

I heaved out a stuttering breath. "Joe promised me he wouldn't kill you. Knowing him, the account will be his by morning." I waved down the beach, where yards behind him, a group of men waited in the shadows under a dim streetlamp. Four of them in total, lounging outside their shiny black Cadillac, watching the scene unfold. "You won't be going anywhere soon. You've got explaining to do."

In the time it took to blink, Major's face fumed red-hot, and he lifted his fists. I stumbled back and pulled the gun from a strap on my leg, where it had been securely hidden by my dress. I swung it up and forward. The sight of it left him frozen, both hands in the air.

My hand didn't shake when I said, "I will not be letting another man hit me, not so long as I have a gun in my hand and some fight left in me." I loathed that I was near tears, showing him that I was not a wolf and that I did not belong in that room with the other animals. "All my life men have hurt me, and all my life, before they made me bleed, I convinced myself they were different. For a second, I thought you might be the real thing. A good man." I laughed, distracting myself from the sobbing I wanted to do.

"I am a good man," he said through gritted teeth. "I let those girls go, didn't I?"

"How many more came before them?" I didn't want the answer, I couldn't live knowing the real number. "They could have been girls just like your Georgia peach."

His eyes dropped.

I flicked my gaze back down the beach behind him. "Have a good life, Major, and best of luck. You're going to need it."

I folded the very last blouse into my traveling case and began to close it while Vel sat at the edge of the bed, visibly pouting. It was a dreary November night in Chicago, with rain pattering down against my elongated windows, leaving the water view a hazy, blurry mess.

Vel didn't want me to leave and had taken every opportunity to delay me.

"We should have dinner before you go," she insisted.

I shut the case and ran my hands down my dress to press out any

wrinkles. I shoved the case aside and sat beside her. "I should get some sleep before the train. You know I never sleep well on them. Can you promise me to take care of the place while I'm gone?"

"I'll take care of it," she said with little enthusiasm.

"I mean it, Vel. I know the parties you throw, and I don't want to come back to stains I can't get out of my rug."

"I said I'd take care of it."

"But will you take care of yourself?"

Her eyes were downcast, and I knew I couldn't possibly leave without giving her a much-needed lecture. "Vel?"

"I always survive, Virginia. I did it long before you came along."

I still decided to remind her of the moments that scared me the most. "I won't be here to get you to the hospital when you've drank too much or pick you up from a club you get kicked out of. Or that time . . . I found the bottle of pills . . ."

"Enough," she implored. "I will take care of myself."

"I'm going to send Joe to check in every week."

She groaned in response. "I can't stand him, and I can't listen to another monologue on the importance of opera. He's pompous and unpleasant. Why the torture?"

"He's not your biggest fan either, but you two can help each other. You need someone to tell it to you straight, and Joe, well, he enjoys having something to take care of."

"It's not just that I don't want you to go," she said slowly. "What if, like her, you don't come back?"

My heart thudded because not once had I considered the thought.

"Adonis is a violent bastard," she pointed out. "He didn't get the position he's in without plenty of death, and you're walking right into his arms, just like she did."

"If I don't go, I might never know what happened."

"I don't care about her; I care about you."

She continued to debate with me until I had my things at the door and ready to go. A man waited just outside to escort me, taking my luggage with a friendly smile. Vel's stare grew somber. "You don't leave until morning. Where are you off to?"

"There's someone I need to see before I go."

Sweat began to gather along her brow, and I knew she had more excuses loaded up. The goodbye was painful, making my chest feel heavy. I longed to sit back down with her but wondered if I'd ever be able to get back up again. "I want you to know something," I said before she could get a word out.

"Yes?" Her voice was tense with impatience.

"I'd look for you."

With tears in her eyes, she watched me off, and I decided, with great effort, not to look back.

The driver cautiously dropped me off at the massage parlor, with the promise to return bright and early to see me to the train station. The rain had let up, leaving behind a cool mist coating the streets of Cicero with a shiny glow. The night was alive with the sound of music and laughter spilling from the surrounding clubs, tempting me into one last hurrah. If I drank enough, I'd forget about the women in the barn, Major's betrayal, and all the other unspeakable memories I'd gathered in such a short amount of time.

I'd stumble into the car in the morning with a throbbing headache, but at the very least, I'd forget for a moment. A night.

I resisted the urge and walked through the doors I once called home.

"Well, well." Miss Suzannah placed her hands on her hips firmly and gave me a look over, her brows perked and her mouth in a wicked grin. "Come back for a job, have you? I've missed my little laundry girl." The resentment in her tone was evident. She'd been enraged when Joe stole me to live as far away from her as possible. She knew then what I knew now: He needed to isolate me, mold me into a woman who could climb her way to New York.

There was a strong chance if he hadn't forced me to say goodbye to her, I wouldn't have gotten this far, but the sting was still so fresh.

She gave me another look over, eyes narrowing as she reached out to touch my fur coat. "All this from Joey Ep?"

"I bought it," I told her proudly. "I make my own way."

"Then what are you doing back here?"

"I'm off to New York tomorrow."

"But there's not a smile to be seen." She lifted my chin to gaze deeply into my eyes, and I felt as if my soul were exposed. With it, all the secrets staining it. "What have they done to you, Gin?"

"If you knew what I'd done to get here, you wouldn't recognize me."

She smoothed a hand down my back. "I will always recognize you. There's not a damn thing you can tell me that will ever change that. You hear me?"

I knew my eyes had started to water, but I swallowed to coat my dry throat, hoping to keep the emotions in check. Joe hated it when I cried.

"I thought I might stay the night," I suggested, trying to find my voice again.

"I needed your room, new laundry girl, but hers is still there."

"You've been getting my payments, then?"

"I have," she said. "Payments every month to . . ." She paused, recalling something. "What did your letter say? To not move a damn thing?"

I smiled, and she looped her arm in mine and walked with me, waving at one of the men stationed at the door to grab my bags. I retreated into Madeline's space for the night, taking in all the little things that had made up her life before she'd signed her deal with the devil. The room was small, cramped, with peeling floral wallpaper and a threadbare rug. There was nothing glamorous about it, nothing expensive, but it felt warm. I sank into her bed, reached out to switch on the small radio next to her bedside table. Freddy Martin's "April in Paris" came on, and I thought about all the times she swore she'd make it to Paris to see the chestnuts blossom.

Miss Suzannah came in shortly after with dinner, a stew she whipped up to help the girls put on some weight when they arrived to her thin and weak. It consisted mostly of potatoes, but I didn't complain. We ate quietly until she prompted a series of questions I dreaded answering but felt some relief in telling someone. When I finished explaining the events that had transpired, starting from the racetrack to now, another dreadful realization hit me, one I'd carefully avoided facing.

"I think she's dead," I voiced aloud.

Miss Suzannah was startled by the four words, and like Joe, I saw the sparks of defense pulling at her eyes—she was going to explain away Madeline's survival because how could any of us truly give up until we knew for certain?

"These men," I said, interrupting her before she could start. "They're not forgiving, or good, and when they feel wronged, they hunt. They hunt like animals. The girls in the barn, I know that was just a taste of what really happens. If New York found out Madeline was spying . . . or worse, she had evidence against them, they'd kill her."

I stood from the table, leaving my spoon behind in the mushy potato soup. "That means everything I've done to find her, all of it, well . . ." I choked on my own words. "What was the point of it? She's never coming back."

Miss Suzannah dashed toward me, leaping from her seat to take me by the shoulders and shake me from my mad spell, but I was already gushing with tears.

"If she is dead, you find out who did this to her," she told me firmly. "You get everything you can on New York, you get the information she died for, and you give it to Chicago. You're right, they are exactly what you say. They are hunters, they are monsters, and you will have given them all they need to unleash themselves on New York."

I kept shaking and crying, trying to find words, but my mouth came up dry.

"If that is all you can do to avenge her, that is what you will do . . . and then you will get out and never look back."

I hadn't even considered what was going to happen after this, where

I'd go, but I had money. Plenty of money. If they let me go, I could start over anywhere, do anything. I felt a pinch of hope and held on to it, using it to calm myself down.

Later that night, while sleeping in her bed, I dreamed about Madeline saying goodbye for the last time. I hardly recognized her in her green mink coat and blonde tendrils pinned up in a stylish fashion. Her heels clicked against the floor when she walked, and I sat there, watching her pack and dress, envious of her next trip. Her next postcard.

"Last trip for a while, Gin," she said with a smile. "You and me, we're taking a vacation when I get back. Anywhere you want to go." With "April in Paris" on the radio, she leaned down to where I sat on her bed, and her eyebrows lifted with a suggestive wink. "How does Paris sound?"

I peppered her with questions, which she dismissed with grins and childish shrills. Her world was changing, and I was convinced then, despite her assurances, it wasn't going to include me.

I burrowed deeper into the blanket around my shoulders. "Have you considered what's going to happen when he loses interest? This joe you're seeing? We've talked about a life that didn't depend on a man's money, don't you remember that?"

She leaned down to adjust the strap of her shoe, then studied herself rather critically in my floor-length mirror. "I remember, Gin."

"Are you going to marry him?"

"Goodness, no," she said. "Can you trust me, please? And you'll let me know the next time Georgie starts sniffing around? I'll have my man pay him a visit."

I only nodded because, despite a feeling inside me, a deep warning so present and demanding, I wanted to trust her.

I wish I hadn't.

Chapter Thirteen

New York, my new home, was a creature all its own—vast and flourishing—a glittery chaos of soaring buildings and bustling life. The maze of noisy streets, shops, and alleys expanded as far as my eyes could see. Leaning into the taxi door, I strained to get a better view of the congested city, with towering skyscrapers looming above, but the relentless sun hindered my view. Just as I wondered if the busy men in pinstripe suits had ever experienced the depressive slums that Chicago faced, we passed a soup kitchen with a line wrapped around the block. A harsh reminder that not so long ago, months really, I was waiting with them.

The taxi came to a halt at the Waldorf Astoria—the largest hotel I'd ever seen. "Joey Ep has you set up in a room here," said the driver while exiting. "Until you find yourself a place of your own."

I paused for a moment to observe the man, who I'd assumed was just another taxi driver when I flagged him down at the train station. He opened my door and then proceeded to the trunk to get my luggage. I flagged a porter, but he dismissed him with a shake of his head.

"You work for Joe?" I pulled my coat around my shoulders tightly as the piercing air hit my face.

"I work for Chicago," he revealed with little emotion, waving me forward with my luggage in both his hands. "I'll help you get checked in."

"I can take it from here."

He resisted. "It's no trouble. He wanted me to make certain you got to your room safely with all your things."

I scanned him over once again. "Tell him I got here safely, but no more of this." I motioned to him with my hand. "I have a man watching out for me the entire time I'm here, and what does that say about me?" I shook my head firmly. "We've got to play this right . . . and that means I'm an independent woman here. No men watching out for me. No eyes but my own."

He swallowed, visibly nervous at the notion. His lips parted in protest, and I could only guess what was going to come out—something along the lines of, *You'll need me in this big, giant city because you're only a woman.* I didn't give him time to start the sermon. "Thank you."

I waved again for the porter, and he retrieved my luggage in a rush.

"Wait!" my driver called back for me, handing over a black bag, zipped closed. "I was told to give this to you."

I pulled back the zipper one inch to reveal a sparkling array of jewels. I closed it and took the bag with a nod.

I stepped into the hotel with a steadfast pace, not slowing through the opulent lobby, and proceeded straight to the reception desk. My mind was all business, even when it came to getting settled in my room. I didn't look through the entire wardrobe Joe had shipped ahead of time or walk the room to take it all in. I wanted to get this over with and treat New York like a much-needed exit from the Chicago Mob.

There was a small envelope next to my bed with a grand in cash, and before I could take my clothes off for a quick bath, there was a knock at my door. "A package for you, miss."

I opened the door, and a tall, gaunt bellboy handed me a simple white box with a bow. I tipped him and sent him away, then tore off the bow and pulled open the box, finding rows of arranged bills, stacked to the brim, with a note inside:

Spend and return.

With love, Joe

I put the box down on a small round table near the door, then moved to the windows to pull back the thick curtains to get a better view of the city. My mouth went dry, every nerve in my body alive and tingling.

The telephone rang, and my heart hammered.

I answered it quickly.

"Settled in?" Joe's voice, ironically enough, was in my ear.

"I was just thinking how delighted I am to be away from you."

"You should have told me you're having Vel stay at your place."

"Where is the fun in that?"

He made a sound of irritation through the phone, a single gruff sigh. "You've got dinner plans tonight with Adonis at a joint called the Barbetta. Someone will be by to pick you up in a few hours. He was told you'll have around ten thousand worth of stolen jewelry, and he's supplying a fencer."

"Business as usual."

"Plans of your own already?"

"I was going to go shopping and spend some of that money you sent me."

"Let Adonis take you shopping."

I huffed into the phone. "You're the only man I know with good taste in clothes, so I'll pass on that."

He paused for a moment too long, and when he finally did speak, I heard hesitation in his voice. "Should I be worried about you, Virginia? Can you do this?"

"Have a good night, Joe."

I dressed for a night on the town—an emerald silk low-back gown with a scoop neckline and matching gloves. The fabric hugged my hips in all the right ways but left just enough skin to drive his imagination. I painted my lips, powdered my face, and added blush to my cheeks, then sprayed a rose scent along my neck. To top everything off, I slipped on my stylish black pumps. I didn't realize how nervous I was until I brought my shaking hand to my head.

You can do this.

"He's just another man," I muttered to myself, letting thoughts of Major fill my mind until the flighty sense in my stomach turned bitter. I rubbed the back of my neck and then took a deep breath.

I strolled to the minibar to grab a drink, but the knock at my door stopped me in my tracks. I slowly walked to it, giving my escort a full two minutes of waiting before opening it. "I was going to have a drink before I go."

Good thing I hadn't, though, because I might've dropped it at the sight of my escort, staring at me the way I was staring at him. Hungry. Wanting. Alive. Broad shoulders, slick hair, and eyes that could cut glass—a cool blue like the waves on the beach outside my Chicago home. His face was narrow and, in places, unsmooth, and I knew it all too well. In my dreams, I saw him hovering at the foot of my bed, watching me. In my nightmares, I saw him beating a man to death on that desolate street in Cicero.

I'd never forget him.

"Ben?"

How could it be? This wasn't the haunting man I knew, with the overgrown beard and tired look on his face.

"Virginia," he said.

I blinked with surprise, and my cheeks burned hot. "You clean up nice."

A flashy tie, sleek black shoes, and a Louis Roth suit. How could this be the same man from the tracks, or the one who'd killed two people with ease? Chopped them up and discarded them like they were nothing? I shuddered at the reminder.

"Me?" He looked me up and down. "You were beautiful then . . . but now . . . my God, look at you." His eyes brightened, eyebrows perked up. "You've come a long way."

I cleared my throat and found my confidence again in a blink. "What are you doing here?"

A muscle ticked in his jaw. "I'm here to escort you to a meeting with Adonis."

I slipped inside and reached for my handbag, then shut the door firmly. "Lead the way."

There was a swagger in his step all the way to the elevator, but before he could press a button to signal our floor, he held his hand over it and flashed me a stern look. "I know why you're here."

I raised my eyebrows. "Do you?"

"The last dame they sent to distract Adonis . . . well . . . it didn't fare well for her."

He was talking about Madeline, and I was certain my unease was all over my face. I wanted to ask more, but I couldn't give myself away. Instead, my eyes flicked over him slowly, and I flashed him a patronizing smile. "It never gets less amusing."

"I'm sorry?"

"Men thinking they need to warn me when I step into their territory."

He parted his lips to reply.

"But," I continued promptly, "did it ever occur to you that maybe you're in my territory?" I walked past the elevators to the double doors that opened to the stairs. "I don't need an escort, Ben."

"You certainly needed one before," he countered smugly. "Imagine your fate without me . . ."

"As far as I'm concerned . . . we've never met before."

"You've changed," he noted with some disappointment.

"I had to."

I pulled open the stairwell door and rushed down, clutching the end of my dress so that it didn't snag on my heels. I heard the door open behind me, and his feet thundered down in pursuit. "You're driving with me."

I let out a snort. "I'm not."

"You don't know this city."

"I imagine taxi services are the same everywhere."

The impatience left his breathing labored.

I halted in the middle of a step and turned around, nostrils flared. "You don't get a say in anything I do, Siegel. Are we sleeping together?"

The question startled him into a hefty swallow, and he flushed.

"Are we fucking?" I asked, more forceful.

"No," he snapped back with a half grin, and then took two long steps forward, drawing too close for comfort. I stepped back until I was pinned to the stairwell wall with only a few inches between my body and his for me to swivel away. He reached up for my face but didn't touch me. "Unless you'd like to change that? Rumor has it you're good in bed. Did I help with that? Tell me, how many times have you thought of me since that night?"

I lifted my hand to slap him across the face, but he caught me by the wrist, his fingers circling the bone with unrelenting force.

"I'm going to warn you one more time." He leaned in and whispered into my neck, the warmth of his mouth heating my skin with every deep pant. "I know why you're here, and if you do anything that might jeopardize the work myself and my colleagues have done here, I'll take care of you myself."

I pulled my knee up with a quick jerk, slamming it between his legs and using both my hands to shove him off me. He groaned in pain and sank down. He reached for the stairwell railing and gripped it for dear life while using his other hand to tenderly clutch his groin.

I leaned down and ran my fingers through his hair, then took a good chunk and jerked it. "I don't need an escort."

I released his hair and pulled my shoulders back, adjusting my dress and cooling myself down with a deep breath. I turned away and didn't look back, eager to get out of the stairwell and meet Adonis.

He was right. I didn't know this city yet, but I did know one thing: the farther away I got from Ben, the better.

Outside the hotel, I waited for a cab for a few short minutes before it arrived. When it did, I slipped in with a sigh of relief, but before the bellboy could close the door and wish me a pleasant evening, a man shoved past him to occupy the seat next to me.

Chapter Fourteen

"Get out!" I shouted, but it came out as more of a growl.

Ben waved his hand at the cab driver, a signal to get going, and he obeyed, giving me no choice but to endure. I imagined throwing myself out into the street, rolling into incoming traffic. Would I live? Or go down in history as a madwoman, killing herself to prove a point? What a legacy I'd leave behind for all of New York to remember.

Ben adjusted the sleeves of his suit, then cleared his throat. "I will say, you're not what I expected."

"What did you expect?" I dared ask, knowing I wouldn't be happy with the answer.

"For a woman to rise through the ranks in Chicago like you have . . . at the very least, submission. You listened to me before, and it saved your life. Why can't you listen to me now?"

"Only a married man would assume submission is the key to a woman's success. Your poor wife."

His voice was low, ferocious, when he replied, "Don't talk about my wife."

"You just pinned me in a stairwell. You want to respect your wife? Stop sleeping with other women."

His fingers curled into his palm, and he slammed his hand against the door, but then, all too quickly, he stretched his fingers back out and placed them on his knee. One steady breath later, he said, "Did you fuck your way to the top then? That's the rumor going around."

"Just a rumor, nothing more." I thought about everything I knew, all the information I'd collected on Ben over the months we'd spent apart. "Let's talk rumors, then, Bugsy Siegel."

He shuddered at the use of that name, one he was rumored to hate.

"Did you murder Tony Fabrizzo because he was going to expose you to the feds?"

He pulled his shoulders back, straightening. "You should be careful what you say out loud in this city. You're a stranger here, Hill."

"Fabrizzo was writing a memoir about you and your little kill squad, wasn't he? It's a shame what you did . . . tricking a man into thinking you're law enforcement to lure him out of his home. I could write a story all my own, couldn't I? About what you did that night in Cicero."

I watched his fingers curl into his palms repeatedly. "Just a rumor . . . talk . . . nothing more."

"If that's a good enough answer for you, it's a good enough one for me."

I wanted him to stop, but I knew he had no plans to.

"You're here to distract Adonis, right? That's the only reason Chicago ever sends a woman to do a man's job."

I groaned outwardly, letting a dramatic sigh escape my lips. "What do you want from me?"

"The truth."

"The truth?" I turned to face him, and he stiffened at my gaze but didn't return it. "I'm here because I'm good at what I do."

No reply. Nothing for the remainder of the car ride. The cab stopped at 321 West Forty-Sixth Street, in front of the Barbetta. I memorized where I was, the buildings and streets around us, feeling an unwelcome sense of apprehension. I didn't know this city, or this man. Chicago and New York were supposed to be waging peace, but with so much war, was peace truly possible?

Was I walking into a trap?

"I apologize," said Ben, breaking the silence. "I assumed things I shouldn't have, and I've made an ass of myself. Can we start over?"

I folded my arms across my chest but, to my own surprise, couldn't force a sarcastic rebuttal. "Depends."

"On what?"

"If the apology is sincere."

"You don't know me well, yet, Virginia, but I don't apologize."

"Just like you don't lie to women?"

He recoiled at the reminder.

"So, this is painful for you, then?" I weighed in, brows arched. "This apology?"

"Very," he expressed with a huff.

I grinned a little, looking past him out the window. "Apology not accepted, but you're free to try again some other time. Take it or leave it."

He shook his head, but I could see his upper lip twitch like he wanted to smile. He got out and jogged around to open my door. We walked side by side but with just enough space to suggest that though we were arriving together, we were dining separately.

The restaurant was as classy as the San Carlo, only less old-fashioned, with gold embellishments on a coffered ceiling.

The atmosphere was smoky, and the dim lighting cast a glow on a dozen empty polished wooden tables and velvet upholstery. The walls were rich, textured in deep shades of burgundy and gold, with mirrors every few steps reflecting the lights from the chandelier. It had all the glamour Madeline would have adored.

In my mind, I could hear the clink of glasses and the buzz of conversations. I could see a man on the stage with a saxophone, desperate to be heard over the symphony of chatter and noise. Strangers at the bar, meeting for a drink. The taste of an amber cocktail in my mouth. I imagined the lively New York I'd witnessed on the drive in, crammed into the space, but found only a desolate man standing at the center of it all, waiting for us.

The host, familiar with Ben, gave him a nod and gestured me to a single table in the middle of the restaurant, where one man in a stylish wool tweed suit sat with a half-empty drink.

Contrary to Ben, who, when he wasn't killing a man, was a Hollywood type of handsome—flashy, dreamy—Adonis reminded me of Joey Ep. A cool, rugged, dark kind of attractive. His face was clean shaven, his hair thick and jet black, and though he knew I was staring at him as I approached the table, he didn't give me his dark-brown eyes until I sat down in front of him.

"Virginia Hill?" His voice was smooth and mysterious.

I didn't blink when I said, "Are you expecting someone else?" I glanced around at the empty tables with a soft huff. "A lively place you have here, and a dreary start to my trip."

His eyes narrowed, and he ordered me a drink with a snap of his fingers. The waiter arrived a few minutes later with a cocktail. I ignored his now-ominous stare and took a long, satisfying sip.

Behind him, Ben was at the bar alone with a cigar. He flicked the ash from the end into a crystal ashtray next to his drink, then blew out a plume of smoke that filled the surrounding air, making him look almost ethereal—as if he'd come straight from heaven . . . or rather, hell, with looks to kill and a woman to ruin.

Men like Ben, with the power to make your mouth water and your breath hitch, were the wrong sort. I knew it. I'd known it since the moment he slipped into my life and then out my window, but the fascination stuck. He was a sticky piece of gum I desperately wanted to peel off the bottom of my heel, but little chunks of him stubbornly remained.

He caught me looking at him, and I jerked my eyes back to Adonis.

"I've heard things about you," said Adonis, promptly breaking the silence.

I gave Adonis my full attention as I said, "I've heard things about you, not all favorable."

His eyebrows lifted a little. "I heard what you did to Riddle . . . sold him out."

I startled. I didn't like the reminder, or the idea that such a private exchange between myself and Chicago had made its way to New York. "What of it?"

He folded his hands. "Let's just say I'm not thrilled at the idea of doing business with someone who betrays her friends so easily."

"Riddle wasn't my friend," I clarified, and though I wasn't choking on my words, the very suggestion that Adonis had spies in Chicago was enough to leave my legs shaking. I stopped them with a pat to my knee.

"Lovers, then? That's even worse."

I didn't answer the question directly. "Riddle betrayed my trust. I don't like liars . . . or thieves. He stole from Chicago. If I'd kept that information from them, and they found out? They'd have buried me."

"They didn't bury Riddle."

"Because he's a man, and rich. He can make mistakes, but I can't."

I noted Ben turn a bit, stubbing out his cigar to focus on our conversation. A rush of excitement pummeled me, and I found myself pursing my lips in Adonis's direction to stay on task.

Adonis tilted his head. "Can you not see why it would be difficult for me to want to work with you?"

"I was under the impression neither of us had much of a choice in that. You want peace with Chicago, I'm the key. We want peace with New York, you're the key."

He chewed his lip a moment and contemplated my words. A single waiter came to take our order, but Adonis snapped his fingers, a motion that scared the waiter back into the kitchen. "I don't think this is about peace. I think they sent a beautiful woman to distract me, spy on me, see what they can gather about my operations here. Anything they can use to hurt me."

My stomach rolled. I had hoped I'd be dealing with idiots. Men who ignored the rules of reason for a pretty face. But Adonis had already been through this once, and he had no intention of making the same mistake twice. "I'm here to do a job. Fence some goods, broker peace, and set up a good relationship with New York."

"That's what they told you, maybe," he agreed. "But that's not all they want from you."

I laughed a little. "You think I'm just a puppet?"

"I've heard enough about you to know you are anything but," he defended brashly. "You're the first woman to rise in the ranks in Chicago, and I have no intention of insulting that hard work. The racetrack scams, transporting the jewels from the Chicago heist, even what you did with Riddle. It's impressive, and it doesn't matter to me how you did it, the accomplishment is a marvel."

I pulled my shoulders back firmly, not accustomed to powerful men paying me compliments outside of what I looked like. Now he had my attention, my full attention. "Thank you."

"But I don't want any trouble either. It is natural for me to assume they sent you here with ulterior motives. Just look at you." He gestured his finger up and down with a heavy sigh, then folded his hands. "I'm not blind. I have a weakness . . . they know about it . . . so they send you."

My eyes flicked over him slowly, then I took another long sip of my cocktail. "You want my truth? I was so bored in Chicago that when this job came up, I jumped at the opportunity to escape. It's the same routine every day in the same city, so I thought New York would be fun. I thought working with you would be exciting."

Quite suddenly, his tense features eased. Was it far easier for him to believe that I was just a bored, spoiled woman from Chicago searching for a thrill? Could he accept that? Could he trust that?

"How about we make a deal?" he suggested. "You help me with a few things here, I'll arrange fencers for your shipments from Chicago, and we'll work together."

"A deal?" Again, my eyes moved to Ben. The last time I made a deal, I ended up watching him mutilate two dead bodies. I cringed but hid the reaction with a quick drink. "Go on."

"There's a man who owes me a hefty gambling debt. He can be seen most nights at the Stork Club, where he has friends in high places. These friends protect him . . . which is how he keeps evading me."

"What does any of this have to do with me?"

"You go to the Stork Club, acting as if you're just there to have fun, find him . . . lure him back to your place, then I'll do the rest."

"Lure him?" I arched my brows.

"It shouldn't take much . . . a woman like you paying him any attention."

"And if he doesn't take kindly to being tricked?"

"Ben will go with you."

I resisted the urge to glance past him to the bar. "Why not you? It's you and me that are supposed to be working together."

"He knows my face, but Ben, he just got back from California. He won't see him, or you, coming." He looked at Ben briefly, then tilted his head in a mute salute. "When I need something done the right way, I got guys I send in . . . but when I need something done the wrong way, I send in the Bug."

The Bug?

I shook my head. "What is it that you want done the wrong way?"

His lips thinned. "Sometimes to teach a man a lesson, you have to get creative. But not to worry, he won't hurt you or let anyone else."

That I trusted.

I tried not to let the disappointment reach my voice when I said, "You're putting an awful lot of faith in him. You two good friends?"

He tsked and rolled his eyes. "I can't stand that fuck, but you know what they say, the people we hate the most are often the best business partners."

"I haven't heard that."

"Did you and Joey Ep always like each other?"

"I don't want to talk to you about Joey Ep."

He thrust out his chin and leaned in. "Why is that?"

"Because we're not friends . . . This is just business."

He studied me solemnly before signaling Ben over. I didn't give him my gaze and instead focused on my drink.

"Let's have dinner, then you two can head off?"

Ben pulled up a seat with a confident swagger. "Never thought you'd ask."

For a terrible instant, I panicked. Was I in over my head between these two?

I breathed deeply, and Ben took a sip of his drink, eyeing me through the glass. The ice clinked as he finished his last drop.

Adonis raised his own glass. "It'll be nice to see what you're made of."

I scoffed aloud. "You better hope you never see what I'm made of."

Adonis grinned wildly, enjoying this far too much for my taste.

After we ate, I followed Ben to the front of the restaurant, where a sleek Mercedes-Benz was waiting for us. He hurried to the passenger door to open it for me, and I visibly rolled my eyes before sinking into the motorcar. Of course he had the wheels to match his heavenly looks.

"You know the plan?" He started the motorcar and drove off, leaving me on edge, fingers drumming against my knees like a nervous little girl. I tilted my head and ran my hand down the back of my neck, massaging away some of the tension. When I didn't answer, he continued with, "Get in, tell them you're here to collect the cut for Adonis, and then wait for me."

"Wait for you?" I arched my brows, then let out a short laugh. "You're not going inside with me?"

"You want to dance or something?" He grinned, far too confidently.

I decided against his plan quickly. "I have no intention of telling him a damn thing about you or Adonis."

"Then what's your plan?"

"I want you to go in with me. At least through the entrance . . . If he wants to talk to me alone, you can keep your distance."

"What makes you think he'll be interested . . . seeing you with me?"

"Men want what other men have," I answered dismissively. "You're simple creatures."

He stifled a laugh. "You really hate men, don't you? All because of that ex-husband? You should have let me kill him."

"I don't want to talk about him." In fact, I wished I'd never said a word about it in that car with him, but I was vulnerable that night, blubbering on.

He paused and gave it some thought. "It wasn't just him, was it?"

"Leave it alone, Ben."

"Let me guess, your father was a son of a bitch? It's always the father. Ain't nobody in the world that can fuck a woman up worse than her father. I got two girls of my own."

The reminder that he was married with children did a number on my unwanted attraction to him. "I imagine you're doing a great job," I muttered wryly. "Make certain you teach them the throwing-women-into-walls trick, that'll do wonders for their adolescence. Never mind what you did to me in Chicago."

I noted his hands tighten around the steering wheel until his knuckles turned white.

We arrived at the Stork Club shortly, a swanky nightclub I'd only ever read about in magazines. A bouncer waited out front but recognized Ben promptly with a nod. He moved into the club as quickly and deadly as a serpent—ready to sting with me on his arm.

Guests dressed in top fashion waved at him and stared at me. When did the grizzly stranger at the tracks turned killer become a Manhattan celebrity? I pulled my shoulders back and searched for my confidence. My strength in playing a part. This was just another scene, a moment.

A man in a corner room darted between the white-clothed tables and dancing couples, but Ben called him out with a shout. "Reggie!" He left me for a moment to rush and embrace him, but Reggie remained still as a board, shaken by the hospitality.

"I'm going to pay, Ben."

Ben pulled back and patted his cheek.

"No business tonight, Reg."

I moved in behind him, refusing to be left alone, just in time to hear Ben say, "Good to see another castoff, eh? They tossed me when I came back. I draw too much attention, you know."

Reggie's eyes brightened. "They tossed you? *The* Bugsy Siegel? Was it Adonis?"

"It's always Adonis." He lowered his voice and leaned in. "Told me I need to lie low . . . But you know what I say? I'm going to have some fun, make some fucking noise."

Reggie grinned wildly and pointed at the table to his left. "You've got to meet my new girl. We're catching a plane to California tomorrow morning. I bet you've got friends out there now, maybe you could point us in the right direction?"

A dolled-up girl in a tight red dress popped up from the table to join them. Ben held out his hand and gathered both of hers for a brief kiss. "Amber," she said in a voice as dolled up as her face.

I stared at the scene in pure disbelief. There was no way Reggie was falling for this.

"I got plenty of connections," answered Ben confidently. "I'll set you both up in my house in Beverly Hills. You'll love it!"

Amber's entire face heated with excitement. I imagined the same way Madeline's had when Joe presented her with her first metallic-gold lamé gown, which seemed to cement her ever-growing desire for finer things and plenty of money. A desire that had led to her disappearance and, if I wasn't careful, mine. I'd never deny that I liked fashion, the feeling of silky dresses on my skin and stylish hats on my head, but thanks to Madeline, I knew the cost.

I felt bad for Amber, but worse for Reggie. Ben was a pure chameleon, moving from scene to scene, blending to become whatever was needed with an enigmatic, frightening charm.

"Who's this?" Reggie maneuvered around Ben to greet me.

"My date," declared Ben with a grin. "Virginia, this is Reggie and Amber."

"Pleasure is all mine," I managed with a terse smile. The evening powered on much like a theatrical play. Ben engaged with Reggie, promising him great things in California, while Amber gushed about how she wanted to be an actress. *Don't we all, Amber.*

I picked up my cues from Ben, deciding to play the doting girlfriend, even if only for a few short hours. The sooner this was over, the better.

I kept my composure until Ben pulled me into him for a dance. A swing band on the stage started to play "It Don't Mean a Thing," and I felt like making a dash for the club exit. "I don't dance," I lied, as he swung me in with little regard.

"There's no way those hips don't dance."

I opened my mouth to protest before we moved into a side-by-side position, and then hand to hand, where sweat was already building in my palms. "Keep talking about my hips and I'll give your boys another kick."

"You don't take compliments well, do you?"

"Depends entirely on the compliment." I glanced back at Reggie and Amber a few feet away, dancing close, laughing between stolen kisses. "It's not going to work, you know, the seducing him into coming home with me. He's in love with her."

Ben arched a brow, catching my hand a moment too long during an up-tempo step forward. "How do you know?"

"I can tell."

"Shall we test his love?" Ben's hand began to wander down the curve of my back, toying at the fabric of my dress just above my bottom. I reached around to snap his hand back up where it belonged. I opened my mouth to offer an alternative to the plan, something that didn't involve my body, but he silenced the words with his lips.

In the darkest depths of my mind, I had imagined kissing him before. I didn't understand that woman, the one attracted to a beast, and I desperately tried to bury her. If I didn't, the shame would eat me alive. And yet, even in my fancies, the ones I drank away most nights, it was never like this. His mouth was feverish on mine, all-consuming, devouring my lips.

I resisted the heat and pulled back, but his hands predicted my movements, reached up, and coiled around my face. I eased into it, allowing my heart to thud erratically while his mouth explored mine.

It felt like he was trying to burn his taste into my lips and tongue, brand me, and make me never forget. I feared I wouldn't, so I shoved at him until I had enough room between us to speak. "There's another way. He's drinking . . . Let him keep it up and lure him back for a nightcap?"

His eyes were still closed when he said, "Will you be joining us?"

"For what?"

"For the nightcap? I know you're not like most women, but I'd prefer not to have a witness. Again."

I stopped mid-dance. "You're going to kill him?"

He gave me a wan smile. "What did you think was going to happen?"

He pulled me back into the dance, and for the moment, I allowed him to shepherd me forward. "If you kill him, Adonis isn't going to get the money back," I reasoned.

"Money isn't the point anymore. He's shown us a great disrespect."

I glanced past him at Amber and Reggie again, dancing far more closely than Ben and me. There was a carelessness to them, a foolish kind of bliss. If they were less beguiled, they'd be far more alert to Ben's scheme. I searched my feelings but couldn't place them, somewhere between worry and envy. I hadn't looked at anyone like that since Georgie.

Ben blinked, slowing our swing to follow my gaze.

Something dawned on him, leaving his eyes wide and knowing. "That's it . . . I think I finally understand you, Virginia Hill." His full lips curved into a smile. "You believe in love, the real kind."

I snapped out of my haze with a short laugh, my eyes narrowing. "You want me to hate you, don't you?"

"You just keep getting more interesting." He glanced at Reggie and shook his head. "He's not in love with her, trust me."

"You have a wife, but you kissed me in the middle of a room of people, so forgive me if I don't believe you're the love expert you claim to be."

He didn't miss a beat when he pulled me back in, my chest pressing against his, and I'd never felt more like a rag doll. "I love my wife because she gave me my daughters . . . the most precious things in the world to me. I love her because she is dedicated, strong . . . and unwavering in her devotion to our family. But I'm not in love with her, and that's for the best. Friendship sustains a marriage, not passion."

And suddenly, he had too many sides for me to possibly count. The whiplash of ever-changing personalities made my stomach twist. His lips hovered above mine now, and though every instinct inside me wanted me to flee, I remained steadfast. I wasn't going to let him kiss me again.

"That was strangely wise," I complimented.

"Friendship isn't always fun, though, is it?"

Again, he let one hand slide up from the curve of my hip to my face, but I pushed away his hand in a snap. "No more games, Ben. Let's get this over with." I took a step away from him to exit the throng of dancing couples.

I approached Reggie and Amber with the most engaging smirk I could manage. "We're taking the party to my place. Care to join?"

Reggie perked up at the thought while Amber remained unconvinced, cautiously looking back at Ben, who had already pulled another woman into a dance. "We really shouldn't, catching a flight to California tomorrow morning. I'm spent."

"We need Ben," he assured her. "He's got the connections we could use out in California. If he wants us to drink with him, we do it. You want to be an actress, don't you?"

Amber chewed her lip, and I got the sense she was the brains between them. More so, there was something inside her, something strong and ever present, warning her that the situation could be dangerous. That Reggie owed the Outfit, and Ben used to be a part of it, and though everything seemed casual . . . maybe it was a setup.

I would warn her now, save another woman, but where would that get me? I wouldn't earn the trust of New York or find out what had happened to my missing friend. I couldn't take one step forward and three steps back anymore.

I ignored the itching desire to do something, say something.

Ben, likely sensing Amber's hesitation, joined us with a clap of his hands. "I could use something stronger to drink." He reached out and patted Reggie on the shoulder. "I'll give my friends that call. You two will be exceptionally happy in California. Isn't that right, Virginia?"

"Exceptionally," I chimed in with the most convincing smile I could manage.

Amber finally nodded gingerly. "Sounds like fun. We'll follow you in our car."

I grinned a little. She was still wary—driving alone meant escaping if things went wrong. We might be able to outsmart Reggie, but we weren't going to be able to outsmart her.

We headed to pick up our cars, two by two, shifting through throngs of traffic and lines wrapped around the club. I leaned in to ask Ben the plan, still not entirely aware of it, but he took two of the longest steps forward I've ever seen and snatched Reggie by the neck with dangerous precision. One hand held a gun firm against his back. "Get in, Virginia, you're driving."

Amber panicked, but before she could release the bloodcurdling scream inside her throat, Ben said, "Scream and I'll shoot him dead here and now." He tilted his head to the left. "Keep your mouth shut and run."

She did without hesitation.

Ben grinned my way. "Told you it wasn't love."

I stiffened with regret, jerking around to see if anyone had noticed the scene. Aside from the quick cast of eyes to observe Ben's vehicle, there was no sense of panic.

I placed a hand on my hip firmly. "You could have told me this was your plan all along."

He shoved Reggie into the back seat without breaking eye contact, keeping his gun trained on him, finger steady on the trigger. "You told me the original plan wasn't going to work because of love, didn't you? We had to improvise—and I had to prove to you that this fuck doesn't love anyone but himself."

"Listen, Ben, I'll pay it back," pleaded Reggie from the back seat. "I'll pay it all back!"

"Keep your mouth shut," he snapped, then leaned in to thud the gun against his temple, a strong enough force to knock him out cold. "There's this abandoned warehouse not too far from the Lyric Theatre. That's where I'm taking him. I'll drop you off for a late show, then pick you up when I'm done."

I choked back a laugh at the assumption. "I'm going with you."

He ran a hand over his face. "I don't want you to go with me."

"Why?"

"Because I don't want anyone, especially you, to see what I'm going to do to him."

"Can't be any worse than what I've already seen."

"It will be."

A heavy coldness slithered down my spine, and again, my mind flashed back to Wayne.

I could hear Adonis in my head questioning my motives. This was his game, and if I was too weak to play, I wasn't going to last in New York. I snatched the keys from his hand. "I'm going with you, Ben."

He pressed his lips together firmly, singing out his next words: "Say my name again?"

I threw a punch into his arm. "Fuck you!"

"I'm squeezing some money out of him long before I put the bullet in his chest."

"You think he's got money stashed away?"

"He wasn't going to California with nothing. He owes us, so anything we can get back before we kill him, the better."

"I'm going with you; we're finishing this—"

"No, we're not," he cut me off abruptly. "You're a marvel, Virginia, and that's the truth. But women can't be mobsters. You don't have what it takes, and believe me, that's a good thing." He sighed, his expression haggard, then searched my gaze, assessing, looking for something. "Now, will you go to the theater with me?"

I felt a chill seep into my bones, along with his words, so concrete. Burned forever in my mind: *"Women can't be mobsters. You don't have what it takes."*

You
Don't
Have
What
It
Takes

"Certainly," I said, with the best smile I could manage. "I'll meet you there."

"I'll drive you."

"I'll meet you there." I tossed him his keys, turned around, and walked away, waiting until I heard Ben's car speed off before searching the roadside for her. Amber. She was waiting in a black Ford, crying in the front seat. Ben was going to beat the location of the money out of Reggie, but Amber needed to get out of town, and fast. If anyone knew where the money was, she did. Several minutes passed before Amber cleaned her face and started the engine. I signaled for a cab and jumped in the first one that stopped. "Follow that car," I instructed.

Chapter Fifteen

The cab stopped at the Hotel Edison on West Forty-Seventh Street, where I waited until Amber went in before getting out myself. I paid the cab driver and walked inside the lobby, passing leisurely seated guests on my way to the elevators, biding my time. Amber entered the arriving car and just as she leaned forward to press a button, I stepped inside with her. The doors closed behind us before she had time to panic.

I decided to breathe—one lengthy breath.

Her cheeks, wet with tears, burned red. "I don't have anything to do with him!" She leaned against one of the four walls as if my eyes were guns, and though I had no intention of hurting her, I didn't show it. "Honestly, we've only been together a month."

I lifted my hands in mock surrender. "I'm not here to hurt you."

"How can you expect me to believe that when you show up with Bugsy fucking Siegel?"

My gaze dropped. "Believe me, if I had it my way, things would've gone very differently tonight. That's why I'm here. Reggie owes money, a ton of it. You two were taking some to California, weren't you?"

Rather foolishly, she said, "I don't know about any money," and something inside me—my father's well-buried rage—flared. Ben's words burned into my mind on repeat. Then my father, taunting me while he beat me, promising me I'd never amount to anything. Nobody thought I could do this, despite everything I'd given up. There was too much risk for me to fail.

I didn't want to be a violent woman, and yet, I rushed into her, shoving at her shoulder, giving her a quick slam against the elevator wall. I put pressure into her shoulder tissue with my nails until she shrieked.

The sound made me tremble. I was not my father, and nothing about this moment made me feel powerful.

I released her shoulder and stepped backward with a gulp, hoping just the idea that I could be violent was enough to scare her. My voice was low but urgent. "I want us to help you, but I need you to stop lying to me. Ben will be here within the hour, given Reggie lasts that long. You want to run, fine, run . . . but they'll find you. I can help you, but you have to help me."

She touched her tender shoulder. "How?"

"I'll get you out of New York, somewhere safe."

The elevator doors opened, and I took a deep breath, preparing myself if I needed to chase her. I'd have to take off my shoes, but I was a good runner. I'd had plenty of practice.

The doors started to close again, but she put her hand out to stop it. "It's in our room, packed away."

I stepped out of the elevator, dizzy and on edge. It took all my composure not to curl up on the ground to settle my nerves.

I'd done it. I'd gotten the money, or at least, the location of it.

Amber led the way through a hallway of gold-trimmed mirrors to her room. Inside, she opened their luggage and pulled a leather bag from among a throng of clothing and shoes. She flashed me a look at the cash inside, then threw it onto the bed. "It's not nearly what he owes . . ." Her voice trailed with disappointment. "I'm so stupid, you know? I wanted so badly to be an actress that the moment Reggie said he could take me away, I didn't think twice. Not even when he told me that he was on the run."

"You're not stupid," I told her. "I married the first man who told me he could give me a better life . . . make all my dreams come true."

Her eyes flicked to me, watery but hooked.

"He lied, just like Reggie here."

I reached into the bag and fished out a single roll of cash. I grabbed her hand and placed it into her palm. "Catch the first train out of here." When she didn't answer, I continued, "Pack a bag and go before Ben gets back."

Her hands shook violently while she packed up. When she was ready, I walked her out front, where a taxi immediately pulled up to take her away. When the cab was gone, I rushed back inside the room and flung myself down on a chaise next to a window overlooking a busy terrace. I watched the hotel guests stroll and chat, eagerly waiting for Ben's inevitable return, until finally, one hour later, he hurled open the door.

I kicked my feet up, using the bag of cash as a footrest.

"Virginia?" My name came out of his mouth brusquely. He smoothed his hands through his frazzled hair. "What are you doing here?"

"I followed Amber here."

He looked around in raw, sweet confusion. "I told you to meet me at the theater."

I shifted my position from leaning to sitting up, pulling my shoulders back. "If I hadn't shown up when I did, Amber would be long gone with the cash. Because you underestimated her—like you did me." I stood up and took slow, determined strides toward him—the muscle in his jaw tensed with each step.

"Now tell me again, Ben, that I don't have what it takes."

He didn't reply, at least not out loud. I retrieved the bag and pushed past him to the hallway, but he grabbed me by the arm with a soft, almost delicate pull—a complete shift from our earlier encounter. "I'm taking that bag to Adonis. I don't trust you with it."

I gave him a bored look in return. "So you can tell him you did all this by yourself?"

His eyes stayed focused, sweeping downward, trained on my exposed neckline. "You did good, but you're not going anywhere with that bag of cash."

“I’m taking it to Adonis. I have something to prove here, you don’t.”

“Give me the money, Virginia.”

I surveyed his expression, growing colder by the second. Something wasn’t adding up—why did he want it so bad? Unless . . .

“You had no intention of giving this money to Adonis, did you?”

He took a heavy step toward me.

“You want to keep it.”

He shrugged dismissively. “He wanted a body, and that’s what I’m going to give him.”

I decided at that moment I was going to run. I jerked past him and bolted for the stairs. I reached for the stairwell door quickly, but it was locked. I turned to the elevator. I hit the button repeatedly until the doors opened, then slid in.

“Virginia!” Ben’s fingers pried the doors to stop them. He reached for me and the bag, but a pleasant-looking elderly couple joined us, halting him mid-step.

He ran his fingers through his hair again, nervously this time, and flashed them a warm smile. “Good evening.”

They nodded in acknowledgment.

I focused on the doors, not giving Ben or the couple my eyes. They opened again at the lobby for the elderly couple to exit, but Ben tried reaching across me to close the doors before I could slither away. “Get out of my way.”

“Give me the cash.”

I threw myself past him and fled through the lobby to the hotel entrance, where the chilled New York night—full of bustling people and motorcars—brought me all the relief I needed. I lifted my hand to call for a car, wanting nothing more than to bury myself in my sheets and turn off the lights.

“I’ll drive you back.”

My feet ached from the cat-and-mouse game, and I just wanted this to be over with. “If you want this cash, you’re going to have to kill me, and let’s face it, you don’t want to do that. If you wanted me dead, I’d be dead.”

"I don't want to fight with you anymore," he finally revealed. "You earned that cash. You should get credit for it."

"Don't toy with me, Ben, I'm tired."

"Let's get you some food."

"I already ate, and I'm not going anywhere with you."

"Fine, fine. At least let me drive you back, so I know that you . . . and the cash got back to your hotel in one piece."

I struggled because I was quickly losing my fight. "Just a drive, then, nothing else?"

"Just a drive."

He was the quietest I'd ever seen him on the drive back but insisted on walking me to my room. I opened my door with an exhausted sigh.

"You're still not afraid of me," he declared. "Why aren't you afraid?"

He asked as if he'd spent hours thinking about it, and truthfully, I didn't have an answer for him.

"Maybe I am," I reasoned with him. "Or maybe like you said, I'm just fucked up." I couldn't begin to make sense of it, but the longer it lingered inside my head, the more I tried to put it into words. "Something inside me has to be broken if I find men like you comforting. I hate myself for it. I hate that I've never known anything different."

His eyes hardened. "You think I'm like all the others?"

"I think you're worse."

The air grew thick between us. "I might hurt you," he said, voice serious but gentle. "But I won't let anyone else do it."

A knot formed in my throat. "How romantic."

"I don't think romance is in the cards for us."

"Then what is?" I pressed.

His breath slowed; I could hear it. "Understanding, perhaps. You're the only woman who has seen every side of me, and sometimes, that terrifies me. One moment, I wish I'd never met you, and another, I don't know what I'd do if you disappeared again. When I think about you and Adonis together, I feel . . ." He paused, and a muscle in his jaw ticked. "I don't want you in New York."

"I'm not going anywhere," I said, absolute.

The heaviness of the conversation weighed on me. When he didn't reply quickly enough, I pushed on the door. "I want to get some rest. We'll tell Adonis what happened tomorrow."

I closed the door to his steady gaze, but he talked through it. "I'm scared of death too."

I stopped and listened.

"Everyone says I live crazy, on the edge . . . but the truth is if I'm not moving . . . if I'm not on to the next thing, I'm thinking about the nothing after all this."

I didn't respond but placed my hand on the door. He choked back a quick cough. "I underestimated you. You're good at this, but you can't stay in New York. I need you to listen to me, just this once."

"A kiss doesn't mean you get to tell me what to do. I'm not leaving until Chicago tells me to leave. Good night, Ben."

Another long silence. "Open the door, Virginia." My name slipped from his mouth firmly, as if I were a child in need of reprimanding.

I took a deep breath, collecting myself, reaching for the door, but my instinct stopped me. He was bad news, entirely too hot tempered, and I couldn't get involved with him. He'd given me every reason not to open the door. Why did I want to? When was I going to fix what was broken inside me?

I eased it open. "Don't say my name like that."

I watched his breath hitch, his jaw shudder. "How would you rather me say your name?"

"I'd rather you not say it at all."

He stepped inside, edging through the door. "No more apologizing."

I pressed my lips together firmly, trying to ease the tension building between my legs. "I didn't invite you in, Ben."

"Not with words, you didn't."

He closed the distance between us and lifted me up into his arms, pulling my legs around his waist with ease, holding my gaze. He leaned up to kiss me, but I dodged his mouth, refusing to give him my lips again. I couldn't do this, my head knew it, but my legs clung to him, desperate.

A growl escaped him, but I still didn't give in.

I continued to hold his eyes as he carried me across the room to the bed and sat me on the edge. He got down on his knees in front of me and glided one hand up my leg, slipping his hands into my girdle and giving the fabric a pull. Then, he took me by the hips and jerked me toward him with a force that sent my back down onto the plush sheets.

He spread me wider, open for him, exposed, and my legs shook. "Look at you," he mused, using his thumb to play, circling and pressing. I thrashed up, reaching down for his hand instinctively, mostly to prove to myself that I tried to stop this.

"Settle," he said with a grunt, then looked me in the eyes, waiting for my approval. "It's just skin."

The consequences plagued me—what was going to happen if I did something I wanted? Joe had said Adonis didn't like sharing his women, and getting involved with Ben the night I arrived was going to get me tossed back to Chicago in a walk of shame.

I was starting to sweat, could feel it collecting along my stomach and legs.

"Virginia," he repeated my name, and I released his hand.

I arched my back with anticipation, and with one final grin, he buried his face between my legs.

His tongue set me on fire, and then his fingers slipped inside me. He was primal, responding to every nerve in my body as if he were an expert. He kept a steady motion with his hand, applying just the right amount of pressure that made my toes curl.

This was too much, too intimate. He was married, and awful, and killed with the same fingers that seemed desperate to break me.

And yet, I was there, nearing a release I couldn't have resisted or stopped. It was happening quickly, violently, and Ben sensed it. His fingers twitched inside me, then slowed to keep me on the edge, where I was miserable.

His tongue left me, and his face peered up. "Not until I tell you to," he said. "Virginia, look at me."

I moved to my elbows and gave him my eyes in the haze, both stubborn and yielding to his commands. "Ask me to let you," he told me. "Beg me to let you."

His pace quickened again, and my stomach twisted. His free hand took hold of my thigh, digging into the flesh. Then, his fingers clawed up to my stomach, pressing into it, settling my thrashing hips.

"C-can I?" I asked, struggling to find some sense of normal breathing. Everything in my body felt tight, ready to explode.

"Say my name when you ask," he said, prolonging the moment in a dreadful way.

Bastard.

"Ben, please, can I—"

I couldn't finish the words, throwing my head back to ride the pleasure. All the tension in my body shattered with my resolve, and I moaned for him.

He'd told me I would beg, and back then, I'd cringed at the thought. Now, I'd shamelessly beg him again.

"Good girl," he said with a grin, tasting his fingers, watching my legs shake. "I knew you liked me."

I started to pull my knees together, but he didn't give me a moment to breathe, not a single second. His tongue dove back in with newfound intensity, and I thought I might shatter again that very minute. My mind grew foggy, and I slipped into some forgetful haze I didn't understand, didn't know, but for tonight at least, welcomed.

He got me to break three times before I shoved his head away from my legs and fell back on the bed, letting out one breathless heave after another. I forced my toes to uncurl and then my fingers to spread from being clamped inside my palm. I peered around to see Ben, breathing just as heavily as me, lying on the floor in a daze. I waited for the guilt to follow the pleasure. I shouldn't have let him do that to me, and if Adonis found out, who knew what was going to happen?

But the pleasure remained far too powerful to make me feel anything else. At least, not yet. I was too deliriously sated. But when I closed my eyes and allowed my breathing to calm, my mind reeled with images—Ben's bloodied fists, the mangled bodies in his trunk, his hands wrapped tightly around my face, squeezing.

I pulled my dress down, forcing myself up and to the kitchen bar, yet I couldn't make my hands work to fix a drink. Ben jumped up to help me, but I took a step back to keep my distance. My body was still on fire, craving his mouth, but my mind was alert. I'd made a mistake, and I couldn't let myself make it again. "You should go."

"There's a bar at the hotel. Have a drink with me?"

"I shouldn't."

"Just one?"

I was in no position to deny a drink. "One drink."

Down at the bar, surprisingly busy for near midnight, I ordered a nightcap, and Ben ordered a beer. A strange, awkward silence followed. The kind that could only happen between two people who'd just done something very intimate but who didn't intimately know one another at all. "Was it the ex-husband who started it or the father?"

I didn't understand his question entirely. "What are you asking me?"

"Who hit you first?"

"I think you know the answer to that."

"You still talk to your father?"

"Not since I left Marietta."

He sat quietly, considering my words, and I wondered what he was going to do with them. "You're not killing my father," I told him.

"Not until you ask me to," he said playfully, but his expression didn't match his tone. "I got to know, it's been itching at me since Chicago—why did you get into this line of business?"

Inside, everything sank. It would be so easy to tell him the truth, and I felt a sense of vulnerability with him. I wanted to act on it, but I didn't let my guard shake. "That's always the question, isn't it? Would you ask me that if I were a man?"

"Why do you assume I'm asking because you're a woman?"

I sipped my drink. "You said it yourself. Women aren't cut for this line of business."

"I was wrong," he admitted glumly. "I'm interested. Explain to me how a Southern belle ends up here. What made you wake up one day and think, *I want to work with the Chicago Mob*?"

My gaze dropped, and I scrambled to find the words, a lie I could make him believe. "My mother used to say, 'Girls like us take what we can get,' and I believed her. But I had this friend . . ." My voice shook, so I took a drink to clear my throat. "She taught me something else . . . that maybe I could take what I wanted, if I accepted the risk." A soft laugh escaped my lips. "I never thought pretending, being whoever I needed to be to survive, would be useful to someone. And yet, here we are."

He turned the barstool to look at me more closely, his knees grazing mine.

"The money is good too."

He nodded in agreement. "The money is nice."

I pressed my lips together in deep thought, touching on things I'd never voiced out loud before. "Sometimes I can't look at myself in the mirror, but I am someone. Someone important. My name means something. That's power, even if it came with a price."

I thought more about it and came to the bitter conclusion it wasn't a lie. Despite the requirements of the job, I had come to find a sense of belonging in my position. When I was done with this, what then? Who would I be? The idea of losing my name, and all that came with it, made my skin crawl.

He cleared his throat and ran a hand down his face. "Do you want out?"

I arched my brows. "Do you?"

"I never stood a chance." He shrugged casually. "Lansky saw the potential in me when I started cheating pushcart peddlers on the Lower East Side. He trained me, and when he put a gun in my hand . . . everything changed. There's no escape for me." His lips pulled into that same enigmatic grin, but it didn't reach his eyes. "At least, not by my own choice." He took another long chug of beer before signaling the bartender for another. "But you still have a chance."

"I've made some mistakes too."

"Am I one of them?"

I grinned into my glass. "I haven't decided yet."

"You seemed to enjoy yourself."

"You're not the worst."

He gave me a slow, sideways look and reached out to touch my knee underneath the bar top. I straightened my shoulders to keep myself from shuddering.

"Can I stay the night with you?"

I shook my head and shifted my position on the stool to throw my knees in another direction. "No."

"It would be fun," he reasoned. "I'm headed back to California next week. What do you have to lose?"

I could feel my cheeks heating red. "Contrary to the way you live your life, not all of us can just have fun and say fuck all to the consequences."

I stood up in a rush and breathed out with sudden regret—heavy in my stomach until it was knotted there. Major's betrayal was too fresh. I wasn't here for Ben, and I wasn't going to let another man distract me from finding Madeline.

He stumbled off the barstool to chase me, but I pivoted quickly and raised my hand before he could open his mouth to protest. "Don't." A few of the bar patrons cast us a look. I smiled through my words, lowering my voice significantly when I said, "This is over."

I didn't sleep. Every time I closed my eyes, I could still feel Ben between my legs, and when I sat up to catch my breath, I was carefully balancing on the line between panic and fear. A raw disappointment in myself settled in my stomach, and my heart hammered in my chest. The sweat trickling down my neckline left me shivering. Why hadn't I controlled myself? What if he told Adonis?

I nodded off again until a pounding at the door jerked me from sleep. I reached for my robe and inched to the door, painfully unaware whether I was still asleep or not. I assumed it was Ben, of course; he didn't strike me as a man who liked no for an answer. But instead, I found a dapper, polished Adonis standing in his place. The bright hallway light bathed his skin in a warm glow, and I knew this had to be a dream. Certainly, he wouldn't show up at this hour looking like he was ready for a night on the town.

He looked me up and down. "You're not dressed?"

"Should I be?" I inquired.

"Ben told me everything."

A jolt of fear ran through me. "He did?"

"Ben got the man; you got the money. A deal's a deal. I'll show you New York. First stop is breakfast, but before that, one more test."

"What time is it?"

He pulled up his sleeve to check his watch. "Three in the morning."

I stood straighter.

"Well?" He pressed his lips together, waiting, smiling, and I decided then and there to snap out of this Siegel haze and focus on the mission. Spy on Adonis, earn his trust, see what kind of information I could give Joe to use against him.

Find. Madeline.

I breathed out everything that had happened with Ben, the uncertainty in myself, the feeling of being overwhelmed and lost in a new city, and breathed in the confident, marvel of a woman Adonis wanted.

I forced a smile, and a short laugh escaped my lips. I moved into the room, gripped the bag of money I'd collected from Amber, and tossed it at him. "You're buying."

Fifteen minutes into the drive, I watched colorful New York, a vibrant tapestry of sights and sounds, fade into dark, shaded streets similar to Cicero's. A wave of unease washed through me with every block, and I began to wonder what kind of final test he had in store for me. We pulled along the side of a building that looked abandoned, with boarded-up windows and no sign of life. He was first to get out of the car, but I sank into the seat, wishing I had a way to glue myself down.

He opened the door for me and waited, eyes firm, steady. Unmoving. When I didn't get out quickly enough, he reached in and took me by the arm far too violently. "Let's go, Virginia."

He knew about Ben; I was sure of it.

Panic laced through me like poison, and I thought I might cry, but kept my shoulders back. If he wanted me to beg for my life, I wouldn't give him the satisfaction. My heels struggled on the uneven gravel all the way up to the entrance. I tried to figure out what the building used to be but couldn't judge the tattered remnants by the outside alone.

Through the doors, I could see three men standing around a shaking woman tied to a rickety brown chair. I didn't need to see her face to know who she was.

They'd gotten Amber.

I glimpsed the inside of the building in the dim light from passing motorcars, but I still couldn't judge if it was once a hotel or a factory. I was going to die here, alone in New York, and nobody would find my body.

Among the three men, Ben stood rigid, refusing to look at me.

"Amber here says that you gave her some cash, told her to get out of New York," Adonis began, pacing around the bound woman. Her mouth was gagged with something wool, and she was crying through it. I could hear the muffled sounds.

"I did," I said, not denying it. "Sleeping with a man doesn't make her guilty of his crime. You got your money. What does she have to do with any of this?"

"I like things clean," he reasoned. "No witness, no one talks."

"I don't think she will talk," I said. "I made a judgment call, and I stand by it."

"You're weak," he spat. "You don't belong here. Women can't do this job."

Two of the three men nodded in agreement.

"Women are soft." He leaned down to take hold of Amber's chin. "Women talk." He looked back my way, and his expression made me jump. It was wild—unhinged.

He loved this, and he wanted me to know he loved this.

"I prefer my women soft. I prefer they stay out of a man's world."

"Fuck, you like to run your mouth, don't you," I said with little control, feeling my world go gray. "Does it ever stop?"

One of the men laughed, and Adonis looked at him sharply to silence him.

"Prove me wrong."

"You want me to prove to you I belong in your world?"

"I want you to prove to me that you're loyal, that you're going to be able to make the tough choices . . . that you understand what happens to those who cheat me."

All the color around me faded, and right there at the center of my black-and-white vision was Adonis. An emerging blur of red. If this was the man Madeline got involved with, she was dead.

I didn't know him, but I hated him.

He retrieved a small handgun, implying he wanted me to use it. I snatched it from him and pointed it in his direction. He showed no fear, and the men behind him laughed at the notion I'd shoot. They didn't even pull their weapons to defend Adonis.

"You've proven your point, Adonis," said Ben, finally speaking. "We'll send her back to Chicago in the morning."

Ben took a step toward me, as if he had every intention of retrieving the gun from my hands. The weapon felt heavy, suffocating, no longer steady in my grip.

Back to Chicago meant I'd failed. I hadn't found Madeline or proof Adonis was dirty. I wouldn't be able to use the evidence to get out of the Mob, which meant I'd be doing this for the rest of my life. This frightening cycle of sleeping with dangerous men, transporting stolen goods, lying to everyone until I believed the lie myself. Each realization felt more paralyzing than the last.

It would only get worse from here, I knew it.

Ben had asked me earlier if I wanted out, and I hadn't answered him. Did I like the power and the money? The purpose that came with my name meaning something? Yes. Did I also want out of all this? Real freedom?

Yes.

I turned the gun on Amber. I looked into her eyes, the terror so present and real. A woman I couldn't save or help. The choice had been taken away from me because I'd finally met an adversary I couldn't outsmart or outplay.

Adonis wanted blood as proof, and I had to give it to him.

I spent the next week drinking myself into a blurry haze, stumbling in and out of the hotel room and bar like a raging drunk. I was certain the other guests loathed me when I strolled in, unkempt and smelly. I reminded myself of my father in every way, only he drank for fun. He liked the burn and what the alcohol did to him. I drank to forget.

Her eyes. Her face.

Even her name.

Adonis tried to call on me, but I had the desk clerk insist I was sick and staying in my room until I could recover. Joe called daily, but I ignored the phone and the messages that arrived from the front desk. I even dismissed the maid, who insisted on tending to my room, which had fallen into disarray. I wanted to be alone, in the dark, and try to drown out her face with anything I could find.

Toward the end of the week, Ben unexpectedly showed up. He lifted me from my half-awake stupor on the floor and guided me to the bath. With my clothes still on, he eased me into the water, ensuring I nursed coffee and water to sober up. He prevented any attempts I made to slip back to the bar, taking care of me without uttering a single word. He cleaned me up, held me as I sobbed myself to sleep, and made sure I ate and slept. He became my lifeline, my savior in those dark days. And just when I thought he was a figment of my imagination, I found a note on the bedside table one morning: *Don't make me come back.*

Down in the lobby, Adonis sat waiting patiently for me near the doors. My entire body tensed at the sight of him, but I maintained my composure and moved forward.

"Feeling better?"

"Much."

He nodded, extending his hand, palm out. "No more business, let's have fun and forget about that unfortunate event last week. Shall we?"

Forget. If only I could.

I took his hand. "I could use some fun."

Chapter Sixteen

The months passed like a slow-motion film, and I was playing the role of my career. Adonis treated me to the finest meals, and we danced at the most popular New York nightspots. Every circle, ranging from the dark dealings in bars to poker games held at elite hotels, believed we were an item.

Just as Ben could somehow fool Hollywood into thinking he was one of them, someone who didn't intimately know Adonis might consider him a diplomat or legitimate businessman. He was good at what he did, but being around him made me sick.

The only time I felt any sense of relief was in bed with him, where I could hurt him with my nails and teeth and claim it was just my passion-fueled instincts. He treated me like a possession, issuing demands and relishing in having me at his mercy. I complied, playing my part and pretending to enjoy it. Out of all the men I had been with under the Mob's command, none terrified me as much as Adonis. His brutality was not confined to the world of violence; it seeped into the bedroom. He was not gentle when we were naked, and he pulled his gun often to prove a point, so I filled our days with business to tire him out.

Joe sent shipments from Chicago full of stolen jewelry, clothes, and cash, and Adonis arranged buyers to help me launder the money. He wasn't shy about how he conducted his business, leaving me plenty of moments to eavesdrop on his conversations. I took notes for Joe in a black book hidden under my mattress, full of names, dates, and amounts. Not all the transactions made sense to me, but I trusted they'd be significant to Joe.

After dressing for dinner with a plan to meet him at a restaurant near the hotel, he surprised me at my room with a detour in mind. The tension in my stomach grew as we drove. His surprise could have been a trip to another abandoned building or a shopping spree. I never knew what to expect or how to predict him. The relief set in when we pulled up to a two-story town house in Greenwich Village. He jumped out of the car and walked around to get my door, then whispered something to the driver.

I stepped out and looked around at the brownstone buildings and tree-lined fences before he motioned at the building and inclined his head toward me. "I bought it for you, Princess," he said humbly, but I cringed at the pet name I'd heard at least a hundred times.

"You bought it? I told you I was looking for a place, that I didn't want to rush it."

"It's been months," he reminded me like I didn't know.

I shrugged. "I have high standards."

"I know your tastes," he assured me. "I know what you like. I want you to stay, Virginia." He gathered my hands. "Not short term, long term. Our partnership, it's working for me. Is it working for you?"

Keeping Adonis happy was a circus, in truth. A balance of intimacy and business I hadn't experienced before. It was exhausting on all accounts, but what choice did I have? I'd only just started to fill the pages of my black book with detailed notes.

"It is," I said confidently, placing a hand on my hip. I reached for the lapel of his suit and gave it a tug. "But maybe I'll give you a proper answer after I see inside?"

He pulled me up the stairs and unlocked the door, giving me a long, proud tour.

And even I could admit, the apartment was a beauty. Dark furniture, gray carpet with shag accent rugs, blue walls, and a terra-cotta-yellow sofa. I imagined myself drinking on it after a late business meeting while the bustling New York sounds drifted through my windows. As Adonis reached the kitchen, his driver shuffled through the door. "Sir, a word," he said, rather urgently.

Adonis smiled warmly at me and waved his hand at the place. "Keep looking around, make yourself at home. I'll be right outside."

I'd usually eavesdrop for more notes to scribble down in my black book, but I sneaked upstairs to check out the bedrooms. The master was the first room to my left, where there was a vase of fresh flowers on a rosewood dresser and a tinted coral dressing alcove opposite the bed, where I could easily envision dolling myself up for a night on the town.

And yet, even with how attractive the room was, something felt off. Something I couldn't put my finger on. I searched the feeling long and hard until I spotted a wall opposite the bed, covered with a gray panel. I moved closer and touched it lightly, noting the surface was more of a padding than a wall. Little tacks were stuck into the panel, as if someone had pinned notes or photos they could view from the comfort of their bed.

Someone had lived here before me. Was this where he set up all his mistresses? Had Madeline stayed here at some point?

I sank down to the ground and searched under the bed. Maybe a photo or note had slipped through the cracks? But there was nothing under the bed, not even a small hint of dust. The apartment was clean from top to bottom.

Where would I hide something important?

A small bookshelf was nestled by the window, lined with novels and magazines. I browsed them, noting that while the magazines had been freshly perused, the novels were collecting dust. I stopped at one title, *Vanity Fair.*

I could hear Madeline in my head, her voice light and playful. *"The world would be easier on women if there were less Amelia Sedleys and more Becky Sharps."*

I opened the book, praying for a miracle, something to show me she'd been here. A postcard accompanied by a photo fell from the binding to the floor. A black-and-white picture of Adonis and a woman, standing happily in Times Square. She was wide eyed, with a swanky sport coat on, tailored like a man's suit. Adonis was looking at her with an adoring smile, one he'd never shown me.

Madeline.

She'd stayed in this apartment. I flipped the postcard over to read the scribbled note.

New York, 1933
I'm coming home, Gin

"Virginia?" he called from the stairs, his feet taking lengthy steps up.

I slipped the photo and postcard into my purse and met him halfway down. "It's lovely. My answer is yes, I'll stay."

"Just what I wanted to hear, Princess. I've got business with Ben. He wants to meet at the Barbetta. Care to join us?"

Ben had come and gone over the months, slipping in and out of New York for business before fleeing back to California. We tried to avoid each other entirely. Usually, hearing he was back in town would leave me anxious, dreading our next meetup, but today I was too light—in a state of bliss. I'd finally found the first piece of evidence to prove Madeline had been here, and this was her apartment. For the first time in almost a year, I felt close to her.

I wanted to go back to the hotel and call Joe. There had to be more memories here, something else to lead me to her. But I still had a role to play, and for now, that would require me to smile and endure. "I'm starved. Let's eat."

I ate in silence while Adonis talked business with Ben at the bar, trying not to aggressively stab the steak on my bone-china plate and give myself away. My mind wandered to Madeline and the tactics she'd employed to captivate Adonis. What endearing nickname had he given her? When did their relationship sour?

Ben looked good tonight. His hair was more tousled than groomed, just like it had been when he pulled his head up from between my legs.

I stiffened with regret, hating my mind for replaying the memory. I needed to get out of here. I gathered my legs to stand, but just as I reached down to finish my drink, the doors of the Barbetta swung open violently, unleashing a hail of gunfire into the dining room. The sound of shattered glass reverberated through the air, igniting panic within me. Instinctively, I sank to the ground, seeking shelter beneath the crisp white tablecloth. My body trembled, and waves of nausea crashed over me, forcing bile to rise in my throat.

"Virginia! Out the back!" Adonis bellowed, yanking me from underneath the table with little delicacy. I thrashed, shaking violently. The gunshots were too fresh in my head, a terrible sound on repeat, making me feel like I had no control over my senses.

He took me by the shoulders, forcing my face to meet his. "Go out through the kitchen. Stay in the back alley. Now!"

He shoved me into a run. With a surge of adrenaline, I obeyed, stumbling through the bustling kitchen. Cooks armed themselves with weapons hastily retrieved from hidden corners, readying for the imminent danger.

I threw open the exit door, and sirens blared in the distance, a symphony of warning.

I placed a hand on my chest to steady my heart, then blew out a series of shallow breaths to regain control. I couldn't wait around for Adonis. I was getting the hell out of here.

I compelled my feet ahead but halted when a pair of men jogged down the slender alley in identical black suits. Both had an identical handgun pointed in my direction, and just as I turned to flee back inside, I heard one of them clear his throat. "This his new girl?"

"Look at those hips," growled the second man.

He rushed in front of me, maneuvering between me and the door. My posture went rigid. I considered every single move of self-defense

I'd learned. Between the legs, the eyes, throw anything, kick anywhere. Distract them and run.

I threw a punch, but he scooped me up by the hair faster than I could choke out a screech. "No fighting, girl. We don't want to hurt you, just use you. We got you, we got anything we need from Adonis, now, don't we?"

I pulled at his hand, but the more I pulled, the worse he yanked my hair. I felt thin strands start to rip from my scalp. "You have no idea who I am," I said through my teeth.

He let out a booming laugh. "You're just another Mob whore. Adonis has a collection of them, always coming and going."

The other man, standing by idly, heard something, a whistle down the alley, so they started off with me in tow. I kicked and thrashed into both to make it impossible to drag me without lifting my feet off the ground.

They tried, but I sank myself down, using all my weight to sit on the cold ground like a stubborn child. As one of them lifted me up over his shoulders, I heard two shots. A pop and a pop, then a splatter of something covered my face and dress.

The metallic smell filled my nostrils, threatening my stomach. The man who'd had me by the hair now had me by the shoulders as he stared down at his dead friend. I glanced at his fallen lug of a body and the bullet wound in his neck. It was his blood on me. All over me.

"Virginia, get down!" a voice called.

The man held me close, revolver to my head. My tongue fell flat, and I froze. There was no sad, tragic montage of my life playing in my head. I waited for it, the cascade of memories I'd collected over my short time here, but nothing. Ben eased into view, scanning the scene, and I wished more than ever that I'd said yes to him at the bar that first night. At least then I'd have died in New York doing something I wanted. One thing that wasn't a game or a trick or a part.

"Put down the gun!" the man barked, knocking the barrel into my head.

Ben didn't stand down.

"Ben? I didn't know you were in town."

"Business," said Ben. "What did Adonis do to piss you off, Rico?"

Rico's hold on me eased significantly. "Killed a friend of mine. Tortured him over some business gone wrong."

Ben flashed him a smug grin. "Do you want me to tell you what he said before he died?"

I couldn't see Rico's expression, but I could only imagine. His breathing grew staggered; I could hear it in my ear. I watched Ben, looking for any sense that he was bluffing—I found none. How many people had he killed in Chicago, New York . . . California?

"I'm going to kill her the same way I found him, missing parts," ground out Rico, and I shuddered at the thought, feeling queasy.

Ben ran into the man in a rage, plowing his entire shoulder into his stomach to knock the gun out of his hand. The gun flung to the ground, just out of reach.

I threw myself into the nearest wall, holding my chest, watching them fight with fists and kicks, each trying to get power over the other until both guns disappeared in the struggle. Rico finally got Ben in a grapple he couldn't break, and for a moment, a brief passing breath, I considered running.

But it wasn't Adonis who'd raced to the back of the Barbetta to check that I'd gotten out safely. It was Ben. He could've stayed to protect Adonis, but he went after me.

I reached for Ben's fallen gun and lifted it quickly.

Rico threw a punch into Ben's face, then jumped up at the sight of the gun, looking down the barrel and then up at me with a condescending reproach. "Put the gun down."

I thought about blood staining Ben's crepe trousers, and then Rico's words, still so fresh. "You think I can't shoot?" I gave him a matching condescending smirk. "Because I'm just another Mob whore?"

I aimed at his leg and fired. The raw power of the shot left my hand in a tremble, and I nearly dropped the gun. He screamed in pain, then hit the ground with a thud. I felt out of my body now, drifting back to the scene with Amber. I'd closed my eyes then but heard her screams through the muffled wool in her mouth. I wanted another drink, something to make me forget.

Ben stood up and straightened his clothing, extending his hand to take the weapon from me, but my hand tightened, refusing to relent. I wanted him to be Adonis. I wanted to shoot and take my power back.

"Virginia," he whispered, too cool and causal, as if this bloody mess were nothing new. "Let me do this."

I shook my head, but no words came out of my mouth.

"I know how to kill the guilt. I bury it or burn it with the bodies. Do you know how to kill it?"

He already knew I didn't.

"Let me do this for you."

"You don't need to do anything for me. I can do this myself. You know I can." I held on to the notion that I needed to shake off my feelings for him, toss him aside like all the other men who were poisonous to me. "Stop underestimating me. Didn't you learn your lesson the last time?"

Finally, he extended his hand and reached for my wrist, delicately trying to pry my fingers from the gun. "I'll never underestimate you again. That's not what this is."

"Then what is it?" I growled, unshaken by his touch.

"A favor."

"You've done me enough favors. Eventually, like everyone else, you'll want something in return."

"I don't want something in return."

My mouth went dry. "Then why?"

He didn't look at me when he said, "You know why."

He seized the gun and fired one shot into Rico's head with no hint of emotion in his icy gaze. I turned my head to the door, where Adonis finally ran through with the surviving staff of the Barbetta.

"Virginia!"

Adonis reached out for me, but I recoiled at his touch. "Don't you fucking touch me!"

I left them all in the crowded alley, walked through the debris of broken restaurant windows and empty motorcars to the street. I walked several blocks until my feet turned numb from the pressure of my heels.

I was done with New York and Adonis. I was done with Madeline. If I didn't leave now, with the little information I had, I was going to die here. I'd have no warm memories to hold on to, nothing worth remembering.

Madeline had saved my life that night in Cicero, walked me through my divorce with Georgie, been a friend when I needed one most. But I couldn't die for her, not when I'd done nothing to live for yet.

I packed when I got back to my hotel, tearing through the room, gathering clothing to jam into my traveling case with little organization. My hands were shaking, and though I hadn't pulled the trigger, somehow I got an eerie feeling that Rico's body was going to inhabit my mind just like Amber's.

I was moving to the kitchen bar to make a drink when the phone rang. I ignored it, but it didn't stop. So finally, I picked it up with a long, exhausted huff. "I'm leaving, Joe. I'll see you back in Chicago."

"It's me, babe," said Vel, and her voice was like music to my ears.

"Velma? It's good to hear your voice." And it was. I'd done plenty of quiet complaining about having to care for her like a child, but I longed for her now. I needed a friend.

"I wish I had some better news, but a man's been telephoning for you."

"A man?"

"Says he's your brother Chick?"

My heart dropped, but I kept my voice even. "What did he say?"

"Your ma died," she revealed softly. "They're having a funeral in a few days. You never mentioned your family much, but I thought you'd want to know."

Memories should have flickered through my mind—all the moments that had made up Margaret Hill's life—but I struggled to tap into anything decent. I closed my eyes, and all I could see was her shaking in that barn. My weak, crying ma, who had finally dared to leave my father after years of abuse but still let him back into the house every other night for supper.

"Virginia?"

"Thank you for calling." I finally pulled the words from my throat. "I'm leaving New York. Let's do dinner when I get back to Chicago?"

"Leaving so soon?"

"I almost got killed tonight." I pressed my hand to my rolling stomach, still a mess of nerves. "I stay here any longer and I'll be joining my ma in a casket."

"Take care of yourself, now. When you get back to town, we'll have some fun."

I hung up the phone and tried to focus on packing, but a heaviness filled my chest as if every emotion I'd so carefully stored away while pretending to be someone else abruptly refused to go unnoticed.

The fear of the gun against my head and Adonis nowhere in sight.

Madeline's abandoned apartment.

Chick calling around Chicago to find me.

Ma, forever sleeping in a grave somewhere in Georgia.

Ben killing for me, twice.

I broke down, tossing the glass to the floor, finding strange comfort in watching it shatter into a thousand pieces. A tap at the door made me want to throw another glass to ward off my visitor, but I was certain it was Adonis, and I didn't plan on missing the chance to tell him exactly how I felt about him.

"Don't bother, Adonis. I'm leaving this fucking city and you with it." I heaved open the door to Ben, still in a messy state from the tussle.

"Bad time?" Ben joked, giving me a wide, enigmatic grin.

"I was just packing." I left him, and he took the open door as an invitation.

"Adonis told me about the apartment he got you."

I laughed richly. "You mean his former girlfriend's apartment?"

His mouth went slack at the words. "What are you talking about?"

"Madeline," I said, and saying her name aloud filled me with sweet relief. She'd been my secret for too long, someone only discussed in private rooms. A name the men here wanted to forget.

Ben changed at the mention of her, tensed. "You knew her?"

"I knew her," I told him. "I know a lot more than you think. And in the beginning, I thought that knowledge gave me some kind of power. But now I see that's a lie because what fucking use is a secret when there's a gun to your head." I caught my hands shaking while trying to shove my traveling case shut.

Ben drew closer, and his mouth turned downward. "Virginia—"

"Don't!" I lifted my finger to stop him mid-step.

His posture went rigid. "I don't want you to leave."

"Why not? You're not here long, anyway. You need to get back to your wife in California." The bitterness tasted foul on my tongue, and I loathed that I envied his wife even for a small instant.

"I don't want to do this with you," he pleaded, voice uneven. "If this is your last night in New York, I want to spend it between your legs, in your arms, with your voice in my ears."

All the muscles in my body tightened, and I blew out a shallow breath to hold myself together. I couldn't tear my gaze from him, even when every bone in my body begged me to walk away.

"No," I said, as firmly as I could manage, but it came out rather weak.

"Give me one good reason," he insisted, looking me up and down with slow determination.

"I can name more than one." I placed a hand on my hip and finally averted my eyes over his shoulder, training them on the door. "Aside from the fact that you are married, you are a pompous, violent bastard, with nothing to offer me but a fun night. The mess that follows? I'll have to deal with it on my own. This is all just a game to you, Ben. I'm just a game to you."

"You really believe that? After what just happened, you think you don't mean something to me?" He closed the space between us, and his hand glided up my arm, but instead of the chills that would usually follow, my mind did something dark. My memory, still so fresh from tonight's bloodshed, flashed back. The men in the alley and the thump of the barrel against my head.

I shuddered and pulled away. "Leave, Ben! You just shot a man, the second man you've killed in front of me. I imagine there's been a dozen more, at least. Who was Rico talking about? Who did you torture and cut up?" Through wrenching sobs, I managed my next words, far more damaging than the first. "And how fucked am I to want you? You are wrong, Ben. You are a bad person. I wasn't always like this, I used to be good."

He lifted his hands up in mock surrender, eyes scanning the room until he spotted the broken glass. "You are good. Good people can be made to do bad things, but that doesn't make them ruined or wrong. The world is not made of people who fit into one side or the other."

"And where do you fall, Ben?" I challenged his own logic.

"I am ruined," he said, with no sense of unease or question behind the words. "I am a bad person."

I know, I acknowledged to myself, but there was still that lingering sense of want, and sympathy, all entangled together to create the woman I was. Drawn to broken men.

His eyes stared into mine. "But when I'm with you, I feel like . . ."

"Like what?" I pressed him on.

"Good," he said simply.

"When I'm with you, I feel out of control," I snapped, "and I can't afford to lose control. You make a mistake, and they say, 'Oh, that's just Siegel being Siegel.' I make a mistake, and I end up just like Amber."

I had to get out of this conversation and far away from him. I didn't know what was in store for me when I got back to Joe, or if any of the information I'd collected on Adonis would free me of my obligations to Chicago. All I knew was I couldn't stay.

"My mother died," I revealed. "I'm going to go bury her."

He opened his mouth, maybe to offer me condolences, but I pointed to the hotel door without giving him a chance. "Goodbye, Ben."

Chapter Seventeen

I settled into a seat near the bar just as the train rumbled to a delayed start. I focused on the smooth ride delicately rocking my rolling stomach until I sighed with contentment. I watched the cityscape turn into a scenic countryside of rolling hills and verdant fields stretching vast and endless, giving me an entirely different view of New York. Despite the clattering of the wheels along the track and the occasional high-pitched whistle, I knew drifting into a slumber would come easy now that I was long gone from Adonis.

I rang Joe before I checked out of the hotel to let him know I was leaving, not giving him a second to question why. I could still hear him cursing when I hung up the phone but didn't let the thought of his disappointment linger.

I was leaving New York, and there was not a damn thing he could have said to change it.

I studied the ticket in my hand quietly. What was I going to say about my ma at her funeral? *Rest in peace, Margaret Hill. You weren't the best mother, but at the very least, you made me one hell of a wedding dress.*

I closed my eyes, surrendering to the gentle rocking of the train. The barkeep shuffled over to join me with a fresh smile.

"Can I get you anything, miss?"

I placed the ticket on the mahogany bar top. "You know how to make a Georgia mint julep?"

He nodded, briefly glancing down at the ticket. "Preparing yourself for Georgia?"

I forced a smile. "You have no idea."

He mixed up the drink and placed it on a cocktail napkin in front of me. I could smell the whiskey and mint before my lips touched the edge of the glass.

"I'll have the same," called a voice beside me, and I choked on my whiskey at the sound.

I twisted around, then let out a sigh of defeat. He was sporting a yellow pinstripe suit with a matching fedora, an almost unrecognizable look. I'd grown so accustomed to his dark suits and underworld style—the dreary, challenging fashion of the Mob. A statement of sleek, unmatched intimidation.

Finally, I found my voice and asked, "What are you doing here, Ben?" I looked him up and down. "And what are you wearing?"

He took off his hat and placed it on top of the bar, then ran his hands down the front of his suit. "Thought this would be more suitable for Georgia. Maybe I'll find myself a sweet little farmer's daughter and settle down. Raise some, um . . . cows? Chickens? Goats?"

I held in a laugh because I wasn't going to give him the satisfaction. Only two perfectly mad individuals could laugh hours after they'd both shot a man in a dirty New York alley. "Start another family? At this pace, you'll have one in every state."

A muscle in his jaw ticked. "You never miss a chance to remind me that I'm married."

I lifted my hand and pointed to his ring finger, where the ring was absent but a pale outline of where it once was remained. "Thought you might need one, given you've lost your ring."

The bartender placed his drink down in front of him, and Ben didn't waste a second. He took a long, satisfying sip before declaring, "You can't bury your mother alone."

I forced out a mocking laugh until I turned to face his soft eyes. "We weren't close."

"You weren't close with your own mother?"

"Go back to New York or California, or wherever the hell you're supposed to be."

"I'll go back when I'm ready, and I'm not ready yet." He rolled his shoulders, clearing his throat and glancing behind us at the window, where the moving landscape had created a blur of colors.

I kept my eyes on my drink when I asked, "Do you actually believe that?"

"What?"

"That we have the control to make our own choices?"

He gestured at the train. "You made this choice, didn't you? I'm sure Chicago isn't happy that you're abandoning your responsibilities in New York."

"I'm certain Joe will make me pay for it somehow."

"What about Adonis?"

"Fuck Adonis."

He only half smiled. "Let me come with you."

"No," I said quickly, but still, as I refused him, I couldn't help but wonder. Would I like his company during this leap into the past? Did I really want to be alone to face it all?

He reached for his hat, paid for his drink, and tried to get off the barstool. I stopped him with a quick grab at his wrist. "Fine, but play nice."

I knew I'd regret it. I had begged him to leave me alone in New York, but now, the thought of him slipping away again left my chest tight, shame coiling in my stomach. I didn't have anyone to hold my hand while I mourned my mother—nobody but Ben, who'd openly admitted that he'd eventually hurt me.

His mouth quirked to the side. He flicked his wrist and took me by the hand, then lifted it to his mouth for a quick kiss. "You tell me what to do, and I'll do it."

The barkeep cleared his throat to get our attention, and a younger me would have flushed red with embarrassment knowing he'd likely overheard our conversation.

"Can I get you another, miss?"

"Sure," I said, glaring at Ben. "He's paying."

We arrived in Marietta late the following afternoon at a barren, dusty train station. I stepped off the platform with Ben in tow, trying not to stiffen at the sight of it. When I left with Georgie, my younger brothers and sisters had waved goodbye, sobbing every inch the train crackled by. My ma and Chick had sat on a hard wooden bench just feet away from the train, unmoved, refusing to believe I'd leave without seeing it for themselves. I breathed in the faint scent of magnolia, a reminder of the world I'd left behind five long years ago.

Ben glanced around at the few stragglers waiting for departure, then gathered my traveling case from my hand. "You know where you're going?"

"Short walk from here to the house."

"Walk?"

I kept a blank face when I replied with, "It's just a few miles."

Three miles, to be exact, and my feet ached with every passing step. I shuddered out of my New York furs, finding sweet relief in the occasional cool breeze. March in New York was still bitter most days, with the occasional snow. I'd never walk outside without one of my furs to keep my shoulders warm. Georgia wasn't scorching, but the humid air made me feel sticky, as if the fabric of my dress might mold to my skin at any moment. Ben didn't complain, even as the miles stretched on. He held the suitcase, taking in all the dust plumes and wafts of animal manure without complaint.

When we finally arrived at the wide-open pasture leading to my family's dilapidated farmhouse, I grew flighty. Did I really need to be here to bury her? Chick could handle it without me. He'd always handled things well enough without me.

"This it?" Ben placed the luggage down on the dirt road.

The white-paneled house with broken shutters sat on a run-down farm with nothing left but a stray chicken, pecking out holes in the screened-in porch. Once upon a time, there had been a well-tended garden and too many dogs to count. I'd run out the back door when Pa started raging and wait on the porch for it to stop, a couple of dogs by my side. Sometimes it didn't stop all night.

The screen door opened with a slam, and Chick raced down the steps. I remained frozen, watching him dash up the dirt road in a stained cotton shirt and trousers, with the biggest smile on his face. He probably had holes in his shoes, no money, and nothing to his name but this run-down house.

How could I have left him so long without a word?

I had money, more than I knew what to do with, and I had never once sent anything home.

The guilt crept in, nearly rendering me to tears, but I managed to return his smile when he finally reached me. He scooped me up in his arms and twisted me around, then set me down with a gentle laugh. "My God, Gin, look at you! You look like a dream. Thought maybe Loretta Young was finally comin' to kiss me." He jerked his eyes to Ben, shifting from welcoming to defensive in a snap. "Who's this? Your man?"

He stepped forward, standing half a foot taller than Ben, with muscles groomed from years of manual labor, hoping to scare him.

"A friend," Ben answered kindly, and I breathed a sigh of relief that he'd decided to play nice. "I'd like to be her man, but she keeps saying no."

For a moment, Chick said nothing, but then let out a booming laugh. "That's my sister, always giving them a good chase." He returned his gaze to me, placing both hands on my shoulders firmly. "Took me so long to hunt you down. I didn't think you'd make the funeral."

"I should have written," I said. "I should have called."

"When Georgie came back without you, I thought . . ." He paused and swallowed. "You know, I thought maybe something happened to you."

My thoughts of regret grew, so I changed the subject. "I want to pay for her funeral."

He bowed his head slightly. "It's covered, Gin."

"Covered by who?"

He hesitated, scratching the back of his neck. A sign he was planning a lie.

"Be straight with me, Chick. Who is paying for her funeral?"

I knew the answer, but I needed to hear it.

"Pa," he finally muttered. "And because Ma never really divorced him, he gets the house and the land. Cotton and me . . . we tried fightin' it, but no use."

"He gets the house?" My voice hitched, and instinctively, Ben reached for my hand. "Grandpa left her this house. Where are you going to stay? What about everyone else?"

"The boys are married off, living in different parts. The girls too. Only Ruth left, and Pa said she could stay with him if she wanted to handle the cooking and cleaning."

"Over my dead body," I ground out.

Chick lifted both his hands. "Let's just get through this together. You can stay here for the night, and I can take you to town in the morning. Old man Davis has an inn across the street from a brand-new theater they opened last year. Call it a movie palace." He glanced to Ben with the same cheeky smile. "Just got to find me a date."

Ben and Chick started to chat back and forth about movies and women, while I stared at the house, thinking about all the blood Mack Hill had spilled teaching us lessons over the years. He couldn't get this house.

I'd lost Madeline, with no sense of finding her the justice she deserved. Adonis had won that war; my father couldn't win this one.

"Chick, you mind taking us to the inn now? I don't want to sleep here."

He straightened up, gathering our luggage. "Just don't go leaving without saying goodbye, Gin."

I gave his arm a reassuring squeeze. "I'm not going anywhere, Chick."

Old man Davis made us rent two rooms because we weren't married, and Chick got a laugh out of the interrogation. Ben's room was across the hall from mine, but I snuck in and locked my door with a good night, desiring nothing more than to be alone. Chick wasn't having it, though, thundering his fists against the door until I let him in.

The room itself was devoid of character, filled with mismatched furniture that seemed out of place. In one corner, a rocking chair caught my attention, reminiscent of the one my mother used to own.

For a moment, I saw her again, rocking and singing one of us to sleep, but Chick's heavy steps jerked me back to the present.

I peeled off my shoes and sat on a round, worn-down chaise near a dust-covered window. It overlooked the theater palace he'd mentioned, and I considered seeing a show. *Top Hat* was playing, starring Fred Astaire and Ginger Rogers. Would a musical cheer me up?

Chick sat down on the bed, picking at the ends of a homemade quilt. "You got a plan, don't you, Gin?"

I chewed my bottom lip. "I think I might set the house on fire. He can claim the rubble."

"Ain't you tired of hating him? Hating him never done anyone any good."

I leaned forward. "Is he still drinking, Chick?"

He nodded.

"Then I'll never stop hating him, and Ma."

His eyes enlarged at the words, like I'd punched him in the chest.

I remained stoic when I continued, "She still loved the bastard, even when he beat her black and blue in front of us."

His shoulders slumped. "What are you doing, Gin? I called Chicago, they said you were in New York. What kind of job takes you to both of those places?"

"The kind of job I can't talk about," I admitted to him, taking a deep breath. "I'm going to bury our ma, but then I have to go."

"Back to New York?"

I gave him a tense grin. "Back to wherever they need me next."

"They?"

"They."

"You're not gonna tell me anything, are you?"

"You don't need to know what I do. Only that I'm going to take care of you."

"Georgie will be at the funeral. He's got a new wife, a baby on the way." He thought about it for a moment.

I couldn't decide how I felt about the news because I was too cold, too angry. If I closed my eyes right now, I'd see that house burning to the ground. "Let's hope he doesn't hurt her the way he hurt me," I said.

"Georgie doesn't seem like the type."

"They never do."

He sighed. "That could have been you, Gin. I thought that's what you wanted when you left. A family."

"I just wanted to leave, Chick. Georgie was a way out." I looked back out the window, imagining a little girl with Georgie's face. I thought about holding her tiny body in my arms, not knowing what to do with her—how to protect her. "You would have known that if you really knew me."

He blinked with surprise, but before he could speak, I said, "But I don't think I even knew me back then."

"Well, one thing hasn't changed."

I arched my brows.

"You still scare me." He squared his shoulders and got off the bed. "Just don't do anything that will make our lives harder here. This town might not mean much to you, but it means something to me. This is my home."

As he departed without uttering another word, I collapsed onto the bed, my mind caught between thoughts of violence and the need for sleep.

The next morning, a symphony of birds chirping outside the window abruptly roused me at six o'clock. I mustered the strength to gather my scattered thoughts as I sifted through my collection of dresses. The photograph of Madeline and Adonis slipped from the pile, tumbling to the floor. Another wave of guilt hit me. I couldn't decide if I should hold on to hope or bury her photo and postcards with my ma.

I continued to study her swanky suit before opening my door to knock on Ben's. He opened it with squinty, gummy eyes. "It's not even morning."

"It's six a.m."

"Chick said the funeral is at ten."

"I want one of your suits."

He scratched his head. "For what? Chick and I aren't the same size."

"For me."

He looked me up and down. "We definitely aren't the same size."

I pushed out a frustrated laugh. "Just give me a suit, Ben. I'll pay you back for it. I've got to get going if I'm going to get it fitted in time for the funeral."

A flicker of doubt crossed his features. "You're wearing a suit to your mother's funeral?"

"Something colorful."

"Pinstripe?"

"The one you wore yesterday?"

He nodded.

I grinned. "Perfect."

We arrived at the funeral ten minutes late to a sea of black-clad men and women mourning over her grave. She was buried under a large red maple in mid-bloom. I walked up the cobble path with Ben on my arm, both of us dressed in suits—his black as a show of respect and mine a pin-striped yellow as a show of defiance. My unspoken sentiments on the life of my mother. I adjusted my sunglasses as the crowd whispered, many momentarily pausing their sniffling grief to cast me glares.

I smiled in return, then greeted the pastor with a firm handshake. "Sorry we're late. Please continue."

Startled by the handshake, he cleared his throat and opened his Bible to resume his passage. Chick stared with his mouth open wide a few feet away, but my other brother Cotton struggled to contain his amusement. They looked almost identical but never agreed on much. Chick was friendly, small-town. Simple. Cotton was a troublemaker, with a mind of his own. Even his suit was slightly unkempt, and the woman on his arm was weeks away from delivering a baby, but there was no ring on her finger.

I scanned the crowd for Ruth and spotted her surrounded by a huddle of children.

"Everyone is staring," muttered Ben into my ear. "That's the idea, right?"

I nodded firmly, but despite the display, I interlaced my fingers with his when the pastor listed Margaret Hill's greatest achievements: her children.

It was over in minutes, and I found it so strange that her life, all those years of memories, could be summed up so quickly. What would they say about me? Who would even be there?

Ben, somehow sensing my deepening thoughts, squeezed my hand. And as if on cue, Mack Hill appeared, a picture of confidence and swagger, despite his graying hair and balding scalp. It had been nearly five years since I left home, but six since our last encounter. He'd showed up in the middle of the night to start a fight with Ma and I hit him over the head with a frying pan, cracking open his forehead. Even in the bright Georgia sun, I could still see the scar. A reminder that no matter what he said to me, he was still the same bastard I wanted to beat to death all those years ago.

The closer he got, the older he looked. His face was narrow, eyes heavily lidded, and even though he had a smile pulling at his lips, I already knew the second he opened his mouth, I'd smell the alcohol.

Maybe Chick could stop hating him, but I sure couldn't.

"You know how to make an entrance, Gin." He placed both hands on his bony hips and flashed Ben a grin. "Second husband or third?"

Ben threw a punch so fast that I didn't even see his hand fly into Mack's face. I wouldn't have known it had happened if Mack's nose didn't gush blood all over my suit. I stepped away to look at Ben with a low growl.

"Why did you do that?"

He held out his hand, stretching his fingers before curling them into his palm, giving me no explanation aside from a curse under his breath.

Mack tried to fight back, jumping to attack, but Chick and Cotton showed up in time to gather him by the arms and pull him off.

Chick pointed a finger at me. "I asked one thing of you! Don't make trouble. The sheriff wants to make me a deputy next month. How am I going to explain this?"

Ben cleared his throat. "I didn't know, Chick. We won't make any more trouble for you."

"You're the same crazy bitch," growled Mack, holding his nose to stop the bleeding.

When I finally found my voice, I looked at Chick and said, "Who are you going to defend when you're a deputy? Men like him?"

His face went stricken, and Ruth ran between us before anything else was said. "Enough of this, all of you. Chick, take Mack home. I need to get these children back to the schoolhouse, but we'll all have a family dinner tonight." Her eyes, always so bright and blue, looked to me with nothing but hope. Of course she'd become a teacher. Ruth Hill, so patient and kind, freely displaying her compassion when I struggled to find any. "Will you come, Gin? Please. It's what Ma would want."

I blinked back bitter, angry tears. "I'll think about it, Ruthie."

"No!" Mack bellowed, joining us only to say, "None of you are welcome in that house again."

"Pa," reasoned Cotton, clutching the girl beside him. "Anna is due any day now."

"Give us a week or two," pleaded Chick. "We'll find something else."

Mack glared my way but spoke aloud to all of them: "Don't come anywhere near my house. As far as I'm concerned, you're all dead to me now."

I raised a skeptical brow. "I'd wager we've always been dead to you."

Mack stormed off, leaving Cotton and Chick in a flustered rage.

"I asked one thing of you, Gin. We just needed some time to find a place of our own."

I shrugged. "We'll buy a new house."

Cotton rolled his shoulders back and laughed. "With what money?"

"I'll buy it. One for each of you."

"You could use a new car too," added Ben, pointing to Cotton. "Something good for the family. I'll take you shopping tomorrow. I've got great taste."

Cotton's eyes brightened. "A new car?"

Chick's face held no such wonder. "How are you making money, Gin?" He surveyed Ben, as if he were putting something together in his head but couldn't vocalize it yet. "You don't need to take care of us, we've managed this long without you . . . We'll be fine."

"Speak for yourself, Chick," argued Cotton.

I narrowed my eyes. "No more barely getting by. I'm going to fix everything. You don't have to like it, Chick, but it's happening."

Chapter Eighteen

Chick insisted on giving us a ride back, but I refused, wanting to walk. Georgie met us near a flower shop with a bright awning and a sign directing the townsfolk to my ma's funeral. He was the same lanky man, only this time, he had a petite, brown-haired woman in a yellow cotton dress hanging on his arm, observing me cautiously.

My mind turned on me, and I imagined her bruised, hiding his beatings from the world. Could children really change him? Children hadn't changed my pa. I tried to find something on her, a mark to prove that he hadn't changed. That this cycle of abuse would continue no matter who he married. But I found nothing—no mark, no bruise, no sign of unhappiness in her blissful expression.

"Good to see you again, Gin," he said warmly, reaching out to shake Ben's hand. "That was one hell of a punch you gave old Mack. You ask me, bastard could have used a few more."

Ben gave him a tense grin, glancing between us both slowly.

"You two old friends?"

"This is my ex-husband, Georgie," I told him.

"This is the ex-husband?" All the charm was gone in a single breath, and I knew who I was dealing with and what he was capable of. The only thing I didn't know was how to change him, how to get him to snap out of it and not react with violence. I held his hand tightly, interlocking our fingers.

He eased up, shoulders settling, then smiled from ear to ear. "Someone got Virginia Hill to walk down the aisle?"

Georgie chuckled, giving me a long stare. "It's not walking down the aisle that's the problem. It's trying to keep her. You leaving soon?"

"Just here for the funeral," I answered.

"Don't let Mack ruin your visit. There's nothing you can do to change what's happening. Even if you contest the will . . . do you really want that old house?"

"I want it for my family," I said quietly. I was still lost looking at Georgie and his wife, a strange mirror into a world and life I could have had. I thought about my belly, round and growing, and the longing left me daydreaming. I knew I didn't really want that life with Georgie, but some part of me did long for it.

"Virginia," said Georgie, "you think we could talk sometime before you leave?"

His wife pulled at his arm to get his attention, and I cleared my throat, gathering myself. "We should get going."

I walked in silence to the inn. Ben was quiet beside me until I tried to slip into my room without a word. He jammed his hand between the door and the frame. "You're angry with me."

"How observant," I said, trying to pull his hand away. "I can take care of myself. If anyone gets to punch my father, it's me."

"I don't know what came over me."

I let out a short snort. "You know exactly what came over you. You don't think about anything you do, you just do it."

"Forgive me."

"Tell me something, Ben, how many times do you get to ask for forgiveness before I stop forgiving you?"

He cocked his neck, and his face flushed red. "Tell me something, Virginia, do you still love your ex-husband? Because the way you looked at him made me want to kill him." His face hardened, and the charming nature he'd casually displayed since the train ride disappeared. A startling reminder that I was traveling with a man who murdered without question. Somewhere, there was a graveyard of bodies with no headstones and only one thing in common: Benjamin Siegel.

I took a deep breath. "I might hate Georgie more than my father, though it's hard to know anymore. Both treated me the same, and both have somehow ended up with everything they've ever wanted. A dreamy little life."

He gave me a smile that felt condescending. "Is that what you want? A little life here?"

"Don't tease me, Ben, not now."

"You didn't answer the question."

"I don't know what I want."

"But I know what I want," he said, hand ghosting up my arm. "I hit your father because he hurt you. You want me to kill him? I'll do it with a smile on my face. He dies, Chick gets the house . . . everything works out." He didn't blink when he asked, "Will that make you happy?"

I felt my stomach drop. I wasn't this woman, this person who made a call on who lived or died, certainly not when that person was family. My own blood. Yet, the lingering feeling resided, pressing. I wanted my father dead; I'd wanted it for years. I prayed at night the drinking would kill him and we'd wake up to him cold in a puddle of his own vomit. Ma would mourn him, but only long enough to bury him. Her life would have been different, more than just the collection of dreary memories I have of her.

"I can't." The words came out a stutter, messy, uneven.

"What you said back in New York, about your name having power? Do you remember?"

I remembered everything. "Yes."

"How often do you use that power?"

Not enough. "I'm not like you," I told him, and myself. A knot formed in my throat. "I'll remember Amber until the day I die . . . the look in her eyes, Ben. I can't do what you do."

His eyes sharpened. "Then let me do what I do."

I looked away from the seriousness of his gaze, but he tenderly cupped my chin to pull my eyes back. I waited a long minute before pulling the words from my throat in a barely audible whisper. "Hurt him, hurt him bad. Then run him out of town."

There was no cheeky smile in response, no sign that he took any pride in what I'd asked of him. Instead, he released my chin, walked into his room to retrieve a briefcase, then met me back in the hallway. "I'll let you know when it's done."

"You're going now?"

"I'm going to sneak into the house, wait there for him."

"I want to go with you."

"I don't want you to see it."

I frowned. "I'm going with you."

Mack returned late that evening with a bottle, sinking into the run-down sofa in the living room. The radio crackled with static as he absentmindedly listened to its distorted tunes. Ignoring the disarray surrounding him, he propped his feet up on a small table. Ma's favorite bluebird cup, still filled with stale coffee, sat on a table.

Ben and I watched from the kitchen, where I couldn't help but stare at the hanging rack of pots and pans to the left of him. I reached for one quietly. "This is the one I almost killed him with." I gazed at the innocuous pot for a long moment. A chilling reminder of the darkness inside me, the depths of that rage I so desperately tried to control.

His face, cold and detached, changed at the mention of it. He shut his suitcase, filled with an assortment of knives and guns, and scooped up the pan from the rack, cleaning off a few motes of dust along the surface. "I like it," he said, holding it tightly and swinging it in the air for practice. "Sentimental, you know?"

Straightening, I studied him warily, searching my mind for any pinch of regret. There was still time to stop him.

Ben must have sensed my reserve because he was quick to whisper, "Last chance, Virginia. Is this what you want?"

I squared my shoulders and looked past him. I delved deep into my memory, desperately searching for a fragment of compassion, a flicker of redemption that could save Mack Hill from the clutches of Bugsy Siegel. But all I saw was the blood on that sofa from my mother's nose and the nights he spent dragging us to the barn to sleep in the cold as punishment.

The words slipped out coldly: "Do it in the barn."

Ben moved between the shadows and threw the pan into my pa's face, knocking him to the ground with a thud. Moonlight filtered in through the dim house from the cracks in the windows, illuminating the gore of it all. The blood and the screaming. Only it wasn't from Ma this time or my siblings—it was him.

Our worst nightmare.

A figure we dreaded in the day and the night.

When the screams stopped, the dead silence pulled me back to the moment. Mack was still breathing, just a mess of cuts and swelling flesh. Ben dragged him by the legs out of the house, through the door, and down the porch steps. I followed the trail of blood, stopping at the last step to take a seat like I used to.

Ben took him to the barn and shut the door. A light rain fell, washing some of the blood off the porch steps.

I soaked in the house for the first time since I arrived. The broken porch swing needed fresh paint, the cracked windows and hornet nests hanging from the eaves removed. There might be mice inside, judging from the filth, and I knew there were leaks in the roof likely flooding the interior every time it rained. So, why did this place mean so damn much to Chick?

What memories did he have here that I didn't?

When Ben finally left the barn, he walked through the rain back to the house in heavy strides. He folded up his shirtsleeves, stained in blood, and the rain glistened off the skin of his forearms. I took a sharp breath and thought about New York. His face between my legs. Then, we were still very much strangers.

Now, we were more. I couldn't possibly deny it any longer.

And though everything inside me warned against it, even the rain and the barn and the musky air—all too familiar to my mistake with Riddle—I started to strip my clothes. Shoes first, then stockings, and when I looped around to tug at my zipper, he stopped to watch.

Blood rushed to my head, and my chest tightened. His eyes wandered over the length of my body, his chest pulling up and down in heavy, shallow breaths. He wanted me as badly as I wanted him, but something inside him, just like the warning inside me, stopped him.

We both stared at each other for several long, tense minutes, the rain soaking him while I stood half naked on the porch, exposed but unshaken.

If you want me, Ben, come and get me.

He moved again, faster, nearly running at me, stripping away his clothing piece by piece. Our mouths collided first, wet and full of need. He lifted me up, wrapping my legs around his waist to carry me into the house. Weightless in his arms, I bit and kissed his mouth and then the skin of his neck until he groaned in response.

He sat me down with a thud on the kitchen table next to a vase of wilted flowers. I ripped at his damp shirt and tugged at his trousers. He trailed kisses down my neck and breasts, licking the skin below my navel until I took him by the hair and urged him back to my mouth again. This time, he held my head in place so my lips couldn't escape his.

Even when I felt him inside me and moaned into his mouth, he didn't relent. He kept my mouth on his, our wet foreheads pressed together. My legs trembled with every thrust in my ma's dusty kitchen, where I'd spent years hiding from my pa's wrath. I burned this moment into my brain, praying it would ruin all the others.

I felt him for the first time, dragging my nails over his shoulders, where my fingertips grazed old wounds. Smooth skin to uneven tissue—healed and broken. His body was a landscape of bad decisions, and now, so was mine.

"Fuck." The word came out of his mouth low, strangled, and his hold on my head weakened.

I snaked my hand into his hair and pulled with force, leaning up to whisper into his ear, "Not yet. I want you to ask me, Ben."

His eyes, squeezed shut, opened to stare into mine deeply. He was close, I could feel him inside me tensing, pulsing, each thrust slowing while he strained under the pressure. The table rocked beneath us, creaking against the hardwood floor.

"Ben," I moaned his name, and he growled into the nape of my neck.

"Virginia," he uttered. "Can I?"

The shift in power left me smiling, and I curled my hand around his neck, keeping our eyes steady, locked. "Yes."

We finished together and collapsed on the floor, where the door, still cracked open, pulled in drafts of cold, wet air. I turned over to bury my face into his side, knowing that soon, that pleasure-fueled haze I entered when I was with him would vanish. When it did, I'd feel wrong again, and dirty. I'd question everything I thought I knew about myself.

I wanted to keep that dreadful time from coming as long as I could.

"Again," I ordered him, and we found a new spot in the house. I was desperate for him, but more desperate to erase the memories staining this house and the power they held over me.

That night, we cleaned up the blood with soap and water, scrubbing the stained floorboards until they gleamed. We gathered the soiled rags and, with a sense of finality, entrusted them to the flames of the hearth, watching as they turned to ash. Ben spent an hour working on the broken-down truck until he got it running, then tossed Mack into the back with a bag and a small bundle of cash for food.

"I'll drop you off closer to town. Stay at the inn until I return. There's a train tonight that will take him to California. I have an associate there that will put him to work and keep an eye on him."

"What kind of work?" I asked, still breathless from the kitchen and the deep cleaning.

He didn't smile but walked around the truck to kiss my forehead. "He'll stay busy and away. Let's get you back before your family starts looking for you."

Ben dropped me off and left in a rush. I snuck in through a back door and got to my room without alerting old man Davis. I took a long bath, rinsing off any blood between my fingernails along with the lingering scent of Ben.

I imagined Joe's face, pinched with disappointment, staring back at me. I let the thought remain too long, giving me shaky anxiety until I heard the door of my room open and close. I threw my legs out and wrapped my body in a robe before slipping out to find Chick, toying with a newspaper in his hand.

"I knew I recognized him," he finally said aloud, breathlessly.

"Who?" I tightened my robe. "I'm trying to bathe. Think you could come back when I'm done?"

His sweaty brows perked up, and he straightened the crumpled newspaper. "Bugsy Siegel!" He hit the paper with his finger, slamming it down. I reached for it. The article had a picture of him, following a list of his rumored violent exploits. I didn't know what to say to my brother. I could lie, but it was right in front of him.

"What do you want me to say?" I finally asked.

"Tell me you're not caught up in all this? That this money you've come into isn't from him?"

I paused, weighing my response, until I decided I didn't want to pretend to be someone I wasn't. Not here. "It's not from him," I said clearly. "It's from me."

He didn't blink. "What?"

"I've earned it working for the Mob. Sometimes I launder money, sometimes I cross borders with stolen merchandise. Occasionally I find myself spying on a crime lord . . . and who knows what the future will bring."

His mouth went agape. "Why are you telling me this?"

I stepped closer and reached for his hand. "Because I don't want to lie to you."

"I want to be an officer, Virginia." He pulled his hand away with a frown. "I want to work with the law. I can't have a sister working against it."

I looked at him deeply through narrowed eyes. "I thought you wanted to be an actor."

"Childish dreams."

"Are they? If you want me to send you to California, I can."

He hesitated. "I have a life here, Gin."

I startled. "A life? You want to live and die in this town having done nothing? Nothing exciting, nothing fulfilling. Nothing you dreamed about?" I couldn't make my own dreams come true, whatever they were, but at the very least, I could help him. I had to do something with my money, and running wasn't an option.

Maybe some good could still come out of all this.

"Is this what you dreamed about? Have you read what they're saying about Siegel? He's a murderer." He came to some quick conclusion in his head and walked to the door. "You're not leaving with him. I'm not letting him get anywhere near you."

As he reached for the doorknob, I stepped forward to stop him from leaving, my voice low and ferocious when I uttered, "You're going to forget this conversation. Tomorrow, we'll find you and the family a nice, big house. A few cars." I picked at his shirt. "Some new clothes. Everything you need to start a new life here in this same dreadful town that you seem to love so much."

For a moment, he just looked me dead in the eyes, waiting, maybe hoping I'd change my mind. Then he squared his shoulders and turned away from me. "What happens if I get the sheriff involved? Tell him there's a big fish in our small pond. What happens then?"

I craned my neck to look up at him, matching the challenge in his eyes with my own icy reserve. "You're not going to do that, Chick. Not if you care about this town. I'm trying to protect you."

"Who is protecting you? I know you, you wouldn't do something like this for money . . . you wouldn't make a choice like this. Why did you do it? What happened that left you so desperate? Was it Georgie?"

He wanted answers, and I longed to tell him about Madeline. The reason why I'd done this, and how, despite all the wrongful acts I'd committed in pursuit of her, I'd still found nothing. All of this was done for nothing.

But if I said it out loud to him, it would be real.

"Just keep your mouth shut."

Another tense moment of silence passed between us until something inside him relented. He ground his teeth in response before uttering, "Your funeral, Gin."

Later that evening, a knock on my door jolted me from my thoughts, and when I opened it, Ben stood there, looking presentable and clean. There were no visible traces of dirt or blood on his hands, but I couldn't help but conjure dark scenarios. The image of him dragging Mack to the barn, returning to the house drenched from the rain, his hands gripping my waist, his face buried in my neck, and the way he felt inside me, replayed in my mind, refusing to fade away.

We silently made our way to a cozy little diner near the theater, where we sat down to supper. However, the food had no flavor, and an uncomfortable silence hung in the air.

"What's on your mind?"

"Chick came by," I told him slowly. "He knows who you are."

He raised a brow while sipping at his Mason jar of sweet tea. "Should I be worried?"

"I handled him."

He smiled but didn't reply.

"Shouldn't you be going?"

"I'm not done here."

As much as I wanted the words to die in my throat, they erupted bitterly. "What about your family?"

He shrugged, far too casually. "I'm not done with yours yet."

Chapter Nineteen

The next two weeks flew by in a blur. I took the opportunity to purchase a beautifully renovated Victorian home for the family. No one mentioned Pa, or where he'd run off to. The new house boasted intricately carved woodwork and stained glass windows that illuminated the rooms with a kaleidoscope of colors. It sat on expansive landscaped grounds, complete with a charming pond teeming with fish. I furnished it with pieces from a shop in Marietta but traveled to nearby towns to explore different options.

I created the home I never had, but I still felt this lingering itch of missing the city. Even in the mornings, when a light mist encompassed the land, creating a quiet stillness only present in the countryside, I found no peace. I longed for the bustling streets, the vibrant energy, and the constant rush of life that only urban living could provide.

I moved in Ruth and Chick, but Cotton and his wife took the old farmhouse. Instead of living in the main house, Chick had set himself up in a cottage behind the house and didn't come out when Ben was around.

One warm Sunday morning, I gathered the courage to call Joe just before slipping out of my room for breakfast.

"Done burying her?" His voice was somehow cold and warm at the same time.

"She's in the ground," I told him.

"When are you heading back to New York?"

"I don't know if I am."

Silence, then he cleared his throat and said, "Chicago wants you back in New York next week. You don't get to decide when you're done, Virginia. Take a few more days, but you have to go back to New York."

"He put me in her apartment," I revealed. "He gifted it to me."

Silence.

"He gave you Madeline's apartment?"

"Yes. I was nearly killed, Joe. Had it not been for Ben, I'd be dead. That's not what I signed up for. I don't want to go back."

"Ben?" He repeated the name, giving it a moment of thought. "Siegel?"

"Yes," I said, trying to keep my voice even.

"Is he there with you?"

My nerves made my hands itch. How did he know?

"Is he there with you, Virginia?"

"Yes."

"I'm on my way." The urgency in his tone frightened me. It wasn't the Joe I knew, so accustomed to chaos, so calm during the storm. I knew he didn't like Ben, but why did he feel the need to rush to Georgia?

"I'm perfectly fine, Joe."

He was gone, leaving me on edge, wondering what kind of trouble I'd need to defuse when he arrived.

I hung up quickly, reaching to pinch the bridge of my nose. I stood and raced for the hallway, prepared to tell Ben to leave. He couldn't be here when Joe arrived. How would I explain any of this? But when I opened it, he was standing stark naked with a wide, cheeky grin.

I placed my hand over my mouth and laughed into it, searching the hall for any wandering family members.

"Come here," he beckoned.

It took considerable focus to keep my eyes on his. He took me by the hair, pulling me in for a kiss. Inside the room, we moved from the bed to the floor, naked and sweating. Time passed, but I didn't keep up with it. We rested every few hours, had a drink, then found a new place in the room to explore. Finally, I awakened at the bottom of the bed, our legs were tangled together, but I was comfortable and warm.

I sat upright, painfully aware I was running out of time. Mid-sleep, his hand moved to my lower back and rested there. "Don't go."

"I need to clean up," I told him, leaning down to kiss his mouth. His hand moved from my back to my neck to deepen the kiss.

"One more time," he whispered.

I took him by the chin and shoved him down, breaking our mouths. "Joe is on his way."

He sat up stiffly. "You told him I was here?"

"A mistake," I said. "I know you two don't get along. You should leave," I implored with a wave. We didn't have time for soft goodbyes. I'd already lost too much time wrapped up in his arms.

He leveled a serious gaze at me, holding on to my shoulder to keep me from leaping up. "He's going to want you back in New York, you know that."

"I couldn't avoid him forever." I shrugged, as if it were nothing, when really, I dreaded the conversation coming. The bitter reality was that I hadn't accomplished anything in New York and I'd likely be punished for it. I maneuvered around his pressing hand, stood up, and searched for my dress. "I'll grovel to Adonis, explain my behavior as grief, and get back to work."

"I don't want you back in New York."

I stopped a moment, toying with my dress, considering his words. We'd managed to come this far without sentiment, and I didn't want to cross the line now. After all, there was no future for us. No world where we ended up together. I repeated the words at night to remind myself not to get in too deep, and yet, I could hear the emotion in his voice.

The longing in his words.

We'd gone too far.

"We both knew this was going to end. Let's end it on our terms . . .

not theirs," I reasoned. "The honeymoon is over, Ben. I need to finish what I started in New York."

He sprang up and began to rustle through his clothing, opening drawers and shoving items into the luggage case on the floor. I wiggled into my dress, found my undergarments and stockings, then tried to slip out of the room.

"The last girl, the one before you, she didn't make it out of New York alive," he said coldly. "I don't want you to be next."

The shift in his voice hadn't gone unnoticed, sending a chill along my arms and legs. It occurred to me now, but should have long before, that every side of Ben was temporary. I wasn't speaking to the flamboyant gangster with a confident swagger . . . I was speaking with a killer. A killer who knew the person I'd spent months trying to find was long dead.

"Madeline," he continued when I said nothing, and the way he said her name unnerved me. "She's dead, Virginia, and I need to know if you found out information you shouldn't have."

I shook my head because I must have heard him wrong. How had the conversation gone from him caring about me, longing for me to stay in Marietta, to a deadly threat if I didn't give him what I had on Adonis?

"I don't know what you're talking about," I lied.

"You do," he insisted and took a terribly long step forward. "Joey Ep sent you to spy on him, just like her. Adonis should have learned his lesson, but there's a good chance he didn't, so I need to see what you have on him. Madeline had a notebook filled with transaction dates, conversations, numbers that didn't add up. She had proof Adonis was stealing from Chicago."

She had far more information than I did. Adonis hadn't slipped up in the months I'd been working with him—every dime and nickel added up. It was the very reason Joe wanted me back in New York. I didn't have my proof yet.

I stood speechless, pointing to my luggage. Ben drifted to it, searched the front pockets, and retrieved my notebook.

He didn't open it. "I need to destroy it so that nobody suspects you. That's the only way I can keep you safe."

My ears heard the words, but they were jumbled while I tried to comprehend them. I couldn't stop thinking about what he'd said before, that Madeline was dead. So resolute and unshaken.

"How do you know she's dead?" My voice broke.

Something dawned on him, and his eyes narrowed. "In New York, you said you knew about her . . . I just assumed you meant that you knew everything." He left the words dangling, confusion setting into his features. "Who was she to you?"

"How do you know she's dead, Ben?" I repeated the words, but my mind already knew the dreadful answer.

"Answer me, Virginia. Who was Madeline to you?"

"A friend," I yelled, and the relief was all-consuming. I'd spent months hiding what she meant to me, months keeping her my secret. "She's the reason I did this . . . joined Chicago. She went missing, and I was going to do everything I could to find her because when I had nothing . . ." I paused, my voice breaking. "She was my friend, Ben . . . She was my friend and you—" I couldn't say it out loud because that would make it true. That Benjamin Siegel, my stranger from the tracks, had killed my best friend.

"You did it, didn't you?"

His eyes were soft, possibly the softest I'd ever seen. A gentle glimmer adorned those baby blues I had thought about every night for months, but when I looked down at his hands, my stomach churned with nausea. In part, because I knew it to be true—he'd killed her in cold blood—but also because I couldn't muster enough anger to hate him.

Why couldn't I hate him?

"I didn't know who she was to you," he answered instead. "She had information on Adonis, dangerous information. I had to get it from her before she took it back to Chicago, before she gave it to Joey Ep and he took it higher."

I leveled a stony gaze at him. "Is that why you got on the train to follow me here? Were you going to kill me if I had information? Just like you did her?"

"No." The word came out breathlessly.

"I don't believe you."

He looked down at his hands, then shook his head. "I don't understand. Joey Ep let you join to find your lost friend? Why would he do that?" I could see the confusion twisting his features.

"He wanted to find her just as much as I did," I said, but somehow, I felt like I was about to learn the most devastating fact of all, one that far outweighed the pain of Ben's revelation. I felt it, that sense that I didn't know everything, that I'd been too quick to believe all the words Joey Ep had spewed at me that desperate night in Chicago.

"That's impossible, Virginia. I left her body in his hotel room as a message."

Denial sank its teeth into my flesh, and I let it poison me. "No, you're lying. He didn't know what happened to her. Why would Chicago hire you to watch Wayne at the racetrack if you'd killed one their own?"

"This war is private . . . between Joey Ep and Adonis. Only the three of us knew what happened to Madeline, and we had all planned to keep it that way."

It couldn't be true. I had encountered plenty of awful men since joining. They were liars, manipulators, devoid of any goodness. I knew that, but I had always held a soft spot for Joe. He had taken care of me from the very beginning, and he was just as desperate as I was to find Madeline. He offered me hope when I had lost my own, guided me, and even shared drinks with me on nights when I didn't want to be alone. He was a friend.

Could it all have been an act? Was he merely grooming me for his own personal revenge, knowing that I could have met the same fate as Madeline?

How had I not seen it? Why had I been so quick to trust him?

Ben took another step forward, reaching for me, but I recoiled, nearly leaping across the room to the opposite side of the bed, desperate to get away. "Don't, Ben. Don't come any closer."

"I was just doing a job," he reasoned. "The job isn't who I am."

"Do you tell yourself that so you can sleep at night?"

His eyes widened.

"I want you to leave. I don't want to see your face again."

He was wounded by the notion—it was so painfully clear in his taut chin—but he rushed to his suitcase instead. I prepared myself to leap from the window if he drew a gun, but instead, he withdrew a black notebook. One eerily similar to the one Joey Ep had given me when I left for New York.

"This is hers," he said. "This is all the information she had on Adonis. It's evidence he cheated Chicago out of large amounts . . . and it's what Joey Ep wants."

I blinked back more tears. "Why did you keep it?"

"I take it with me when I go to New York," he admitted. "I'm on a leash, and I can use it against Adonis when I want something from him." He tapped the book. "But you can use it to get out. Give it to Joey Ep."

"And start another war," I pointed out.

"Maybe," he said. "Maybe not. It's impossible to know. The totals are small in the grand scheme of things, and this book only proves Adonis is a problem, not all of New York."

The very thought of Adonis taking a bullet gave me some reprieve, but Joey Ep getting everything he wanted couldn't possibly be in the cards. Not after what he'd done.

Ben placed the book on the bed and began hastily gathering his belongings, stuffing them into his suitcase with little regard for order. He dressed quickly, leaving his shirt unbuttoned and clutching his hat in his hand. "Use it, Virginia. It's the very least I can do for you . . . You have to believe me, if I had known . . ." he pleaded.

"I don't ever want to see your face again," I reiterated, needing him to understand, to hear it this time.

He left with a cold, detached gaze, and I watched from the window as he stormed out of the house. Alone, with nothing but Madeline's book to console me, I sank to the floor and wept. My chest heaved with such intensity that I feared I might never find a steady breath again.

Madeline was dead, killed by Ben. Joey Ep had known about it long before he offered me the deal in the parlor. I had been played, used, and manipulated. I had unknowingly signed my life away based on a lie.

Reaching for the book, I clasped it against my chest. I had lost all control over my life the moment I agreed to Joey Ep's terms, but this book, *her* book, offered me a semblance of power. I would never see my friend again, and there was nothing I could do to change that. However, I could ensure that Joey Ep's plan, the one he'd had since the moment he sent Madeline to New York with a secret agenda, would never come to fruition.

I waited for Joe to arrive later that evening. The house was empty aside from Chick, who insisted on waiting outside the kitchen in the hallway, carefully positioned near the swinging door with a gun and a steady hand. I thumbed my hands along the book until I heard Joe's tender steps. A knock at the door. I didn't answer.

He wandered around the house, peeking into windows until finding the side door. He turned the knob with ease and walked inside, a visible sense of relief in his expression. He kept his gun drawn as he spoke to me. "Is he here, Virginia?"

"He's gone," I said.

He lowered his weapon but didn't look convinced. "You're certain? Did he hurt you?"

"He's gone, Joe."

He took a breath, finally taking a moment to gaze at my Victorian treasure, meticulously noting all the details of the kitchen, including the molding. "I can see why you haven't left yet. You've done well here. But I bring good news, another opportunity."

"Oh?"

"There's a position in Mexico we think you'd be a good fit for. It's more pressing than this business with New York."

His eyes met mine, and the look of admiration dissipated. Though I was certain Joey Ep couldn't read minds, somehow, in that instant, he seemed to possess that ability. With just a glance at my face, he knew everything, the most crucial being that I had learned the truth.

"Maybe some travel will do you good?"

"Business as usual?"

He clicked his tongue disapprovingly. "There's no room to slow down." He gazed at the black book, and his eyes brightened. "Is that everything you collected on Adonis? Even if you didn't get proof, I'm sure there's something I can use in there."

"This is all Madeline collected," I countered. "You would recognize the differences if you hadn't given us matching books. But then again, you didn't want us to be different, did you? You only needed a woman with a body and a hint of desperation."

A subtle twitch appeared on his upper lip.

"I got this from Ben," I continued when he said nothing.

"You stole it from him?"

"No, he stole it from her dead body." I uttered the words with a somber darkness that sent shivers down my spine. "But you knew that too, didn't you? Since she was left for you to find."

A chilling transformation overcame him, his once-soft expression turning icy, his gaze now unwavering. His breath quickened, and I wondered if the man I'd come to understand and predict had a similar rage to Ben's, always waiting to be unleashed. Instead of losing himself, he blinked his body into a relaxed state, and his shoulders eased.

He moved to the table to sit in front of me, just as he had that night at the parlor when we started this together.

"You have questions for me," he observed. "Ask them without all this emotion and drama."

I wanted to hurt him . . . Did he feel anything? Did he ever feel anything?

"You knew she was dead."

"That's not a question, but yes, I knew she was dead. We both knew, in many ways. I just used your hope against you. It kept you sharp and determined."

Speechless, I fought to find my voice. "You manipulated me."

"I used you," he confirmed. "I not only saw your potential to rise in this organization, but I saw an opportunity. I wanted to bring down Adonis."

"You never cared for Madeline."

"I loved Madeline."

"You loved what she could do for you."

"Regardless."

My eyes watered. "I could be dead just like her. What would you feel then?"

He rolled his eyes dismissively at the fleeting display of emotion. "I would mourn you, but then I would use what you collected to bring down the man that did this to both you and Madeline."

"You did this!" I shouted, balling my hand into a fist. "You killed her. Not Adonis, not Ben, you."

He sat in quiet reflection for some time. "You don't have to admit this now, certainly not to me, but you are exceptionally skilled at this. Perhaps you despise yourself when you lie down to sleep, but you have achieved more than I ever anticipated. You are the first of your kind. Don't you see that?"

I saw nothing but red. "You want me to thank you?"

"I want you to understand. I needed something from you, but you needed something from me. You were lost, you had no direction, you clung to this woman, this *friend*, you hardly knew. Divorced, poor, and alone. I gave you this fate by trick, but this fate gave you everything." He lifted his arms at the Victorian home. "This fate can give you even more if you let it." He motioned at the book. "But if you want out, you just have to give me that book."

I absorbed his words, realizing they would become the foundation I would depend on in the years to come. He didn't know it yet, but I'd already made a choice, one he had no say in. "Where is she buried? I want to visit her," I pleaded, fearing he would confess to disposing of her body in a dreadful manner, making it impossible for anyone to find her. Aside from her mother, I was the only person who had ever gone looking for her. I prayed he'd give me something to give her. A place, a grave.

"Ottawa, Illinois, a small city near the Fox River," he revealed. "There's a cemetery there, it's pleasant."

The relief made my chest sink. "Why there?"

"My mother is buried there."

"I burned it," I stated icily, devoid of any trace of emotion, just as he preferred.

"Burned what?" he inquired.

"The evidence."

I opened the book, revealing a tattered mess of pages reduced to ash and scribbles. I had ripped out every page—notes, writings, the list of numbers—and set them ablaze.

The horror in his eyes made me smile through the pain in my chest.

"What have you done?" he exclaimed.

In a frenzied motion, he seized the book from my grasp and hastily flipped through the frayed pages near the binding. It didn't take long for him to come to the bleak realization that all hope was lost.

"I burned everything, including my own notes," I declared. "It's a shame, really. Ben claimed Madeline's book held all the evidence you'd need to bring down Adonis."

He broke, standing from the table to take a violent step toward me. I didn't shake or show any sense of fear. I had angered him, but I held on to the belief that he wouldn't hit me. He'd use women, manipulate them to get what he wanted, but he wouldn't touch me.

At that very moment, I couldn't decide which was worse.

"Why would you do this?" He couldn't make sense of it. "This was what you needed, Virginia . . . This evidence could have freed you."

I hardly recognized my voice when I replied, "I don't get my friend back, you don't get your war. That seems fair to me."

"A chance like this isn't going to come along again," he reminded me, disregarding my words, as if he still didn't believe them. "You wanted out, this was it. Now . . ."

"We're stuck together." I finished his sentence with my long-lingering fear. "As you said, I'm good at this. Someday, Chicago will make me a deal and I'll give them my terms, but you won't have a chance to fool some other poor woman into joining you. I might not have control over my life, but I can make certain I'm the last one of me. No other women will die for you, you sick fucking man."

He pulled his gun again, lifting it to my head, and I stared him down, unblinking. His resolve was spilling out of him through the violent shake of his hand.

"Go on," I taunted him. "Pull the trigger, Joe, but who will Chicago send to Mexico?"

His mouth opened, but no words came out.

"Relations with Mexico are important in order to keep the drugs moving in and out freely. At least, that's what Guzik pitched me over the phone a few minutes ago when I told him I was bored in New York."

"You already spoke to Guzik? Without speaking to me first?"

"I called him after Ben left. Mexico will be expecting me in a few weeks."

"We're supposed to be partners, Virginia."

"I work for Chicago now, Joe. You don't give me orders anymore."

He seethed, tossing his gun to the ground with a growl, and it thumped against the tile. "I don't understand," he said breathlessly. "You had everything you needed to escape and you burned it to spite me?" He then held my gaze steady, searching for something—some explanation to sort it all out.

In a rush, I played through the moments leading up to this, the brief longing for the small life Georgie had built here, a baby growing in my stomach. Then, the orders I'd given Ben, watching him drag Mack out to the barn. The money I'd given my family to start fresh, and the relief in their eyes, knowing they wouldn't have to fear being hungry. Train rides through glittering cities, lavish dinners, my name meaning something.

"Good people can be made to do bad things, but that doesn't make them ruined or wrong." Ben's words settled on my tongue, and my eyes lowered. I didn't want to be Georgie's wife again, or Mack Hill's daughter. I wanted to be Virginia Hill. "Who would I be without this, Joe? There's no job in the world that will give a woman this kind of power or money."

He blinked with surprise, then the cool contempt returned to his features. "You are good at what you do," he said curtly. With a deep sigh, his mouth settled into a flat line, and the tension in the room eased. "Shall we discuss Mexico in more detail?"

Part II

Chapter Twenty

MEXICO, 1939

"Any messages?" I inquired, peeling my hat off my head and using it to fan myself. The hotel clerk, a slightly disheveled man, scurried about behind the counter, searching through a pile of papers until his eyes lit up with recognition. I studied the intricate mosaic patterns and murals on the wall behind him. I'd been in and out of Mexico for five years, but I still found ways to get lost in it.

He retrieved a large envelope with my name elegantly written across it. "*Sí, señora*," he replied with a nod, extending the envelope toward me. "This arrived for you earlier today."

I took the envelope from him with slight unease. "Who sent it?"

"There was no note."

With a nod of thanks, I stepped aside, finding a spot in the lobby to sit. I sank into a plush armchair near one of the arched walkways, where the scent of tobacco tickled my nose. I waited, crossing my legs and holding the envelope in my lap tenderly. I closed my eyes to concentrate on the soft music emanating from a live band tucked away in a corner of the lobby. The sounds of romantic boleros and lively mariachi tunes blended, and the hint of anxiety making my hands shake faded.

I knew this day would come; it was just business, after all.

I pulled my shoulders back and peeled the envelope open, retrieving the papers inside. I'd seen them before with Georgie and knew what to expect and where to sign. Back then, I'd been eager to pen my name on the line and free myself from him, but today, I felt only a sense of dread.

The Mob had arranged my marriage, and if they wanted the divorce finalized this quickly, my time in Mexico was done.

With the papers were round-trip train tickets to Los Angeles for the next morning. I quickly tucked the papers back into the envelope just as I heard my name across the lobby.

"Carlos," I whispered under my breath, even though he was too distant to hear it.

He entered the lobby, carrying a travel case. His spare hand casually swept through his thick jet-black hair, and his sun-kissed skin radiated a healthy glow. With his strong jawline, deep-brown eyes, and enviable sense of style, I couldn't deny that I had lucked out with my arranged marriage.

He pulled off his wide-brimmed hat and took me by the hands to pull me into him. He smelled of sweat and fruit.

"Carlos. You had a break?"

"I needed a break," he admitted. "The tour is exhausting."

"It's a rumba tour," I reminded him. "You're allowed to be exhausted."

"Let's have dinner. I want to take you out. Do you have any meetings?" He ran a hand down my face, and though I liked to believe I hadn't gotten too close, I sank into him.

Shaking my head, I mustered the courage to share the news I had been dreading. We had worked together to establish the drug trade in Mexico, forming connections with influential individuals and expanding the Outfit's presence in the region. We had accomplished what was asked of us, no matter the sacrifices we had to make. I couldn't possibly accept it was over. But, of course, it was.

"Something has happened," I revealed, wondering if I should wait until after dinner. The matter wasn't urgent enough to warrant immediate attention from Chicago. They had entrusted me to handle it at my own pace.

He looked at me with concern as I handed him the envelope, and he glanced inside without removing the papers. Anger colored his complexion.

"They said three years," he reminded me. "That was the deal, a three-year marriage to complete our work here."

"We did it in two," I said, and though it was nothing to be proud of, my moral code had long since blurred. Chicago wanted Mexico's vast access to opium, and through years of climbing high society and bribing law enforcement, we'd given it to them.

We both knew the marriage had a clock. After Congress passed the Marijuana Tax Act, criminalizing and restricting marijuana, it became more difficult to move drugs effectively. Chicago knew that the authorities would be keeping a more watchful eye and that my life here alone could not continue. I needed a husband, a life, a cover. But also someone who wouldn't covet my position. Carlos used his connections to help me establish myself here, and in return, he was granted freedom outside his country.

The arrangement was simple enough, and yet it pained us both to see it end. He was my friend, my life over the last few years, and the thought of saying goodbye to him for good left me with a hole in my chest.

"When do you leave?"

"Joe sent tickets to Los Angeles for tomorrow."

"Tomorrow? Why Los Angeles?"

I shrugged. "He didn't say, but they're round trip. I'll be back in a few days."

"Let's not think about it," he said, combing his fingers through my hair. "Let's celebrate like we always do, go dancing, make love, watch the sunset."

I nodded gently.

I awoke in a flush, peeling Carlos off me to scurry out of bed and look at the papers on the handwoven rug. We had dined at our favorite spot, danced until my feet throbbed, and made love for the first time in months, perhaps the last. I picked up the papers and held them tightly, consumed by an awful feeling I couldn't ignore. What if once I signed the papers, they disposed of Carlos?

I liked to believe they wouldn't, but he knew too much. He was my insider, my friend, my partner in crime. But if he was no longer useful, what good was he to Chicago?

I gazed around our apartment. I sank into the worn leather armchair near the window, glancing at the paintings on the walls from local artists we'd collected over the years. From the ornate wooden chairs to the carved coffee table adorned with Indigenous motifs, every piece told a story of our time together in Mexico.

I heard the blankets shuffle, and two feet landed on the Talavera tiles. With only the gas lamps casting their gentle light through the window, he appeared as if from a dream. I'd miss the strength of his arms, the faint smell of the clubs lingering on his skin, the way he knew every inch of my body because he was so very careful with his own. But above all, I would miss the solace of knowing that despite the dark deeds we had done for the Outfit, he'd proven to me that marriage wasn't the enemy.

I'd just picked the wrong man.

I made a silent vow to protect him, and the only way I knew how to do it was to make him run.

"Let me into your head, *mi amor*," he whispered, lowering himself to his knees to meet me at eye level, gently placing his hands in my lap.

"I have this feeling that they might . . ." I struggled to get it out. "That they might kill you."

The words left him guarded, tense. "Why would they do that?"

"If the marriage is over, if Mexico is over, what can you do for them?"

"Maintain things," he reasoned, though I could sense he had no idea what that meant. He had many talents, but I wouldn't trust him to negotiate with criminal figureheads or make deals that made his stomach roll. He was too soft for this business, and if I knew it, so did Chicago.

"I don't want that for you," I said evenly. "What kind of life did you want before me?"

"I just wanted to dance." He shrugged humbly. "My family wanted me to follow their path, to serve God devotedly, marry a good woman, and stay in one place."

"Imagine their disappointment."

"We could stay married," he offered. "Refuse to sign the papers? I'll follow you to wherever they send you next. We make a good pair. They see that, don't they?"

I smiled in response, not wanting him to know how wrong he was. If they'd served me the divorce papers, a husband wasn't required for the next job.

"You can't come with me," I told him as firmly as I could manage. "You can't come with me because I care about you, and if they know it, they'll use it against me. You make me weak, and I can't be weak."

He seemed to grasp it, and yet defiance lingered in his eyes. I reached for his face, pressing my forehead tenderly against his.

"I have some cash for you, enough to set you up nicely. I want you to sign the papers and leave while I'm gone. I'll tell them that you ran off with your mistress."

"You want me to run?"

I gave him a resounding nod. "You're not to call me, write me, nothing. We are dead to one another."

He rose to his feet and shook his head in disagreement. "You're telling me I have no say in this? You want me to pretend the last few years didn't happen?"

"That's what I'm saying, Carlos."

"I'm not signing them." His eyes held a sense of darkness I hadn't seen before, and I began to wonder if he'd find a way to disappoint me like all the others. "I sign those papers, and they'll sell you to the next man, or the next, or worse, forbid you from marrying again because your body is valuable to them."

I glanced out the window. "I like to think my mind is important too."

"I am not laughing, Virginia."

I gathered my thoughts for a brief moment because if I were to look into his soft eyes, he'd be able to see the lie in the words I collected inside my head. I had to bury every tendril of emotion and hurt him badly. Otherwise, he'd hang on, desperate for some ending where we wound up together forever, nestled in a sleepy town in Mexico with nothing but love between us. I had imagined it before, hoped this endeavor would last longer. That after our years were up, they would ask me to stay and maintain the operation. But they had only wanted me to establish their presence here, to set down roots. They would never trust a woman to lead the operation long term. I was once essential, and now, they wanted me gone.

I stood from the chair and pulled back my shoulders. "I needed someone in Mexico with the connections to get me started. You worked all the clubs, and you made all the introductions. I needed you then."

"But you don't need me now," he concluded, and I noted the small tremble in his lower lip. I was breaking his heart, and I knew I had to break it further.

"We are not friends, or lovers, or husband and wife. We built a life out of necessity. It was all business, Carlos. You were paid, given a tour, and our marriage allowed you to freely travel, but now it's over."

He didn't believe me; it was evident in the furrowing of his eyebrows and the annoyed gaze he leveled at me. He knew me well enough to see through my facade, but I persisted. "If you don't sign, they'll make you."

He walked to the front of the bed, where we had carelessly thrown the papers while undressing. Retrieving them, he crumpled them up and defiantly tossed them to the ground in front of me. "I'm not signing."

We fought for the rest of the night, and I indulged him while he played out various scenarios in his mind, desperately seeking a solution that would allow us to stay together. Each one had the same outcome—we weren't forced to separate, to be without one another, but I had already made my decision.

I'd spent two long years getting to know him, caring for him. If the only way to protect him was to stay away, nothing he said was going to change my mind.

After Carlos was long asleep, I slipped off to a bar a few blocks away. It was around three in the morning, but the bar still had a man outside the door observing anyone who ventured too close. It was a small joint, private, with a select guest list. The man at the entrance gave me a nod and opened the heavy wooden doors. Inside, the smell of spice and tequila filled my nostrils, and though there was a single guitarist playing, none of the patrons were dancing. They sat at round tables, scattered about, discussing business over candlelit tables, the flames casting lively shadows of *papel picado* strung along the ceiling.

The barkeep smiled warmly and started to mix up my favorite rum cocktail. He gestured his head to a door near the bar. I slipped through it, down a smaller hallway, into a room at the back. It held one round table, made by hand, etched with a triangle pattern. Some days, there were three to four chairs; tonight, just two.

My guest, Luis, sat with his eyes closed, drumming his fingers to the music. He inhaled the air when I walked into the room. "Little Red," he said in a low voice, eyes opening to greet me. He ran his fingers along his trimmed mustache and then through his tousled short hair. "This meeting was spontaneous. Are you safe?"

I eased down across from him, and not a moment later, the barkeep brought me my drink before slipping out of the room like a shadow. "Maybe I just missed you," I teased, and he grinned, a sense of relief washing over his features.

"Are you finally going to leave that dancer?"

"He's been useful to us," I defended. "We wouldn't have half the reach we have without his connections."

"I'm aware he *was* useful," he said. "He's no longer useful, though, is he?"

I took a drink, deciding to change the topic rather quickly. I pulled the clutch from my hip and placed it on the tabletop. "The divorce papers came this morning. I suspect I'll be done in Mexico soon."

His breath hitched, and the charismatic smile left his face. "When?"

"I'm not sure. I'm headed to Los Angeles tomorrow. They'll tell me more. But I wanted to let you know, and make sure our arrangement is—"

"I started this operation with you," he said, cutting me off. "I have no intention of letting it fail."

I'd come here to create a drug trade, establish a connection between Chicago and Mexican high society; I'd done one better. Luis was chief of the narcotics police, and I had him in my pocket. Money bought him, but our partnership kept him loyal. I had doubts, a lingering uncertainty, that the moment he was forced to do business with someone else, his dedication would slip.

I stared at his face, long with disappointment. "Luis."

He didn't give me his eyes.

I squared my shoulders and stood, moving around the table in slow anticipation. I reached out for his face, and he shuddered against my touch, eyes closed. I dragged my nails through his hair, down the skin of his cheek. "You're going to be good, aren't you? I can trust you, can't I?"

He leaned into my hand and reached up, fingers clutching my wrist, holding my fingers against his face. "I'll be good, but I'll expect a payment for inconvenience."

I grinned and tilted my head, gesturing to my clutch. He reached across the table and opened the bag, skimming through the cash. Usually, his face would light up at the money, but his lips turned down. He reached for my hand again and brought it to his face. "Stay with me tonight?"

"Carlos is home," I said, then took him by the chin. I moved down to kiss him, and his mouth tried to devour mine, as if he were tasting me for the last time—and he was. "But I'm here now," I whispered against his mouth, and he sucked in a fast breath. He stood, took me by the hips, and moved me across the room to the nearest wall. The aggression had startled me at first, and every tryst with him left me on edge, uncertain if he'd leave behind marks I couldn't hide from Carlos, but I'd come to understand him over the years. He'd never hurt me, knowing the consequences that would follow, but he loathed my control over him, how my body seemed to make him do things he didn't want. He felt pleasure in punishing me for it.

He took me against the wall, hand on my neck. When it was over, my legs were shaking against his hips, and he looked amused that I couldn't quite catch my breath. I scrambled for my clutch and pulled out a round compact mirror to check my neck; no bruising, but the flesh was red. He bent his head low against my collarbone and trailed kisses, covering the red with a diamond necklace. "Do you like it, Little Red?"

I thought about stabbing him as a farewell gift, and the image brought a smile to my face. Chicago would rage—he was too important. Appeasing him was essential; I knew it. That didn't stop my mind from wandering. I touched the diamonds with my fingertips, then turned my head to look him in the eyes. "It's lovely. Thank you."

I arrived at the train station with little time to spare. Carlos and I raced through the hazy veil of steam pillowing along the platform, traveling cases in hand, and reached the attendant just as he was preparing the last passengers to board. My eyes felt sunken, the lack of sleep leaving me dizzy. I breathed myself calm while Carlos handed off my luggage and reached out to kiss me.

I met his lips with as much enthusiasm as I could manage. "You'll do what I told you? Go home to your family for a few days?"

"Yes," he said. "But I'll be here to pick you up when you return." He pushed some hair behind my ear. "I'll sign the papers then."

I rolled my eyes, exhausted with his stubbornness, but too tired to fight him. When I finally settled into the plush velvet seat of the first-class carriage and the train rocked into motion, I watched him fade in the distance—his image blurring into the Mexican landscape.

My eyes grew heavy, and I wanted to sleep all the way to Los Angeles. I eased into it, allowing the train to rock me, until I heard someone clearing their throat in front of me. I opened my eyes, expecting a train attendant with a drink menu.

"Virginia Hill?"

My full name startled me awake. I sat up in my seat and took in his appearance.

Dark, expressive eyes and olive-toned skin. Glossy brown hair, a defined jaw, and a small scar near the right side of his mouth. He wore a black tweed suit and held a fedora in one hand, pressed up against his chest.

He took a seat in front of me.

"That seat is taken," I told him, searching for an attendant. The carriage was rather empty, with only a few passengers lounging about. My stomach lurched.

"I won't waste much of your time, Miss Hill. I'll be getting off at the next stop." He crossed one leg over the other and observed me closely.

"Have I met you before, stranger?" I asked, politely but on edge. He didn't seem tender or welcoming, and the urge to run gnawed at my insides.

"I know all about you," he said simply. "What you've been doing here, bringing in all that dirty business from America to stain my country. The drug trade you created will kill thousands, rip apart families. How do you sleep at night?"

My throat locked up, and I couldn't pull any words out, just stared at him with the same frightening intensity he did me.

"I've been following you since you first arrived. My superiors weren't worried about you then, but when you started clawing your way up Mexican high society, sinking your teeth into powerful men and women . . . I knew you were a viper. Something we needed to get rid of."

"I think you have me confused with someone else."

"You're on a list now, Virginia," he uttered, voice gravelly. "Maybe I can't touch you here because your American friends paid off the right people in my government, but back home, they're watching too. You think you've gone unnoticed, but you haven't."

In all the years of doing this, I hadn't considered that I'd be put on a watch list. That the government would start tracking me, hunting me. I'd always thought myself untouchable, too clever to be caught—too much of a silly little woman to be taken seriously by law enforcement. I had paid off all the right people, had Luis stalking my every move to ensure nobody suspected a thing. "You have me confused with someone else," I said again, stronger now. "I'm a tourist. I don't know nothin' about any drugs."

"You're going to pay for the lives you've ruined. Do you know how many lives? Have you kept track?" His eyes hardened. "Because I have."

"It must be so difficult for you to spend four long years on a case and have nothing to show for it," I said evenly, desperate to control the emotion bubbling up inside me. I tried to stare with no expression at all—to feel nothing. It was how I'd gotten through my years of work here. I treated my body as if it didn't belong to me. Not mine to control or use. The decisions I made with it were handed down to me, so the consequences weren't mine to carry.

He challenged me with a somber expression. "A difficulty we've shared, I think. I've watched you drink yourself to sleep every night for years." He looked up and shook his head. "You hate yourself, and that is a greater punishment than any man can execute—it is divine."

I felt still, paralyzed, unable to retort or move. His words wounded me, burrowed inside me and nestled there. He pulled something from a brown satchel beside him, a book. A Bible. He placed it beside me.

I opened my mouth, my eyes watering. *Say something, Virginia.*

"We've launched an investigation into Luis." He stood, placed his hat on top of his head and tipped his head a bit. "I think it would be best if you stayed in Los Angeles."

And as quickly as he'd arrived, he was gone.

Everything around me began to blur and spin, and even when I tried to level my breathing, center on a steady rhythm, it just grew more erratic. I couldn't begin to explain what was happening to me, but the terror of it was overwhelming. Consuming.

I sank to the floor, placed both palms down and flat. The hum of the train shook my fingers, a rumble that didn't grow in strength or change. "Breathe," I told myself, "just breathe."

I could hear the attendant in the background, reaching out for me, a string of pleas. When I finally felt my heartbeat sync with the train, I looked up at the attendant and forced myself to smile through the panic. "I'm swell, but I could use a drink."

Chapter Twenty-One

I stepped off the train, keeping Joey Ep's orders in mind—to meet at Chasen's. Los Angeles breathed new life into me, its sun-drenched, bustling streets a stark contrast to my quaint and comfortable Mexican home. Mexico was a tapestry of history—easy to navigate, rich in culture, but at times, dull.

Here, the influence of Hollywood was everywhere I turned, from the skyline of buildings down to the street signs. Initially, I contemplated heading straight to the restaurant, but the allure of the palm trees and the scent of orange blossoms diverted my path.

I'd spent the train ride considering the man, his threats, the Bible he left beside me to haunt me. I was raised in church but was never close to God. I felt too much like his castoff, another little girl he didn't have time for in a world of little girls. Since Madeline, and the deal I made with Joey Ep, he seemed even farther away. Was there truth in the man's words? Was I being watched? On some list with the brutal men I did business with? I had taken Mexico by storm, but at what cost?

I'd thought so long and hard about that, my head was pounding.

I needed a distraction, and Los Angeles felt like just the right medicine. I indulged in some shopping, opting for small boutiques that offered unique fabrics and designs instead of the larger department stores.

Each store held a treasure trove of fashion possibilities, tempting me with their curated collections. I spent money, big money, until I couldn't carry all the shopping bags, forcing me to check into my hotel early.

Approaching the front desk, a friendly concierge greeted me with a warm smile. I gave him my reservation details, and he swiftly began my check-in process.

"Welcome to Los Angeles," I heard someone say behind me, a voice I'd recognize anywhere.

I turned around to face Adonis, his charcoal-gray suit impeccably tailored, his hair slicked back, and his lips curling into that familiar twisted smile. It had been years since I last laid eyes on him, and yet, the deep-seated loathing I held for him remained. Memories flooded my mind, images of his hands tangled in my hair, of my knees sinking into the plush carpet of a hotel room. The scent of his skin, the way he nibbled at my neck. The disapproving click of his tongue echoing in my ears and the haunting image of Madeline's New York apartment. Gunshots. Smoke. New York's intimidating views. Ben between my legs.

But mostly, I saw *her*, the woman I killed in cold blood just for him.

"Adonis." His name came out a hiss. I hadn't the faintest idea why he was in Los Angeles, and I didn't want to know. I retrieved my room key and walked past him.

He blocked my way, hands up in the air in front of me. "I'm here for the same reason you are," he insisted. "Business. Turns out Joey Ep and I have a common enemy."

"Unlikely," I said. "He'd rather shoot himself dead than be stuck in the same room with you. I don't blame him."

My bold response seemed to catch him off guard. "I thought you would miss me," he taunted, a self-assured grin spreading across his face. "We had quite the time in New York, didn't we?"

"I had a great time in New York," I lied with a bright, endearing smile. "Best fuck of my life."

His grin widened, his teeth gleaming. "I knew there was something special between us," he boasted, his hand reaching out to brush a loose tendril of my hair. In an instant, I seized his wrist, my grip firm. I wanted to break his hand, but instead, I gently kissed his knuckles and lifted my eyebrows.

"I could use a little stress relief, want to come to my room?"

I stared at his naked body on the plush bed of white, hands tied to the bedposts in secure knots. He moved his arms around, but with little panic. He tested the strength of the scarves I'd used before his mouth inched back into a smile.

"Tight enough?" I asked.

"Tighter," he said with a sigh of pleasure.

I continued roping the knots.

"You're different," he noted, somewhat breathless. "I like what Mexico did to you."

I tightened the knot even harder, and he grunted in response. "Am I enough like Madeline for you?" I asked, losing the playful disposition I'd used to lure him up to the room.

His eyes narrowed, and I watched him visibly swallow. I had not once spoken her name in all the time we'd spent together in New York.

"You knew Madeline?"

"I loved Madeline," I countered. "She was easy to love, wasn't she? It's too bad she's dead."

"Virginia," he said quickly, nearly stuttering. "I don't know what Joey Ep told you—"

"Shut up," I said.

He began to thrash, and though I couldn't hear his heart racing, I could see it. Every nerve in his body was on alert. "What is this? Untie me. I'm supposed to escort you to the meeting with Dragna. Something happens to me . . ."

Dragna. The name rang a bell in my memory. The Capone of Los Angeles. Why would Joe arrange a meeting with Dragna and Adonis?

The confusion weighed on me as I tried to piece together what any of this had to do with me. "What is this meeting about?" I asked.

"Dragna wants your help with something."

"With what?"

"I don't know, Virginia, I wasn't privy to the information. He asked me to make sure you arrived safely." He looked up at his hands and clenched his fists. "Are you going to fuck me? If not, untie me."

I inched forward, sitting on the edge of the bed to give his cheek a slap. He thrashed again, this time trying to buck himself off the bed. "I was raised on a farm," I said. "You're not getting out of those knots until I untie them."

"This isn't a fucking game. Let me go!"

I leaned in, my voice laced with cool determination. "I never said it was a game."

"Just wait," he threatened. "I'm going to hurt you for this. You know what I'm capable of, what I mean to this organization. I say the word, and you're done, Hill."

"Four years ago, I would have believed you," I said, with little emotion. "But then I established a working relationship with Mexico. I did what the men of this organization could not. I am not expendable, but you, another Italian mobster with an itchy trigger finger and nice hair? A dime a dozen. There are a hundred like you . . ." I reached down and took hold of his chin, making sure our eyes met. "But only one of me."

His crude expression and tense face softened. I could see the flicker of vulnerability, the loss of the bravado he survived on. "You didn't like me, but you liked being in bed with me. Best fuck of your life, remember?"

"I wasn't talking about you," I clarified, my voice dripping with contempt. I moved to the bathroom, finding a white washcloth with the neatly folded towels. I returned to him and stuffed it into his mouth, muffling any further protests. Leaning down, I whispered into his ear, my words taunting and soft, "You're not the only man I fucked in New York."

I didn't bother changing for the meeting but touched up my hair before leaving the room. Back at the front desk, I asked for privacy, instructing the concierge that we wouldn't need cleaning for the next few days.

"Three days?" he asked, with a hint of confusion. "Are you certain?"

"Let's make it four," I said with a smile. "We haven't seen each other in a long time. We have so much catching up to do."

He caught on quickly and cleared his throat. "Of course."

I arrived at Chasen's to find Joe and Jack Dragna seated in a leather booth near the back of the restaurant. The wood paneling behind them cast a shadow over the entire corner, creating a darker atmosphere around them. They stood out, and judging from the looks of the nearby patrons, they didn't mind it.

As I made my way through the crowd, I couldn't help but notice the walls adorned with photographs of celebrities who had dined at the restaurant. A glimpse of Katharine Hepburn's image caught my eye, triggering thoughts of Madeline. The pain of her loss briefly touched my chest, but I closed my eyes and pushed the emotions aside. In Mexico, her memory felt distant, but here, where she thought all her dreams would come true, she felt so close. If "April in Paris" were to start playing, I'd know she was haunting me.

Joe stood up and greeted me with a kiss on the cheek before pulling out a chair. He had already ordered a cocktail for me.

I observed Jack Dragna. He commanded the room, exuding a sense of authority and confidence. He sat with impeccable posture, his shoulders squared, and his head held high. His piercing eyes locked onto me, studying my every move, while he maintained a polite smile on his face. I looked down at the steak in front of him, cut in neat lines, almost identical to Joe's plate.

I was dealing with similar men, and that gave me a sense of ease.

Joe cleared his throat, searching behind me as if looking for someone.

"Adonis is preoccupied," I told him.

He gave me a hard stare. "What did you do, Virginia?"

I took a sip of my martini. "He's tied up in my hotel room."

"Tied up? He knows the importance of this meeting. Shall I ring the hotel?"

"He's tied to the bed, Joey Ep. I doubt he can answer the phone."

Dragna let out a booming laugh. "You are an enigma, Miss Hill."

"Virginia," I said. "Now, what is this meeting about? Adonis mentioned we all have a common enemy. What does that mean, and what does any of it have to do with me?"

Joe looked down with distaste. "Do you have the divorce papers?"

I pulled them out from my clutch and unfolded them, flattening out the lines, waiting for the look of confusion to settle in. "He didn't sign them?"

"He said he wasn't going to."

"We can make him," said Joe, folding the papers back up in a flushed rush.

"We're not going to hurt him," I said, a declaration I wanted known. "If you hurt him, I will become very unpleasant, Joe. He's stubborn, but not a risk. Give him time, and he'll sign. The marriage isn't going to change the way I do business."

"It's important for you to be divorced for our business here. We need to leave Mexico behind," said Dragna, finally adding to the conversation with a revelation I never saw coming. What use was I in LA? What could I possibly do for Dragna, who knew very little of me? I quickly decided that I didn't want to engage in small talk. I just wanted the truth, and I wanted it fast.

"My business in Mexico isn't over," I said in a rush, then looked to Joe. "You bought me a round-trip ticket."

"Things have changed," he said evenly. "You're staying in LA."

An image of Carlos waiting at the train station with a bouquet of flowers in his hand made my stomach roll. "What am I doing here?" The words came out louder than intended, but both men looked at each other with a nod of approval.

Dragna proceeded to share his history, recounting his ascent in the Los Angeles crime family and his close business ties to New York. He painted a picture of a man who started with nothing but achieved everything, conveniently omitting the key methods he used. Extortion. Bootlegging. Narcotics. Gambling. Like all the men before him, Dragna viewed me as simpleminded and uneducated. Good for one thing. However, I recalled every conversation about Dragna, every newspaper article that had been published.

As Dragna's narrative continued, I listened attentively, piecing together the fragments of his criminal empire, still unable to figure out what he could possibly want from me. "I don't want a history lesson," I cut him off quickly, and I could have sworn I heard Joe gasp.

"I want to know why I'm here." I looked Dragna in the eyes.

Dragna cleared his throat, visibly taken aback by the abrupt shift in conversation, yet maintaining a veneer of politeness. "I am interested in purchasing your contract with Chicago," he revealed. "I'd like you to move to Los Angeles and work for me."

"I wasn't aware I had a contract," I said. "I assumed the promise of death was all the contract Chicago needed to get what they wanted."

"Virginia," Joe interjected.

"Joe," I responded firmly.

"Everyone has a contract, even Joey Ep over here."

I looked at Joe with surprise—another secret he'd withheld from me.

"Why do you want my contract?" I asked, trying to fathom Dragna's ulterior motives.

"If you are willing to do business with me, I am prepared to purchase your contract and transfer its ownership to you," Dragna proposed. Sensing my hesitation, he was quick to add, "You would have complete control over it, Virginia."

"You'd be done," Joe finally chimed in, his tone resolute yet hopeful.

"You want me to be done?" I asked tautly. Joe wouldn't be offering me a way out without reason, certainly not after Mexico.

"Anslinger," he said, voice low. "Commissioner of the FBN. He's launched an investigation into several of our own, and his hunt has leaked into Mexico. He's desperate to tie everything together, and I fear your name might be somewhere in this mess."

The man on the train had been telling the truth. "You're . . ." My throat locked. "You're certain?"

"We need to get you far away from their investigation," he advised. "No more traveling, no more Mexico."

I felt the rage inside me growing, a subtle pounding against my skull. "All the work I did in Mexico to keep myself safe, to protect Chicago's investments, and you bums couldn't manage to keep my name off a list?"

Joe cleared his throat in response. "We're working on plugging the leak. In the meantime, you can move here, have a little fun, finish this business with Dragna, and then you're—"

"Done?" I said the word again because I couldn't quite believe it, or imagine it. Back in Marietta, I hadn't wanted the simple little life I'd been on the run from since that first bus to Chicago. Now, five years and countless sleepless nights later, the regret of that choice often plagued me. I knew then that money and power were going to give me a better life, give my family security, and I knew the cost was myself.

I'd have to give up everything that made me good and live with the guilt.

Now the choice was in front of me again: I could do anything, be anyone. Find myself all over again. My heartbeat thrummed, but I didn't let the thought consume me. I still didn't know what Dragna wanted.

"What do you want me to do?" I asked them both.

Dragna unfolded a copy of the *Los Angeles Times*, and the front page displayed the disturbing news of the German troops' invasion of Poland. He turned to a smaller article that caught his attention, titled "Hollywood Gunman," and there, in black and white, was Ben Siegel's name. My heart fluttered involuntarily, the mix of emotions leaving me tense. I remembered my last encounter with Ben, when he confessed to taking Madeline from me. The pain of that betrayal clashed with memories of our bodies tangled up on a creaking wooden floor.

I'd kept tabs on him, heard the rumors of his progress in Los Angeles—establishing the West Coast rackets, his close involvement with the wire services, and his goals for a gambling enterprise—but I wasn't going to tell them that. "What's your problem with Siegel?"

"Siegel is encroaching on my territory, seizing what is important to me and making a spectacle of it," Dragna stated, his tone brash and determined. "He never does anything quietly, and while he may be effective, he is a loose cannon. Unpredictable and uncontrollable. This forced partnership I have with him will inevitably end with one of us dead. Preferably him."

I knew he could see it on my face, evidence of my weakness for the Bug, but I played the fool. "How do you think I can help you? I have no love for the man."

Dragna glanced at Joey Ep, their silent exchange conveying information with a mere nod. "I've been told that you and Siegel have a history. I even have a source that says he visited Mexico several times over the last few years."

It was news to me—I hadn't heard a word from Ben since Marietta. I felt a flutter in my stomach. I'd longed for him on more occasions than I cared to admit—imagined him in place of Luis and Carlos. I shuddered away the thought. "I never saw him in Mexico. Perhaps your sources are wrong."

"My sources are never wrong," said Dragna.

I blinked, understanding the conclusions but unwilling to admit them out loud. When I said nothing, Dragna continued, "I need to find a weakness in him, something I can exploit to bring him down. At present, he's untouchable, enjoying the favor of Lansky. You help me with this, and your contract is yours, along with a nice payout."

A wave of nausea washed over me, prompting me to down my drink in one swift gulp. Without uttering a word, I left the restaurant, the sound of Joe's footsteps trailing close behind as we emerged onto the street. "You think I don't see that it's also an opportunity for you? You want Ben dead."

"This is just business," he said evenly. "Ben's death is advantageous to you."

"How much did Dragna pay for my contract? How much did he pay Chicago for me?" I huffed at the thought, my face heating. "After everything I've done for you, for them, I'm still just a number to be sold to the highest fucking bidder?"

"That's not true."

"I can say no, then?"

"I wouldn't recommend it. You need to stop traveling, settle somewhere. This is a good deal. You can start over here, have some fun with Siegel in Hollywood. Maybe audition for some movies." His mouth quirked up at the thought. "You'll have endless resources at your disposal, and then when it's over, a payout large enough to set you up anywhere you want. All you have to do is—"

"Send a man to his death," I uttered.

"Kill a killer," he corrected me, his tone a bit too strong.

A passing couple cast a puzzled glance in our direction. I found a bench across the street from a lively theater and took a seat, placing a hand on my chest. Joe settled beside me, maintaining a comfortable distance between us. "I've arranged for Vel to come stay with you and help you like she did in Chicago."

I hadn't even given him my answer, and he was already making plans. I groaned inwardly but remained silent, my gaze fixed on the theater marquee showcasing the latest films. The vibrant colors and titles painted a picture of a world so different from the one I'd come to know in Mexico. I knew I could be comfortable here, regardless of the goals Dragna had for me. Los Angeles reminded me of Chicago, not as busy, but promising.

After a prolonged silence, I disrupted the stillness by cautiously vocalizing my fear—the only one that mattered.

"I don't know if I can do it," I admitted. I liked to believe I didn't have a soft spot for Ben, but my chest ached at the idea of bringing him down.

"You care for him," he said like he'd always known.

"He could see through this all."

"That's not the woman I mentored," he countered brashly. "You do not let anyone see the real you."

"I don't even know who the real me is anymore, Joe. I think we're long past your manipulation tactics of big words."

He looked away in thought. "It wasn't always manipulation. You have done nothing but impress since the day you pulled that gun on me. I made a mistake with you, I know that." The words were icy and calculated as usual, but I sensed truth in them.

"I also know you've found comfort in the idea that I killed Madeline, and while I did send her to New York, unprepared and alone, I wasn't the one with my hands around her throat. I wasn't the one who took her life."

I shuddered at the grotesque and unsettling images. I had spent years in Mexico distracted and busy, and now I had to face it. The god-awful truth that Benjamin Siegel had killed Madeline. My Ben, my stranger, and in some twist of fate I could never have predicted, bringing him down was my only hope of escape.

I searched for something, anything to stall my answer. "Do you ever think about your soul?"

His eyebrows lifted. "My soul?"

"There was a man on the train . . . He told me I was being watched. That he couldn't bring me down in Mexico, but he made certain my name was with the right people here. Then he gave me a Bible."

Joe folded one leg over the other, giving it some thought. "I thought you seemed on edge when you arrived. All this self-loathing because a man with a badge said you were a bad girl?"

I flinched at his cold tone. "Someday we're going to have to answer for our crimes."

"What crimes?" He let out a short laugh. "Show me proof you've done anything but sleep with men you fancy and spend money you're given? There's no proof. Do you want to know why?" He leaned in closer to me. “Because I am good at what I do. Perhaps you’ve hated me much of our career together, but I have protected you.”

“You can’t protect me in hell,” I shouted involuntarily, deeply considering the Bible—the man’s words. My soul.

“Who’s to say?” his voice snapped back. “We’ll be there together.”

My mouth went agape. I was somewhere between tears and laughter, a strange balance of emotions.

“Honestly, you couldn’t have picked a worse time to have a religious epiphany.”

“I can’t stand you, Joe,” I said, teary and repressing a smile. “You couldn’t just sit here and make me feel like a whole person again, could you? Stroke my hair and tell me everything will get better?”

“It will get better,” he said, with stiff awkwardness. “There, there. Now, are you ready to finish the job?”

Ben was a job that started at a racetrack in Chicago and should have ended in Marietta. My memory of him was sharp, unforgiving. A collision of lust and lies, all heaped together in my chest. I could still feel the sting years later.

“What about Carlos?”

“I’ll have some friends pay him a visit, make him sign.” I opened my mouth to protest, but he was quick to stop me. “They will persuade him without violence.”

I tried not to imagine all the things they’d use against him to get him to comply. I buried the thought because he was just another man to add to my collection of broken people I longed to save. I wasn’t certain of anything, but it had taken Joe years to find me this offer. This chance. What if I never got another one?

I didn’t know how or even where to begin, but somehow, I was going to bring down Ben and be free of the Mob forever.

Chapter Twenty-Two

I settled in at the Ambassador Hotel, and for the first time in four years, I saw her again. Madeline. There she was, strolling about the grand lobby, heels clicking against the marble floor, blending in so beautifully with the Hollywood glamour around her. She wore a red backless dress, and the light from the ornate chandeliers above bathed her flawless skin in a gentle, ethereal glow. Whispers of admiration rippled through the patrons near the reception desk as she passed by, her presence commanding attention. When she ascended the grand staircase, all eyes watched.

Somewhere between the swaying palm trees, manicured lawns, and lavish furnishings, I'd found her again. I followed her up the staircase at a distance, drifting quietly, unremarkable in comparison. Nobody looked my way or stepped aside to give me space to walk. For the first time since I joined the Outfit, I was just Virginia again.

To make matters worse, when I looked down, I was wearing my uniform from the San Carlo. Surely, this was a dream? I continued briskly until I lost her at the top of the staircase. The Ambassador Hotel blurred around me, a mushy block of colors, murals, and Hollywood memorabilia. Suddenly, the lights that made her skin glow burned my own. I raced now, moving to catch up with her just as she entered her room, giving me only a glimpse of her red gown sliding through the cracked door.

I swung it open, deciding that if this was a dream, I didn't want it to end so soon. But when the hotel door gave way, slamming against the coat closet behind it, I felt every nerve in my body tense.

She was on the bed, thrashing and clawing at his hands the same way I had fought Georgie the night Madeline saved my life. Even now, I could feel the pressure around my neck as if I were experiencing it all again.

She cried and screamed, and he hovered over her, squeezing tightly, jerking her body until she stopped fighting. Until she was gone. The room was still, eerily quiet, and I didn't make a sound, not even when Ben's eyes jerked my way.

"I told you," he said. "I don't want you to end up like the last girl."

I awoke to the sound of the phone beside me, a melodious tone that had my head pounding. Sitting up in bed, I glanced wearily at the tall windows, trying to gauge how long I had been unconscious. The late hour was evident, yet the distant strains of music drifting from the Cocoanut Grove reached my ears—soft jazz mingling, with the energetic tunes of a live band.

Taking hold of the receiver, I steadied myself. "It's late, Joe."

"I signed the papers," said Carlos.

I breathed myself awake. "Did they hurt you?"

"They wanted to," he replied, his tone cryptic. "But Joe told me that this was a smart opportunity for you, and that I would complicate it."

I couldn't judge how much he knew by his voice. "You were such a fun complication, though," I admitted, seeking refuge in the memories of our late-night dance lessons and his infectious laughter. I drowned out the images of Madeline and replaced them with him. Our first meeting to our very last, just days ago. I hadn't mourned him yet, and in a way, I didn't want to.

There was a good chance I couldn't recover long enough to pull this off.

"I am not laughing, Virginia," he said, the way he always did when I used humor to avoid feeling anything at all.

"I'm glad you called."

“I’ve called you, slept with you, danced with you, nearly every night for two years,” he expressed, his voice tinged with both longing and uncertainty. “It’s all I’ve known, and now I’m just supposed to do something else?”

I choked back what I wanted to say and said, “You’ll learn to love someone else, Carlos.”

“Maybe I’ll wait for you here in Mexico. You’ll see me when you come back?”

If I had it my way, Mexico, Chicago, all of it, would be long behind me after my time in Los Angeles, but for the sake of not breaking him any more than I already had, I said, “Of course. Get some rest, finish the tour, and go home to visit your family.”

“After our runaway marriage, I doubt they’ll see me.”

“If I’m out of the picture, you’re right with God again.”

I could have sworn I heard him grinning through the phone.

“Good night, Carlos.”

I didn’t recognize Vel when she met me at the Cocoanut Grove nightclub the following night. Her hair was cut, her eyes were sharp, and her skin glowed. Even the way she walked, with newfound confidence and grace, left my mouth agape. I didn’t even wave for her when I spotted her.

She took a moment to search before rushing over to me, tugging me off my chair at the bar to pull me into her embrace. I looked her over again. “Something is different about you?”

“Me? What about you?” Vel laughed heartily, her booming laughter filling the air. “How could you get married and not invite me? Even worse, I had to hear about the divorce from Joe.”

“It was a whirlwind romance,” I lied, and she eyed me seriously.

“I wrote you.”

“I know,” I admitted, a tinge of guilt coloring my words. “I read them, but Mexico kept me busy.”

"Did you read the last letter?"

"I didn't," I admitted. "I'm awful, forgive me."

She extended her hand, and it took me a moment to grasp why until I noticed the absence of a wedding ring. All that remained was a faint outline on her finger, a reminder of what had been. "I got divorced, and it was the best decision of my life," she declared, her eyes shining with a newfound sense of liberation. Again, I couldn't manage the words.

"Virginia! Say something."

"I'm proud of you," I finally said. "When did you decide to do it?" In all the time I'd known her, divorcing a Mob man had been a nightmarish thought. The fear kept her in line, but the unhappiness left her chasing her next drink to numb herself. Those memories remained etched in my mind as if they had happened yesterday.

"A year ago," she said happily. "It got messy, but I made it through. It was in the papers, so dealing with the press has been a real drag." A moment of silence passed between us, in which I motioned at the chair next to me and the bartender joined us. I waited for her to order a cocktail, but she surprised me further when she called out, "Club soda."

"You're not drinking?" My heart thundered in my chest.

"I'm still drinking," she said with a roll of her eyes. "Just less."

Then, before I could take a sip of my own cocktail, she reached for my hand and squeezed. "Thank you, Virginia."

"Don't you dare give me credit for the divorce, you did that all on your own. I remember how complicated the system is for women and the courts. I know it wasn't easy and you could have used me." I cursed myself for avoiding her letters, Chick's, and every reminder of the people I'd left behind.

"No," she corrected me. "Thank you for taking care of me then. I was hardly functioning most nights, and there's a good chance if you hadn't been there, I'd have drowned in my own vomit." She cringed at the thought.

I started to protest further, but she shushed me with a wave. "Now, how can I help you? Shall we have some fun like we did in Chicago? Host parties, tour the town, create enough chaos to get people talking?"

I smiled at the reminder of those memories, which, despite occurring only a handful of years ago, felt like a lifetime away. "This is different," I told her, unable to hide the uneasy edge in my voice. "The man Joe wants me to target, he already knows me. He's known me for years. He'll see through the charades."

"You're giving him more credit than he deserves. All men can be played. Maybe a challenge in comparison to others, but not impossible."

I finished my drink, and the bartender replaced it within a few minutes. I closed my eyes and drifted to the sounds of the live band, thinking briefly of Carlos and the sway of hips. He danced in my mind until the images grew violent, and I saw Ben hovering over Madeline on a plush white bed. Vel snapped her fingers.

"Virginia?"

"You're right," I declared. "There's a way to get to him, I just don't know how yet." But I did. Ben Siegel had only ever wanted one thing since the moment we met—me. If I surrendered to him, body and soul, I'd be able to bring him down. The only question, the only sense of doubt lingering inside me, was could I follow through?

"You're telling me I've come all this way and you don't need me?" Her mouth dipped into a frown.

"I do need you," I admitted softly. "In Chicago, I needed an accomplice. But here, I just need a friend. Could you stay for a while?"

The idea left her face pink with delight.

We spent the next few days together, shopping, exploring Los Angeles, and recounting all the men we'd collected and the experiences we longed to forget with them. It had been years since I'd done anything with a female friend, and I didn't want it to end. When the invitation came, a special delivery from Joe himself, I dreaded opening it.

"A party hosted by George Raft," he told me. "Siegel will be there."

Vel joined us at the breakfast table, snatching the invitation from my hands, and I felt a sense of relief wash over me. Suddenly, I could breathe again. "George Raft? The actor? You have to take me with you."

Joe eyed Vel and then me, a silent exchange of looks that said it all—he wasn't pleased to be entertaining her presence. "She's not going anywhere," I told him, and his jaw tensed.

"You'll go alone," he instructed, and Vel tossed the invite on the glass table. "Adonis will escort you, as we discussed."

I grinned at the reminder of where I'd left him. "You found him?"

"Some poor woman cleaning the room next door heard strange noises," he said, and though he wasn't smiling, his voice was lit with amusement. "Not one of your finest moments, Virginia."

I took a long sip of my juice. "I beg to differ."

Finally, a modest smile tugged at the corners of Joe's lips, but he quickly shook it off and pointed to the invitation. "This is your chance to see him again. Make it count."

"Why is some actor entertaining criminals?"

"He's not some actor," Vel urged. "Haven't you seen *Scarface*? *The Glass Key*?"

"Virginia has been busy," said Joe in my defense.

Vel sighed. "I'll remedy that. We'll get you back in touch with everything Hollywood so you can make real conversation. Imagine Raft finding out there's a guest at his party who hasn't seen one of his films."

"When is it?" I took hold of the invitation again.

"Two days."

I took a deep, steadying breath. I wasn't ready, and it showed. Joe reached across the table, his hand hovering uncertainly over mine. I didn't realize he was trying to offer me comfort until his fingers gently brushed against mine. "Good luck, Virginia."

He retracted his hand and stood, straightening his suit with a pull. The strange gesture didn't bring me any ease or confidence, but I did consider that maybe everything Joe had said, his admission of grave mistakes and his determination to make amends, was not merely another fabrication.

"It was Ben, wasn't it?" asked Adonis as we strolled toward the actor's home, my hand linked with his arm. The residence exuded the same glamour and charm that characterized all the houses and hotels in Los Angeles. Decorative moldings, wrought iron accents, and stucco adorned the exterior, capturing the city's signature style. Los Angeles had a distinct personality—everything was grand, big, and often too bright.

"That's why Dragna and Joey Ep wanted me in on the plan but wouldn't tell what you had to do with it." At this point, he was talking to himself. "You fucked Ben in New York, behind my back."

"We hadn't fucked yet," I countered with cold precision. "But he spent some time between my legs."

Adonis seethed, his grip on my wrist tightening as he shifted our linked arms. "You're a—"

"Whore?" I finished his sentence with a hiss. "That word means nothing to me anymore, Adonis. And frankly, I don't have the time or patience to deal with your little-boy antics. You want to take down Siegel? You need me." I pulled my arm away, adjusting it properly. I didn't want the Hollywood elite to get the wrong impression.

He remained tense but followed my lead as we entered the venue. Unlike the raucous parties and nightclubs I had frequented over the years, the atmosphere in the room was subdued. Men and women mingled leisurely, sipping drinks and discussing the latest Hollywood gossip. Initially, I felt out of place, but I quickly adapted, allowing Adonis to guide me around, introducing me to Raft and his acquaintances.

Raft had a strong jawline, high cheekbones, and dark eyes. If I hadn't known he only played mobsters, I'd have assumed he was one of us.

Among the throngs of Hollywood elite, Ben stood with an enigmatic smile on his face. He talked with them, smiled with them, drank with them. I couldn't make out the conversation, but his enthusiasm was contagious, leaving him crowded.

"There's your Jew bastard," spat Adonis, and the moment he laid eyes on Ben, he found someone else to look at. A woman at the far corner of the room next to the red velvet drapes.

"You want him dead because you two shared a woman? That hardly seems like a just cause."

"I want him dead because Benjamin Siegel is a problem."

"How is he a problem? If Siegel can do more for Los Angeles than Dragna, isn't it in the best interest of the Outfit to allow him to take over the territory? To force Dragna into retirement?"

"It's not that simple."

"Then explain it to me."

Adonis smiled, but it didn't reach his eyes. "The Bug is the best in this business. He can kill a man, then persuade that same man's best friend to work for him. It took you four years in Mexico . . . Ben could do it in months. He's a freak of nature. He can be anyone he needs to be, and there will never be another one like him."

"But?" I pressed, awaiting further explanation.

"He's a wild card," he continued, lowering his voice while retrieving us each a drink from a man walking around with a tray of champagne. "Unpredictable, loud, and he always wants more. He will make money, then lose it, arrange deals, and break them. He reaches too high, and eventually, he will lose Lansky's favor. Do you understand what I'm telling you?"

I gave him my eyes, but no response.

"Ben Siegel is not going to live to be an old man. He's going to be killed one day; if not by us, by someone else. Don't get too close." He pulled me into his body, hand resting on the curve of my back. "Now, let's put on a show."

He positioned our bodies so that he leaned into my neck, whispering sweet nothings, while I kept my eyes fixed on Ben. I waited anxiously, my heart racing, until his piercing eyes met mine. With that same primal look I had grown accustomed to, he forcefully pushed through the crowd around him.

"He's coming," I muttered, my voice barely audible. "He's not happy."

Adonis lifted his mouth from my neck, the cool air revealing that his kisses had been genuine and not mere pretense. He turned around just in time for Ben to slug him in the face. Reacting swiftly, Raft rushed to the scene, speedily guiding him away as though this act of violence was an everyday occurrence.

Raft exchanged a few words with Ben, and the two engaged in a heated conversation until Ben visibly began to calm down. Adonis wiped the blood from his split lip, wearing a taunting smile. Suddenly, the once spacious venue felt small and suffocating, with all eyes on me, questioning what I could have possibly done to provoke the two men. Sweat began to bead down my neck. I blinked, remembering to put on a show. I reached for Adonis, and Ben reached for me. His fingers circled my upper arm to pull me up and close, where our faces were inches apart—breathing the same warm air.

"What are you doing here with him?"

"You're fucking embarrassing me," I gritted, and with a pull, freed my arm. I left through the front doors, past the wrought iron fencing, searching the quiet street for my car. I timed him following—fifteen seconds.

"Virginia," Ben called behind me, nearly breathless.

There was no turning back now.

"Ben," I said his name sharply, facing him head-on.

He sighed, as if my mere presence exhausted him. "What are you doing here?"

"I was invited," I said simply.

"I mean here, in Los Angeles."

"Business."

"With Adonis?"

"Unfortunately, yes."

"Come back inside, I'll make you a drink. What happened in there, I'm sorry." He took a deep breath, and then, as if trying to keep his voice merry, he said, "Let me give you a proper welcome to my city?"

"Ben . . ." I paused a moment, gathering my thoughts. "I just want to get some sleep. We'll forget it ever happened in the morning."

Again, I tried to leave, finding my Cadillac and reaching for the door. He persisted, stepping up to the car to stop me. "What happened in Marietta? I gave you Madeline's journal—"

"Don't say her name," I demanded, and he turned his eyes to the road.

"I gave you the journal so you could use it to get out. Then, six months later, I hear you're in Mexico."

I exhaled. "I don't want to talk about Marietta. I've spent years coming to terms with the fact that I slept with my best friend's killer. I don't want a reminder."

"You could have been done," he said, dumbfounded. "This all could have been over for you. Why didn't you just give Chicago the journal?"

I didn't want to talk about it, not yet. I hadn't expected us to jump right back into the moment we left frozen in time in Marietta—where he stood with his hands up, his eyes pleading for me to understand, and then his final offer to free me that I didn't take.

"That journal didn't promise me nothing."

He shook his head with a confused look. "You could have been done."

"All that journal did was tell me that men are liars, and that the Mob will do anything to keep its secrets. There was no safety in turning it over. I can't trust anyone but myself. When I want to get out, I'll get out." My words came out hard, focused, but my eyes felt watery.

A tender look overtook his face.

"Don't look at me like that, Ben."

"Like what?"

"Like you feel sorry for me."

"I learned my lesson," he said, raising his hands defensively. "I won't be calling you a soft dame again."

I kept my lips from curling. "I didn't know you'd be here." Lie number one. "I'm a fan of Raft." Lie number two.

"Let me introduce you, then?" He offered me his hand, and Joe would have had me take it. But Benjamin Siegel knew me long before I was good at this. He'd suspect something if I gave in too willingly, so instead of giving him my hand, I threw it across his cheek.

"I meant it when I said that I don't ever want to see you again."

Chapter Twenty-Three

For the first time in my life, I was out of control, and the sleepy city of Los Angeles was to blame. I knew getting close to Ben again wouldn't happen overnight, which meant taking back what I'd said to Vel and establishing myself in Hollywood. He had to believe my presence here was just another job.

I settled into a bungalow at the Beverly Hills Hotel and later leased a house in the Valley. Each new residence sparked rumors about my mysterious and sudden wealth, and the papers buzzed with speculation. I immersed myself in the glamorous world of movie sets, collecting Hollywood friends, partying until the early hours of the morning, and sleeping through the day. I indulged in every drink, every drug, and in just six whirlwind months, I made a name for myself.

"You're doing this to spite me," Joe accused, pulling back the curtains of my bedroom window and allowing the harsh sunlight to flood the room, jolting me awake. I gasped and sat up, shielding my eyes from the light, my head still throbbing from the effects of last night's seventh cocktail.

"Good morning, Joe," I said groggily.

Joe stood, his posture rigid, his arms crossed tightly across his chest with a disapproving scowl. I knew a lecture was coming, but I had little energy to spare. "Can we do this in a few hours?"

"Six months and you've gotten nowhere with Siegel."

"I wouldn't say that." I threw my body back down with a dramatic plop, and Joe walked over to strip the blanket off my head.

"You've certainly had fun with others, haven't you? Errol Flynn, and let's not forget about the drummer. What was his name?" He tossed a rolled-up newspaper onto the bed. Vel joined us in the bedroom, wearing the same dress as the night before. She perched on the edge of the bed, scanning the newspaper.

"Gene." Vel swooned. "He was a dreamboat." She studied the *Los Angeles Times*, flashing a black-and-white photo of me and Gene enjoying a night out. "They can't get enough of you." Vel cleared her throat. "'Nobody knows where her wealth comes from, but her spending habits rival that of her celebrity friends.'" She paused, and I knew she was about to read something unflattering. Since my arrival in Los Angeles, I'd had the displeasure of reading one desperate journalist's column after another. They wanted a story, even if it meant making one up.

"Go on," I muttered from underneath the blanket.

"They're calling you a red-haired Mae West."

I felt heat rush through me and sat up, needing to read it for myself.

"None of that is important." Joe dismissed it with a wave. "Why am I not seeing you and Siegel in the papers? What's the delay, Virginia?"

"I can't help it if he's not interested," I said while continuing my read of the article.

"Flip the page," he said.

I turned the page and found another article detailing an altercation involving Ben and Gene.

"A fight after one of his shows," said Joe. "Siegel caught him on the way out, slugged him, and threatened him. You're the only connection between those two men."

Vel shrugged nonchalantly. "Maybe Siegel doesn't like good music."

"Don't you have somewhere to be?" Joe's voice grew sharper.

I nodded at Vel, and she left the room while holding Joe in a glare. When she was gone, I rolled the paper back up. I slunk out of bed, heavy and unsteady. "I know what I'm doing, Joe. Ben would suspect me if I just threw myself into his arms after what he did to Madeline. He knows he'll have to earn me again, and the best way to keep his interest fresh is reminding him that other men have me."

"There's something different about you here. I can't describe it, but I can see it."

"I'm having a good time," I said firmly. "That's the difference, and it's not a crime. Haven't I earned it? This job is going to take time, years even. So, settle in and trust me to handle it."

My bold tone seemed to catch him off guard, but he straightened himself up and gave me a nod. "Promise me you'll keep your wits about you."

I took a deep breath and finally stood up, allowing the room's spinning sensation to settle before walking over to Joe. I placed a hand on his shoulder, looking him in the eyes. "Tell me you trust me."

He hesitated for a moment, his gaze searching mine. "You don't trust me," he countered.

"With good reason."

"That's fair," he conceded.

I gently nudged him to the side, creating enough space for me to squeeze past and reach the curtains to shut them.

Two weeks later, I stumbled into my house close to two in the morning to find someone waiting for me. The entire house was scattered with a collection of things I'd bought in Los Angeles. Furs, jewelry, shoes. I had been cautious in the past, carefully stowing everything away in boxes and hiding them in closets. But I was surrounded by Mob figures here, each checking in weekly for progress updates. They kept tabs on me, ensuring I arrived or was delivered exactly where I needed to be, giving me a false sense of security.

Two men had slipped past all that and stood at the center of my living room with bags loaded with items they'd collected from my house.

I had drunk too much, as usual, but any sense of wanting to drift off to bed was stripped from me. I stood on alert, watching the masked figures stalk toward me.

"You have no idea who you're stealing from."

"I'll take the fur off your back," he said lowly.

I obliged, knowing my revolver was in my coat. I reached into a pocket with one hand and inched out of the sleeve with the other, not breaking eye contact with them. One of the thieves seemed to read my body language and lunged at me. I panicked and fumbled, my hand slipping from the pocket. The man had me in a flash, his gun pressed to my temple, his grip firm. "Take off your coat," he shouted, and thumped the gun against my head.

I cried out from the broken flesh, feeling the blood start to stream down my face.

"No," shouted the other man, exchanging a look of horror between us both. "We're not supposed to fucking touch her. He said don't touch her."

The man holding me fished the gun from my coat. "I should have let her kill us? He didn't say she had a gun."

He? I looked them both over. "Who put you two up to this?"

"Shut up," ground the one holding me.

The other man walked up and reached for the gash in my head, surveying the depth of the wound. His eyes started to water. "You've fucked us!"

Tears sprang from my eyes—I was frightened and angry. I wanted it to be over. I didn't want to die over jewels and clothing, items I'd bought and given away over the years with each new fashion trend. "Take what you want and leave," I said, heart pounding in my chest.

The one holding me shoved me to the ground, and I held my knees to my chest, hearing them shuffle in and out of the house until they were gone, leaving the door wide open.

The next morning, I woke up early to clean the gash on my head, blotting the dried blood and adding a clean bandage. I hesitated to go downstairs and relive the scene, but the moment I reached the last step, a knock at the door startled me.

I raced back upstairs for my revolver, nestled on my nightstand. By the time I got back downstairs, the knocking had stopped. I moved to the window next to the door to find nobody there, only a few neatly wrapped packages outside. I eased the door open—three packages total and a note on top. I picked up the note and opened it. Inside a mess of dark-red smudges and fingerprints was Ben's handwriting.

I told them not to touch you. I'm sorry.

I heaved and crumpled the note, squeezing it tight in the palm of my hand. I peered into the boxes to find all my stolen items and lugged them inside before locking the door. I wanted to hurt him, and I wanted to drink.

The phone rang all day, and I knew it was him. I didn't pick up, just shut my bedroom door to drown out the sound. Later that evening, when I'd had too much and my throat burned, the pounding started. I imagined his fists, curled up, slamming against the wood.

When it finally stopped, I watched his shadow stalk the house from window to window. My gun was glued to my right hand, and in my left, a half-empty glass of whiskey. "I'll kill you, you sick son of bitch," I muttered to myself, inching to the back door.

He violently shook the handle of the door, and I got closer, my ribs feeling like they were going to strangle my chest.

"Virginia," he said, as if he could smell me from the other side. I leaned into my negligee, sniffing the lacy fabric for reassurance.

"I was desperate, a desperate man," he said honestly. "How else did you expect me to get your attention? They were going to take your things so I had a good excuse to return them. They weren't . . ." He let the words hang a moment. "They weren't supposed to touch you. They won't touch you again. Now, open the door so I can grovel properly."

"I've got a gun," I told him.

"Your old revolver?"

"Get off my property or I'll kill you with it."

"You really want to kill me?"

"You're a bastard."

"I try to find you in other women," he said, breathless. "You're always in my head . . . I can't get you out. When you went to Mexico, I wanted you to stay there." He paused, then continued, his voice heavy. "But then you showed up at the party, you came to me."

"I'm here for work," I said. "Get it through your thick head."

"You're here for me," he said, and if the words hadn't sounded so much like a plea, I'd have assumed he was on to me.

"I hate you, Ben," I said, though my voice was hardly convincing. My mind reeled with the memories of our first meeting to our last. How Ben, my stranger, had turned into my monster. The disturbing images of him strangling Madeline replayed in my mind like a recurring nightmare. "What kind of person would I be if I didn't hate you?"

"You don't hate me." He hit the door again. "You want to, but you don't. You can't. I want to forget about you, but I can't. Los Angeles is mine." His voice shifted, rising, the confidence making him breathless. "I'm going to run everything, the movie business, city hall . . . I'll run the politicians. We can do this together, run this whole town. This isn't freedom, but it's the closest thing I can give you. If you're with me, if you're my girl, they can't force you to be with someone else. I did it, baby, I'm on top of the world."

I mentally noted it all, finally understanding why Dragna feared him. I had seen Ben kill with ease, convince men to follow him and women to sleep with him. But now, he was something else entirely. A Hollywood terrorist that would only grow stronger. I'd played the game too well—lured him in and now I was facing the consequences. He'd hired men to rob me, and those men had hurt me, but I knew he was capable of worse. I couldn't possibly trust him inside my house, alone with me.

"There, you groveled," I countered, desperation creeping into my voice. "Now you need to get off my property. I'll decide when I want to see you again, Ben."

"Open the door."

"I'm going to shoot you, you hear me?"

He stepped back, and I thought I might have scared him off until I heard his entire body crash against the door, breaking the hinges and frame. The force sent him barreling through, and I stifled a scream before firing the gun. The bullet flew past him through a window, shattering the glass. He didn't even flinch, and his eyes turned feral. "Put down that fucking gun."

I found my voice, pulled it from my throat, and took an unsteady step backward. "Get out of my house! You're out of your mind if you think I'm going to forgive you." I fired again, aiming past him, just wanting to startle him—the gun was empty. I stared at it, horrified. It was supposed to have six bullets in the cylinder, but I knew I had more in the kitchen.

The rage changed his face, turned him into the monster I knew so well. He wasn't going to let me get away with two shots.

I fled for the kitchen, reaching the drawer that held the bullets. I had it open before his hands found my hips, his grip bruising my flesh. He pressed my body into the drawer, forcing it shut. His face buried into my neck, mouth on my ear, sending a chill down my spine. He gripped my wrist hard, adding just the right amount of pressure. I winced and the gun dropped to the linoleum.

"All night at the clubs," he accused, his voice tinged with resentment. "All the men—do you do it for business or to provoke me?"

I forced out a resentful laugh, trying to pry his fingers from my hips. "Why do men always assume everything I do revolves around them? I'm having a good time in a new city."

"You're doing it for attention," he growled. "Now you have it."

He flipped me around, and sat me firm on the kitchen counter, sliding my negligee up my hips, clawing at the fabric to get it out of his way. I knew what he wanted, and for the moment, I let his mouth settle between my legs.

I looked over my shoulder, panting, searching the kitchen. I frantically reached for one of the knives by the sink. I gripped the wood hilt, held it high above his head, battling the pleasure of his tongue, his mouth. My body had missed him, but my mind crafted hauntingly satisfying images of him bleeding—sharp cuts to his back. Blood pooling on my kitchen floor, his body cold. I'd call the authorities and tell them I'd shot an intruder . . . all the stolen boxes were still there in the kitchen. A robbery gone wrong.

Tears sprang from my eyes. Could I do it? Dragna wanted him dead, after all. He kept licking me, slipping his fingers inside me, and my head felt dazed. A cloudy mess of passion and hate. The knife was slipping, my grip less firm. The feeling of wanting him was painful, leaving me queasy. I fought the desire with reminders of Madeline on soft sheets, cold and alone and dead.

He's a killer who knows your body. Nothing else.

He grunted, and I knew he could sense how hard I was working to resist him. He picked up speed, desperate to break me. Using just his fingers now, he lifted his head up, eyed the knife, and grinned. Then, he took me by the chin, our mouths inches apart. "Give me what I want," he said, his voice both bitter and pleading.

I knew I should, that the plan was to entrap him and bring him down, and yet my mind was unyielding. I didn't want to accept I'd come so far to end up right where I started, at his mercy and out of control.

"Now, Virginia," he panted, squeezing my chin tighter before leaning in to kiss me. His mouth, devouring and steady, broke me. I cried out, angry at myself, and him. He moaned in response, a mix of relief and pleasure. He reached up and took the knife from me, then tossed it down with the gun.

I trembled, and again, he tasted his fingers, then his eyes rolled. When I said nothing, just stared at him, loathing him down to the way he breathed, he combed through my hair, and pressed our foreheads together. "You want more, baby? All you have to do is say it."

I knew what he wanted—the question wasn't about sex. He needed confirmation that I'd forgiven him, that I wanted him, despite everything he'd done. That I could accept the monster and live with Madeline's ghost. My bottom lip quivered, and I thought I might cry again.

I nodded against his head in response, but he waited. He needed to hear my voice; he was a glutton for it.

"I want more," I whimpered.

He gathered me up, holding my gaze while we drifted up the stairs to my bedroom. He laid me on the bed, quietly stripping me, the silence between us tense. He crawled on top of me, hovering above me. "Tell me what you want me to do."

"I want you like this," I said without thinking.

There was nothing forceful about it, nothing primal. He insisted I look him in the eyes, and when he leaned down to kiss me, it was tender and slow. He wasn't trying to fuck me, break me; he was trying to make love to me.

My stomach tightened at the idea. He spread my legs apart, finding his spot between them but taking one of my thighs to lift one leg higher. He moved inside me, holding my mouth on his. His pace was slow, as if he'd memorized the precise rhythm needed to make me thrash under him. Every tense nerve in my body eased under him so that I could feel everything. And just like before, when he had a way of making the world disappear around us, I forgot about the mission, the job.

With each passionate thrust, as my fingers dug into his hips, I came to the dreadful realization that it didn't matter if I had him right where I wanted him because if wasn't careful, Ben Siegel would have me too.

Chapter Twenty-Four

1940

"No," I said simply, and his eyes, lit with wonder, lowered. He stood naked at the foot of the bed, pacing, rambling on about a wild idea, one of the many he'd had over the last few years. Only this one was too big, and too terrifying.

"You're saying no?"

"I'm saying no."

"Don't you understand what this could do for us? A luxury casino? Not just for the poor man gambling to make a few bucks in a little fucking adobe in the desert that smells . . . but for the elite. The very elite we walk around with every day. Not just gambling either. Restaurants, pools, a garden . . ."

"A garden?" I grinned.

He threw his hands up wildly. "Showrooms. Imagine it now, Virginia. The profit, the ease of laundering money. No more sitting at the races."

I lowered deeper into the bed, pulling the sheets over my bare breasts, wanting to return his enthusiasm in some way. "Come back to bed, Ben. We'll talk about this casino in the morning." I looked out the window of my new home in a quiet residential neighborhood, where I prayed the neighbors in the house across the street weren't peeking inside at this late of an hour. "You really need to get away from the window."

He walked straight over to it and stretched.

"God! Ben!" I flushed with embarrassment. "You're going to make me never want to leave this house, you know that, don't you? I already get strange looks when I'm checking the mail."

He just stood there, hands on hips. "Why are you saying no?"

"Get away from the window."

He turned around instead, flashing his pale cheeks to the world with a grin.

"Tell me first."

"It's not like you have ever taken my advice . . . You always run the opposite direction. You do exactly what everyone tells you not to do. What does it matter why I'm saying no?"

"Because this is for us," he said, easing beside me, pulling me into him. "This is going to change everything. I need you to see it."

I shifted around to look into his eyes and saw it. All the hope he stored there, the vision. But two years together had given me perspective on the brilliantly destructive nature of Benjamin Siegel, and the words Adonis had uttered that night at Raft's party. Against my better judgment, and my mission to ruin him, I told him the truth. "You're bad with money."

His mouth fell open. "I've seen the way you spend, Virginia."

"What I mean is"—I placed my hand on his chest—"you're bad at paying it back. How many of your little celebrity friends do you owe now?"

He shrugged. "They've got it to spare."

"They don't ask for it back because they're terrified of you."

"I'll be able to pay it back," he urged, confidence spilling from his mouth. "They'll see that the investment is worth it. Why don't you see it?"

My expression changed, I felt it. "Because you're not borrowing from celebrities this time. You're borrowing money from the same men that made you, Ben. You know what they're capable of if this all goes wrong."

His hands cupped my face in response with not a glimmer of unease to be seen. "I'm untouchable, Gin . . . and with this, I'm going to be at the top of the fucking world."

"Not if you're dead." I pulled away, and the very words shook my core. He was supposed to die at the end of this awfully twisted game, yet saying it out loud made me flinch. I left the bed and searched for my robe. "Do what you like, Ben, but I'll never approve of it."

He leaped from the bed, taking me by the hips to keep me from slipping away. "Just say it."

"Say what?"

"That you love me."

I rolled my eyes, stifling a laugh. "Vain, as always."

"Virginia Hill is in love," he sang the words.

I shoved at his arms.

"I think I've loved you since the moment I met you," he uttered, and the playful demeanor between us diminished quite suddenly. "I think I'll love you until they bury me."

"You think?" I muttered the two words weakly while he trailed kisses down my neck.

He moved his lips to mine, pressing our foreheads together tenderly. "I think."

I opened my mouth, waiting for the words to come. I had lied plenty to men, but I couldn't lie to Ben. Even worse, what if I said the words and came to the dreadful realization that they weren't a lie? That I'd fallen for a dead man? I cringed at the thought, battling my emotions.

"We should sleep," I told him. "Aren't you due on set tomorrow?"

"Come with me?"

"I have things to do here," I said, motioning at my house. I was newly moved in and longed to shop and furnish the rooms—make this place my own.

"You love going to the sets," he reminded me. "I'll take you shopping after."

I watched Ben move throughout the back lots, holding the script in his hand, fussing over some lines with one of the actresses. The crew responded when he was near, taking his input as if he owned the studio. I didn't know the extent of his hold over the union, but it was strong enough to keep the production in his favor. Amid the sea of producers, cinematographers, lighting technicians, and set designers, I lost sight of Ben. I had come so often that I knew everyone's job and how they did it.

Out of all the exploits shared with Ben, including racetrack scams and gambling, being here was my favorite thing to do.

"Shall I take you for some lunch?" Raft asked, sitting next to me to watch. "You've been here for hours."

I gazed at him, my shoulders in such a state of relaxation that I wouldn't dream of moving. "I'm enjoying myself."

"We could get you a supporting role," he suggested. "Have you ever thought of being on the big screen?"

"No," I said. "I had a friend who wanted to, but she never made it." I stayed quiet, observing the set, wondering what kind of role Madeline would have played if she were here. It was a warm day in Los Angeles, and I kept drifting back to when I thought I saw her years ago at the San Carlo, the last time she'd felt real to me and not a ghost walking the halls of my dreams.

"It's a tough industry."

I made sure Ben wasn't anywhere in sight before asking my next question: "How did you get involved with this? With Ben? You two are so close."

Raft subtly shifted in his seat, betraying a flicker of unease. His gaze darted around the set, scanning for Ben's presence, before he finally responded, "It was all very exciting in the beginning, and given the roles I play, Ben was a great character study."

"When did it go from a character study to friendship?" Though, I hardly considered what they had a friendship. Vel didn't ask anything of me, but Ben demanded everything from Raft.

"At some point, I got in over my head." His voice was light, but he shifted in his seat and looked around the set for Ben again. "What about you, Virginia? How did you get involved with this lifestyle?"

I grinned widely. "Oh, I love it. I came from nothing, and now I have everything." I motioned at the film set. "I'm living the dream, Raft."

Raft's eyes narrowed in response, his intense gaze lingering. "Are you certain you don't want a role on set?" He leaned in. "You're quite good."

We both smiled at that, and though we'd said nothing out loud to imply we felt like prisoners, we knew the truth. We talked longer about his career, his travels, and shared some laughs.

Sometime during the conversation, I looked back to the set to find Ben in front of a city backdrop, arms crossed, watching us both with a look that could kill.

That evening, at his home on Delfern Drive, Ben remained silent until we sat at the dining room table, discussing the film. I half-heartedly picked at my grilled steak and spinach until I couldn't take the tense air between us. I studied the dining room, the long table we sat at, imagining his daughters and wife eating alongside him. He'd sent them away on vacation, but I always felt their lingering presence in every room of this house.

"Did you mention to Raft your plans for the casino?"

He said nothing, and with only the scraping of his fork on porcelain, I kept pushing. "You know he'd invest."

Nothing.

"We were discussing the set," I said.

He took a bite of his own food and turned the page of the script. "He's attracted to you, and you know that. You like that, don't you?"

I rolled my eyes. "I'm not every man's taste, Ben. A man talking to me doesn't mean he's attracted to me. Raft offered me a supporting role."

"What would you know about his movie?"

With a scoff, my mouth pulled into a grin. "I know everything you know about that set, maybe more."

"What is that supposed to mean?"

"That you make everyone uncomfortable the second you walk in," I said.

He paused his script wrangling and leaned back in his chair, his expression pensive. "I haven't come this far by concerning myself with people's comfort. I don't want you talking with Raft if I'm not there."

The audacity of such a demand had me laughing. "You don't get to decide that." He'd already made me send Vel away and insisted on attending every party I did. If he wasn't involved in the conversations, he'd force himself in, just to keep me isolated. All to himself.

"Fine," he concluded. "How about this? If I catch him talking to you again without me around, I'll beat him within an inch of his life. Then we'll see how comfortable I make everyone on that set."

I rose abruptly from the table, causing the plate to tremble beneath the pressure of my palms. "You're married, Ben. You brought me back to your family home to fuck me. And even if I could somehow forget about that, you'll fuck anyone that can give you something, most importantly, money. If you want to talk about my men, let's talk about your women." It was the first time I had uttered the words aloud, and though they tasted bitter on my tongue, relief washed through me. For the past two years, we had maintained this arrangement where I silently pretended to be his sole woman, all the while knowing that his weekly disappearances were to be with someone else.

I had grown accustomed to it. The other women served as reminders that despite all his efforts to prove he was different from the men before him, he wasn't. There was no fairy-tale ending with Ben, he'd all but proven it over the years, and I had never been so driven to ruin him.

"Sit down and eat," he said, exasperated with the conversation, his usual response when he knew he couldn't win.

I shoved back my chair and left the dining room to retrieve my coat, deciding that anywhere would be better than here. At the very least, I needed the cool night air to settle my racing heart.

I could hear his chair scraping against the floor and his footsteps hurrying behind me, but I wasn't prepared for how swiftly he reached the coat closet. "I just need air," I told him while slipping into one of my favorite Persian lamb coats. I turned around, and he stood rooted at the door, blocking me from leaving.

"Why do you always wear that coat?"

"I like it," I said.

"Adonis got that for you in New York," he revealed, a fact I wasn't aware of and found difficult to believe. I had never kept track of who gifted me what, and this coat held little significance to me other than its beauty and warmth. "First Raft, now Adonis, who else are you fucking?"

"Get out of my way, Ben," I ground out. "It's a damn coat."

"It's more than that. Who else, Virginia?"

He reached for my hand, circled my wrist, and jerked it up between us. "This ring? Who gave it to you?"

"Vel. It was a goodbye present."

"You've had it on for years." He shook his head. "Did Joe give it to you? They say you two secretly married at one point . . . Is this his ring?" He tried pulling the ring from my finger.

I attempted to shove past him but then felt the tight knot of his fist strike my stomach with a force that knocked the wind out of me. I collapsed to the ground, gasping for breath, clutching my abdomen as it swelled beneath my hand.

He sunk down to check on me, whispering apologies into my ear. His entire face, red with fury moments before, was pale and sickly. With shaking hands, he promised me he'd never do it again, but I knew it was a lie. I'd come so far since Georgie, yet I felt just as weak as I had back then. With a scream so feral that I choked on it, I balled my hand into a fist and threw it into his face. I clawed and hit until I couldn't anymore, until my hands shook, and the room spun.

The next morning, I was sleeping in when Ben heard the doorbell and hurriedly left the bed. Seizing the opportunity, I slipped out of bed and grabbed a robe, silently descending the steps of the house. I positioned myself by the banister, straining to listen as I heard him yelling at Mickey Cohen from his office. I was thinking about getting closer when the office door slammed open, and the two men began to argue in the foyer.

"How did he know?" demanded Siegel. "How did Dragna know we were coming?"

"I don't know, Ben," said Mickey. "All I know is he wasn't there."

"He wasn't at his favorite spot, the restaurant he goes to every day at the same time? Conveniently on the day we're coming for him?"

A moment of silence hung in the air until Mickey suggested, "Maybe someone tipped him off."

"That's not possible," Ben stated, causing my heart to sink. I huddled in a curled position, attempting to control my breathing. Until last night, I had been compliant, submissive to his lifestyle and needs. There was no reason for him to suspect me.

"We've got to stop all this," said Mickey. "The DA is closing in on Dragna. Let them handle him; we can't keep making so much noise. Ben, listen, I'm hearing rumors that they're going to arrest you for Greenberg's murder."

I heard him scoff. "Let them, ain't no evidence."

"You need to get a mouthpiece lined up."

"I got a lawyer."

"Maybe go to Vegas for a few weeks, keep scouting."

"You want me to run?" His voice was dripping with contempt. "I've made a name for myself in this town, and if I want to make the casino happen, I need my connections here. If they take me to trial, I'm fighting it. In this town, I'm guilty until proven innocent."

I left my perch on the stairs and slowly made my way back to bed, sinking into the sheets. I waited until he returned to bed, his arm finding its place under my waist as he started kissing my neck. "How can I make it up to you?"

I shrugged. "How do you always apologize?"

His wicked smile returned, and he disappeared under the sheets, pulling my legs apart and getting lost between them. I stared at the pendant light on the ceiling, a glass globe surrounding the bulb, counting the minutes.

Three days later, I woke to another pounding on the door and slipped out of bed in a rush. I inched open the door and found Raft standing in a panic, sweat beading down his forehead. "They arrested Ben this morning," he said, breathless. Hungover, I let him inside, the light streaming in through the windows causing my head to ache and pound.

When I didn't respond quickly enough, or match his labored breathing, his eyes narrowed. "Did you hear me, Virginia? They arrested Ben, charged him for some murder."

"I heard you," I said, sinking my fingers into the side of my temple to relieve the pressure.

"The police will come here next." His voice was hard and pleading. "We need to get you out of here, somewhere away from all this. But first . . ." He paused, reaching out for my shoulders. "First, I need you to show me where to find Ben's guns. He said to check the library."

I shuddered away from him, my head spinning. "Why do you need his guns?"

"He told me to come get them." His voice turned hoarse. "He wants me to clean up the house before they get here."

"Shouldn't you be checking the home he shares with his wife and children?"

"He said they were here."

"Raft," I said his name slowly. "You get caught up in this and your career is over."

"And if I don't do what he says? What happens to me then?" He rolled his eyes, his brief moment of acting over. He cared about Ben's arrest just about as much as I did. "Just tell me where to find them."

I crossed my arms over my chest. "I'm not going to do that."

He shook his head tersely. "Why are you fighting this? We're all he's got right now, and if we don't do this, and the guns get to evidence . . ."

"Ben goes away for a very long time." I finished his sentence, my voice light. "All our problems are solved." It had slipped out, really, but the relief I felt saying it made a smile pull at the corners of my mouth. Could it be that easy?

For a moment, he looked as if he wanted to keep probing me, but grunted in frustration instead. He left me and moved to the library, throwing down bundles of books and moving furniture. Half an hour passed before he turned to face me. With a fresh drink in my hand, I plopped down on the chaise near one of the long windows, giving him a leisurely smile.

"Virginia, do you know where they are?"

I gestured to one of the shelves he'd emptied. "There's a button under that shelf."

He felt around along the wood, pushed the button to reveal a hidden panel with a large box inside it. He opened the box slowly, his hands shaking. Along the trove of things that mattered most to Ben—watches, cuff links, and various items from his women—were two guns, a revolver and a Colt.

I took a swig, watching intently. Raft reached in and then out. He didn't want to do this; it was evident in the way he moved. The hesitation in his hands, his labored breathing.

I stood to meet him at the shelf. "How about the police got here before you did? I'll tell him that's what happened myself. I'm very convincing."

He glanced at me with some surprise. "You want him to go away? You two have been inseparable for years. Don't you love him?"

"Do you love him?"

His face looked pained in response. "I'd love him more if he didn't terrify me."

I passed him the drink, and he accepted it.

"Let this play out," I advised. "I don't see him finding a way out of this one."

"And if he does?"

I didn't want to consider it. "Finish the drink and leave out the back before anyone sees you."

"Did you see the papers?" Joe asked, pushing them across the table to Dragna. "He's seeing Wendy Barrie, taking her to dinners. The police are allowing him to leave as he pleases. They say he's eating like a king in jail."

I picked at my eggs, glancing down at the front page of the *Examiner.* A picture of Ben and Barrie. She was in a sleek evening gown, smiling at him the way most women did. She was all high cheekbones and full lips—soft around the edges. I tried not to imagine him hurting her, bruising her delicate flesh, but the image played in my mind without consent.

"I hear she's pregnant," I said, and they both looked at me. "Just a rumor."

"Poor dame," tsked Dragna. "I like her movies. She's good in that one . . ." He searched for the title. "Sherlock Holmes."

"*The Hound of the Baskervilles,*" I muttered. My mind reeled, playing scenes from the movie and her role in it. A young woman, surrounded by mystery and lies—a curse involving a demonic hound. Did she know she had her own hound now? I blinked away the thought. "How are things with the trial?"

"Reles is due to testify in November. He'll put him away," said Joe.

Abraham Reles was a Mob man turned government informant, and the lead testimony needed him to close the deal on Ben's trial. "And when that happens," I said, trying to carefully navigate my words as I shifted my eyes to Dragna, "what happens to my contract?"

"I know you've worked hard, Virginia," said Dragna, and I waited for him to add some kind of stipulation. A final request. Instead, he lifted his juice and silently toasted me. "When Ben is found guilty, your contract is yours."

We finished breakfast, and Dragna left, leaving Joe and me alone in my kitchen nook. I tried not to let the excitement get the better of me. Ben could still find a way out of this somehow, couldn't he?

Joe shifted in his seat, and I finally looked at him for the first time that morning. He was stiff, toiling with the napkin in his lap, a faraway look in his eyes. "Joe?"

He gave me his eyes, and I knew something was wrong. A secret, something he intentionally hadn't shared with Dragna.

My heart skipped a beat. "What's happened?"

"There's a complication with Reles," he revealed, peering at me cautiously. I didn't like where this was going. "Allowing him to testify is risky."

I waited for him to elaborate, but he didn't.

"Joe." I said his name cold, firm.

He blinked slowly. "The very information that could put Siegel away could also put Adonis away. He's a dangerous leak. He knows too much."

"You've watched us discuss this trial for weeks over breakfast, and you've been keeping out that you're conspiring to get rid of Reles?" I felt the sting of betrayal, but more so, the heavy disappointment that I'd thought, even for a moment, we could leave Ben to the justice system.

"It's out of my hands," he reasoned.

"No," I said, but the word came out strangled.

"Siegel is one problem, Virginia. If Reles testifies, Chicago is at risk. You are at risk." His voice hardened, and I knew a decision had already been made.

He cleared his throat. "Reles will be dead before the trial. He's hunkered down in a hotel right now, but some of the police guarding him have been paid off. I hear they plan to throw him from the sixth-floor window."

Dread ran through me. If Reles didn't testify, Ben would be free again. I'd have to return to playing my role, quietly plotting his death in the dark, waiting for another moment like this to come. What if it never did?

"You and Dragna will have to find another way to bring him down."

I reached for my coffee cup, half empty, and threw it to the floor. The sound of the porcelain shattering didn't faze Joe. He continued reading through pages of the *Examiner*, unmoved by my act of violence. It happened too often now.

"You can't do this to me," I uttered, bottom lip quivering.

"Go home, visit your family. Take some time away. You need a break."

"I'm not going home until I'm done," I ground out.

"Slow down, Ben!" A scream tore from my lips as the streets of Los Angeles became a hazy blur around us, my heart pounding in my chest. I couldn't die, not today. I wasn't ready. I shoved at his arms, gripping the wheel, until he turned off, plummeting into my neighbor's manicured lawn. I leaped from the car, holding the wet earth with my hands, breathing in the cool night air. He stumbled out, clutching the newspaper in one hand.

"Not guilty," he declared and laughed at the notion, his words a drunken slur. He screamed down the street, waved the newspaper wildly at houses until lights started switching on and strangers began peering through windows.

I gathered myself, found my footing, and then stormed off, looking around frantically for my house. I was desperate to get away from him, and the second he spotted me leaving him, he rushed down the road after me.

"Don't come near me, you bastard. You could have killed me!"

"You know I'd never let anything happen to you. Why aren't you celebrating?"

"Celebrating you killing a man and getting away with it?" I yelled, just as loud, screaming it for the world to hear. I didn't care, didn't feel anything but anger. It gnawed at my insides, twisting the muscles in my chest until I felt like my heart might burst. I wanted to break things—I wanted to break him.

"Not so loud, Virginia." He moved fast, and so did I. I could see my house in the distance, less than a block away. His voice was hushed. "I had to do it to protect us, don't you see that? I had to plug the leak."

I just kept running, the sound of his voice making me itch. I found my home, sprinted up to the door, and threw it open. I turned around to slam it shut, but he lodged his foot inside and gave it a solid kick. The door crashed into my nose, and the gush of blood that followed sent me into a fury. I shoved it closed again on his foot, over and over again. He cursed at me, battling my strength until he used his hip and shoulder to gain advantage.

The door burst open, and the fury etched on his face, in his eyes, warned me to flee. I listened.

I sprang for the staircase, clawing my way up, finding my room, and shutting the door again.

"Open the fucking door, Virginia!"

I curled behind the bed, heard his fist slamming into the wood, splitting the doorframe, and I knew his knuckles were wet with blood. With a final split of wood, he reached around to unlock the door and stalked the room for me. I drew my knees into my chest. My face, tearstained and red, stayed buried between my legs. I could hear his breathing, staggered and uneven, feel him looming above me like the shadow he'd been for years.

He lowered in front of me and slowly placed his hands on my knees. I flinched in response.

"You're scared of me," he said, puzzled and hurt by the notion. "You've never been scared of me."

I couldn't stop my shuddering breaths long enough to give him a response.

"Virginia, breathe," he said, forcing my face up. I could taste the blood coming from my nose. "I need you to breathe." He took my body and pulled me close like a rag doll, and I let him. We sat there, curled into each other with so much blood, sweat, and tears. A true horror scene, one I couldn't have predicted if I'd tried. "That's it."

I forced myself to ease into him.

"I'll take you anywhere you want to go," he whispered into my ear. "We'll step away from everything . . . just us. Tell me where you want to go."

I just wanted to be done, a fresh start somewhere new. I wanted a life that was slow, with no man in sight.

I wanted Ben dead.

"Anywhere with you," I said the words as if I'd rehearsed them a hundred times, and in many ways, I had.

Chapter Twenty-Five

1945

Joey Ep stared at me from across the room, and his gaze said far more than his mouth ever could. "It's risky holding a meeting here," he advised, scanning the tastefully decorated home that Ben and I shared.

"He's still in the desert, shouldn't be back for a few days."

Joe approached me, his hand reaching out to touch my face, lifting my chin to examine me closely. His eyes took note of the blemishes I had concealed, but the bruising cast a shadow under my eyes that I couldn't hide.

With little emotion, he asked, "When did it start?"

I shoved his hand away. "Let's keep this business."

Soon after, Dragna arrived, and I led them both to Ben's office before closing the door behind us. These meetings occurred every few months, but this one was arranged on short notice. Dragna took a seat in one of the leather chairs by the window with a frustrated huff. "What's happened?"

"There's a property he's bought, swindled from a little old lady. It's a motel, and he wants to turn it into something bigger, a hotel and casino."

"This isn't news," Dragna said. "He's got plenty of clubs already in the desert. He's making money, big money."

"He wants more," I said simply.

"Not surprising," Joe added. "You wouldn't call us here over Siegel getting another property. What is it about this plan that you're not telling us?"

"It's expensive," I said, emphasizing the word. "Lansky is on board but has no idea what Ben is planning. Everything he wants, it's going to cost money." I walked over to the desk to retrieve some of Ben's notes. "He's already had the blueprints redone twice for nearly a hundred grand. He thinks he can get Lansky to agree to a million-dollar budget, but his plans are going to cost more."

Joe joined me at the desk, picking up the collection of bound notes and ideas, all written in Ben's handwriting. He meticulously examined the numbers, evaluating the costs associated with each idea Ben had jotted down. The luxurious dishware, the Tiffany lamps—this desert gem was going to come with a staggering price tag. When he finally grasped the expenses, his eyes lit up.

"I'll have a meeting with Lansky," proposed Dragna. "I'll stop this before he can get too deep into the construction."

"No," I said strongly, wondering why he couldn't see what I saw. "Back him, Dragna. I'm investing too."

"Are you mad?" He shook his head at the notion. "We're trying to bring down the Bug, not let him continue to build his gambling empire."

"This will end him," Joe concluded, and I felt like I could finally breathe again.

"What do you mean?" Dragna's eyes narrowed. "Make me understand this, both of you."

"He's going to spend too much," I said. "He's going to keep building and keep going until his dream is a reality. He will swindle the actors, the studios, the politicians . . . He's already promising shares of the casino to his friends."

"And have either of you entertained the idea that maybe it all pays off?" Dragna said, his frustration evident in his hand gestures. "That Lansky wants to fund this venture because it's going to work? Because it is a gold mine?"

"The success of the casino will not change the fact that he is making promises he can't keep," I pressed on. "When Ben sets his mind to something, he follows through . . . and I've never seen him so passionate before, not about anything other than . . ."

Dragna arched a brow. "Other than?"

"Me," I concluded.

Both men remained quiet, contemplating my proposal. In the tense silence, it finally dawned on me that we were missing a key figure. "Where's Adonis?"

Dragna looked out the window and pulled a cigar from the inner pocket of his suit. "Business in New York. He'll be back tomorrow. I'll update him." Again, the silence continued until both men looked my way.

Joe sighed deeply. "We all have to agree to support this, and then when it inevitably fails, we must also agree to contribute to its downfall."

I nodded in agreement, and though hesitant, Dragna came around. When he left, Joe stayed behind, taking hold of my arm before I could slip away to the bar for a drink. He glowered at me, examining my face. "How often does he hit your face?"

"Men have hit me my entire life, Joe, don't make this into something it isn't."

"I worry you're provoking him," he said. "You know him better than anyone; you know what to say and what not to say."

I made myself a drink, a glass of bourbon, and started to sip it. "I'm not that woman anymore." I finished the drink, and it left my throat burning. "I fight back, and Ben doesn't like it. Then we fuck, and he leaves, and returns a week later with gifts. It's the same thing, year after year . . . and every year, I just get angrier."

Joe reached for the empty glass and set it down on the mahogany bar. "Shall I call Vel to make a visit?"

"No," I blurted. "I don't want her involved with this, any of it. She should have been done when she signed her divorce papers. I'm doing this alone."

"If this hotel is going to be his downfall, he'll only become more suspicious and ill tempered. You need to play nice, convince him you're his greatest supporter. His trust in you is the only way we're going to see this through."

"I know," I said, using my glass to motion at the door. "Now get out of my house."

1946

Three weeks before opening, and over four million in the hole, I watched Ben crumble, desperately seeking money where there was none. I reported everything back to Dragna in detail, with the understanding that we couldn't intervene without raising suspicions. Now we all just waited. With the promise of using the casino for Mob-related interests, everyone had invested in Ben's grand dream—Chicago, New York, Miami, all the major figureheads. If Ben could pull the Flamingo off, the promise of reward was too great to ignore.

After fourteen months of attending to his every need, aiding in construction, and watching him sell shares to Mob associates and celebrities alike, I could see his dream becoming this ghostly figure, haunting his every step.

"The suites aren't even done," I said, going over the list he'd made weeks ago to ensure a smooth opening. "Where are the guests going to sleep? The lounge isn't complete, there are electrical issues, and our opening act isn't confirmed." I stopped when I noticed he wasn't listening.

He began pacing his suite, only occasionally glancing out the window. Las Vegas was dry but pleasant, a welcome change from the bone-chilling winters of New York and Chicago. I shared in Ben's desperation to see this through, except he would do anything to succeed while I would do anything to watch it all burn. I felt myself getting closer and closer to holding my contract in my hands, and it kept me up at night, stirring.

"The guest stars are pulling out," he revealed. "The opening date, the holidays—they're all saying the same thing."

I placed the notes down and reached out for him, sliding my hands over his shoulders. "Then we get someone else," I offered.

"We need more money," he declared, removing my hands from his shoulders to continue his pacing. I looked down and saw his hands shaking.

"There is no more money."

"You sure you've squeezed every dime out of Joey Ep?"

"Yes," I said with a sigh. "He's not investing any more, he wants me to be done with this." It had slipped out too quickly for me to realize it.

"'With this'?" His lips thinned. "He doesn't want you watching over his investment?"

"Not when he thinks the investment is going to fail," I countered. "Not when you've poured money into all the wrong things. You're going to get yourself . . ."

"What?" His eyes were grave.

I paused, considering my next words carefully. "If you need money, use the two million you put back for us."

"Stop talking about that," he said, voice low.

I had to talk about it, though. I had to keep bringing it up to ensure that it was still there, that at the end of all this, I had the proof Ben had swindled from his own investors. I didn't know the money's whereabouts, but I was certain it existed. Unlike Major, who had been rather careless with his plan to outsmart his captors, Ben was so meticulous that it was unlikely the account was even in his name.

If all else failed, and he managed to turn this casino into the promised land he envisioned, at least that money, the proof I needed, was out there somewhere.

"That's for us, Virginia. That's our money. We've earned it; we're keeping it. I'll find money somewhere else, I always do. It's all paper, but this," he said, extending his arms wide, as if embracing the entire building. "This is going to change everything. We're at the top of the world." His hands moved back to my face, and despite all efforts not to show fear, I shook.

With each new challenge he faced in opening the casino, he directed that anger at me, blurring the line between affection and abuse until I could no longer distinguish one from the other.

"Have you thought about it?" he asked, with our faces pressed together.

"I'm not marrying you," I said again. I wasn't entirely sure the divorce with his wife was finalized, but I recalled Adonis meeting with him to discuss the terms. Ben had swindled her out of money when he first began construction of the Flamingo, and she wanted it back. She'd made her own threats, and whatever she had on her ex-husband was enough to get him to cave to her wishes.

"The account, it's in your name," he said, voice light. "Wouldn't you like to cash it out as husband and wife?"

"My name?" I asked quietly.

His lips curved up, eyes softening. "I've done wrong by you, Gin, but you always come back. You've stood by me when you shouldn't have."

A tremor flooded my body. Was this a romantic gesture or a strategy? If the money was in my name, he could ultimately blame me if it was ever discovered. "Ben, I don't want the money."

"If anything happens to me . . ." His voice grew slow, and he paused a moment before picking back up his thoughts. "You need to be taken care of." He leaned in to give me a quick kiss. "Now, marry me?"

I pinched his arm and forced a smile. "You're already married to this casino."

He gave a tight laugh but didn't deny it.

He returned to scheming, going through the friends he hadn't tapped out yet. I stood back and watched with a smile, hiding the simmering fear that this would never end. I waited for his confidence to buckle, for the pressure to get to him, but whenever I thought he was close to breaking, he'd find some new schmuck to throw money at his dream.

He wanted everything, and it terrified me to think how far he'd go to get it.

Despite the stack of celebrity guests and shows, the grand opening was a disaster. The usual dry weather had turned against Ben, causing storms and delays that left most of the celebrity guests stuck in place or unable to travel. Gamblers filtered in with awe but left shortly after winning due to the incomplete rooms and suites. To make matters worse, three weeks after opening, with building codes not properly met, the Flamingo was shut down. I'd lost track of the fits of rage, the abusive fights, the sheer number of days we'd both drank ourselves into a stupor.

Sometime later that summer, I made my escape to Los Angeles under the cover of night, leaving Ben's hotel suite without a single word. Ben had grown increasingly suspicious, and I knew it was only a matter of time before his paranoia turned toward me. Dragna had sent Adonis to retrieve me, and I couldn't wait to leave behind the desert town that held more memories of bloodshed than prosperity.

Adonis met me at the train station and escorted me back to my house, where I joined Dragna and Joey to discuss our next course of action.

"The hotel is set to reopen in a few months," said Dragna.

"I've crunched the numbers, and he's going to be in the red for a long time," concluded Joe. Still, for the men scattered about Ben's former office, hope was dwindling. I could feel it.

"He has a way of convincing Lansky that he'll bounce back and thrive. He's always got a plan," said Adonis. "Lansky buys into the Bug every time."

"This would be over now if he hadn't been acquitted in the Greenberg trial," spat Dragna. "Lack of evidence . . . how can you have a lack of evidence when all the witnesses keep turning up dead?"

I looked to Joe and Adonis, wanting them to feel the pressure of my gaze. They were the reason he had been acquitted, a secret they felt entirely fine keeping from Dragna for the rest of our partnership together. They didn't dare look up at me. They continued debating, while I stared out the window, considering the money. The two million.

I had remained silent for too long, catching Joe's attention. He could read me like an open book and took a seat in the vacant chair next to mine. He gently took the bourbon from my hand, his fingers brushing against my swollen knuckles. "What do you know, Virginia?"

All three men looked my way. I considered the information I knew, and whether it was enough to secure the hit on Ben. I opened my mouth to tell them, reveal the secret account with stolen funds, but nothing came out. Not a word about Ben, and I wasn't entirely sure why. I loathed the hesitation inside me, this ever-growing feeling that despite all he'd done to me, I owed him something.

"I heard rumors about a secret account," I revealed. "He's got a couple million stashed away from the investors." Only I hadn't heard rumors; I knew the account existed and was very much involved in the scheme to swindle the money.

"Which investors?" Joe pushed me to continue.

"Never mind who he stole the money from, Joe."

"She's right," said Dragna. "It doesn't matter who, the Outfit will assume he stole from them and could be still doing it."

"Can you get the account information?" asked Adonis. "We need more than just a rumor."

I sat up slowly in the chair, and my throat swelled. I'd come too far to protect him or any man like him. Why couldn't I say it?

"Virginia," Dragna said my name slowly. "I told you not to get too close."

"How dare you," Joe snapped. "She hasn't gotten too close. Virginia?"

"I haven't," I said in agreement. I gathered my head, a mess of emotions and painful images of Ben's wrath. "It's not a rumor, he told me directly. It's in a Swiss bank account under my name. There's roughly two million in it."

All three men dispersed the second I revealed the information, off to achieve the goal we'd been working for since the very beginning.

Two weeks later, Ben returned home with a swagger to his step. The casino had reopened, and operations were going well. He had no reason to suspect his associates were plotting against him, or that I had revealed the stolen money to Dragna.

Ben dropped his bags off at the door, and I waited on the chintz sofa for him, legs crossed, my posture tight. He strolled in with a smile, but it all too quickly faded. That unshakable confidence had finally broken, and I recognized him again. The role I'd been playing, the dutiful girlfriend, was long gone. I wasn't hiding anymore, and he could see it.

"It's over," I told him, and though I gave him no other clues as to what I meant by it, he sank down into the plush chaise opposite of me. The silence between us was heavy. "I'm leaving you, Ben."

He wore an expression of exhaustion. "You'll come back, you always do."

"I can't come back to a dead man."

He studied me, frozen at the words. "It was you, wasn't it?" he said. "The reason Dragna was always one step ahead of me?"

"Before we discuss Dragna, can we agree not to lie to one another?"

He nodded firmly.

"I work for Dragna."

The words made him shudder. "How long?"

"He's the reason I came to Los Angeles. He bought my contract and agreed to sign it over to me if I brought down his enemy."

"You're lying to hurt me," he ground out. "You wouldn't do that to me, not after everything we've been through."

"It's already done, Ben."

A frantic laugh escaped his mouth. "Mickey warned me about you, but I didn't believe it. How long have you been working against me?"

"Since the moment I found out you killed Madeline."

"Her? Again?" He let out a tight, exasperated sigh. "She is dead, Virginia."

"Because of you," I shouted.

"No," he said. "Because she was a spy, just like you. An unfaithful, lying bitch." He stood briskly, his shoulders squared, and I knew what was coming. He'd pull me off the sofa, throw me into something, knock the wind out of me, and hit me until I screamed. I pulled my revolver and aimed.

He froze in place. "You're not going to kill me."

"No, but they are."

"They?"

"The little family you've worked so hard to impress, Ben. They know all about the account, the stolen money."

"You sold me out?" His voice dropped, and with those four desperate words, he looked like a lost child in search of a hand to hold.

"I didn't need to do a damn thing. You were so blind to every mistake in the pursuit of proving yourself. You lied, you stole, and you built that casino on nothing but broken promises. Did you really think they'd let you get away with it?"

He sank back down, staring blankly at the wall behind me. After a moment of stillness, I felt comfortable enough to drop the gun. Then laughter erupted from his mouth, hysterical and scattered. The shift in his demeanor made me tremble involuntarily. I never knew which side of him I could trust, nor how long each personality would last. "They're not going to kill me over two million. What I've done with that casino, the profit it will bring in for them? No. They need me."

"They need the casino, they don't need you."

"Did you ever love me?" When I said nothing, he pressed on, "We said no lies."

"Yes." The word felt so rough going down. I wished I could chew it up, spit it out, and never have to swallow it again. "In my own fucked-up way that doesn't make any sense to me, I loved you, Ben." I paused a moment. "They made you kill Madeline, they gave you an order, and you had no choice. I understand that, even if I hate you for it. I understand it. But then you started beating me, and sometimes when you're doing it, I think you have to stop yourself from killing me too."

He cringed at the thought. "We hurt each other," he spat brashly.

"We fight, and then we fuck, and then we make money and spend it. There's not a soul in this world that understands you like I do, Virginia. Not a man who'd love you like I have, do the things I've done for you." His face tightened with fury. "I have killed for you."

There was no lie in his words. In all the wrong, awful ways, Ben loved me.

My eyes watered, but I stood up before the emotion could seep out of me. "They're coming for you. Maybe you have a day, a week, a month, but they're coming." I began to walk past him, intending to go to my bedroom to finish packing my things—two suitcases stuffed to the brim with clothes. I'd get the rest later. He hurriedly followed me, his hands reaching out to grab me, to twist me around. He took hold of both sides of my face and pulled me close. I flinched but didn't fight him.

"We can still go, we can run," he said with a breathless plea. "We catch the first flight, keep the money for ourselves. They don't know where it is yet, it's still ours."

I didn't give him an answer, but the tight grip he had on my face worried me. I reached for his hands, closed my eyes, and focused on my breathing. My lack of fight seemed to give him hope; his grasp on my face grew slack.

"You're not going to give up your precious casino for me."

"You never asked." He pushed a tendril of frizzed red hair behind my ear. "We've done things to each other, horrible things, but I am not your monster. I have protected you, haven't I?"

I didn't want to revisit the beginning, but my mind played tricks on me. The mistake with Wayne and the chance he gave me to survive. My fleeting time in New York, where I wouldn't have made it without him. Tangled up on the floor of my childhood home in Georgia. All of the images that should have left me warm were overshadowed by a painful collection of years. Those memories were too sharp and unforgiving.

I couldn't love Ben Siegel because if I did, I'd be killing myself.

I let him take me to bed, where there wasn't the slightest hint of dampened passion, and awoke to a call from Joe.

"You need to leave now," he said. "Adonis will be there shortly. Catch the first flight to Chicago and go to Miss Suzannah. She's waiting for you."

My heart throbbed with intensity. If he was giving me direct orders to leave, the hit had been called in. Siegel wouldn't survive the week.

Ben stirred beside me, and I muttered, "I'll call you later, Vel," before hanging up. His hand rested on my lower back, but his eyes were closed. I leaned down to kiss his forehead and slipped out of the room. I gathered my suitcases and waited outside, and Adonis pulled up a few minutes later. He leaped out of the car and ushered me inside, tossing my bags into the back.

On the way to the airport, he handed me my ticket with explicit instructions: "You're not to answer his calls anymore. The account was in your name, and Lansky didn't like it. He thought you might be involved with Siegel's schemes. Dragna assured him otherwise, but we can't take any risks. You'll stay in Chicago for a while, and then Joe wants to send you to Europe. The farther away from this mess, the better."

I hadn't realized I was trembling until we arrived at the terminal, and Adonis reached over to take my hand. He retrieved something from the inside pocket of his suit, a rolled-up contract I had been waiting years to see.

Unrolling the paper, I checked the signatures. Dragna had signed, leaving an open space for me to sign next to him. I let out a shaky breath, holding the contract so tightly that my fingers began to sweat, leaving imprints on the paper.

Adonis reached over and held my arm to steady it. "It's over, Princess. It's over."

Standing outside Lady Luck, I gazed at the building, my mind filled with disbelief at how quickly time had slipped away. Stepping inside, I inhaled the stale, cramped air, finding a strange comfort in its familiarity.

It was bigger than I remembered somehow, and less forlorn. The joes were better dressed and the girls less vacant eyed. Or maybe that was just my memory playing tricks on me, and it was still the same cut-rate whorehouse it had always been. When I lived here with Madeline, we had spent every night dreaming of something more, and now, I just wanted to sink into my small room on my bed with thin sheets. I wanted to wake up in the morning to busy Chicago streets outside my window and the girls shouting at one another from across the hall.

Miss Suzannah met me in the foyer with a warm embrace. Her face had new and old wrinkles, her eyes looked tired and worn, but she still had the stern air about her that told me she was still holding down the place.

"Did you find our girl?" she asked over coffee that night.

I gave her a nod and handed back her revolver.

One month later, Miss Suzannah and I embarked on a journey to Ottawa, a quaint town nestled near the banks of the Fox River in Illinois. Joe had given me directions to settle in a small motel, just across the street from the cemetery. I stared at the wrought iron gates from our shared room, where Miss Suzannah and I sat in silence that night and into the following morning.

After breakfast, we walked across the street and through the gates. A wave of intense vertigo struck me, and I let out a long, shallow breath. I strolled with her tentatively down the paved, winding path between graves and sun-blanched headstones. Aside from the rustling of leaves, the only sound in the air was the faint crying of mourning men and women, hunched over new graves. I could smell the freshly turned earth from here.

I searched for her name and found the headstone beneath an old oak with a fresh bouquet of roses resting atop. "Did you come to see her this morning while I slept?" I asked Miss Suzannah, and she shook her head.

I searched the bright cemetery until I found him, Joe, standing against a tree in his exceptionally fitted suit. Miss Suzannah glared his way but didn't make any trouble.

He slowly walked to meet us while I stared at her name on the headstone for so long that the sun started to burn my skin. He delicately placed a hand on my shoulder, and the weight of the last thirteen years hung between us. The lies we had told, the shared desperation, and the woman we had both lost.

Joe handed me a fresh newspaper, still warm from the press. The headline blared, "Bugsy Siegel Murdered in Hail of Bullets," and I gazed at the picture of him before placing the paper near the gravestone. "Siegel was just one man," said Miss Suzannah, breaking the silence. "The Mob is going to kill hundreds more women before it's destroyed, if it ever is. One man isn't going to make a difference."

Joe challenged her with thin, narrowed eyes. "The goal wasn't to take down the organization, it was to free Virginia. It's done." He turned to face me, but I couldn't deny Miss Suzannah's words buzzing around in my head.

Adonis had said the same thing, but again, I didn't know if I believed it. I didn't know if a paper with signatures was the freedom I desired. How much of the last thirteen years was going to haunt me for the rest of my life?

"You're set to fly to Europe," he told me, retrieving the plane tickets from the lining of his suit.

I took the tickets slowly. "When should I come back?"

"Not until they're done investigating the murder. I'll call in a few weeks to check in."

Drawing in a deep breath, I turned to confront him directly. "Don't ever call me again, Joe."

Back in Chicago, Miss Suzannah and I prepared a package to send to Madeline's mother, Doris, with all her postcards and a detailed letter about where to find her grave. We packaged what was left, her clothing and trinkets.

"What's this?" Miss Suzannah asked from the other side of the bed that had once belonged to Madeline. Other girls had stayed in the room over the years, but she'd kept everything the same.

I folded up the last cream day dress and tucked it into the package before looking up. There in her hands was Madeline's black book, the one I'd told Joe I'd burned. I stared at it, then back up at Miss Suzannah. She opened it slowly, skimming through pages and pages of notes, and then, her face changed. "You've been keeping notes? Virginia . . ." A pause, then she swallowed. "You've been keeping track of everything? Every bribe . . ."

"Every murder," I added. "Every shady deal done by every Mob associate I've met."

I walked around the bed and retrieved the book from her hands, reclaiming its weight. Miss Suzannah covered her mouth, a mix of awe and terror on her face. "What are you going to do with it?"

"Insurance," I said firmly. "They don't go after me; I don't go after them."

"You could bring them down, Virginia," she said, pointing it out as if I didn't know that.

"And then I spend years in hiding? Running?" I shook my head, deciding that for the first time since I signed my life away to them, I was doing something for me, regardless of the lives lost. "I'm done with the Mob. All I want is to sit on my front porch and watch a Georgia sunrise with a cold glass of tea." I held the book to my chest, sighing at the dreamy scene I'd imagined.

We continued packing, dropping the topic until she asked, "Will I ever see you again?"

"Not if I can help it." I gave her a smile, one she returned warmly.

Epilogue

MAINE, 1950

I moved through the market leisurely, carefully selecting two plump lobsters for our dinner from a vendor with a kind, weathered face. There was a warm glow in the stalls while I listened to a fishmonger announcing the catch of the day. In my basket, I had gathered an assortment of flowers, fresh fish, and aromatic spices, the weight of which grew heavier with each passing minute.

Insisting on taking the burden from me, Hans reached around to grasp the basket with one hand, while his other hand gently caressed my growing stomach. The baby hadn't moved since I arrived at the market, lulled by the rhythm of my feet, but Hans's voice was enough to get a small thump out of him.

"There she is," he mused, eyes bright.

"He," I insisted. I didn't know how I knew, but I leaned into the instinct. The enticing aromas of grilled sausages, freshly baked bread, and the ever-present scent of the ocean tickled my nose. By day, the coastal town buzzed with activity, but at night, the ocean view and the sound of the waves kept my night terrors at bay.

I'd been all over the world, but none of it compared to Maine. I'd even gotten used to the salty tang in the air, compliments of the nearby water.

"Let's go home," he said, looking down at my feet. He couldn't see them through my shoes, but he knew they were swelling. I had two months left, but each day felt longer than the last.

"Not yet," I said. "I like being in the market." It wasn't shopping in New York or Los Angeles—I didn't wear jewelry or furs, and I liked it. I liked being no one here.

"Not much longer, then," he reasoned, his gaze fixed on the Maine sunset, wearing an unusual expression that bordered on distress. I had noticed it earlier when he took a hurried phone call, but I had chosen to ignore it. My trips to the market were my favorite time of the week, and I didn't want them ruined with bad news, but now I felt compelled to ask.

"Who called earlier?"

His smile returned, but I could sense there was more to the story. "Nobody important."

"They said something," I countered. "I can see it all over your face, Hans, and I'd rather know now than at dinner. You know how much I like lobster."

He grinned, finding my stomach again with a soft pat. "A man named Joe," he revealed quietly, and I was thankful he was holding the basket because I'd have dropped it.

"What did he say?" I dared to ask.

"He said he was an old friend of yours."

"A bad old friend," I told him, the only words he needed to get a glimpse of the past I'd told him about when we first met.

"He said that you needed to prepare yourself, that you'll be subpoenaed to testify in the Kefauver hearings." I knew all about the hearings, a special US Senate committee charged with investigating organized crime. Reporters had been ringing over the last few weeks, desperate for interviews. It was only a matter of time before they showed up at my doorstep, ruining my little hideaway.

I forced a smile to comfort him. "Good thing I don't know nothin' about nothin'."

He didn't look convinced. "You'll be under oath, Virginia."

A sharp pang pierced my chest, and my throat tightened so much that I struggled to swallow. Three years had not been enough time. I had only just found Hans and begun to build a life with him. A family.

"Let's go home," I suggested, and though he didn't press the topic on the way to our cottage bordering the water, I knew he needed more—some sense of assurance this wouldn't end our lives and leave our son without a mother.

At dinner, I savored the meal of lobster dipped in melted butter with a fresh green salad. Once I finished eating, I left the table and made my way to the porch, its weathered boards creaking softly beneath my feet. I considered the questions they'd ask, the timeline of events they'd make me live through again—everything I had done just to feel this fleeting moment of peace. It was foolish to think I could escape it all.

I breathed in the air, watched the ocean meet the rugged shore, and began to cry—wrenching, ugly tears. The baby danced inside me the way he always did outside in the fresh air, and I cleaned my face as if he could see me already.

Hans joined, taking a seat in a chair beside me. He reached for my hand and held it, again allowing me to think and not pushing me. But I knew I owed him answers.

"I'll ask them to hold my testimony until after the baby is born," I said. "That will give me some time with him."

"Are you going to tell them what you know?"

"I can't," I said.

"You're going to lie under oath?" His disappointment wasn't lost on me.

"I don't have a choice." I reached down to tug at the fabric over my stomach. "If I know nothing, they can't charge me with anything. They need me to be a whore, Hans. They need to think I slept with these men to better myself, not because I was in league with them. Do you understand what that means? What they'll think of me? What the world will think?"

He shifted in his chair, but I couldn't read his expression.

"The press is going to feed that story. Virginia Hill, the Mob whore," I continued brashly. "They'll come after you, after our family, but it's better that way. Better I be a loose woman, a laughingstock, than lose you both."

He ran a hand down his face, lips pinched together tightly. "I don't want this for you, for our family. How do we know this is the end of it?"

"We don't," I said with little hope. I had thought it was over three years ago, but now, I wondered the same thing. Would it ever end? I took another steadying breath. "If something happens to me—"

"Don't," he interrupted. He left his chair and sank down in front of me, hands on my legs. "Nothing is going to happen to you. You'll testify, put on a show, and then come back home to him."

I smiled warmly. "Him?"

He gave one of my hands a kiss. "Who am I to argue with Virginia Hill?"

Author's Note

Virginia Hill was found dead in 1966, and her death was ruled a suicide. Her name is still recognizable more than half a century after her death, yet she remains a one-dimensional figure, with little known about her beyond the men she slept with. In telling Virginia's story, I tried to stay true to the known facts while letting my imagination fill in the blanks. Two resources that were immensely valuable in my research were *Bugsy Siegel: The Dark Side of the American Dream* by Michael Shnayerson and *Bugsy's Baby: The Secret Life of Mob Queen Virginia Hill* by Andy Edmonds.

To this day, many believe she was killed for what she knew and the threat she posed against the Outfit. While it's impossible to know her true motives for joining the Mob, the facts paint a clear picture. She was smart and driven and rose through the ranks of an organization dominated by men, and when Siegel died, she settled down to start the loving family she'd never had. She was both a criminal and a victim, but most importantly, a survivor. I hope I did her justice.